THE
DIVIDING
LINE

THE DIVIDING LINE

RICHARD PARRISH

 A DUTTON BOOK

DUTTON
Published by the Penguin Group
Penguin Books USA Inc., 375 Hudson Street,
New York, New York 10014, U.S.A.
Penguin Books Ltd, 27 Wrights Lane, London W8 5TZ, England
Penguin Books Australia Ltd, Ringwood, Victoria, Australia
Penguin Books Canada Ltd, 10 Alcorn Avenue,
Toronto, Ontario, Canada M4V 3B2
Penguin Books (N.Z.) Ltd, 182–190 Wairau Road,
Auckland 10, New Zealand

Penguin Books Ltd, Registered Offices:
Harmondsworth, Middlesex, England

First published by Dutton, an imprint of New American Library,
a division of Penguin Books USA Inc.
Distributed in Canada by McClelland & Stewart Inc.

First Printing, January, 1993
10 9 8 7 6 5 4 3 2 1

 REGISTERED TRADEMARK—MARCA REGISTRADA

LIBRARY OF CONGRESS CATALOGING-IN-PUBLICATION DATA:
Parrish, Richard.
    The dividing line / Richard Parrish.
    p.   cm.
    ISBN 0-525-93561-4
    I. Title.
    PS3566.A757D5   1993
    813'.54—dc20   92-20049
                                                              CIP

Printed in the United States of America
Set in Simoncini Garamond
Designed by Eve L. Kirch

Dedicated to
Stewart ("Sandy") Richardson
and
Joshua Ben Parrish

וּבְמָקוֹם שֶׁאֵין אֲנָשִׁים הִשְׁתַּדֵּל לִהְיוֹת אִישׁ.

and, of course,
to Pat

Haud ignara mali, miseris succerere disco.
—Virgil

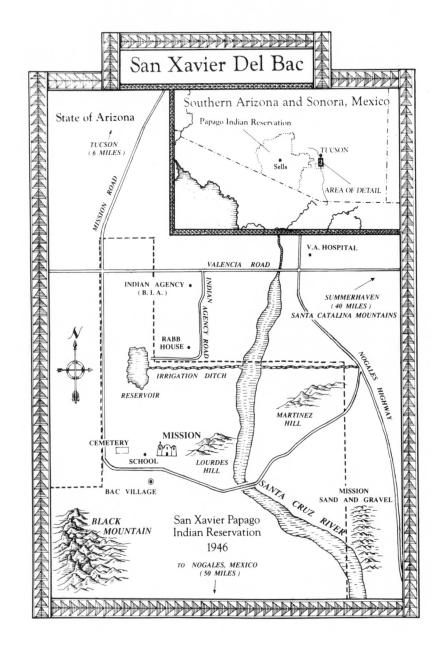

San Xavier Del Bac

State of Arizona

↑
TUCSON
(6 MILES)

MISSION ROAD

Southern Arizona and Sonora, Mexico

Papago Indian Reservation

TUCSON

Sells

AREA OF DETAIL

V.A. HOSPITAL
•

VALENCIA ROAD

INDIAN AGENCY •
(B. I. A.)

INDIAN AGENCY ROAD

SUMMERHAVEN
(40 MILES)
SANTA CATALINA MOUNTAINS

RABB
HOUSE •

NOGALES HIGHWAY

IRRIGATION DITCH

RESERVOIR

MARTINEZ
HILL

MISSION
🏛

CEMETERY
•
SCHOOL

LOURDES
HILL

◎
BAC VILLAGE

BLACK
MOUNTAIN

SANTA CRUZ RIVER

MISSION
SAND AND GRAVEL

San Xavier Papago
Indian Reservation
1946

TO NOGALES, MEXICO
(50 MILES)
↓

N

CHAPTER ONE

They drove toward Tucson through tiny desolate towns which all looked the same, mere dots on the map, a couple of ramshackle slumpblock buildings, a faded yellow-wood railway office, two gas pumps in front of a tumbledown tin shed with a broken red Coke machine next to it. The droopy little towns had oddly bold names, like Beaumont and Corpus Christi and Lordsburg, and the most incongruous of all was a pustule of a place, debouched from a flat, vast, rocky moraine, with just a railroad crossing and a rickety clapboard shed, named Garden of Gethsemane. They drove quickly through the Garden, fearing that the car might break down and that they would have to spend even one extra minute here. They had the dismal feeling that they looked like Okies from *The Grapes of Wrath*, two water bags hanging from the steaming radiator cap of the wheezing mud-splattered De Soto, a spare tire roped to the top of the car.

As they neared Tucson, they waited anxiously for the harsh terrain to soften, to ameliorate, and they expected to see handsome cowboys in great felt hats with shiny silver concho belts and big blue steel Colt .44s strapped to their hips, and menacing Indians covered with red-and-black-and-white stripes of war paint, dressed in loincloths and carrying lances adorned with scalps and eagle feathers. They looked right and left for sprawling ranches with elegant black stallions and huge herds of brown-and-white-spotted cattle grazing on abundant pastures of emerald rye grass. That was the Wild West they had become familiar with from the movies, *My Friend Flicka* and *Stagecoach* and *Arizona*. But they didn't see any of that as they drove into Tucson in June 1946. They only saw an occasional skinny jackrabbit in an endless expanse of heat-shimmering desert and prickly pear cactus and ocotillo and ragged mesquite trees and straggly clumps of famished sagebrush, all bent under a fierce, scalding, relentless sun.

Tucson was a hot, dry, dusty little nothing of a town. There were no cowboys, there were no Indians; there weren't any cows or horses or stagecoaches. There were only burnt sienna dogs with lolling ocher tongues curled up beside parboiled pink people sitting on parched wood porches, hiding from the sun, swatting mosquitos and horseflies and drinking beer or Coke or lemonade and wiping their faces with soiled red handkerchiefs.

The Book of Genesis said that God had created the world and the sun and the moon and the stars, the heavens filled with birds, the seas teeming with fishes, and the dry land upon which flourished all of the fruit-bearing trees and over which crept the reptiles and the wild animals and the cattle of the fields. And the king of all creation was man, for to man God gave the privilege of subduing the earth and wielding dominion over the fish in the sea and the birds of heaven and every living thing that moved upon the land.

But in this country, mere man had dominion over nothing. The story told in Genesis seemed to belong to another place, a greener, cooler, sweeter, gentler place. Here it was the sun that was the subduer of the earth and all that was thereon. It bore down pitilessly, cracking the land, parching the trees and the shrubs and the cactus and the wildflowers, subduing with its ferocity the reptiles and wild animals and the cattle of the fields. And especially man. No man could stand unshielded in the relentless, dazzling, scorching furnace of the afternoon sun. The

sun demanded that all living things wilt before its fierce coun-
tenance, for here it was God, tangible, fearsome, essential, not
some ephemeral, elusive spirit like the disembodied God of the
Bible. The sun god had to be cajoled so it would not remove
its life-sustaining warmth from man, and placated so that it
would not destroy him. For in this place the sun was king of
all creation.

~~~~~

Their pants and the backs of their sweaty shirts stuck to the
cracked leather seat of the De Soto when they parked and got
out of the car in the center of Tucson. They knew it was the
center because it was the only four blocks with buildings higher
than one story. The tar from the asphalt streets boiled up in
little black bubbles like sand crab holes on Brighton Beach.
They ate chicken fried steak at Georgette's Diner next to Johnny
Gibson's Barber Shop. Then they went for a tour of their new
hometown. Ronstadt's Hardware was across the street, with big
posters on the windows advertising all the equipment you need
for your vegetable harvesting and the latest in insecticide sprays
to keep the weevils off your cotton. On one corner was Penney's
Catalogue Showroom, and on the other was a department store
named Levy's. In the windows were female mannequins in light
cotton housedresses and male ones in beige-and-gray-twill work
pants and shirts.

"Fancy place," Joshua mumbled.

Hanna nodded grimly. Only Adam still appeared to cling to
a shred of the enthusiasm with which they had left Brooklyn.
He looked with hope at his father, waiting for a word of
assurance.

Joshua was broad through the shoulders and tall, and his
square jaw and deep-set eyes were just a little gaunt. His eyes
were bright blue and gentle under heavy brows, and his forehead
rose straight up to a widow's peak. His short-cropped dark
brown hair was limp and straight, moist from perspiration in
the intense afternoon heat, and flecked with just a touch of gray
over his ears and at his temples. He had the look of a scholarly,
good-humored man, big and lean, who had become pale and

solitary from years of being cooped up in a musty library. He was dressed in black wing-tips, black wool slacks, and a starched white long-sleeved dress shirt, limp and wrinkled and sweat-stained from hours on the highway in the boiling car. The cuff of his left sleeve was safety-pinned to the yoke of his shirt, since his left arm was gone from just below his shoulder. His skin was too light to protect him from the desert sun, and he looked like he had just become aware of it and was concerned because he knew that his children were also too pallid for this place.

Hanna was fourteen years old and looked like her mother. She was dressed in tan shorts and a white cotton halter top and brown suede sandals. She had mink brown curly hair and pellucid gray-hyacinth eyes and a porcelain delicacy that was one of her mother's special gifts. But her face was troubled. Her life had changed abruptly, overnight, and she stared at the ugly mannequins wearing the cheap clothes in the shop window. Why couldn't everything be like it once was?

Before Daddy had gone off to the war, he was a big, handsome man. Women had always glanced at him, even when they were with other men. But when they picked Daddy up at the veterans hospital last year, he was thinner than he'd been when he left three years before, and his rich chocolate brown hair was flecked with a little gray, and he sometimes used a cane and limped a little with his left foot. And he didn't have a left arm. But it wasn't just those things that made him seem so different. It was his eyes.

His crystal blue eyes that had always sparkled with humor and warmth were now just lusterless shards of colored glass, ink dense, melancholy. And the saucy youthful grin was gone. When he smiled at her and kissed her, she saw that his eyes didn't brighten up and gladden his whole face like before the war. He just kept on looking sad. He looked her up and down and nodded approvingly and pursed his lips and said that she was growing up and would soon look just like Mommy. Then his eyes kind of misted up. Mommy had been dead for over a year, but the thought of it still made him blink back his tears.

Daddy rarely smiled anymore, and then only with his cheeks. He looked sad all the time. Hanna and Adam slept in twin beds in the spare bedroom, and Hanna could hear her father telling Grandma and Grandpa stories about a concentration camp. When they were whispering in the living room, and Hanna was supposed to be sleeping, she could sometimes hear Daddy talking about what he had seen, how many helpless people the Germans had shot and starved and gassed and burned up in ovens.

And Daddy coughed all of the time now, a hacking deep cough that sounded like a gunshot in a barrel and burned his throat. The doctors at the veterans hospital told him that he must go to a warm dry climate. Brooklyn weather was giving him a chronic bronchial irritation, and since he had an injured lung he had to be very careful. Arizona was a great place, the doctors said. The veterans hospitals in Phoenix and Tucson were where the army was sending vets with tuberculosis and asthma and other lung ailments, because the climate was genuinely therapeutic.

Hanna didn't want to leave her friends and especially the sloe-eyed boy with strawberry blond hair who sat behind her in homeroom. They had gone under the boardwalk at Brighton Beach, and he had kissed her and brushed his trembling fingers over her swimsuit top, and she had never felt this way about a boy before. But she knew deep inside that Daddy needed to get away, or he would get sicker, much sicker. So she said, sure, why not? And tried to look like she meant it. But now she was sorry that she hadn't stayed in Brooklyn with Grandma and Grandpa. Tucson sure wasn't like in the movies. When would Daddy get cured and have enough of this crummy place so that they could go back home?

They got back in the car. The steering wheel was fitted with a special shifting device that made it possible to drive with only one hand. Adam sat in the backseat staring gloomily out the window at passing cholla cactus and creosote bushes and tumbleweeds. His mood had soured in the moments since the reality of Tucson had fully dawned on him. He was eleven years old and looked like his father's son, with the same shaped face and eyes and straight brown hair and already broadening shoulders and long legs. He wore a T-shirt and baggy blue cotton trousers with an elastic waist. He had on a pair of black Keds sneakers, the laces untied and loose.

Joshua studied the directions that he had received in a letter and drove south out of downtown Tucson on Sixth Avenue past the Veterans Administration Hospital, three miles to Valencia Road, then west just over two miles to Indian Agency Road. The asthmatic De Soto stirred up puffs of hot dust like smoke signals from the dirt roads. The Bureau of Indian Affairs was in a hundred-year-old sprawling adobe building with a flat roof and tiny windows. There were four much smaller adobe houses strung southward down the road like a sulky quartet of dingy offspring.

Edgar Hendly, the head of the Bureau of Indian Affairs, was a rotund little man with a dyspeptic frown permanently etched onto his bulbous, florid face. Despite the heat he wore a rumpled gray wool suit and once-white dress shirt and stained black silk tie. There were wide sweat patches under his arms. He had an oddly effeminate mannerism of continually smoothing his few wisps of gray hair over his sweat-glistening bald pate, like a vain actress nervously petting her coiffure with fluttering fingers.

Joshua stood with him in front of the bureau, and the short, heavy man looked him up and down. "I didn't know about all this," Hendly said wanly, pointing at Joshua's arm and the cane he held in his right hand. "You able to work?"

"I'm able."

"This is pretty rough country out here," Hendly said, his voice trailing off. "You shoulda told me." He looked away and shook his head with a mixture of anger and embarrassment.

"I'm able." Joshua's voice was strong, insistent.

"What happened to ya anyway? Ya got pretty bad bunged up."

"What the hell's the difference?" Joshua jutted his chin out. "I can do the work."

Mr. Hendly studied his defiant, angry eyes and shrugged. "What the hell," he mumbled. He rode with the Rabbs down to their new home, the last of the four adobe houses. Hanna and Adam looked around inside in shocked silence. It was tiny, a kitchen and living room and three miniscule bedrooms. On the side of the house, fifty or sixty chickens cackled gratingly inside a bedraggled wire coop.

"White Rocks," Mr. Hendly said, pointing with evident pride at the chickens. He seemed oblivious to the nauseating stench which hung thickly in the air.

Hanna was almost catatonic. She had gone, in less than two weeks, from an eleven-story apartment building on bustling Brighton Beach Avenue, with all the store signs in Yiddish and a soda shop with chocolate phosphates and a beautiful beach out the back door and Coney Island about a mile down the boardwalk, to this, the most dreary horrible little mud shack she had ever imagined. In fact, she had never imagined that people lived in places like this. She held protectively onto Adam's hand, and they stood in the front yard next to their father while Mr. Hendly babbled on in that funny Western accent.

They walked across the rutted dirt road in front of the house to an irrigation ditch about fifteen feet wide and ten feet deep. The water was less than a foot deep in the bottom, a muddy ten-foot-wide rivulet, and the overweight sun and stinging hot wind bludgeoned the tiny wavelets into a million silvery dagger points. Evaporating water shimmered up in a nacreous mist that pinkened everything up to about five feet over the ditch and then dissipated into the dazzlingly clear, burning air.

"This is the northern boundary a the San Xavier Del Bac Papago Indin Reservation," Mr. Hendly said. He paused a moment and his voice became grave. "There was a body floatin in that there ditch just two days ago. A thirteen-year-old Papago girl. Ya might hear some folks say that she didn't drown, that she was murdered, strangled prob'ly. But don't ya pay no heed to such fool talk. Nobody's ever gonna be able to prove it no how. And how could ya ever find the killer on the reservation, ten thousand Indins that won't hardly even talk to a white man, let alone turn in one a their own. Anyway, as long as them greasers just kill each other, they ain't no danger to us."

He looked at the Rabbs and smiled, revealing tobacco-stained teeth. But it was a troubled smile, as though he were trying to convince himself that what he said was true. Hanna's eyes widened in fright. She looked from her father's drawn face to the nervous, forced smile that the BIA superintendent gave her, and she could hardly keep from bursting into tears. Mr. Hendly took a pack of Camels out of his shirt pocket. He gestured toward Joshua, and Joshua shook his head. Hendly lit a cigarette and inhaled deeply.

He looked gravely at Hanna and Adam. "Don't you kids be a goin onto the reservation, you hear me now? That's the Indin Nation, and white folks ain't welcome over there." He etched a boundary line in the dust with the toe of a scuffed brown wing-tip. "Most a them people got nothin to do but drink all day and get mean. They're poor as all hell—oops, sorry for my sharp tongue, little lady, but mind good what I tell ya."

Hanna was only half hearing Mr. Hendly's words now. She felt dazed, lost. And he talked with such a funny thick Western accent, like Gabby Hayes. Except what he was saying wasn't so funny, not so funny at all. She was scared of this place.

Mr. Hendly pointed across the half-mile-long barren field on the other side of the irrigation ditch. "That there church yonder is the mission a Saint Francis Xavier. It was built in seventeen ninety-six by Jesuits from Spain. The monks gradually converted all a the Papago Indins to Catholicism, but ya cain't never cleanse all the paganism outta them greasers.

"The dry bed a the Santa Cruz River runs about a quarter mile east a the mission yonder." Mr. Hendly pointed. "There used to be a whole lot a water in it, but now farmers up north a us here draw most of it off to irrigate their fields. That sprawl of a dozen or so ocotillo and brush houses with mud and grass roofs is the center of the village of Bac, meanin 'by the waters.' The Papagos call it *Wahk*. This branch a the Pima Indians has been here by the Santa Cruz River for centuries, livin on prickly pears and saguaro fruit and a few skinny cows and farmin beans. Which is why they're called Papagos, 'bean people.' Them people are all fat 'cause they live on tortillas and beans fried in pig lard, and they stink like the devil 'cause they only got one set a clothes and never heard a takin a bath. The smart ones go through sixth grade at the mission school yonder"—he pointed again and took a long drag on his cigarette"—and then they stop their schoolin. Don't need much book learnin to pick cotton and dig ditches and drink mescal till their eyeballs are floatin. They don't want nothing to do with us neither. And you sure don't wanna end up a floatin in that there water. So just mind you stay on this side a the irrigation ditch and leave them people alone."

He frowned and shook his head. Then he ground the cigarette butt into the dirt with his shoe.

"You wanted the Wild West and wide open spaces, Mr. Rabb," Mr. Hendly said with a shrug. "Well, here they are." He spread his arms out expansively around him. "I guess Tucson ain't exactly what ya'd expect from the movies. It's just a little town with twenty-five thousand Meskin Catholics and fifteen thousand redneck Baptists like me, and we don't do much mixin with the few thousand Papagos who was here a long time before any of us." His voice was tinged with sarcasm. " 'Ceptin me 'n you, a course, cause it's our job."

Hanna stood in stony dejection. Tears streamed down Adam's dusty cheeks.

Mr. Hendly's voice softened, lost its acerbic edge. He turned to Adam. "I got a son just your age. He'll be goin with you to school next year, but he ain't got many friends. Tough to, you know, 'cause we live so far outta town here. And it's mostly just Meskins out here anyway." He shrugged his shoulders resignedly. "He's sure been anxious to meet you. Why don't you come on over to the house with me and meet him?"

"Go on," Joshua prodded gently.

"I have to help unpack," Adam mumbled, clinging more tightly to Hanna's hand. He wiped the tears from his cheeks.

"Naw, that's okay. Hanna and I can do it just fine. You run along now. Come on home around six, and we'll see about going out somewhere nice for dinner."

Adam frowned and then nodded his head in reluctant obedience. His sneakers scuffed up little explosions of dust as he walked up the road with Mr. Hendly.

Joshua turned to Hanna and tried to smile reassuringly. He watched her walk toward the car, and he felt suddenly guilty, selfish, for bringing her to this wasteland. This should be her time for parties and sock hops and boys. Those lissome legs, the flowering body of a woman. She was a real beauty. But he had brought her here to a yard full of dirty white chickens and choking dust and searing heat and nothing. He shook his head slowly and pursed his lips as she walked disconsolately to the trunk of the car to help unload the suitcases.

But despite the initial shock of it, Joshua knew that he needed this place: the hot sun and the clear dry air and the cleanness of the unbounded desert, empty of memories of Rachel and Brooklyn and all the things that were gone and unrecoverable. Those memories had almost destroyed him.

He had gone to a bar near Prospect Park one night after work, and he had drunk too much, much too much. He saw a woman sitting at the bar who looked like his wife, the same brown hair and complexion, the same slope to her bare shoulders, and he went over to her to talk. But she was sitting with a man, whom somehow Joshua didn't notice, and when Joshua sat down and said, "Hello, Rachel," the man got up from his barstool and came around to him and said, "Hey, gimp, you don't just walk up to Betty without you pay me ten bucks first."

Joshua had hit him so hard that he knocked out three teeth and broke his nose and lower jaw, breaking two fingers on his own hand. Joshua's father had to go to the jail at four in the morning and pay a $168 fine for drunk and disorderly. Luckily, it was a pimp that Joshua had hospitalized, so nobody pressed charges. And Joshua and his father had ridden morosely back to Brighton Beach in an almost-deserted subway train, and his father said that Joshua ought to get out of Brooklyn, go somewhere new and fresh where he wasn't haunted every day by memories of the past. And Joshua grudgingly agreed. He felt like he was dying here; he was bitter and angry and had forgotten how to smile and enjoy anything. And when they got back to the apartment, Joshua's mother reluctantly said the same thing. She didn't want him to take the kids away, away from them and Brooklyn and their school and their friends, but she knew that it had to be because Joshua wouldn't leave them behind. But he was troubled in a way that wasn't suddenly and miraculously going to clear up with a couple of pills and magic potions, and they all knew it. And if he didn't go away it might get worse. God only knew what he might do, what might happen. There was a raw corrosive violence in him that was frightening.

So Joshua had talked to Phil Rourke, one of the veterans hospital orthopedic surgeons, who said he knew a doctor at the VA in Tucson, had served with him in England during the war. Phil contacted the doctor, and within weeks, Joshua had a lead on a lawyering job. The Tucson office of the Bureau of Indian Affairs and the Federal Office of Land Management needed a lawyer to do part-time work in exchange for a modest salary and free rent on a small house attached to the bureau. It was at least a start, and part of the deal was that he could use his office the rest of the time to try to build up a private practice. And there was plenty of room on the property for raising chickens and having a goat for milk and a few rows of carrots and lettuce and onions. Just what Joshua needed. Get some mud under his fingernails. Get plenty of warm dry air into his chest, and sunshine to burn his memories to dust.

The Hendly house was a large square adobe building directly behind the Bureau of Indian Affairs. The house was at least three times larger than Adam's new home. Behind it was a rickety wooden shed with a corrugated tin roof.

Inside the shed, a shaggy-haired blond boy was currycombing a huge dappled-gray horse. Mr. Hendly made a two-word introduction, "Jimmy, Adam," and walked back toward the bureau. The boys cocked their heads slightly and appraised each other.

Jimmy was wearing a faded pair of Levi's tucked into high-topped cowboy boots of tan suede calfskin, a red-and-blue-and-yellow-plaid cowboy shirt with pointed snap pocket flaps, and a battered brown felt cowboy hat. Sweat had stained and soaked the hatband so often that the lower part of the crown was dirty black. The horse appeared to be sleeping on its feet, head down, eyes closed, its skin rippling beneath the stiff bristles of the curry.

"Charger," Jimmy said importantly. "He used to belong to the Seventh Army down on the Mexican border by Bisbee. Now they use jeeps, so Dad got him for me."

"Can I comb him?" Adam asked.

"Sure. Here," Jimmy said, handing him the curry. "Where you from?"

"Brooklyn."

"Where's 'at?"

"Next to New York."

Jimmy looked puzzled. He screwed up freckly cheeks and squinted in thought. "I thought Pennsylvania was next to New York."

Adam stuck out his chin. "Well, so's Brooklyn."

Jimmy still looked a little skeptical. "Y'ever ride a horse?"

"Sure I did. Lots."

"Wanna ride him?"

Adam wasn't about to admit that he didn't know how. "I don't have boots or nothing," he said.

"Aw, that's okay. I ain't got no saddle, so you gotta ride him bareback anyway. And all I got for a bridle's a hackamore."

Jimmy went to the corner of the shed and pulled a rope hackamore off a nail on the wall. The bitless bridle fit loosely over the horse's head and had a single rope rein below the jaw. He handed the end of the six-foot rein to Adam, and Adam led the listless horse out of the stall.

"Let's go over to Lourdes Hill," Jimmy said.

"Where's it at?"

"Right next to the mission yonder." Jimmy pointed to the small hill to the left of San Xavier Mission.

"We aren't supposed to go there. Your dad said not to."

"Whattaya, fraidycat? Just 'cause some Indian girl got drownded, my dad gets all upset. But I ain't scared."

"I'm not neither scared," Adam said indignantly. "But your dad said that girl might've been murdered and we can't go over there 'cause it's dangerous." Adam stopped walking, and Charger immediately lowered his head and snorted and closed his eyes, asleep on his feet.

"How's he gonna find out, less'n you tell him?" Jimmy eyed Adam belligerently.

"I wouldn't do that," Adam said, his eyes flashing with the insult.

"Okay then, let's go. I'll get my gun."

"Wow, you got a gun?" For the first time, Adam was truly impressed.

"Sure I do. All us guys do. It's a Daisy."

Jimmy walked back inside the shed and came out a moment later with the BB gun. Adam's eyes were riveted on it. It was a beauty, lever action, sleek black steel with a shiny brown wooden stock, just like one of those Winchesters the cowboys always had in the movies.

"Can I hold it?" Adam asked.

"You sure you know how?" It wasn't a question, it was a challenge.

"Sure I do!" Adam said, putting just enough petulance in his voice to be convincing but not sound like a liar. He had once shot Johnny Rivkin's Daisy, under the boardwalk on Brighton Beach. Got a sea gull that was sleeping in the nook of two support beams.

He dropped Charger's reins, and Jimmy handed him the BB gun. Adam fondled it lovingly, fitting his hand around the neck of the stock. He put his index finger into the trigger housing and squeezed the trigger gingerly.

"Come on," Jimmy said, taking the air rifle back. "We'll go hunt buffalo."

"Buffalo? There's buffalo here?" Adam's eyes widened.

"You'll see," Jimmy said. A knowing smirk wrinkled his cheeks.

Adam stood beside the drowsing horse, whose back was way over Adam's head, and he wondered how he was going to get up. Jimmy came over to him and made a step by interlacing his fingers. Adam put his left foot into the step, and Jimmy heaved him up onto Charger's swayback. Adam swung his right leg over, steadied himself upright, and couldn't help smiling smugly at his accomplishment.

Jimmy led the way through a rocky field of sparse mesquite. Recent monsoon rains had given life to straggly clumps of bear grass and careless weed and occasional wildflowers. The ground had dried and cracked and curled like old leather. The boys picked their way through the mile-wide field and came to the irrigation canal.

Charger began climbing reluctantly down the steep side of the ditch, snorting, puffing, and he lowered his head and minced downward with short jerky steps. Adam clung hard with his knees to the horse's fat sides, but he began to slide forward over the horse's lowered neck. He gripped a handful of mane, but it didn't help. He slid straight down the neck and toppled • over the horse's head onto the edge of the ditch bottom. He got up quickly and rubbed his muddy knees, embarrassed to look at Jimmy, who was whooping with laughter on the other bank. Charger kept on walking, oblivious to anything but getting out of the ditch.

"Gotta hold on good 'n tight when a horse lowers his head and goes downhill," said Jimmy.

They walked a half mile across a barren field to a cemetery about a hundred yards square. It was half full of six-foot-long mounds headed by whitewashed wooden crosses. Many of the mounds were studded with bunches of cut flowers, merry white chrysanthemums and vermillion hibiscus and yellow daisies. The cemetery was surrounded by an old barbed-wire fence that had long since fallen into disrepair. The wood staves lay decaying on the ground. Strands of barbed wire were embedded in the soil, and the barbs stuck up in bunches like small patches of thorns.

Adam gave Jimmy a leg up on Charger, and they trudged around the cemetery to the dirt road that led in front of the mission to Lourdes Hill. No one was around. They passed the small igloolike houses of bear grass woven around frames of ocotillo staves. In the distance were occasional low square houses of adobe. Unfenced chickens clucked and strutted, pecking at the ground. A few goats lay motionlessly under lean-tos, chewing their cud, staring placidly at the boys and the horse.

The front of the mission was an ornate brown plaster façade

framing two heavy wooden doors. The rest of the mission was white stucco. One of the two tall church steeples was topped with a round plaster cap and a tall black steel cross. The other steeple lacked the cap and spire, as though the construction had never been finished.

They walked past the mission and up the ten-foot-wide path on Lourdes Hill. A pair of bronze lions sat on two tall cement pillars as they reached the top of the hill.

"There's the buffalo," Jimmy said.

"Where at?" Adam asked.

"Down yonder, by the Santa Cruz River." Jimmy pointed with his BB gun a few hundred yards away toward a quarter-mile-long thin strip of green along the western bank of the riverbed.

Grazing on the thin green patch of earth were two scrawny brown cows. Just beyond them past a bow in the river were several tall cranes and great clouds of billowing dust from some excavation in the riverbed which Adam and Jimmy couldn't see. The noise from the excavation was barely audible, muffled by the distance.

"They don't look like buffalo to me," Adam said.

"What's a guy from Brooklyn know?" Jimmy dug his boot heels into Charger's sides, and the horse walked slowly toward the river. Adam walked beside the horse.

About thirty yards from the stolidly grazing cows, Jimmy let out a war whoop and kicked Charger hard. The horse began loping toward the cows, who looked up at the unwelcome intruder with huge startled brown eyes. Jimmy took aim at the first cow and shot it in the rump. Adam could hear the compressed air expel from the barrel, and he saw the cow whip its tail around like it was flicking flies. Charger passed the cows ten yards away at a slow, arthritic gallop. Jimmy cocked the rifle and shot at the second cow and missed. Charger circled around for another pass at the unhappy quarry. The cows began trotting away from the horse, up the riverbank toward the dust clouds of the excavation. Jimmy loped beside them and shot the trailing one in the shoulder. It flinched and began running faster.

Jimmy reined in Charger and walked the snorting horse back

to Adam. The cows reached the edge of the straggly Bermuda grass pasture and stopped running. They stood looking warily at the boys and the horse.

"You wanna take a couple a shots?" Jimmy asked, climbing down from Charger.

"Yeah, I guess," Adam said, not enthusiastic for the cow hunt, which seemed kind of cruel, but he was dying to get his hands on the BB gun.

Jimmy climbed down from Charger and gave Adam a leg up. Adam steadied himself and Jimmy handed him the BB gun. Just the touch of it was enough to make a guy smile. He spread his legs and brought them into the horse's sides with a loud thump. Charger snorted resignedly and began trotting toward the cows. Adam took aim with the BB gun at the lead cow, but the gun was going up and down, and he couldn't control the horse with the rein in his left hand and shoot anything just using his right. The horse passed fifteen yards away from the wary tail-flicking cows and stopped at the end of the pasture. Adam turned in the saddle and shot at a cow. The BB struck it in the withers, and the cow turned and started running down the pasture toward the irrigation ditch.

Feeling like Buffalo Bill, Adam walked Charger back to Jimmy and slid down from the horse. "You see me get him that last time?" Adam gushed, handing the rein to Jimmy.

"Hey, you boys!" came a high-pitched woman's voice from the direction of Lourdes Hill.

"Aw cripes! Old lady Antone," Jimmy said. "Them're her cows. Let's get outta here!"

A large Indian woman in a shapeless faded brown sack dress with gray stringy hair bouncing around her shoulders came running toward them wielding a long broom. "I tell you plenny times, stay away my stock!" she screamed, now only fifteen yards away. "I tell you father, you Hendly som bitch!"

There was no time to remount Charger. Jimmy started running toward the irrigation ditch, holding hard onto the horse's rein. It was about 150 yards away, and Adam reached it first, panting for breath, clutching the BB gun protectively in front of him with both hands like a priest with a golden chalice. It took Jimmy and Charger another couple of minutes. The old Papago woman was far in the distance, standing with her broom laid back over one shoulder.

"Is she gonna tell on us?" Adam asked as Jimmy came up.

Jimmy shrugged his shoulders and took the gun from Adam. "So what?" he said.

"My dad might murder me," Adam said.

"Quit bein' a chicken. He ain't gonna find out."

They crossed the muddy ditch near Indian Agency Road. Hanna was standing by the chicken coops and saw Adam cross the ditch just fifty yards away. And then he saw her, standing there with her hands on her hips, staring at him, and he had the sudden impulse to run back down into the ditch and hide. But then Jimmy would laugh and call him a fraidycat. So he trudged reluctantly toward his new home, his face down.

As he reached the house, Hanna came up and stood stiffly in front of him. He shuffled to a stop and raised his face and met her hard stare. Ever since Mommy had died, Hanna had taken upon herself the responsibility of being Adam's mother.

"You were over there on the reservation, even though Mr. Hendly told you you couldn't go there." She wagged her finger at him accusatorily.

"No, I wasn't," he mumbled.

"Don't lie, Adam!"

"Well, Jimmy made me go," he whined.

"Did he tie you up and drag you there?"

Adam lowered his face.

"You have to start acting like a man, Adam," she scolded him gently. "Daddy's sick and you can't upset him."

"Are you saying Daddy's still crazy?" He studied his big sister carefully, a little fear showing in his eyes.

"No, not crazy," she said, not wanting to frighten him, and knowing that he didn't fully understand. "He's just real worn out emotionally from the war, you know, and Mommy dying. He's real nervous and frazzled."

"Yeah, I know," Adam mumbled. "He's been writing in that book of his, like he did a couple of months ago when he was acting real strange. Sometimes he spends hours writing in it."

Hanna's face was grave.

Adam studied his sister. "You think he'll be okay?"

"I don't know." She shook her head. "I just don't know. But you've got to act right and not worry him by doing bad things."

He hung his head again and walked into the house. His father was sweeping the rough wood living room floor when Adam walked in.

"You meet Jimmy?" his father asked.

"Yeah, sure. He's got a horse and a BB gun."

"You get to ride the horse?"

"Yeah, it was really neat."

"Be careful. I don't want you getting hurt." He looked carefully at his uncharacteristically reserved son. "Where've you been to get your sneakers all muddy?"

"Aw, just out playing." He looked away from his father.

Adam always looked away from Joshua when he was telling a story. Joshua eyed him cautioningly. "Don't be going on the reservation. You heard what Mr. Hendly said. A girl drowned in the ditch."

Adam shook his head resolutely. "Dad, you think I could have a Daisy? All the guys got one but me."

Joshua smiled at the earnest look his son gave him. "Well, we'll see about it. Go on, get washed up now and let's scout around Tucson." He watched his son walk into the bathroom, and somehow, for some reason, the day no longer felt so heavy.

CHAPTER TWO

T he next morning Joshua dressed in a gray sharkskin suit and white shirt and blue silk tie and black snap-brimmed fedora, and he felt ridiculous walking up the dirt road to the adobe bureau. He stamped the dust off his black wing-tip shoes outside the front door.

It was only a few minutes after eight, but the waiting room of the bureau was already full of Indians, men, mostly middle-aged, all wearing straw hats and Levi's and cowboy boots and varicolored cowboy shirts. They sat quietly on folding metal chairs along the wall. In the last chair next to the dimly lit corridor sat a nun in full black habit with a white scarf around her hair tied behind her neck.

Joshua walked up to the receptionist behind a sliding window and knocked. A severe-looking woman, thirty-five or forty years old with light brown hair in a bun and a pinched face, looked up warily.

"I'm Joshua Rabb." He tipped his hat to her and held it against his chest.

The woman opened the sliding window and smiled broadly, showing a mouthful of large yellowish teeth. "You say you're Mr. Rabb?"

"Right."

She signaled him to wait where he was and closed the window. She disappeared and emerged a moment later from a door at the end of the corridor.

"Mr. Rabb," she called.

Fifteen pairs of obsidian eyes, cold and opaque, and the nun's brittle green eyes, followed him intently as he limped down the hallway.

The receptionist was short and scrawny. She wore a dun-colored dress with a high tight neck that fell straight down over her flat chest and reached almost to her ankles. She held out her hand to him. "I'm Frances Hendly," she said as they shook hands. "Edgar told me you got settled in yesterday. I hope everything's all right."

"Yes, just fine, Mrs. Hendly." He'd tell her about the chattering swamp cooler fan later.

"Call me Frances," she said, giving Joshua what he imagined she thought was her most alluring smile. With her square teeth and strong jaw, she resembled unfortunately the braying mule Joshua and the children had seen yesterday in a field beside the road.

"Your office is down here at the end," she said, leading the way down the long ill-lighted corridor.

She opened the last door, and sunlight assaulted them through the window behind the desk. The office was about ten feet square and had an army desk, olive drab metal with a serial number stenciled in yellow on the side, an oak swivel chair, and a matching straight-backed desk chair. The bookshelf covering the entire wall on the left was navy, battleship gray metal with a stenciled number in black, filled with rows of black-spined books. *CCH Federal Lands* was the title on each of the books on the top two rows. *Collected Indian Treaties* filled the third row. The bottom two shelves were piled full with manila files. The desk was uncluttered. The room was dingy musty adobe, and the two-foot-square window behind the desk glinted hotly with sunlight.

"The sun will be out of the window by ten o'clock. It won't get too hot in here," Frances said.

"Fine, looks just fine," Joshua said. Ever since arriving yesterday, he had gloomily pictured his office as a mud-floored
closet with decaying adobe walls. He had guessed right.

"Those Indians and Sister Martha are all here to see you, Mr.
Rabb."

"Joshua, please call me Joshua."

She smiled at him with those huge teeth, and he thought she
fluttered her long eyelashes.

"They've been waiting out there since I opened up an hour
ago. You ever deal with Indians?" Her face became serious and
pinched tight.

"No, never have."

Her eyes squinted a little. "They don't talk much, just stare
at you. One of them will do most of the talking, but that doesn't
mean he's the leader, just that he can speak English. A lot of
them aren't even American citizens. Their tribal lands reach
down into Mexico and they just go back and forth like there
isn't even a border. The leader of this bunch is Francisco Romero, a real rabble-rouser. And that nun with them, she really
stirs them up." She eyed him askance. "You a papist, Mr.
Rabb?"

"Joshua, please. No, I'm not."

"Well, then you won't feel bad about treating her like she's
got to be treated. She's a terribly pushy troublemaker."

"What do they want to see me about?"

"Mineral rights. That's been the big problem around here for
a while now. That's why Henry Carboneau left. Just got sick of
the constant hassling by the Indians."

"Henry who?"

"The lawyer that was here before you, Carboneau. Just picked
up and left about three months ago, him and his wife and year-
old kid. We have no idea where they went. They didn't even
wave good-bye to Edgar and me. Strange guy."

"Well, let's see how long I last," Joshua said.

"Oh, you'll be just fine. You just keep smiling that way and
you'll charm them and the sister to death."

Joshua thought he saw those eyelashes fluttering again, like
a coquettish schoolgirl. God save me, he thought.

"I'll send them in if you're ready."

Joshua shrugged. "Yes, fine." He walked behind the desk and whisked the layer of dust off the chair with his hand. He sat down, and the chair squeaked, but it held his two hundred pounds. There was a yellow legal pad on the desk and several pencils. He shook the dust off the pad.

The nun entered first and stood directly in front of the desk. Joshua appraised her unsmiling face. With a little makeup she'd be pretty. She was medium height and might have been very well built, although who could tell under all of that black cloth? Her face was well tanned and strong, a cleft chin and high cheekbones. She was probably about thirty-five years old.

The men slowly entered his office. It was too small for all of them, and several remained in the corridor outside. Ten of them and the nun stood close together around the front and sides of the desk.

"You Mr. Robb, the new lawyer?"

"Rabb. Raaab."

"I am Francisco Romero. We come see you very important thing for us, mister."

Romero was an old man with pure white hair spilling around his shoulders, which contrasted sharply with his glistening black eyes and sweat-shiny deep brown leathery skin. He was short and gaunt and his eyes squinted almost shut as he looked at Joshua framed against the sunlit window. He looked extremely sinister to Joshua, wrinkled and wiry and clad in stiff filthy clothing. Not a guy you'd want to run into in a parking lot in Brooklyn. Or Tucson. He was wearing a plaid sweat-stained cowboy shirt and faded Levi's and scuffed dusty cowboy boots. He didn't remove his straw cowboy hat. The acrid smell of stale sweat assailed Joshua's nostrils.

"What can I do for you?" Joshua tried to smile pleasantly.

"We got problems Mission Sand and Gravel Company, they stealing minerals under riverbed and putting mine tunnel into bank, they got no right, mineral rights is Papagos'."

"What kind of minerals?"

"Dunno zackly. We think maybe silver, maybe gold."

Joshua raised his brows. Silver was fixed by the government

somewhere around $1.30 an ounce, and gold was $35 a fine troy ounce. Hell of a lot of money.

"What makes you think there's silver or gold there?"

Romero shrugged. "Whatever it is, mineral rights is Papagos'," he said. "You here protect our rights. We need money from minerals, tribe need money. Our people very poor."

"Well, then, why don't you go over to the Sand and Gravel Company yourselves and find out what's going on?"

The old man spoke Papago for a moment, looking around at the grim-faced men. Several of them muttered something incomprehensible, staring hard at Joshua. Though he couldn't understand the words, the tone of disgust was perfectly clear.

"You not understand, mister," Romero said. "The company is own by Senator Lukis. He have private army there. We no can go there."

"Senator?"

"Yah, yah. Senator Lukis. He state senator here fifteen twenny year. Now is federal, in Washington. Everyone afraid argue with him." The old man stared harshly at Joshua.

"Where's the company located?"

"Right in bed of Santa Cruz River by big oxbow across from Martinez Hill. You go out Nogales Highway just mile and half from here, you see cranes, trucks, rock crusher."

"How long has it been there?"

The old man wrinkled his brow in puzzlement and said something in Papago to a considerably older man next to him, who appeared to be at least seventy years old, although his shoulder-length hair was shiny black just slightly mottled with gray. He sucked in his leathery jowls in thought and grunted a few words in Papago through almost toothless gums. He was about five foot eight, a few inches taller than Romero, and thirty or forty solid muscular pounds heavier. He and all of the Indians were dressed almost identically in faded Levi's and worn boots and straw cowboy hats and plaid shirts. The only differences were the colors of the plaids. They looked like the stiffly posed platoon of aging Indian scouts in a photograph Joshua had once seen in a history book about the Old West.

"Macario say is maybe fifty year, maybe longer. Father of senator start company."

"Why do you say it doesn't have mineral rights?"

Romero looked around at the others in disgust, his chin quivering. He muttered a few words that sounded like grunts.

"You Bureau Indian Affairs lawyer, mister. You supposed know our rights. We got treaty with United States government, we got federal law, 'Dawes Act,' we got contract with company, mister. We got rights to minerals, mister. You get our rights." He gritted his teeth and stared balefully at Joshua.

Joshua looked at the sour faces and suddenly felt that he should be back in Manhattan, in a big law firm library, safely behind a shelf of books researching the sterile intricacies of the law of principal and agent as it applied to the decisions of bank vice presidents as to corporate investment of employee pension plans.

"What exactly do you want me to do, sir?" Why the hell was he calling this old man "sir"? It had just come out of his mouth without thinking.

"We want you talk to company, talk to senator, not let them steal."

"Well, Mr. Romero, I apologize to you for not being as knowledgeable about these matters as I should be. I've only been the BIA lawyer for ten minutes"—he glanced at his watch for emphasis—"and it's going to take me a while to catch up on my homework. I'm going to look into this matter." He said it in his "well, it's time to be off now" tone of voice and rose slowly from his chair. It was always effective with New York clients. They knew that it meant that it was time to leave, and attorney and client could work up an overly earnest handshake at the door and a counterfeit congenial pat on the back.

None of the Indians budged.

"We been shit on by BIA a long time, mister. We no be shit on no more." Romero pointed a finger at Joshua. "Senator Lukis try to get new cheap contract with us for subsoil rights. We tell him go to hell. He is bad man. Now he try make you do something, or maybe he try make new federal law says he got mineral rights. You protect our rights, mister." He lowered his hand

and glowered at Joshua. Then he turned slowly around and left Joshua's office. The other Indians followed silently.

The nun remained standing in front of the desk.

Joshua smiled at her. "Something else, Sister?"

She shook her head disgustedly, frowning in mortal disappointment. "I watch you sitting here breathing through your mouth trying to keep from choking on the smell of the Indians, their stink of poverty and despair, and all you can do is spout the same platitudes as your predecessor." She spoke fluently, but a heavy French accent made her a little hard to understand: *"ees spou de same plahdeeTOODZ."*

He didn't know what to say, and he didn't want to let his anger erupt. He spoke softly. "I'm really sorry that I gave that impression, Sister. I didn't mean to."

"You are so uncomfortable with these people that you act like an aristocrat paying insolent lip service to stable boys." *(". . . eensolent leep serVEEZ . . .")*

His eyes flashed with the insult. "I've apologized, Sister," he said slowly. "That's it. I'm not going to fall down dead with guilt. I didn't intend any insult." He stood up abruptly, and his chair spun back into the wall with a crash and fell over.

"Very dramatical, Mr. Rabb, very histrionical indeed." She sat down slowly on the straight-backed wooden chair. "Now that the preamble is over, I would like you to assure me that you will act immediately on behalf of these people to stop Lukis and his son from stealing the tribe blind."

"Jesus Christ!" Joshua exploded angrily. "Why don't you give me a little time to get my bearings around here?"

"Please don't blaspheme, Mr. Rabb," she said in a soft voice.

He pulled his chair upright and sat down. He pressed his hand palm down on top of the desk, gritted his teeth, and swallowed down his anger. "My apology, Sister. Now why don't you give me a little time to get my bearings."

She stared at him with eyebrows raised for a moment, studying him. "I suppose you're not even a Catholic?"

"Right."

"May I ask," she said slowly, " 'Joshua Rabb,' that is a Jewish name?"

He looked back at her blandly, saying nothing.

She sighed disgustedly. "All our people are devout Catholics, Mr. Rabb. And they live in mud and grass huts with no electricity or water. It's typical of the BIA to send someone who is totally unfamiliar with our way of life and our problems and probably never even met an Indian before."

Joshua stared at her coldly. "My salary is two dollars and thirteen cents an hour for fifteen hours a week." He strained to control his temper. "That's one hundred and twenty-eight dollars a month, Sister, with a tiny little mud house thrown in. It's hardly a job any expert on anything would fight for. I came because I want to be here, and so do my children. That's the best I can do for you. I'm sorry I'm not what you wanted. But for the moment I'm all you've got."

The nun's voice became entreating; the confrontation left her opaque green eyes and they softened. "To understand my people, Mr. Rabb, you must yourself know suffering and privation. Have you read the poet Virgil?"

Joshua sighed wearily. "I had to read part of the *Aeneid* in college years ago."

She had a haughty schoolmarmish look in her eyes. *"Haud ignara mali, miseris succerere disco."* She stared at him. *"Not unaccustomed to misfortune, I have learned to succor the downtrodden."* She kept her fixed stare on his eyes. "Frances Hendly told me you're from New York City, Mr. Rabb. A fancy corporate lawyer in Manhattan. Very impressive indeed, Mr. Rabb. But out here we don't need suits and ties and shiny shoes. We need someone who understands and feels the suffering of oppressed people. I'm afraid you're not going to be very happy here, Mr. Rabb. And we certainly won't be very happy with you."

The nun stood up and walked quickly out of his office.

Joshua sat staring at the doorway, slightly shell-shocked.

Edgar Hendly walked in. "I see you've met Sister Robinette and her band of merry men."

Joshua grimaced.

"Well, Senator Lukis called. He'd like to see you at eleven. I told him I thought it'd be all right."

"Yeah, no problem."

"Come on, I'll drive you over to the mission, introduce you to Father Hausner."

"Is he the priest over there?"

"Well, he's one of them," Edgar said. "There's usually a coupla monks or friars over there too. But Hausner's the boss. The 'Superior' is what they call him."

"What kind of a guy is he?" Joshua asked.

Edgar shrugged. "Just an average guy, I guess. Only reason I have much to do with him is that the Mission Sand and Gravel contract has to have the approval of the mission superior. Not a legal requirement, but somethin we've always done. The missionaries know their Indins and know what's fair when it comes to dealin with em."

Joshua nodded. "This contract seems to be right in the front of everybody's mind."

"You bet it is. It's only a three-year contract because a some quirk of the Indin laws or treaties or somethin. And there's never been a big deal made about it till this year. Now all of a sudden, it's like the biggest thing in the world, and that nun bitch got them Indins stirred up like a nest of hornets. Well I ain't gonna stand for it." He was working himself up, and blood rose in his cheeks. "I been runnin this bureau for fourteen years without trouble, and I'll be damned if some lesbian papist bitch gonna stir up a bunch a dissidents and go complainin to Washington and get me in hot water." His breathing was labored, his skin blotchy, and his lower lip quivered with ill-suppressed rage.

Joshua walked over to the bookshelf and began thumbing through the manila folders. "Well, maybe I'd better find the contract and read it over before I meet any more people wanting to discuss it. It must be somewhere in this stack of files."

"Yeah, all right. Come on down to my office when you find it." Edgar walked out of the office, and his lumbering steps echoed down the terra-cotta tiled hallway.

There was no such file in the bookshelf. Joshua pulled out the last volume of *Collected Indian Treaties*, which contained the "Index of Statutes and Descriptive Word Index" and looked

under "Papagos." There were numerous entries, and Joshua got
a pen and small pad out of the inside pocket of his jacket and
jotted down the references under "San Xavier Del Bac." He
replaced the index and pulled out volume 2. He read President
Grant's Executive Order of 1874, which withdrew 71,000 acres
of land around the Franciscan mission from the public domain
and reserved it for the use and benefit of the Papago tribe, and
the Executive Order of 1916, which established the Papago
Indian reservation as a 2,800,000-acre nation covering a huge
area of southern Arizona. Joshua pulled out volume 3 and
opened it to the "Dawes Act of 1887." He tried quickly reading
the "Land Allotment" provisions, but they were much too com-
plex for instant comprehension. He laid the open book down
on his desk. He'd get back to it when he had the chance.

He pulled open the side drawers of the desk. Nothing. He
opened the small top drawer and there was a single manila file
inside. The dog-eared label read "Mission Sand and Gravel."
Inside was a three-page, single-spaced typed document which
had the heading "Bureau of Indian Affairs, Licensing Agree-
ment." It was signed on the bottom of the third page by Jacob
Lukis, President of Evelyn Enterprises, Inc.; Edgar Hendly,
Superintendent of the Bureau of Indian Affairs; Henry Carboneau, Legal Officer for the Federal Office of Land Management and Bureau of Indian Affairs; and Macario Antone,
Chairman of the Papago Tribal Council.

Was this the same Macario who had been here fifteen minutes
ago? No, couldn't be. The one who signed this contract is—or
at least was—the chief of the tribe. The one who was in here
a few minutes ago was just a member of a ragtag band of
troublemakers. At least that's what Mrs. Hendly said.

Heavy footsteps clumped down the corridor again. Edgar
Hendly looked exasperated. Sweat rolled down his forehead
and cheeks and wet his too-tight frayed white collar. His fat
neck bulged around the collar.

"That gott damn Romero and Antone and that fag nun have
been to see Father Hausner already. I just got a call from him
wonderin what in the name a God we was doin with Lukis's
contract. Hausner gets about seventy-five percent of his church's

budget from Lukis as a tax-deductible contribution, and he don't want nobody tippin his cart over. That damn Franciscan takes a vow a poverty and then lives like a gott damn Turkish sultan with his little harem a nuns. Him and them three nuns who teach in the school are just like one a them damn Mormon patriarch families with alla them wives!"

Joshua stared at the wheezing fat man. "You have a whole lot of regard for these people out here."

Edgar snorted maliciously. "Shit! I was raised on a ranch just two miles on the other side a Nogales Highway yonder." He pointed toward the window. "I know these people, grew up with em. The Indins are a bunch of thievin little bastards, and the papists ain't any better, except they blame everything on the Devil and the Indins blame it all on the white man. When I was eleven, my pa died a tuberculosis. Nobody lifted a finger to help us or gave us a slice a bread. And the Indins robbed us blind, took our chickens, livestock, even our tools. The land was so poor we couldn't even sell it. Had to move on into Tucson and go to work for peanuts cleanin the Cattleman's Hotel downtown. Lived in a little room no more 'n the size a this office. My ma, my younger brother, 'n me. I know all about sufferin. I know all about hunger. But we made it, bootstrapped ourselves up. Not the Indins, though. Hell no! All they do is piss and moan about how much the white man owes em. Shit! We don't owe em a gott damn thing!"

Joshua picked up his hat.

"Better leave that here," Edgar said. "Your head'll get so hot wearin a felt hat around here in the summer that your brains'll explode."

The mission was about half a mile away across the irrigation ditch and the barren cotton field, but to reach it by car was a roundabout bumpy three-mile ride on rutted dirt roads.

"You're gettin your 'acculturation girl' this mornin," Edgar said.

Joshua was in a deeply glum mood. He stared at the road ahead and wished it was the Belt Parkway and that he was heading back to Brighton Beach.

"I said you're gettin your acculturation girl."

"Oh, sorry. I was just thinking about something. What kind of girl?"

" 'Acculturation.' It's required by law. All the BIA employees gotta take one a the reservation girls into their homes. They work as domestics for no pay, and they learn white folks' ways and language and how to integrate into our society."

"Where am I going to put her? The house isn't even large enough for Hanna and Adam and me."

"Oh, don't worry none about the girl. She'll sleep on the floor in your daughter's room or out in the chicken coop for that matter."

"Who is she?" Joshua asked.

"Macario Antone's granddaughter."

Joshua turned his face toward Edgar. "The chief of the tribe?"

"Well, he was. Up until a year ago. But he's old now, well over seventy."

"Was he one of the men who came to see me this morning?"

Edgar nodded.

"But your wife told me they were just a bunch of troublemakers."

"She hit that on the nail head," Edgar said, looking at Joshua and nodding. "Just exactly what they are. Old Macario's gettin senile, can't go with the flow, you know what I mean? Gotta make big issues outta nothin. He's gonna get his brains blowed out one a these days, more 'n likely by one a his own people. The copper company down by Sahuarita ten miles south a here laid off nineteen Papago miners last week. Afraid the rabble-rousin on the reservation was gonna spill over into the mines and the Indins would start talkin union and collective bargainin and alla that shit. A lot a the farmers and ranchers round here are afraid to hire the greasers anymore to do the fieldwork like they used to. And that's even makin it worse on the reservation."

The car rumbled to a stop in a cloud of dust in front of the mission. The great wooden doors were wide open, and they could see a man in bright green vestments standing on the altar holding a chalice out before him. They heard monotonal chanting in Latin. They walked to the open doors, and the nave of the church was filled with forty or fifty kneeling women. There were no chairs or benches. The altar was extremely ornate, rococo, in stark contrast to the bare simplicity of the nave and narthex. The apse walls were covered in gilded columns and colorful frescoes of Jesus and Mary and saints whom Joshua couldn't identify, except for St. Francis, because he had birds on his shoulders and a lamb in his arms. In numerous niches were plaster statues. At the rear of the apse was the largest one, of a priest in very fancy vestments. A statue of Mary stood in a niche above him, saying a benediction over him. The beauty and richness of the apse were almost physically shocking in contrast to the desert desolation that lay outside.

The priest gave communion wafers to the women who passed by the rail in front of the chancel, and then the mass ended. The priest signaled with his hand toward Edgar and walked into the sacristy. The women filed silently out of the church.

Edgar and Joshua walked through the nave, climbed the steps to the chancel, and went into the sacristy on the right. The priest's arms were lifted from his sides. A tall stocky man in a brown cassock with the cowl covering his head was standing behind the priest taking off the white linen amice. He folded the amice carefully and laid it on a wooden chest. He took a cotton rope cincture off the chest, circled it around the priest's ample waist, and tied it on the left side with a simple knot.

"Edgar, how nice to see you," gushed the priest and flashed a great smile of ecclesiastical love. He held his right hand out palm down, fingers spread, like Joshua had seen in photographs of bishops or cardinals kneeling and kissing the Pope's ring.

Edgar bussed his lips on the priest's hand, giving Joshua a brief glance of embarrassment. "Father Gerhard Hausner, this is Joshua Rabb, the new BIA lawyer."

The priest turned slowly toward Joshua. His hand was still stiffly extended, and Joshua took it and shook it hard in a vigorous handshake. The priest's wooden smile didn't change at all, but his pale blue lachrymose eyes seemed to darken. He was almost as tall as Joshua, overweight and wheezy like a tall version of Edgar, and somewhere around fifty years old. He wore a faded brown linen cassock. He had short, graying brown hair, and his furrowed face was burned beetle brown by the sun.

"How nice to meet you, Mr. Rabb," the priest said, withdrawing his hand from Joshua's grasp and flexing his fingers gingerly. "We've so looked forward to meeting you." The other priest or monk or whatever he was stood silently in the dim shadows in the corner of the sacristy.

"This is Brother Boniface," Hausner said.

Boniface remained in the corner of the sacristy. Joshua nodded to him, but the man made no gesture of greeting.

"Rabb, Rabb, now what kind of name is that?" Hausner mused. "Maybe short for Rabbinowitz or Rabbinsky or Rabbi." He laughed with phony pleasantry. "We get so few *mazzochristi* here."

Joshua had heard the slur before: "Christ killers." A nice bit of Italian slang. But it had somehow sounded much less ignominious on a Brooklyn street corner with a bunch of guys in front of a candy store telling dirty jokes than it sounded here in this mission south of Tucson, in the middle of nowhere, from the mouth of this leering priest.

"I had very little to do with that, Father Hausner. I'm only thirty-six years old."

The priest studied Joshua's unsmiling face. "Yes, yes," he drawled pleasantly, "just a funny word I picked up from my friend Father Vinitesto at the seminary in Santa Barbara." He stepped toward Joshua and put his hand on his shoulder and gestured out the sacristy with his other hand. "Come, Mr. Rabbinowitz, I'll give you the ten-dollar tour of my mission."

"Rabb," Joshua said, not moving. "Raaab. I don't know why so many people here have trouble with my name. R-a-b-b," he spelled it slowly. "A very simple name."

"Yes, of course," the priest said, shrugging off the exchange as meaningless. "Now come, Mr. Rabb, I'll show you around, and you'll be able to see for yourself just how important Senator Lukis is to my mission here and to the welfare of my flock."

He led the way out of the sacristy and through the side door of the nave. They walked out of the mission grounds to the dirt road in front. The priest stopped and pointed to the small hill just thirty yards east of the mission. The path up the hill was guarded by two bronze lions. Atop the hill's summit was a huge whitewashed wooden cross.

"That's Lourdes Hill. The lion statuary and a chapel at the top which I'll show you some other time were built about forty years ago to celebrate the great miracle at Lourdes. By the way, I understand you had a visit from our Poor Clare."

"Who?" Joshua asked.

"Sister Martha Robinette, she's a sister of the Poor Clares, from Paris."

"Oh, yes, yes. I met her just a little while ago. Strong-minded woman."

The priest grimaced. "Yes, she thinks women should be allowed into the priesthood and that the Pope's authority is too strong."

Joshua said nothing.

"She also has some unfortunately misguided and silly notions about the best way to run the mission and to handle our Indians. She's been here at the mission for eleven years now, longer than any of the rest of us. So she takes great pride in telling us all how we should handle Indian matters." He stopped and looked soberly at Joshua. "Pride is a sin, Mr. Rabb. And when it arises to true arrogance, it is a mortal sin indeed."

Father Hausner turned to his right and walked down the road away from the mission. Joshua and Edgar followed.

"Our nuns live here"—he pointed to a small stucco building—"but this is our pride and joy." He stopped in front of an obviously newly constructed cinder-block building about the size of a house trailer. "Our new elementary school. Our nuns teach grades one through six, and we've got twenty-nine students now."

The priest turned to Joshua and stared hard. "This wouldn't be here if it wasn't for Senator Lukis. His construction company built the school. His influence helps get us army surplus food to feed our children. His money finances many of the good works of the church here, on behalf of these Indians. He is the best friend the Papagos have." He glared at Joshua. "Am I making myself clear, Mr. Rabb?"

Joshua nodded and pursed his lips. He wrinkled his brow, as though in deep contemplation. "Yes. I think I've got it."

"Ah, you're a kidder," Father Hausner said, chuckling avuncularly. "I can see you're a kidder. We'll get along just fine, won't we, Mr. Rabb, now that we understand each other." He extended his hand to Joshua, palm down, fingers spread. Joshua stared coldly at him and didn't move.

"Yes, indeed. A real kidder," the priest said, turning abruptly on his heels and striding away.

Joshua and Edgar stood silently watching the priest disappear into the mission.

"Well, he's a real charmer," Joshua said.

"Yup. Been puttin up with that self-righteous asshole for four years now. The guy before him was pretty decent, but he got valley fever so bad they had to move him, somewhere in Michigan I think. But this guy's a downright shithook."

Joshua chuckled. "Edgar, you have a real talent for crisp nononsense descriptions of people." He eyed the fat, sweating man. "I wonder how you've been describing me?"

"Ain't had a chance yet. See me next week."

Both of them laughed.

"The way Father Hausner talks about 'our Indians,' " Joshua said, "it sounds like he thinks he has some kind of direct authority from God on how to deal with them."

"You ain't heard nothin yet. Wait till you meet old Jacob Lukis. Now there's a man who don't brook no interference with carryin out God's plan, and he'll tell you right to your face that he's the one been designated to carry it out!" He squinted a little at Joshua. "By the way, rumor has it that he's one a *your* boys, of the Mosaic persuasion." Edgar paused a moment to let the revelation sink in.

Joshua looked at him quizzically. "Is that why you hired me for this job?"

"Naw, hell no!" Edgar said, shaking his head vigorously. "Them Lukises would never admit it nohow, not anymore. Why hell, they're all lily-white Episcopalians now, go to St. Phillip's in the Hills church up on River Road where all the fancy swells go. But they say Jacob's pa Simon was a immigrant peddler from Austria or Poland or somewheres like that who came out to this territory way back in the eighteen seventies and started mercantile stores all over, Nogales, Tucson, Phoenix. They say Jacob's ma was the Mexican girl who cooked for old Simon Lukis, but no one really knows. They still got the stores in Phoenix, two of em I think, but the one down here is now Goldberg's, some friend a the old man's who bought him out before he died. Anyway, Jacob has half a Tucson in his pocket, construction, the sand and gravel company, a hotel, a lotta land, who knows what all. And he's a senator to boot. But ye cain't resent it none. He's a good-enough man, sure done right by me."

They started walking slowly back to Edgar's car. "How come Jacob Lukis is the only one you have anything nice to say about?"

"Well, I reckon he gave me my chance. I worked for him at the Cattleman's Hotel my ma cleaned for, and when I got outta high school, he made me manager. Then he put me on as a bookkeeper for his holding company, Evelyn Enterprises, named after his ma—or Simon's wife, anyway—and I became his business manager. From nothin to somethin in eleven years. Then fourteen years ago, when he was first elected a United States senator, he got me this appointment as head a the BIA. I reckon I owe old Jacob one hell of a lot, yessir, one gott *damn* hell of a lot."

They got into the car, and Edgar drove over the rutted road back to the bureau.

"You say he's coming over at eleven?"

Edgar nodded.

"Well, then, I won't have to wait long to meet God's messenger."

Edgar snickered maliciously. "A course I ain't made no mention yet about Steven Lukis, the senator's son. Now there's a piece a shit that stinks for a mile in every direction. You be smart and stay far away from *that* low-life pervert."

Joshua looked over at Edgar to see if he was joking, but there was no humor in the man's face.

"That fat little turd's fifteen years younger 'n me and don't know jackshit about nothin. But whenever the senator was outta town, little Stevie would come down to the Evelyn Enterprises office and start shoutin orders and give everybody a ration a shit like he was the only white man in a room full a niggers. Someone once asked him where 'n hell he got off actin like a big shot when he wasn't no more 'n a piss ant spoiled kid, and Steve says, 'Well, I guess I was born in the right crib!' Imagine that?" Edgar scowled at Joshua. "We all wanted to take one a them crib slats and shove it up his ass and spin him like a top."

Joshua couldn't help laughing, despite Edgar's grim seriousness. "You are one hell of a gifted poet, Edgar. I'm talking Longfellow, Byron, Keats."

Edgar nodded and smiled. "You know, the real reason I hired you is because you have an eleven-year-old boy in the sixth grade, and I wanted my son Jimmy to have a white boy to play with for a change. And now I know I chose good, 'cause you're a man who can see the true inner beauty in another human being."

Both of them laughed.

CHAPTER THREE

First the three people had just been slowly bobbing specks in the long cotton field, specks growing against the whitewashed stucco of San Xavier Mission behind them, framing them in a dust-hazy timeless picture of sere desert and tremulous waves of heat and boundless time. Fuzzy figures in a sepia daguerreotype. Then they loomed closer and closer until it looked like they were going to come over this way on purpose, actually cross over the fifteen-foot-wide, ten-foot-deep irrigation ditch that divided the Papago Indian reservation from Tucson as abruptly and uncompromisingly as the Atlantic Ocean divided Brooklyn, New York, from Lisbon, Portugal.

Hanna Rabb watched them approach. She stopped throwing corn kernels on the dirt for the squalling chickens to eat. She had never seen Indians before—not real ones—and she was frightened. Her father was at the bureau down the road, Adam was off playing with Jimmy, and there was no one around but her. A fourteen-year-old girl from Brooklyn was no match for a war party of marauding Indians.

But they didn't look like a band of Geronimo's renegades. A very pretty girl probably in her late teens or early twenties walked with her head down, seeming to try to hide behind the woman in front of her. The girl was tall and slender and wore threadbare Levi's and a faded blue chambray work shirt and was barefooted. Her shiny black hair was in a long ponytail. The woman was tall and broad-shouldered and very fat with her gray hair in a bun. She wore a plain housedress of unbleached muslin, dirty, sweat limp in the hundred-degree heat. The man riding on the ancient sorrel horse looked as old and as bent as the horse. He kicked it hard, and it picked its way gingerly through the muddy ditch, stumbled a little, then up the other side to the edge of the yard.

Hanna dropped the rest of the corn out of her apron, and the chickens squabbled crabbily around her sandaled feet. She backed up hesitantly toward the house and stared warily at the intruders. The man had a leathery-jowled, russet-colored face that showed no age other than old. Maybe sixty, seventy, eighty, maybe more. He wore a battered straw cowboy hat pulled low over his forehead. Straight black hair with dabs of gray fell to his shoulders.

The man said something in Papago to the girl. She stared at him and then lowered her face. He spoke sharply to her. She raised her face slowly and looked past Hanna.

"My grandfather asks if your father is home."

Hanna shook her head. "No. He's at work, probably won't be home till noon for lunch."

The girl translated. The old woman soundlessly squatted down. The man settled back in the saddle and pulled his boots out of the stirrups, easing his weight on the horse's back. The girl squatted behind the old woman.

They were immobile, like three bronze Indians in the Museum of Natural History. Hanna backed through the screen door of the little house and closed it quietly, as though not to startle the statues. She stared at them for a moment through the kitchen window. The Indian girl started doodling idly on the ground with a stick.

The hands on the red clay rooster clock on the kitchen wall

showed ten-forty-five. Hanna went to the screen door, hooked it closed, and left through the wooden door at the opposite end of the house. She ran to the Bureau of Indian Affairs to find her father.

Joshua was sitting at his desk reading the Dawes Act when Hanna burst in.

"Daddy, there's Indians at our house!" She looked at him urgently, her eyes wide.

"What do you mean? Settle down, honey."

"There's an old man and lady and this girl a little older than me."

"Oh, I forgot," Joshua said, standing up from the desk and reaching for his cane. "She's our acculturation girl."

"Our what?"

"Acculturation girl. She's going to live with us for a while."

Hanna's mouth fell open in shock. "What?"

"Come on. Let's go meet her. I'll tell you on the way."

Adam and Jimmy sat on the gently sloping bank of the reservoir at the far western end of the irrigation ditch about a half mile from Adam's new home. Here the water collected in a pond about ten feet deep and thirty feet wide. Jimmy had touted it as the best place around to get frogs and tadpoles, and this morning Adam had seen more of them than he'd ever seen before in his whole life. They had each caught a big whopper of a bullfrog and had races for an hour. They had also raced against each other for over an hour, underwater, crawl, breast-stroke, butterfly, and the corkscrew, which Adam had taught Jimmy in just a few minutes. Then they lay back on the bank and baked in the sun.

They were both hungry, and the sun was high enough that it must be around lunchtime. They walked slowly back toward Indian Agency Road. As they neared Adam's house, he saw his father and sister entering the front yard from the direction of the BIA and walking up to what looked like some Indians.

The horse and rider hid some people on the other side, and

all that the boys could see were a couple of pairs of legs. As they came into the yard and walked to where Hanna and Joshua were standing, Adam recognized the Indian woman with the broom who had chased them away from her cows yesterday.

Adam froze. Oh no, she told Dad.

Jimmy obviously assumed the same thing, and he took off running toward his house.

"Adam, come on over here," his father said.

Adam was too scared to budge. He stared at the old woman as she turned to look at him, and he could see the flicker of recognition in her eyes. Oh God, I'm sorry, I swear I won't do it again.

"Come here and meet our friends Macario and Ernestina Antone and their granddaughter, Magdalena."

No one seemed to notice the abject terror in Adam's eyes. He shuffled toward his father, waiting for the old lady to clop him on the head with a broom. Nothing happened. His father put his arm around Adam's shoulders and pulled him close.

"This is my boy, Adam. Adam, Mr. Antone was chief of the whole Papago tribe until he retired last year."

"How do you do, sir," murmured Adam looking down, afraid to catch the woman's eye.

"This is Ernestina Antone," Joshua said.

"Hello," Adam mumbled, not looking at the old woman.

"And this is Magdalena, their granddaughter. She's going to come live with us for a while and help with the chores around the house."

Magdalena stepped self-consciously toward Adam and smiled, a little embarrassed, a little frightened.

"It's nice to meet you, Adam," she said in a soft voice.

"Hi," Adam said and smiled back. She was beautiful, like those Indian maidens in the movies, black shiny hair and big black eyes and dark skin and tall and slender.

"Please come into the house and we'll get to know each other," Joshua said. "I'm sure Hanna has some lemonade in the icebox."

Hanna nodded. Magdalena turned to her grandparents and translated. The old woman looked up at her husband, and he nodded almost imperceptibly. He got off the horse slowly and handed the reins to Magdalena.

"Could I?" Adam said hesitantly to the girl. He turned to his father. "Could I tend to him, Dad?"

"That's not up to me, son. You'll have to ask Chief Antone."

Adam looked at the old man. Without waiting for any translation, Macario said a few words to his granddaughter in Papago and she handed the reins to Adam. He led the horse to the other side of the chicken coop, where there was a pile of old hay yellowed by the sun.

Joshua led the way into the house. The Indians came into the living room followed by Hanna.

"Please sit," Joshua said, pointing to the old couch.

The three Indians sat down close together. Joshua sat on the only chair, a threadbare overstuffed armchair.

"Why don't you tell your grandfather he can take off his hat and make himself comfortable," Joshua said.

Magdalena looked a little ashamed. "It's the Papago way, Mr. Rabb. The men don't take off their hats in someone else's home. They think it would be very rude, like taking off their shoes."

"Oh, oh, well that's okay," Joshua said, trying not to offend. "Just however he's comfortable." He smiled reassuringly at the old man.

Hanna came into the living room and handed glasses of lemonade to the chief and his wife. She went back to the kitchen and came out with two more glasses. Then she sat cross-legged on the floor next to her father's chair.

The old man said something to Magdalena. "My grandfather says that he is honored that I will serve the new lawyer and his family. He is grateful for the opportunity for me."

"Oh, it's our pleasure, please assure him of that. We'll all learn from each other." Joshua looked at Hanna, and she was staring in rapt fascination at the beautiful Indian girl.

"I have prepared for you a writing about myself on this form the BIA gave us." Magdalena reached into her back pocket and pulled out a folded sheet of paper. She unfolded it carefully and got up from the couch and handed it to Joshua.

It was a mimeographed form titled "Curriculum Vitae of

Acculturation Program Participant." In the various spaces provided, she had written the information in pencil in careful and
fluid cursive.

"You write very well," Joshua said.

"Thank you," she said, sitting down again next to her
grandfather.

Joshua read the form. "I see you did your first eight grades
at the Sacred Heart School at Cowlic. Where is that?"

"Near Sells on the Big Reservation. That's the tribal headquarters, about sixty miles west of here."

"And then you went to high school at the Phoenix Indian
School and graduated three years ago."

"Yes, sir."

"What have you been doing since then?"

"I studied at the University of Arizona for two years, but then
I had to come back home, because my grandparents needed me
to help them here at San Xavier. Grandma is seventy years old.
Grandpa is seventy-six."

"Do you have any other family?"

"My parents died, I only have a brother. He is a switchman
for Southern Pacific Railroad. He lives in the shacks near the
switching yard downtown."

"I would think that you'd be able to get a paying job in
Tucson," Joshua said. "We're certainly delighted to have you
come live with us, but wouldn't you be happier earning some
money in town?" He smiled gently at her. She is a pretty girl,
he thought, very delicate.

"No," she responded resolutely. "My grandfather has asked
me to do this. He worked hard to set up this acculturation
program, to help our young people, and now he must show
everyone that his own granddaughter does not hesitate to become part of the program. I will serve you and your family."

"Well, that's fine then. We're delighted to have you." He
glanced at his watch. "Uh-oh, I'm a half hour late for an appointment. I've got to get back to the bureau." He stood up.

Hanna and the Indians stood up as well.

Joshua shook the old man's and woman's hands. He quickly
left through the back door and walked to the bureau. As he

THE DIVIDING LINE   43

came into the reception area, Frances Hendly made a big show of reaching down to the locket watch hanging from a brooch on her blouse and studying the time. She wagged a critical finger at him.

"They're in Edgar's office at the end." She pointed down the opposite corridor from Joshua's office.

He limped down the hallway, his cane tip echoing hollowly like distant gunshots. Edgar's office was about six times as large as Joshua's and had a shiny Mexican ceramic tile floor in a gaudy blue-and-yellow-and-red geometric motif. The desk was large, polished gleaming walnut, and the furniture was several matching walnut armchairs covered in burgundy leather with a burgundy leather camelback sofa against the side wall. The walls were covered with framed lithographs of historic documents, the Constitution, the Declaration of Independence, and numerous government office pictures of presidents.

"What happened to you?" Edgar asked, his face flushed, his eyes hard and unsmiling.

"Sorry, I lost track of the time. Our acculturation girl came with her grandparents, and I was just making sure everything was okay."

"Well, the senator couldn't make it, but his son, Steven, came over to meet you. We been havin a nice chat." Edgar's eyes twitched nervously.

The man in the chair in front of the desk stood and turned slowly to face Joshua. Joshua came toward him, laid his cane against his leg, and held out his hand. Lukis's hand was very small and soft and his handshake was insincere. He was overweight, pudgy rather than fat, a few inches shorter than Joshua, around forty years old. Brown eyes, bushy thinning brown hair, practically no chin. His left eyelid was sluggish and didn't open and close in synchronization with his right eyelid, and it gave him a weird look.

"Nice to meet you, Mr. Lukis."

"Call me Steve, everybody calls me Steve."

Joshua nodded.

"Go on, have a seat, Joshua." Edgar gestured to the desk chair next to Lukis.

"My father and I were wondering when you'd have the first draft of our new contract ready for review."

Joshua shrugged. "I haven't even had a chance to read the old contract through yet."

"Well, we can take care of that tonight. My father would like you to come over after dinner, say, eight o'clock."

"Sure, I'd be happy to."

"You can bring over the contract and we'll go over it and have a few drinks."

Joshua nodded.

"I'll send Buford Richards for you in our car. Otherwise, you'll never find our place. He's our security chief. He'll pick you up at seven-thirty." He stood up quickly and strode out of the office without another word.

Edgar stared hard at Joshua and shook his head. "I told you about that piece a shit. You gotta be real careful with him. And whattaya do? You keep him sittin here coolin his heels like a Indin for a half hour. He's gonna remember that for the rest a his life, and someday he's gonna shove a broom handle right up your ass."

Joshua rolled his eyes and frowned. "I'm really sorry. I couldn't help it. Anyway, I'm their guest for drinks tonight. That should count for something."

"Shit! That don't count for nothin with them assholes!"

Joshua didn't laugh. The look on Edgar's face was completely serious.

"Them Lukises wouldn't waste a spit of tobacco on anybody they didn't expect to pay em back tenfold. I reckon by the time they get done with you tonight, you'll be writin em a contract gives em title to the whole gott damn reservation with the mission thrown in for good measure!"

Joshua shook his head slowly. "Oh ye of little faith."

"Oh, some good ol Bible quotin, huh? Well, I got one for you: 'And the Lord prepared a great fish to swallow up Jonah.' " He looked hard at Joshua.

"Your poetry never ceases to amaze me." Joshua laughed.

Edgar's somber look slowly gave way to a smile. "I get it all from the preacher. My wife drags me to the Southern Baptist revival meetin's ever' Sunday."

~~~~~~

Buford Richards picked Joshua up in a touring Packard precisely at seven-thirty. He came to the door holding his straw cowboy hat in his right hand. His uniform was tan cotton twill with short sleeves. Two small silver stars were on each of his epaulets and a big gold star above his left breast pocket read SPECIAL SECURITY, EVELYN ENTERPRISES. His hair was white, but straight and thick, despite his sixty or more years. He had soft hazel eyes and very pink skin that looked much too delicate for Tucson's relentless sun. Joshua left the children lying on the floor staring in rapt attention at the radio.

Buford Richards nodded an unsmiling hello. He opened the rear door and Joshua got inside. They rode in silence, since the sliding glass partition between the driver's seat and the rear compartment was closed.

They rode over dirt roads to downtown Tucson, then on rutted asphalt to Oracle Highway and north out of Tucson for another fifteen minutes. They turned west off the highway onto a narrow dirt path and passed a huge grove of date palms and another of orange trees, with a rutted cart path between the two that had a hand-painted sign, DESERT TREASURES.

A half mile west down the road they turned into another dense orange grove, the trees all with white-painted trunks, and followed a winding path to a sprawling redbrick house. It had fancy carved double wooden front doors, and all along the front was a veranda of white-painted wood with red and white vining roses in full bloom thick around the railing and rail posts. Parked in front was a mud-splattered Ford sedan with SECURITY POLICE painted on the door. Next to it was an exotic sports car, shiny red, a Bugatti or Alfa Romeo or something like that. Joshua had never seen one before, but he had seen pictures of them in *Life* magazine.

Richards parked in the three-car garage next to a Cord and a Cadillac convertible. He opened Joshua's door and preceded him through a side door into the house. Joshua followed him down a long hallway past several closed doors to a large dimly illuminated room. It had a great stone fireplace in the middle of the far wall. The floor was flagstone. The overstuffed couches and chairs were all upholstered in cowhide with the hair side out, brown with white guernsey spots and an occasional brand showing, so that the room struck Joshua for just an instant like a pen filled with reclining cattle. The only thing absent was mooing. The overhead electric lights were all encased in lantern fixtures so that the den would resemble an Old West drawing room with gas lanterns.

"Come," called out the old man sitting in semidarkness at the far end of a long overstuffed couch. He waved his hand at Joshua.

Joshua walked toward him. Richards held out his hand and Joshua handed him his hat. Richards left the room.

"I'm Jake Lukis," the old man said, extending a bony liver-spotted hand to Joshua. Joshua shook it, and the senator pulled it quickly away.

"You've met my son, Steven." He was sitting to the left of his father. He wrinkled his cheeks toward Joshua in a forced thin smile.

"Yes, I've had that pleasure."

The senator gestured to a large chair and Joshua sat down. The senator's voice was gravelly and deep, an old smoker's voice, oddly deep for such a smallish man. He had great ripples of almost gray hair still flecked with brown, which richly framed his darkly tanned face. He was dressed in a very expensive-looking deep blue silk double-breasted suit and stiffly starched white shirt with an old style stand-up collar and a burgundy-and-white polka-dot bow tie. He called out something in Spanish, and a moment later a young man appeared carrying a tray of steaming coffee mugs. He handed one to each of the men and then walked over to a side table covered with bottles, picked one out and brought it to the senator.

"You lose your pitching arm in the war?" Senator Lukis asked.

"No. Luckily, I'm a right-hander."

The senator chuckled. "Your mug is half full. Fill it to the top with this Kahlúa." He poured his own mug full, handed the bottle to his son, who did the same, and Steve handed the bottle to Joshua. Joshua also poured some into his mug. The thick black liqueur had a rich coffee aroma.

The senator held up his mug in a silent toast, and they all drank. He smacked his lips and wiped them with the back of his hand. "Cigar?" he said to Joshua, pointing to the silver box on the wooden table in front of them.

Joshua held up his hand and waved no.

"So," the senator drawled, "Steven tells me that you were too busy to look into our contract problem, Mr. Rabb."

Was there a trace of accusation in the voice, of hostility in the opaque brown eyes?

"Well, that was this morning," Joshua said. "But I did study it this afternoon."

"How nice," the senator said. "No problems, I trust."

"I just can't say at the moment, Senator." Joshua sipped the hot sweet mixture from the mug. "The only thing appears to be that the BIA and *me*, as its legal agent, don't have the authority to grant mineral rights. I think that can only be done by the tribal council, since the presidential executive orders fully allot all of the subsoil and water rights to the tribe as a whole, and the rights are not subject to impingement by the United States government."

The senator's face went from pleasant to woodenly flat. His eyes narrowed. "We've never had this kind of problem before, Mr. Rabb." The words were squeezed out with obvious considerable effort made to keep them even-tempered. "We've had our company there for fifty-three years in the Santa Cruz River bed, and no one ever hesitated a minute in giving us our contract."

"With all due respect, Senator," Joshua said gently, "that had to do with surface rock and sand. The Santa Cruz originates up in central Arizona and terminates way down in Mexico. Only eight or nine miles of it is on Indian land. So the allocation of the alluvial rock and sand is deemed to be subject to federal management, or at least oversight. But as to the subsoil rights on the reservation itself—which is what you're after in this new contract—I just don't think I have the power to do that."

"You sound like a fuckin shyster lawyer," Steve hissed. "How much do you want?"

"That's enough, Steven!" His father's voice was harsh and deep. "You mind your manners with our guest."

Steve gritted his teeth, and the cheek muscles in his chubby face clenched up like peach pits. His weird eyelid opened and closed slowly.

"Please forgive my son, Mr. Rabb. He thinks money can buy anything. But he doesn't know a man like you does only what he thinks is right. I respect that, Mr. Rabb." He raised his coffee mug in a toast, and he and Joshua drank. Steve sat still on the couch, fixing Joshua with a malignant stare.

"Excuse me a moment, Mr. Rabb. I must look in on Alice and see that she's comfortable." He stood up. "Come, Steven, say good night to your mother."

The younger Lukis got up from the couch slowly and followed his father into the hall. Their footsteps echoed down the long corridor, and then silence descended on the large room.

That hadn't been nearly as hard as Joshua thought it would be. He'd expected Jacob Lukis to be a great big bear of a man who brutalized everyone into submission. Much to his surprise, the senator seemed to be a gentle man, reasonable, and very gracious. Steve Lukis was another story altogether. But at least around his father he was deferential and tame.

Senator Lukis came back into the den alone, looking rather shaken. "I'm so sorry, Mr. Rabb, Alice is having a rather bad night of it. I had so wanted to discuss this matter further. Particularly the issue of surplus lands. Did you have a chance to look over the Dawes Act, Mr. Rabb?"

"Only briefly, Senator."

"Well, this whole surplus lands principle is worth studying, Mr. Rabb." He smiled ingratiatingly at Joshua. "Perhaps you'd do me the honor of joining us again tomorrow night?"

Joshua was at a loss for words. "I, uh, well me and my kids have only been here a couple of days. I think I ought to spend some time with *them* tomorrow night. I'd feel very odd imposing on your hospitality two nights in a row."

"Splendid, then! We'll both have our will. You have dinner with your children, and I'll have Buford pick you up at eight o'clock. We're having several other guests tomorrow night, nice kids, you'll like them. My daughter will be visiting us for the weekend and she's bound to have several of her friends over. They all live in the dormitory at the University of Arizona. They love to come here Saturday nights and have a good meal."

Joshua felt that he couldn't say no. "That sounds just fine, Senator."

"Good, good! I'm delighted. Buford is waiting outside for you at the car." He shook Joshua's hand and smiled pleasantly. "Now be sure and glance at the Dawes Act so we can discuss it, Mr. Rabb."

Joshua nodded and limped down the corridor to the garage. Buford held the door of the Packard open and Joshua got in the rear. The window was still closed between driver and passenger, so they drove the half hour in silence. There was not a single streetlight and very few cars, and Joshua had the sensation of almost complete isolation in the back of the big Packard.

Buford Richards touched his hand to his cowboy hat as he opened the door of the car for Joshua in front of the small house. Joshua nodded. He limped to the house and went inside. It was only a little after nine, and Hanna and Adam and Magdalena were lying on the floor staring at the radio.

They mouthed quick hellos at him and went back to staring at the wooden harp covering the cloth-covered speaker on the front of the big wooden box. As though there were a picture there that they could see if only they concentrated and dreamed hard enough. Joshua sat down wearily on the couch.

"Magdalena weaves baskets," said Hanna. "It's one of the Papago arts."

"Well, that's nice, dear." He smiled at the Indian girl, and she looked very pleased. Her raven hair and glistening ebony eyes glowed in the lamplight.

"They make them out of willow and devil's claw," Hanna said.

Joshua didn't know what either of those things was. "Well, maybe tomorrow she'll show you how."

"*Daa-aad*," Hanna said, chiding him for his foolishness, "it takes *years* to learn how."

"Okay, honey. Tomorrow you can *start* learning. What is it Confucius say? 'The longest journey begins with the first step.' "

Adam giggled. He leaned toward Magdalena as though he were confiding a deep secret. "My dad gets all his philosophy from Charlie Chan movies."

The Indian girl smiled warmly at Joshua.

"Well, I'm going to bed," Joshua said. "Long day. How about you? Isn't it time?" He looked from Hanna to Adam to Magdalena.

"Aw, Dad. It's Friday night, and Magdalena and me are talking about stuff."

"Okay, but not too late. Magdalena's going to be with us for a long time." He looked sternly at Adam. "Nine-thirty, okay?"

Adam frowned and nodded.

Joshua went into his bedroom and sat down on the bed. He could hear the muffled conversation of his children and the Indian girl through the frail wall. "Tucson is a Papago name," the girl was saying. "It's from '*Shuk son*,' which means 'the black foothills.' There's a mountain just a mile west of here we call 'Black Mountain.' And the name Arizona too, that's also Papago." There was great pride evident in her voice. "It's from '*Ali Shon Kam*,' 'The Peace of the Little Springs.' "

Joshua lay back slowly, and the only sounds that interrupted the tranquil night were the occasional muffled voices of the children.

⌁⌁⌁

It was after midnight. Hanna, Magdalena, and Adam were asleep. But Joshua couldn't sleep. His left hip was very sore. Day after day of being cooped up in the car, no exercise, and walking with the limp because of the soreness of his foot and leg from no exercise had all combined to make his hip muscles very painful. Dr. Rourke had chided him constantly to get regular exercise, walk, bicycle, swim, something that got the blood going in his legs. His injured foot was long since completely healed, but if he didn't exercise it regularly it became swollen, and then he'd limp, and then his hip would hurt like hell. He pulled his shoes off and massaged his foot. He took off the wrinkled white dress shirt that he had worn all day, pulled on a polo shirt, and slipped on a pair of sneakers. It was a struggle to lace them with just one hand.

In the front yard he was attacked by the ammonia stink of the chicken coops. He walked slowly up to the irrigation ditch, and there was practically no water in the bottom. There was an incandescent half-moon and a brilliantly starry sky for illumination, and as his eyes adjusted to the darkness he had no trouble seeing. There was something magnetic, tantalizing, about the stately mission across the field, framed in the moonlight. He had been in dozens of medieval cathedrals and monasteries in France and Germany and had even been interested enough to read about their history and architecture. He had stood for hours in the great vaulted nave and choir of the romanesque cathedral of St. Sernin. He had stood in silent awe before the magnificent gothic clerestory wall of the nave in the Chartres cathedral. And at Notre Dame and St. Maclou and Reims and so many others he had slowly learned to differentiate between the massive solidity of the romanesque and the graceful lightness of the gothic.

He walked into the ditch and across the muddy bottom and up the other side to the barren cotton field. He concentrated on walking evenly on both feet, not favoring his left leg. It was about eighty-five degrees and dry, and the muscles in his left hip began to relax and stop aching. There is nowhere this peaceful and deserted in Brooklyn, he thought. Even Brighton Beach is lit up along the boardwalk, and there are always people out, no matter what the time, men strolling, couples kissing on the benches, women sitting at rickety portable card tables playing mah-jongg. And when there was a cloudless night, which wasn't very often, all the lights dulled the stars.

But not here. He stopped and let the beauty and peacefulness of this place flood into him. He did several jumping jacks to get blood circulating quickly in his leg. He felt relaxed and walked slowly to the back of the mission. In what appeared to be living quarters to the right, dim lights from within made the curtains glow on the rear of the stucco building. There were a few low-voltage lights on short stakes in the ground at the back of the mission. They were so weak that they hardly cast any illumination.

I wonder what the church looks like at night. I bet it's really beautiful. He walked around the mission and went up to the massive front doors. They were locked. He walked around the other side and found a small door and opened it quietly.

The flickering light of two tall candles on a wooden table against the rear of the apse was not enough to give life to the colors of the frescoes on the walls of the nave. He walked quietly through the nave toward the apse, to study the artwork up close. Suddenly he heard a noise and stopped. It was a sort of gasping sound coming from the transept. He walked quietly to the front of the nave so that he could peek around the corner into the right side of the dark transept. The noise got louder.

He looked around the corner and saw two forms, illuminated only by the dull light of the candles at the back of the apse twenty feet away. A naked man, big, heavy, was kneeling behind another naked person, who was on all fours. It was too tenebrous for Joshua to make out anyone's features. He caught his breath and held it. Was it one of the nuns? On a wooden table behind the two was strewn what looked like some sort of robe and rope belt and next to it what appeared to be trousers and a T-shirt. His eyes adjusted to the darkness, and then he realized. It was a boy, a small, young boy, maybe eight or ten. Joshua brought his hand up to his mouth to hold back the vomit. The man was groaning now.

Joshua turned quickly away and retraced his steps to the nave door. He went outside and closed the door gently and then leaned up against the rough adobe wall until the wave of nausea left him. Was it a priest? He had no way to tell. And the boy? Who knows? He walked quickly across the field and the ditch.

He went into his bedroom and sat down on the bed without turning on the light. He let out his breath slowly, as though he had been holding it. What am I supposed to do? He thought. Do I go to the church and confront the priest? But it may not have been the priest. Should I call the police? But the police have no jurisdiction on an Indian reservation, only Indian police do, or the FBI with the permission of the tribal council. That much I remember from "Jurisdiction" class in law school. A policeman can't even follow a speeder onto a reservation and give him a ticket, because it's like going into Canada or Mexico, a sovereign nation. So I'll call the FBI in the morning. Is there an FBI office in Tucson? Probably not. Maybe in Phoenix. And what will I say? I saw a man committing a crime against nature with a boy. Is that what it was? Are you certain? I don't know what else it could have been. You're certain, then? Well, I don't know. Was it a couple of Indians? Was the boy white? Are you sure you saw a cassock? It was very dark, right? Well, if you suspected something that perverted, why didn't you go on over and put an end to it? Well, I don't really know, I got sick to my stomach watching it, hearing it. I was in a mission, a Catholic church, and I guess I wasn't really supposed to be, not at midnight, and me not even a Catholic. Damn it! Let me think a minute. I'm not sure I exactly know what the hell happened.

He lay back on the bed and put his forearm over his eyes. A slight wind had come up and was rustling the heavy chintz curtains by the open window. The swamp cooler was droning on with only an occasional clatter. He got up and stood by the window and stared out into abyssal black space, and the only thing that marred the pervasive peacefulness was the too-hard beating of his own heart.

CHAPTER FOUR

The next evening Joshua dressed in his best blue suit with vest and the gold pocket watch and chain that had been his grandfather's and then his father's, that Joshua had gotten as a gift when he graduated from law school in 1935. Joshua's father was a high school German teacher in Brooklyn, and the Depression hadn't put him out of a job. The gold watch had been Joshua's grandfather's, a jeweler in Kiev, and when Joshua's father had left Russia in 1905 after the Cossack pogroms, he had been given the watch as a parting gift.

Joshua said good-bye to Hanna and Adam and Magdalena and left them glued to the same spots on the living room floor as the evening before. As Joshua walked out the door, Rochester was saying something to Mr. Benny.

Buford Richards opened the door of the Packard. His uniform shirt was a little smaller than yesterday's, and his stomach bulged the buttons. His meaty shoulders seemed trapped in the confinement of the ill-fitting shirt. He touched his hand to his hat and nodded as Joshua got into the car.

Once again they rode in silence with the privacy window

shut. The small fold-down bar built into the back of the driver's seat was open, and a decanter of something amber was sitting securely in a round opening into which half the bottle fit. Next to it was a seltzer siphon, and in front was a highball tumbler. It was too hot for ice to have kept, even if there had been any.

Joshua took out the decanter, pulled out the crystal stopper, and sniffed. Scotch, it smelled like. He could use a drink right now. Maybe even two or three. He poured a couple of fingers into the glass and then shot a couple of squirts of soda into it. He settled back for a pleasant half-hour ride.

Four or five fingers of scotch later, the car drove through the dense orange grove and parked in the garage. The Security Police car was again out front along with a gorgeous 1936 or 1937 Pierce-Arrow limousine.

Buford opened the side door to the house and said, "They're in the music room at the far end of the house."

Joshua had left his cane at home. He concentrated on walking evenly and went down the long corridor toward the opposite end of the house. As he neared the end, he heard music and saw light creeping out under the double doors. He opened the door on the right and walked in.

The room was elegantly decorated with a camelback sofa and two Queen Anne chairs of bone-colored satin. The floor was yard squares of green marble ribbed with rose and gray and rust. The walls and high ceiling were paneled in knotty pine. A large shiny black grand piano took up an entire corner of the sumptuous room. Senator Lukis sat on the piano bench next to a stunning young woman with a rich shock of auburn hair covering her bare shoulders. They were all dressed casually. Even the senator had traded his vested silk suit for a Western shirt and beige twill pants and shiny brown cowboy boots. Joshua felt uncomfortable, overdressed.

"Come in, come in, my boy," the senator called out affably.

All eyes turned to Joshua. Steve Lukis's face lacked the rancor of last night. He waved at Joshua. Joshua walked to the senator and shook his outstretched hand.

"This is my daughter, Jennifer," the senator said.

She held her slender long-fingered hand out to Joshua. "Father has told me so much about you." Her voice was deep and throaty. She was one of the most beautiful women Joshua had ever seen. Big almond-shaped black eyes, dark tanned skin, rich curly reddish brown hair, small, white, even teeth and lubricious pouting lips. She was wearing a Mexican bare-shouldered dress with the billowing blouse tied in front. The white cotton swelled out over her breasts and was embroidered with a couple of big colorful parrots or macaws, or some such tropical birds.

"Have a drink, Mr. Rabb. Anything you wish, right over there." The senator pointed to a bar at the other end of the room.

Joshua was already warm from the drinks he'd had on the way over. He poured scotch into an old-fashioned glass and put some ice cubes in it from a small silver ice container. He shot a stream of soda into it from the siphon.

Steve had gotten up and was putting some records on a Victrola. The two girls with him on the couch were young, pretty, but nothing in comparison to Jennifer Lukis. She's a knockout, Joshua thought, an A-1 first-class knockout. The first record was Frank Sinatra with some big band. Mellow and romantic.

Joshua walked back over to the senator and his daughter.

"Your health, sir." The senator held out his glass in a toast.

"And yours, Senator," Joshua said, clinking glasses with the old man.

"Take off that jacket and vest and tie, my boy. Just make yourself at home."

Joshua put his drink on top of the piano. He struggled a little self-consciously out of his jacket and laid it atop the piano. The sleeve was pinned to the shoulder of the shirt. He unhooked his watch chain and slid it and the pocket watch into his pants pocket. He laid the vest neatly on the jacket. Then he pulled off his tie and folded it on top of the vest.

"There, that's a lot better," the senator said. "Now why don't you two kids dance." He gestured toward his daughter.

She looked very pleased, and Joshua was actually excited. The whiskey and the music and the girl made him feel powerful, full of energy. He forgot for a moment that he had only half a foot. They began to dance, and as he tried to whirl her around like he'd seen in those Fred Astaire and Ginger Rogers movies, he lost balance and stumbled against her. She steadied him and held him against her, and they danced very slowly, very close. The scent of her was even more intoxicating than the scotch. He felt himself begin to bulge, to press on his fly, and he rubbed hard against her. She held him even closer.

Steve and one of the other girls were dancing as well. The senator tapped at the piano keys, creating unconnected sounds like someone who had never played the piano. The record ended, and Jennifer pulled reluctantly away. Joshua hoped that the excitement in his pants was not too obvious. It felt like a ponderosa pine had sprouted down there, but when he glanced down, he saw only an innocuous bulge. He giggled, then caught himself. Jesus Christ, I'm getting drunk. Better learn how to hold my liquor. Out of training. Another record began. Doris Day. Jennifer pulled him close, hungrily, and pressed her thighs against his.

"I feel a little funny dancing like this in front of your father."

"Oh heck. Don't be silly. Daddy thinks I'm going to be an old maid, or worse, a professional student!" She giggled. "I'm twenty-four and I've been going to the U of A for six years, and I'm still not going to graduate! Daddy's getting mad at me. He thinks a nice girl gets married and has a bunch of children so he can play with them." She looked into his eyes. "What do you think?"

"I think children are great," he said. "I've got two."

"Yes, I know," she confided in him. "Daddy looked at your personnel record when you were hired by Mr. Hendly. They're real good friends." She hesitated a moment. "Daddy says you were married."

He nodded.

"What happened to your wife?" Jennifer asked, her voice soft and alluring. She pressed her cheek against his chest.

"She died in an automobile accident in New York almost two years ago," he whispered into her hair.

"Oh, I'm sorry," she purred. "Is that how you got hurt?" She put her hand tenderly on his left shoulder.

"It was a long time ago," he whispered.

The song ended, and no one put on another record. "I'll get you a refill," she said to him. "I think my dad wants to talk to you for a minute anyway."

Joshua went over to the piano, and the senator smiled up at him. "I never did learn to play a note of this thing. My mother could play like a saint, though, and you should hear my dear Alice play Chopin. Of course," he said, a sad afterthought, "the arthritis ended that. But she could charm Lucifer himself."

Joshua smiled politely.

"So have you had the opportunity to look over the Dawes Act, Mr. Rabb?"

"I read over it this afternoon, Senator, and especially the sections you told me you were interested in dealing with surplus lands. But I'm not sure I understand what you're getting at."

"Well, my lawyers and my son—I don't know if you were aware that Steven is a lawyer, doesn't practice, but he sure is a fine one—well, they tell me that if the allotments under the Dawes Act are all completed and the Indians get their hundred and sixty acres or eighty acres or whatever they're entitled to, then the BIA can declare any of the rest of the reservation land excess and sell it on the open market. The Federal Office of Land Management then handles the sale."

Joshua nodded and shrugged his shoulders. "But from what I understand, Senator, the 'trust' period has been extended indefinitely and none of the land has ever been declared 'surplus.' "

"Ah, yes. Now there's the issue, of course. The BIA has just never gotten around to declaring any of the land surplus, because there's never been anybody particularly interested in buying a piece of that godforsaken desert. But now, Mr. Rabb, now I have a genuine hankering, a real honest-to-God hankering."

"Yes, Senator, I've heard. Some Indians were in my office the other day claiming that you hit a vein of silver or gold and are getting rich on their minerals." He chuckled as though he didn't believe the story.

"Well, you don't believe that foolish blather by a bunch of

troublemakers do you now?" It was much less a question than a demand.

Jennifer came up and handed him a drink. Joshua sipped it, to gain a few seconds to think.

"Maybe you'd like to show me around the company sometime, Senator. Then I'll be able to reassure the troublemakers. And maybe then there wouldn't be anyone who would gripe too much if your piece of land got declared surplus and you bought it."

The senator's face brightened, and he beamed at his daughter. "This is a clever man, Jen, a very clever man. You mind him close now and see he doesn't get stolen away by Cindy or Janice over there." He pointed to the two girls on the couch and laughed.

Jennifer hugged Joshua's arm and had a dreamy look on her face. "Nobody steals *my* Joshua away."

He felt literally ten feet tall, as rich as Midas. He drank down the drink in a few swallows, and a record began to play. Dinah Shore. He danced with Jennifer, and he felt a little drunk again.

After a minute she said, "I think maybe you drank a little too much, huh, honey? Come on out with me and get some air."

She led him out of the music room. No one seemed to take notice. They walked out the side door of the house into the deep black night, made even blacker because the stars and the moon were blotted out by huge Aleppo pines. She turned to him and brushed her lips against his. Then she kissed him, running her tongue delicately around his lips.

She took his hand and led him about thirty yards away from the house to a small redbrick cottage. She opened the door and they went inside. It was dimly lit by a single lamp on a side table next to a couch. The living room was small, and the couch faced a stone fireplace which took up an entire wall.

"This is my place," she said. "It's really the guest house, but I've lived here for the last ten years, ever since Steve left and got a place in town. Isn't this nice and cozy?" she said, turning to him and snuggling against him.

He felt woozy, really drunk. But for some reason he couldn't remember drinking all that much. She steadied him.

"Come on, big boy. I'm going to put you to bed before you collapse." She put her arm around him and led him into a bedroom. He flopped down on top of the bedspread and fell instantly asleep.

He awoke to her unbuckling his belt and sliding his zipper down. "Oh, I'm sorry, I didn't mean to wake you. You've been sleeping for hours, and I was going to undress you so you'd be more comfortable."

He blinked his eyes a few times and brought her into focus. A lamp was on in the room. He felt a million times better, refreshed from the sleep, and he drew her to him and kissed her.

She stood up and loosened the bow on the front of her bodice. She pushed down the blouse over naked breasts and stepped out of the cotton sundress, nude. Her body was magnificent, smooth, slender, buxom. He unbuttoned his shirt and struggled awkwardly out of it. She pulled off his shoes and socks.

"Oooh," she squealed, "that's a weird foot you have there. You're missing your little piggies!" Both of them laughed.

He hadn't been with a woman since he had gotten out of the hospital, since he had exchanged his arm for a small scarred stump, and he was conscious of her looking at it. But she said nothing, and she didn't look shocked. How incredible that she didn't look horrified at the stump, which reminded him every time he looked at it of a bell pepper, plump and round on top and pinched together and shriveled on the bottom. It was a disgusting thing to have hanging off your shoulder instead of an arm.

She pulled his trousers off. Then she reached to his waist and pulled his underwear off. She kneeled on the end of the bed and worked her lips up his shin, thigh, and took hold of him lovingly and caressed him with her lips and tongue. It took only seconds, and he jerked and shimmied on the bed.

"Oh, baby, you're fantastic," she purred. She lay down beside him and turned toward him. "Now me," she whispered. He rolled on top of her and she wrapped her long slender legs around him and he rocked on her and came again.

It occurred to him for a fleeting moment that Jennifer was

no ingenue. She was as practiced and as willing as a professional whore.

He lay back on the bed, and after a few minutes respite they began to explore each other again. They locked into various positions and angles and she was eager for anything.

Then they both lay back exhausted. "I guess I'd better go. It must be very late," Joshua said.

"Yeah," she said softly. "I wish you could stay with me all night, but my father is a little too conventional for that."

He sat up slowly, swung his legs over the end of the bed, and began to dress. His head pounded from the alcohol, and he became dizzy when he put his head down.

"Will you come back again next Saturday night?" she asked.

"Of course. Will your father invite me?"

"Don't worry about that! He'll invite you and I'll pick you up myself."

He smiled at her and she lifted her hand and wiggled the fingers. "Bye, honey."

"Bye," he said.

It was thick black outside, and he couldn't see anything. He waited for his eyes to become accustomed and then walked to the side door of the house. It was locked. Damn, my jacket and vest are in there, he thought. He walked around the front of the house toward the garage. Suddenly the headlights of a car went on.

"I've got your jacket and vest," someone called out from the driver's window of the Security Police car. "Come on, I'll take you home."

As he got a few steps away, he recognized Buford Richards. He went around the car and got in the front seat.

"Thanks. I thought all my stuff had gotten locked up inside."

"No, no problem. I've been waiting for you."

"Sorry to keep you up half the night."

"Doesn't matter. At my age all I do is eat and sleep and sit on the pot anymore. I don't mind dozing in the car. I've been chauffeuring the senator around for twenty years, and I'm plenty used to it by now."

"I hope the senator didn't mind my flaking out on him. I guess I had too much to drink."

"He's the last guy who'd mind or even mention it. The senator's a great man, and he's taken a heck of a liking to you."

"I'm very pleased. I've taken a heck of a liking to his daughter."

"Yeah, I know what you mean. She's the family jewel. A little wild, but she's the salt of the earth, just like her dad." He looked over at Joshua, studying him. "Listen, Mr. Rabb, let me talk to you man to man. I'm your friend, and I'll just give you about two cents worth of advice. Senator Lukis is a great man. You help him out, and he'll do things for you you won't believe. He's a fabulous man to have on your side."

Joshua nodded. "If it can be done, I'll help him do it. Nothing would make me happier."

"Make it happen, Mr. Rabb, make it be done," Richards said solemnly.

They drove through the deserted dark streets and came to Joshua's house. Joshua reached over and shook Buford's hand firmly. He reached to the backseat and got his hat, vest, tie and jacket, and went quietly into the black house. His head throbbed painfully again, and he went into the kitchen and took two aspirins. The moonlight through the window reflected off the black enameled hands on the rooster clock. It was almost two o'clock.

He undressed quickly and lay down on the bed. He could still smell Jennifer on him, and he wanted her here now. Her delicious taste, her enticing smell. Next Saturday night seemed like a decade away. It had been so long since he'd been with a woman—any woman—that he was still excited. He still saw the look on her face, still felt her touch. He fell asleep feeling as though he'd suddenly been reborn.

Children's cries awakened him: not cries of playing and pleasure but of fear and alarm. He jumped out of bed. It must be mid-morning, since the sun was high in the window. He pulled on his trousers and went quickly into the living room. Adam came running through the front door.

"Dad, Dad! A boy's in the ditch. A boy's dead in the irrigation ditch!"

"Oh my God!" Joshua said. "Let me put on my shoes." He ran into the bedroom, pulled on his sneakers, and ran out of the house with Adam.

The mission bells across the field were ringing out melodiously, and Joshua could see dozens of people milling about in front. Mass was either over or just starting. He ran alongside the irrigation ditch with Adam and saw Hanna and Magdalena about thirty yards away. They were both kneeling at the edge of the embankment. Hanna was crying. Magdalena was grim-faced and silent.

At the bottom of the ditch, in a foot of gently flowing irrigation water, was a young Indian boy. He lay sprawled on his back dressed in a white T-shirt and an old pair of Levi's and no shoes. His face was underwater, purple and bloated.

"Magdalena," Joshua said, "run to the mission and call the police, tell them we need an ambulance. And tell Father Hausner and Sister Martha."

Without a word, she scrambled down the bank, splashed through the water and up the other side and began running toward the mission.

Joshua gently turned Hanna around. "Okay, honey, it's okay. Nothing's going to happen to you. He drowned, that's all. I want you to go back to the house. There's no reason for you to stay here."

Her sobbing slowly subsided. She walked a few yards away and turned around, watching. Adam remained kneeling at the edge of the bank, staring at the body.

"Go on back to the house and stay with your sister."

Adam shook his head resolutely. "I'm no baby, I'm going to stay here with you."

"Adam," Joshua said sternly.

The boy didn't budge. Joshua shook his head and frowned. "All right, just stay up here out of the way." He climbed down the bank and reached down and grabbed hold of one of the boy's thin ankles and pulled him out of the water. The boy's eyes were open wide and rolled back white. His mouth was open. It looked like he had swallowed his tongue. He had burst blood vessels all over his cheeks and on his neck.

He was nine or ten, maybe even eleven like Adam, but smaller. He had a pretty face, delicate features, and very light skin. His thick black hair was plaited with mud. "Jesus, poor little kid," murmured Joshua, and suddenly felt queasy. He swallowed hard and wiped his mouth with the back of his hand and breathed deeply. He stood there just staring at the boy for minutes.

Far in the distance came the sound of a siren. It took ten minutes for the sheriff's department brown-and-white Chevrolet to pull up on the embankment. The deputy got out and climbed down into the ditch. By then Magdalena had returned and was standing next to Joshua in the ditch. She had found Sister Martha in the convent, but Father Hausner was busy saying mass.

Sister Martha was walking awkwardly through the field, her black skirts billowing about her. This time her head was covered in a great white wimple which rocked back and forth precariously. A half-dozen Indian men and women clustered about her. They came to the edge of the opposite bank and stared down at the body.

"*In nomine patris et filius et spiritus sanctus, Amen,*" the nun intoned, crossing herself. The other Indians and Magdalena crossed themselves, as did the sheriff's deputy standing ankle-deep in the water in his shiny black knee-high boots.

"Gimme a hand, huh, pal?" the deputy said to Joshua. He was a burly man in his mid-thirties with a marine crew cut and the stub of a big cigar clenched tightly in the corner of his mouth. He saw Joshua's disapproving look and pointed at the stub. "For the smell, pal. I'm the coroner's deputy. I sometimes get some real stinkers, 'specially here on the res. I gotta keep it to fight away the smell."

Joshua lifted up the boy's ankles with his right arm and braced them between his hip and his arm. The deputy picked the boy up by the shoulders. Joshua backed carefully up the side of the ditch. The deputy swung over as they reached the top and they laid the boy lightly on the embankment.

Magdalena climbed out of the ditch and stood beside Joshua. "His name is Vittorio Ponsay," she said quietly. "He's an orphan. He lives by selling himself to men." She choked out the words and blanched, and tears began to flow down her cheeks. "His sister works in a house of prostitution downtown."

The deputy reached into the boy's pockets. There was nothing in his back pockets. His front left pocket had a rusty Boy Scout knife. From his right pocket he pulled out a gold watch and chain. Joshua's eyes narrowed and he stared at it. It looked a lot like his own pocket watch.

Adam looked up at Joshua and said, "Hey, Dad, looks like yours."

The deputy didn't seem to hear or care. "Looks like somebody paid him pretty good for once," he said. He put the watch and chain into his shirt pocket. "Evidence."

A converted military ambulance came up trailing a cloud of dust. Two attendants pulled out a pole stretcher and rolled the body onto the canvas. They lifted it easily into the back of the van and drove away.

"Well, show's over, folks," the deputy said. "You can all go home now."

Magdalena put her hand out and Adam looked up, hesitated a moment, and then pulled himself up with it and held on tight. They started walking back to the house, and Magdalena came up beside Hanna and took her hand. Tears still streamed down Hanna's cheeks. They walked silently. Adam and Magdalena joined Hanna on the floor in the living room.

Joshua walked into his bedroom and closed the door. He went to the chair with his suit jacket and vest laid on the seat and felt in the vest pockets. Empty. He felt strange, short of breath, hollow. He pulled out both front pants pockets. No watch. Where had he put it last night? He sank slowly down on the edge of the bed and stared at the clothes on the chair. What's going on, he thought, what the hell is going on? He tried to remember exactly what had happened last night, every moment, but he couldn't. Much of it was a blur, lost in a haze of alcohol. Suddenly he was deeply frightened. He sat unmoving, rigidly tense, thinking about his pocket watch. How the hell did my watch get in a dead Indian boy's pocket? I did have it with me last night, didn't I?

There was a knock on the bedroom door. His head snapped up. He was annoyed. Another knock.

"Yes," he called out gruffly.

"Daddy, it's Sister Martha. She wants to talk to you," Hanna said through the door.

The door opened slowly, and Sister Martha came into the bedroom. She closed the door behind her and stood directly in front of Joshua. Her bold green eyes shone with emotion. She was pretty, despite her pained look.

"You know why that boy was murdered, don't you?" Her voice was hard.

"Murdered?" Joshua said. "You're talking nonsense, Sister."

"Yes, murdered. Do you think a strong and healthy ten-year-old boy drowns in a few inches of water? He was murdered by *them* to make sure you do exactly what they wish. Don't you see? It's a warning. They have shown you what will happen to your children if you oppose them, if you—"

"Lower your voice!" said Joshua. "I don't want you scaring my kids to death."

"Did you know that a thirteen-year-old Papago girl was murdered just two days before you and your children arrived here? She was thrown into the ditch in front of your house."

"Yes, Mr. Hendly told me a girl was found there, but that nobody's sure it was murder."

"He's just afraid to scare you, Mr. Rabb. I saw the body of the girl when they pulled her out of the ditch. There was blood all over the insides of her legs."

Joshua winced involuntarily and stared at the nun.

"They killed her just for you. They knew you were arriving any day, and they wanted to show you what will happen if you don't do what they want. And now the boy."

"*They?* Who are *they?*"

"Senator Lukis and his minions."

Joshua studied the nun's face. "You have proof of this?"

She shook her head. "Even if we had proof, no one in this town would do a thing about it. Senator Lukis owns everybody."

She appraised Joshua's look. "But I can see you don't believe me, Mr. Rabb."

He shrugged and frowned incredulously. "I can hardly imagine a United States senator plotting the rape and murder of a teenage Indian girl and a little boy."

The nun's nostrils flared like an angered spaniel's. "You think I'm just a crazy woman, Mr. Rabb? Well, you're dead wrong. Why do you think Henry Carboneau, the lawyer who was here before you, fled from this place? I'll tell you why. Because he was afraid for his family."

"Frances Hendly said that he left because the Indians were hassling him."

"Are you that gullible, Mr. Rabb? Are you really that stupid?" The nun glared belligerently at him.

Joshua returned her stare, anger bubbling up inside of him.

"Do you know Cicero, Mr. Rabb?"

Joshua shrugged. What the hell did Cicero have to do with anything? "I had to read *The Orations* in a humanities class a long time ago."

"O tempore, o mores!" She recited in a slow, grave tone, her eyes closed tightly. *"Senatus intellegit, consul videt; haec tamen vivit. Vivit? Immo vero etiam in senatum venit, fit publici consili particeps, notat et designat oculis ad caedem unum quemque nostrum."* She opened her eyes and peered at him coolly.

"We read it in English, Sister, not in Latin."

"What an age!" she translated, staring intently at him. *"What morals! The senate knows these things, the consul sees them. Yet this man lives. Lives, did I say? Nay, more! He walks into the senate, he takes part in the public counsel. He singles out and marks with his glance each one of us for murder."*

Joshua looked back at her wearily and shook his head slowly. "Are you telling me that Cicero was being prophetic?" he said sarcastically.

Her look turned frightened. "I am telling you that after Cicero was bold enough to perceive the truth and to speak it, they came to his home and dragged him out and strangled him. You must be on your guard."

"Well, I'd say that's one hell of a good reason to keep my

eyes and my mouth shut." He forced a little laugh, but his face was grave. "I just can't believe it. The Lukis family is hugely wealthy, the old man's a United States senator. I can't see them engaging in a murder conspiracy just to steal a few hundred or even thousands of pounds of gold or silver."

She looked at him as though she were chiding a wayward schoolboy. "You foolish man. Judas murdered the son of God for just thirty pieces of silver. Do you think Jacob Lukis and Steven Lukis and Buford Richards wouldn't murder us all for thirty pounds?"

He breathed deeply and let out the air slowly, trying to calm himself. It was a terrifying possibility, and it would explain why his watch was in the boy's pocket. In fact, it was the only rational explanation.

"Sister," he said quietly, "the senator has a gimmick up his sleeve to legally acquire all the land he wants for his company. They don't have to murder a couple of kids to frighten *me*. The senator can go over my head and make it all happen back in Washington, D.C., without so much as batting an eye. I just can't believe what you're telling me."

The nun's face softened. Her voice lost its tone of accusation. "That's because you don't know these people. I do. I've been here for over ten years. I've watched the senator grow old and bitter. I've seen his son go from being a spoiled venal boy to a vicious man inebriated with malice. I have seen the fences go up and the gates get padlocked around the company."

Joshua turned his face toward her and listened closely.

"Do you think the Indians smell bad because they were born that way?" she said. "No. It's because they have no water to wash with. The company built a huge pumping station behind its locked gates and pumps out most of the Papagos' water supply and diverts it to the two housing projects they built across the Nogales Highway. And the fallow fields around the mission, and lifeless barren desert on the reservation . . . Do you think the Papagos are too lazy or stupid or drunk to grow crops? Of course not, Mr. Rabb. But they have no water. You have seen the irrigation ditch, Mr. Rabb. It usually has only a trickle in the bottom, only enough water to grow tadpoles. Ten years ago it was full of rushing water, and there were crops in all of the fields. But then the Lukises took the water for their building projects, and now there is none for the Indians."

Joshua's face was drawn. "If that's all true, why haven't the superiors at the mission complained about it? If the Church made a stink, I'd think a lot of unpleasant attention could be focused on the Lukises."

"Because the superiors are only mortal men," the nun said softly, "and they are susceptible to the same influences as any others. The senator invites them to his home and wines them and dines them and God knows what else and lines their pockets with lucre, and they become as docile as kittens. Father Hausner is a perfect example. The superior before him, Father Benedict, was not like the others. But he didn't last long. The story was that he got valley fever and had to leave the desert for his health. But that was just a story. The truth is that he was slowly being poisoned with arsenic in his food, and we couldn't discover who was doing it, and after a while he was afraid to eat anything, and he almost died of starvation."

Joshua shook his head. "Sister, I simply can't believe all of this. Edgar Hendly told me the man got valley fever. He seems to be very savvy about what's going on around here, and he doesn't share your view that the Lukises are the root of all evil."

She looked at him incredulously. "Edgar is a boob. Not a corrupt evil man, just a pathetic boob. He's the perfect Lukis appointment as head of the BIA. Whatever the senator wants, the senator gets. Period. And such a man you hold up as your expert?"

"Well, there's another sad possibility with the boy's death," Joshua said. "I took a walk two nights ago, and I went into the mission to look over the artwork, and I saw a man and a young boy naked together. It was too dark to make out their faces." He glanced at her, not wanting to shock her. "But I think I saw one of those brown cassocks the priests wear on a table. And the boy could have been this Vittorio. He was the right age and size." But that wouldn't account for the pocket watch, would it? he thought uncomfortably. What's happening here?

She crossed herself and mumbled a few words in Latin. "We are all sinners," she said quietly.

"Well, some more than others, Sister." He shook his head slowly and breathed in deeply. "You know, Sister, I've been here just three days, and I feel like I've been dropped into the center ring of the Barnum and Bailey Circus and I'm surrounded by twenty lions and no one bothered to give me a whip and a chair." He smiled, but it was mostly pained.

"Then you must endeavor to have the faith and the soul of Daniel: 'My God hath sent his angel and hath shut the lions' mouth that they hurt me not, for God found me to be innocent.' " She nodded at him very earnestly, and then she left the room.

He stared glumly out the bedroom window, seeing nothing, lost in thought. He couldn't believe that her perception of the great perfidy enveloping them all was anything more than her own simplistic answer for uncomfortable, unexplained events. She was a nun, after all, married to Jesus—as her wedding band proudly proclaimed—and in her world there was God and the Devil, good and evil poised opposite each other in constant combat. But to Joshua the differentiation had long since lost any sharp focus. People were good and bad at the same time, puzzlingly so, neither saints nor sinners, just people. And he had met Senator Lukis and Buford Richards, and he liked them. Even Steve was no more sinister than any rich and powerful man's son, too self-assured, much too self-important. But he certainly didn't seem to be a demonic incubus, just a plain and simple jackass. And Joshua couldn't imagine any of them plotting the murders of two children. But there seemed to be no other explanation that made any sense. One of them had to have planted his pocket watch on the dead boy.

He sat slumped on the bed, and the missing toes of his left foot began to ache. He automatically reached down to rub them, but he touched only air. He grimaced in frustration. Funny how things that were long gone could still hurt. Like the phantom pain of missing toes; like the phantom pain of battles long since fought.

December 1944. I am lying in a foxhole in a foot of snow in a frozen field near a town in Luxembourg ominously named Diekirch, and my 109th Infantry Regiment is pinned down by what looks like the entire tank corps of the German Army. My company is suddenly caught by surprise by a machine-gun battery set up at the edge of the skeletal winter-ravaged forest. It rakes the exposed foxholes of my platoon with a withering barrage. I think that all of my men are going to be killed. And for reasons I do not fully understand, I crawl through the frozen snow to within forty feet of the edge of the machine-gun emplacement and throw a grenade into the hole and spray the three German soldiers with the entire forty-round clip of my submachine gun. It is as though I am watching myself in a movie theater, and I have no control over my body.

Suddenly two of my men huddle with me on the ground and I can vaguely hear one of them calling frantically with the field radio for a medic, but I can't focus on why. Then I allow myself to fall into an oddly warm sleep. I awake sometime later in an aid station, and it is the first time that I feel the pain. My left leg is no longer frozen, and the bullet wound in my thigh hurts like hell. My leg is in a slinglike contraption hanging from a metal rod over the bunk, and I can see that the four small toes of my left foot are a morbid purplish color, like shriveled plums hanging on a tree limb. I realize that I have frostbite, and then my foot really starts to hurt.

Some medics haul me into an evacuation ambulance and load my shoulder with something that stings a little and soon takes away most of the pain. I wake up in an army hospital in Antwerp, Belgium, and the doctor tells me that I have lost all of the toes on my left foot except the big toe, and that the thigh wound will heal without a trace other than the scar. There is very little pain, and what pain there is slowly subsides after only a few days. A few weeks later they hand me a cane and tell me to walk, and I discover that I don't need the small toes for balance; the big toe is the important one. And after a little practice, I can almost walk without a limp.

Then one day the colonel who is the hospital chief of staff comes to my room and sits down in the chair and gives me a soulful look. I was notified that your wife died in an automobile accident in Brooklyn, he tells me, but I didn't think you were up to hearing about it till now. I'm very sorry, my boy, he says. I'd have medicaled you back to the States, but we're on our last push through Germany, and we need every available man. I've got to send you back to light duty. He stands up, shakes my hand, and walks out, leaving me piercingly alone, staring into space, seeing nothing through tear-filled eyes. What will happen to Hanna and Adam? Are they okay? I am sure that my parents have taken them to live in their apartment on Brighton Beach Avenue, and that they are well cared for. But just the distance from them, just the not knowing, makes me deeply fearful for them. I feel an almost paralyzing despair, for my wife whom I will never see again, for my children whom I will probably never see again.

The day before I'm discharged from the hospital, there is a little ceremony in the general's office. I'm promoted to major and awarded the Silver Star. The citation reads, "for bravery above and beyond the call of duty," but I don't want to remember it. I push it out of my mind, the day, the place, the weather, and the staring surprised eyes of the blood-spattered Germans I killed.

I'm attached as JAG officer to a rear unit of Patton's 3rd Army and traverse the entire waist of Germany into Czechoslovakia. My company is sent around behind the heavy weapons company to guard their rear when they enter a little town named Medzibiez. Intelligence reports that there is a platoon or more of SS troops holed up there. They had been in charge of a prison camp just south of the town, and they had abandoned it when the Americans were a day away. The prison camp is my responsibility, secure it, disarm it, make sure there are no Krauts around. But it turns out not to be a run-of-the-mill prison camp—

Knocking on the bedroom door startled Joshua.

"Daddy," Hanna called out, "Mr. Hendly is here to see you."

Joshua stood up slowly, opened the door, and went into the living room. Edgar was sitting in the overstuffed chair. Joshua sat down heavily on the couch.

"I hear you had some excitement over here," Edgar said.

Joshua nodded. The radio was playing, but in his preoccupation he didn't hear it. He was thinking about his toes. He

was thinking about a horrible place in Czechoslovakia. He was
thinking about a dead Indian boy. He was thinking about his
pocket watch. The pocket watch, what about the goddamned
pocket watch? He saw it vividly in his mind's eye, held up by
the deputy. How the hell can you explain it?

"How'd the kids take it?" Edgar asked.

Joshua slowly pushed his jumbled thoughts into the recesses
of his mind.

"Adam took it fine. But Hanna and Magdalena were really
upset."

"Well, they'll get over it. Unfortunately, we get a Indin drown
out there in the ditch or the reservoir ever' once in a while.
Like the girl last week. Most of em drunks who just fall into
the water and cain't get up. It's too bad when a kid dies. Vittorio
had a hard life for all his ten years. I reckon I'll go down to the
Catalina Hotel tomorrow and let his sister know. She been a
whore down there a coupla years now, since I threw her off the
reservation. Couldn't have her givin syphilis to all the young
bucks!" He shrugged. "Hell of a life some a them people live,
huh?"

Joshua frowned and shook his head glumly. "Sister Martha
told me that the first dead girl was murdered by the Sand and
Gravel Company people over this contract mess. She's really
convinced that it was meant as a warning to me. And now this
boy . . ." Joshua looked hard at Edgar, waiting for a denial.

"Shit, that bitch has a gott damn hard-on for everybody. She's
just a fuckin troublemaker and alla time tryin to protect *her*
Indins. Why in hell would old Jacob or his son, Steve, do
somethin like murderin a kid? All Jacob has to do is get the
law changed back in Washington or hustle a regulation through
the BIA. Wouldn't be the first time he done it, neither." He
nodded reassuringly at Joshua. "Just forget alla that bullshit.
The worst it can be is just some drunk degenerate Indin on the
loose. It happens out here ever' now and then. We'll get him,
one a these days we'll get him." He shrugged his shoulders,
discarding the nun's foolish words. "Anyway, reason I come
over was to tell you that the clinic is tomorrow over at the Indin
Health Services buildin."

"What clinic?"

"One day a month we get a visitin nurse come over here. She gives some shots, hands out a few pills."

"What's that have to do with me?"

Edgar's face had the beginnings of a smile. "Well, the clinic don't, but maybe the nurse does. She's a real looker, Jewish girl from back East. Maybe ya oughta swing by tomorrow, look her over. Cain't hurt."

Joshua shrugged. "I got all the trouble I need."

"Trouble like her is the good kind," Edgar said laughing. "Anyways, there's a sale over to Porter's today, they're openin at noon. Homer Porter's been my friend for years. He's got Western clothes, Levi's, boots, hats. You gotta get your kids dressed up right out here or they'll look like a coupla dudes in them city clothes. Won't set well with the rest a the kids."

Joshua shook his head. "Can't. Haven't got any spending money, just enough for food until payday."

"Hell! I thought all you people was supposed to be rich." Edgar laughed.

"All but me."

"No problem. I called Homer and told him to put you on the cuff for whatever you needed. He's got no problem with that. He'll wait till payday. The store's downtown on Stone next to the big Bank of Douglas."

Joshua was pleased. Shopping would at least take his children's minds off of this morning. "That's very decent of you, Edgar. I guess none of what they say about you is true."

Edgar wrinkled his brow and studied Joshua. Then a smile slowly crept over his face. "The priest is right, huh? You *are* a kidder." He stood up from the couch. "See ya later." He left the house.

Joshua showered and shaved. He dressed in slacks and a polo shirt and his wing-tips and felt almost undressed. You didn't go shopping in New York unless you were in a suit and hat. Out here his head felt naked all the time with no hat. He walked outside and saw the kids sitting on the bank fifty yards up, about where the boy had been found.

"Hanna," he called out. "Adam."

Their faces turned toward him, and he waved his arm in a wide arc for them to come over. They walked slowly toward him, downcast, Magdalena in the middle.

"We're all going over to a Western store to get some clothing, Levi's, boots. Okay?"

Adam's face brightened immediately. "A Daisy?"

Joshua shrugged. "Could be. Depends on the price and what else we have to get."

"Oh wow!" Adam said. "I'm going to get my gun!"

Hanna was also very excited. "Can I get moccasins like I've seen the other girls wearing? And a Western shirt?"

"I don't know why not," Joshua said. "Don't you kids want to have lunch first?"

They shook their heads vigorously.

"I'll have lunch ready when you get back, Mr. Rabb," Magdalena said.

"No, no. You're coming with us," Joshua said. "Much as you want to, I won't let you work for nothing. You'll get something nice too."

A smile stole across her face.

"Let's go." Joshua walked over to the De Soto and they all got in and drove to downtown Tucson.

Adam got two pairs of Levi's and shiny brown Justin cowboy boots. Hanna got two Western shirts and a pair of Levi's and brown suede moccasins with white leather soles called "squaw boots." Magdalena also got a pair of squaw boots and a Western shirt. The faded blue chambray work shirt that she had been wearing hung shapelessly on her. But when she came out of the changing room to model the fitted Western shirt, Joshua's eyes widened. Hanna noticed and smiled mischievously at Magdalena, who blushed and looked away from his approving eyes.

Joshua picked out a pair of cotton twill Western pants with long belt loops and a wide Western belt with a big oblong silver buckle and two matching cowboy shirts. He knew he could never wear a high-heeled cowboy boot on his left foot, so he bought a pair of tan leather penny loafers.

All of them picked out straw hats. And then came Adam's moment of glory. He took a BB gun off the rack and hefted it lovingly. Joshua did a quick total of the prices in his head, over forty dollars, but they needed the clothing. And Adam needed the Daisy. Joshua put one of the shirts he had picked out back on the counter.

"Well, what do you kids want to do now?" asked Joshua as they got back into the car.

"Can we go to the movies?" Hanna asked.

"I don't want to go to a movie. I want to shoot my gun," Adam said.

"Well, you two can go to the movies, and I'll take Adam back home and he can shoot his gun. How's that?" They all nodded. "Where are the movies at?" he asked.

"They're all on Congress Street, back there." Magdalena pointed south on Stone.

Joshua started the car and did a U-turn and turned right two blocks up on Congress. The Fox Tucson Theater on the corner had a Cary Grant movie that neither of the girls wanted to see. Farther down was the Lyric Theater.

"Let's go here," Hanna said. Two Ma and Pa Kettle movies were showing.

"Sure," Magdalena said.

"How much is it?" Joshua asked.

"Fifteen cents," Magdalena said.

He fished in his pocket and handed three quarters to Hanna. "Here's enough for a couple of ice creams and Cokes. It's twelve-thirty now. I'll pick you up out front here at four-thirty. Okay?"

"Okay," Hanna said. The girls climbed out of the car on the curb side and waved good-bye. Joshua pulled away and made a U-turn for South Sixth Avenue.

Hanna walked up to the ticket window and said, "Two."

The teenage girl in the booth gave her two dimes back for her quarters and tore a red ticket off of one big roll and a blue ticket off another. She pushed them through the opening. "One regular, one balcony."

"No," Hanna said. "We both want to sit together down front."

The ticket girl gave her an odd look. "You can't do that."

Magdalena leaned over to Hanna and whispered, "We can't sit together here. I thought you knew."

"Why not?" Hanna asked, looking perplexed.

"She's gotta sit up in the balcony with the rest of em," said the ticket girl.

"Rest of who?" Hanna asked.

"You know," the girl said, looking annoyed, "the rest of the niggers."

Hanna wrinkled her brow and looked injured. "She's no nigger," she said indignantly. "She's a Papago Indian."

"Alls I know," shot back the ticket girl with a hostile look at Hanna, "is that she's a whole lot darker than anybody we're allowed to let sit up front."

"Well, you can't do that. It's un-American," Hanna said, putting her hands on her hips and squaring her shoulders belligerently.

"Hey, you better get outta here or I'll call the manager," the ticket girl said, standing up and reaching for the phone beside her on the counter.

"Come on," Magdalena said, pulling on Hanna's sleeve. "I don't want to get arrested or something."

She pulled Hanna away from the ticket booth. Hanna was seething with indignation. "How can you let them treat you like that?"

"What do you think I can do about it?"

Hanna opened her mouth to say something, but didn't. She gritted her teeth. She walked up to the ticket booth and said, "Give me our money back."

The girl affected a haughty sneer and handed her thirty cents.

"So what do we do now?" Hanna asked.

Magdalena shrugged. "We can go over to Armory Park. There's a hot dog stand and an ice cream stand and Carnegie Library across the street."

Hanna wrinkled her nose.

"Well, why don't you go to the movie at the Lyric, and I'll go see if I can find Nona Ponsay at the Catalina Hotel. I ought to tell her what happened."

"But you said she's a prostitute." Hanna mouthed the word with vast distaste. "You shouldn't be around her."

"I went to school with her at Cowlic. She was two grades ahead of me. And she was a real good friend of mine, up to a couple of years ago when she started doing this. Nothing bad will happen."

"Well," Hanna said, thinking it over, "are you sure?"

"Yes, I'll be okay."

"Then I'll come too."

"Oh no! Your father would kill me."

"I'm not a child," Hanna said, very insulted.

Magdalena studied her. "I know you're not. But you really shouldn't come."

Hanna stuck her chin out stubbornly and put her hands on her hips. Magdalena shook her head and shrugged. They walked to the hotel across the street from the Southern Pacific railroad station. It was a yellow stuccoed building four stories high.

A few men were sitting on couches reading newspapers. The clerk at the desk was tabulating tickets with a noisy mechanical adding machine.

"What is Nona Ponsay's room number, please?" Magdalena asked.

The desk clerk looked the two girls up and down. "Ain't she a bit young?" he said to Magdalena, inclining his head toward Hanna. He didn't wait for an answer. "Two seventeen," he said. "Second floor down at the end." He watched them climb the stairs and went back to the tabulating machine and the tickets.

They walked to the end of the corridor and Magdalena knocked on the door. Silence. She knocked harder.

"Yeah," came a muffled voice from within.

"Nona? Is that you?"

"Yeah. Who is it?"

"Magdalena Antone."

The creaking of a bed. Footsteps on the wooden floor. The door opened a crack, then wider. "What is it?" She sounded scared.

"Can we come in a second?" Magdalena asked.

The door opened halfway. A big, husky middle-aged man was standing by the bed. His nose was a veiny purplish bulb. He had thinning red hair, almost orange, and bloodshot pale green eyes. He buttoned his Levi's and put the belt he'd been holding doubled in his hand through the loops.

Nona had a welt across the top of her right shoulder and on her right cheek. He walked up to her. "Ya do what I tell ya from now on or I'll stuff yer head down the shitter."

"Yes, Mr. Delahanty," she whimpered. He walked down the hall and Magdalena and Hanna went into the room.

Nona closed the door behind them and walked to the bed and sat down. "It's lucky you came. I thought that bastard FBI man was gonna kill me this time," she murmured. "That fuckin pervert! Always wants it in the ass." She glanced at Hanna suspiciously. Hanna was round-eyed with shock. "Who's she?" Nona asked.

"It's okay," Magdalena said, "she's my friend."

On the nightstand next to the tousled bed was a candle burning. Lying in front of it was a spoon.

Hanna was surprised by how beautiful Nona was, delicate features, a rich cascade of curly hair. But she looked like she hadn't slept in days. She had purple bags under her eyes. She hugged a disheveled green cotton nightgown around her and rocked uncomfortably on the edge of the bed.

"I'm making a couple of papers," she said matter-of-factly, her speech slurred. "I need a hit." She held the spoon over the candle flame and the powder in the spoon began to congeal into a thick brown liquid.

"Can't you stop that for a minute while we talk?"

"Okay," she sighed unhappily, "but hurry, I really need the hit. I'm on a bummer."

"Vittorio is dead."

"What?" she gasped. She stopped rocking and focused her eyes with difficulty first on Magdalena and then on Hanna. "What happened? He was just here last night, three or four in the morning. I gave him some money and stuff. He was fine."

"He drowned in the ditch."

She blinked hard and tears came to her eyes. She wept with

loud gasps. Minutes passed, and she caught her breath and stopped crying.

"Where is he?" she asked, her voice hoarse and deep.

"Sheriff took him downtown."

"Can he be buried by the mission?"

Magdalena shrugged and grimaced. "You'll have to talk to my grandfather and Mr. Sanchez."

Nona breathed deeply and nodded. "I don't want the white men to just dump him in a hole with the bums over by 'A' Mountain."

Magdalena nodded. "Talk to Grandpa," she said gently. "I'm sure he'll help you."

Nona picked up the spoon and held it over the candle flame. Magdalena and Hanna left the room.

Hanna was silent, her face drawn, her cheeks splotchy pink. Magdalena put her arm around Hanna's shoulders, and they stood in the hallway near the stairwell. "I'm sorry I took you here. I'm ashamed. I didn't know she did that."

"What was it?" Hanna looked frightened.

"Heroin."

"Oh God," Hanna murmured. "I thought so. Let's get out of here. Don't tell Daddy we were here. He'll kill me."

They walked quickly out of the hotel. A block away Hanna stopped to catch her breath. She stood still and forced herself to breathe rhythmically.

"God, I never saw anything like that. And she's so pretty. God, it was just awful." She looked at Magdalena. "How can you see that and not just want to die?"

Magdalena looked gently at Hanna. "There are many sad things you will see, Hanna, but you cannot die over them. You do what you can to help, but your dying won't help. You can only help if you keep on living. And some people don't want help, and you can't do anything for them, no matter what you want. Like Nona."

She took Hanna's hand like a little girl and they walked slowly away from the hotel toward Armory Park. An ice cream cone was only a nickel, and a Coke was a nickel, and a hot dog was fifteen cents. They sat torpidly on a bench and threw pieces of the buns to squawking, scrambling pigeons. An old Mexican man with a great big guitar came into the park and stood near them and played and sang Mexican songs. Occasional strollers dropped coins in his upturned straw hat on the ground. A skinny man with clown makeup on his face juggled with bowling pins for a while, two, three, four pins, and then walked away. And then came a man with a little suitcase which he set down on a rickety folding stand and did magic tricks, and a crowd of little kids stood around him and giggled and laughed and clapped delightedly at the legerdemain.

Hanna was miserable. Why wasn't she back home in Brooklyn, on Brighton Beach, looking at all the cute boys in their tight bathing suits? Not here, in hell. How *could* she manage to end up in an awful place like this?

She sat on the bench in the drab little park, feeling dour and desolate, wishing that it were Brighton Beach. But it wasn't.

And the exorbitantly redundant sun burned savagely in the powder blue Western sky.

CHAPTER FIVE

Joshua spent the first working hours of Monday morning in the records room at the BIA, culling information about allotments from hundreds of dusty files containing the original documents all the way back to 1890.

The allotments provided for by the Dawes Act had distributed parcels of land to the 363 registered Papagos on the San Xavier Reservation. The ninety-four family heads had gotten twenty acres of farmland, about eighty acres of rocky "mesquite" land, and sixty acres of barren "mesa." All single persons got up to eighty acres of mesa, and married women received nothing. It had originally been basically a ruse to extract taxes from the Indians. Their lands had always been tribally owned and exempt by presidential executive order from taxation or control by the federal government. But under the Dawes Act, once the initial twenty-five-year "trust" period passed, title would pass from the tribe to the individual Papagos. They would then become American citizens, and they would begin to pay taxes on it like any other landowners.

The "trust" period was continually extended, and additional allocations of land were never made. But the original 1890 allotments had created a horrendous morass of fractionated property claims. The problem was that the Papagos did not make wills, so when they died the land was passed on to their heirs by the Arizona State law of intestate succession. One of the Indians had complained to the BIA that if the allotment system remained in effect on San Xavier Reservation, he'd have such a tiny piece of land left that he'd have to be buried standing up. The response from the BIA superintendent, a copy of which Joshua also found in the file, was dated October 17, 1932: "Dear Mr. Suarez: If you and your seven brothers die at the same time, your thirty-eight children will be able to bury you all lying down, but only if you use the same coffin." Joshua assumed that the superintendent had meant it as a joke. And he also assumed that Mr. Suarez hadn't seen much to laugh about.

He rolled up the seven plat maps he had found showing the allotment parcels and walked down the corridor to his office. It was a little after eleven. The phone rang.

"You made a major hit with my little girl," Senator Lukis said. Joshua easily recognized his deep voice.

"I couldn't be happier," Joshua said. "She's a lovely girl."

"She insisted that I call you first thing and invite you for next weekend. We certainly hope you'll join us again on Saturday night. This time for dinner if you can make it."

"I can most certainly make it, Senator. Thank you very much."

"By the way, son, have you thought some more about the 'surplus' issue?"

"Yes I have, Senator. In fact, I'm going to go down to the county recorder's office and check the recorded titles on the reservation. The only thing I can find here at the bureau are the original allotment grants done in 1890. The allotments add up to forty-one thousand six hundred acres, so that leaves almost thirty thousand acres on San Xavier subject to sale as surplus. I've got to check the county records to make sure your parcel wasn't allotted."

"Well, I'm impressed. You're a man who doesn't let moss grow under you. You'll call me when you've verified the status?"

"Of course, Senator."

"Good-bye, my boy."

Edgar Hendly stood in the doorway. "That the senator?"

Joshua nodded.

"He called me a little after eight this mornin ravin about what a great guy you are. I wasn't even done dunkin my first dough-nut." Edgar laughed. "He's after you like a tick on a red bones hound. Have ya deeded him the mission yet?"

"I was just writing in the legal description when you popped in," Joshua drawled. He smiled wryly at Edgar and laughed.

"The senator's as happy as a pig in shit," Edgar said. "What the hell did ya do when ya went over there last Friday, blow the old bastard?"

"Nothing. At least not on Friday. But he invited me back to his house on Saturday night, and I met his daughter."

An odd look clouded Edgar's eyes. "Daughter? Ya don't mean Jennifer?"

"I do indeed. A real beauty."

Edgar gave him a bland look. "Well, to each his own, as the good book says. Got yer ashes hauled, huh?"

"Now, now, Edgar. I'm no talker."

"I wouldn't be talkin about it neither!" Edgar cackled like an old gossip. "Well, lemme know what you're gonna do on the proposed contract. We'll never get no peace around here till we put *that* puppy to bed."

"I'm going down to the recorder's office to check on some things. Probably have a pretty good idea what we can do by tomorrow."

Edgar waved and walked down the hallway.

Joshua drove down Indian Agency Road and turned right on Valencia. Almost to the Nogales Highway he saw the Indian Health Services Building, little more than a small square adobe shack. Several dozen Indians stood outside, beside their horses and mule-drawn wagons and occasional ancient pickup truck.

Why not? Joshua thought. Might as well have a look. He parked in front of the building and drew the curious stares of several Indians. He walked up rough wooden steps into a shock-ingly dismal examining room. A long wooden table covered by a dirty sheet served as the examining table. On it sat a little boy with his shirt off. The nurse had her back to Joshua. She was listening intently to the boy's chest with a stethoscope.

"I'm very sorry," she said, turning to the woman standing beside the table. "I'm pretty sure your son has tuberculosis."

The Indian woman's heavy jowls trembled. She mumbled something that Joshua couldn't hear.

"I'm going to send you over to the sanitarium. It's on Speedway right near Campbell. They have an X ray there." The nurse wrote on a small pad and tore off the sheet and handed it to the woman. "Please go there today. With fast treatment he'll be fine."

The woman nodded morosely. The boy pulled on a soiled T-shirt and jumped off the table. He ran outside and his mother followed, not looking at Joshua. There were tears in her eyes.

"Can I help you?" asked the nurse, turning to Joshua. She had long hair in a ponytail, the color of ripe corn, and soft light-blue eyes. She was about twenty-four or twenty-six years old, wearing Levi's and logger's boots and a crisply pressed white cotton shirt like a man's dress shirt. She is lovely, he thought. Cute little nose. Great figure.

"Can I help you?" she asked insistently.

"Oh, I'm sorry," he said. "I'm Joshua Rabb, the new BIA lawyer."

She nodded, waiting.

He stood staring at her, disarmed by the surprise of her in this ugly place.

"Are you sick?" she asked.

"No, no, not at all. I just came to say hello."

She tilted her head slightly and studied him for a moment. "Well, then say it and let me get back to work. I've got fifty more people waiting outside."

Her voice was harsher than the look she gave him, and he nodded in understanding. "Hello," he said.

"Sorry," she said, her voice softer. "I've got a lot of sick people and almost nothing to treat them with." She shrugged apologetically.

He nodded. An elderly Indian man, supported by two girls, hobbled into the clinic. He sat down heavily on the table, wheezing, and the nurse turned around to tend to him. Joshua left, feeling foolish at his intrusion into the clinic and the offhand manner in which the nurse had treated him. But she is as pretty as Edgar said, he thought. Prettier.

He drove to downtown Tucson, and by the time he reached the courthouse, his shirt and suit jacket were soaked through with perspiration. As hot as hell doesn't exactly describe Tucson in July. After all, Joshua thought, there are many hotter places right here on earth, the Sahara, the Gobi desert, and some of them, like Death Valley, are right next door. So it stands to reason that if hell's supposed to be even hotter than this world, then Tucson must not be too terrible after all. But today was as hot as hell, no matter how you looked at it.

He parked in the big empty dirt lot just north of the adobe courthouse with a spectacular green-and-orange-and-yellow ceramic-tiled cupola trimmed in gleaming blue. The sign on the central door to the north wing of the sprawling building said PIMA COUNTY JAIL. To the right of it, recessed back about ten feet, was a door marked CORONER. And to the left, also recessed about ten feet, was another door with a sign that read RECORDER.

Joshua went into the recorder's office and asked for the plat maps of San Xavier Reservation. The clerk told him that there were none specifically for the reservation, but that they had a book of plats for the Santa Cruz/Helmet Peak area. Joshua took the big roll of maps and sat at a large library table in the rear of the office. The cooler was blowing hard and steady, and he almost dried off. It was difficult and tiring manipulating the large maps with one arm.

After two wearying hours of studying the county plats and comparing them to the Dawes Act allotments, he felt confident that the entire area around the Santa Cruz River was still intact in tribal ownership. He rolled up the county plat maps as neatly as he could with one hand. The clerk grimaced at the untidy result. Joshua left the recorder's office and walked around to the front of the courthouse and up the stairs to the law library. It was deserted. He looked up the Dawes Act in the *Federal Digest* and read several court of appeals decisions that were annotated there. He did the same with the *Supreme Court Digest* and read three decisions. One thing at least was certain: the land allotment plan had been discontinued by 1916, and there had never been an attempt by anyone to have any Indian lands declared "surplus" by the BIA and sold to private bidders by the Office of Land Management. Those "surplus land" provisions of the Dawes Act, if not stillborn, had apparently long since become moribund. And the death knell of the act was sounded in 1924, when all American Indians were granted citizenship. The land allotment/citizenship/taxes scheme of the Dawes Act died completely.

Joshua had wanted to be able to tell the senator to go ahead with his surplus land gimmick, have it declared surplus by the BIA in Washington, and then buy it at auction. But that was now obviously impossible. The only possibility to make the senator happy was for Joshua to sign a contract with him granting him subsoil rights. Edgar would be pleased. The priest would be thrilled. Jennifer would purr like a satisfied kitten. And only the Indians and that crazy Poor Clare nun would raise a stink that it was illegal. But who cared about them anyway? Nobody listened.

Damn, what a lousy situation, Joshua thought. He left the law library and started walking back toward his car.

Suddenly he heard a woman screaming. He turned toward the sound and saw a sheriff's deputy dragging a woman kicking and screaming out of the coroner's office. Joshua froze, stunned.

The deputy backhanded her hard across the lips, and she stopped screaming and began to whimper. The deputy pulled her though the door marked PIMA COUNTY JAIL.

Joshua dropped the roll of allotment maps he was carrying and ran the fifty feet to the jail door and swung it open. There was a row of small cells in front of him, each with metal bunk beds, a toilet with no seat, and a washbasin. They were empty. The deputy came out of the last one and locked the door.

"Yeah?" he said, walking up to Joshua. He was even taller than Joshua and much heavier, no fat, just huge. His once tan uniform looked like it hadn't been laundered in a month and had darkened to brown by the accretion of several layers of filth and numerous applications of food. His face was greasy with sweat. It was boiling hot in the jail.

"That's Jennifer Lukis," Joshua said incredulously.

"Who?"

"Jennifer Lukis," Joshua almost yelled, "Senator Lukis's daughter."

The deputy cast him a strange look, as though he were gazing at a dangerous escaped lunatic. "You outta your mind or what?"

"Look, you reeking sack of pus," Joshua forced through gritted teeth, clenching his fist, "that's a United States senator's daughter you just beat up."

The deputy stepped menacingly toward Joshua. "Whattaya been smokin, shithead?"

"I'm not smoking anything, you asshole. Who's your superior officer? I'm gonna cut your liver out and feed it to my cat!"

Joshua saw the blow just before it landed on his chin. But seeing it wouldn't have changed anything. It was a short right cross with about 260 or 270 pounds behind it. The light disappeared for some length of time. Then he felt the deputy's hands under his arms and felt himself being pulled to his feet. He shook his head groggily. The deputy pushed him, stumbling, down to the last cell. Joshua put his arm up and flopped against the cell bars. Jennifer sat five feet in front of him on the lower bunk. Her lip was bleeding, and she was crying softly and shaking.

"Hey, Nona, this asshole says you're Senator Jacob's daughter. You like that?" He roared with laughter. "Hey, Nona, show him what the senator's daughter'll do for a couple of papers of horse." He reached in his left front pocket and pulled out two small packets of folded wax paper.

She got up shakily from the bunk and walked slowly toward the bars. She held out her hand to the deputy, who did a mock introduction. "Nona Ponsay, the best greaser piece of ass at the Catalina Hotel, meet Mr., uh, uh, well Mr. Shit for Brains anyway. That'll about describe him."

She looked at Joshua with glazed eyes. Mucus was running out of her nostrils in two streams, and she was drooling.

"Ol' Nona here's a regular," the deputy said conversationally. "Today's a little bit different, though. Usually it's just for stealing her johns' wallets. But this time she got all loaded up on horse and went and threatened the coroner with this knife." He pulled a small jackknife out of his pocket. "Demanded he turn over her greaser brother for a decent Christian burial. You get that, Shit for Brains? *Christian!*" Again laughter exploded from him.

Joshua's mouth was open in shock, his eyes wide with bewilderment. "Why?" he said, looking at her. "Why me?"

"For a hundred dollars," she stammered, her voice hoarse and weak. "I gotta do a hundred pigs like him for that much money." She gestured toward the jailer. "This was easy money."

"My pocket watch?"

A look of fear came over her face. "You gonna press charges for me stealin?"

He shook his head. "Just tell me."

"I took it and gave it to Vittorio. He was gonna pawn it."

Joshua walked slowly down the jail corridor and out into the burning, dry air. He steadied himself against the adobe door-jamb. He worked his jaw and decided it wasn't broken. He walked slowly to where he had dropped his plat maps, picked them up, and continued to his car. His head felt thick and turgid, and he couldn't think. What the hell was going on? He'd go to the Lukis house and confront the senator, but he had no idea how to get there, just that it was way north of downtown and a little west. He'd never find it. He suddenly thought of Edgar. When Joshua had mentioned Jennifer to Edgar, it seemed like Edgar knew her.

He drove back to the bureau. It was locked, and he walked around it to the adobe house in the rear. He knocked, and a moment later Edgar came to the door wiping grease off his chin with his shirtsleeve and holding a drumstick in his other hand.

"What's with you? You look like you got a prickly pear caught in your shorts." He looked at Joshua with alarm.

"Do you know Jennifer Lukis?"

"Yep." Edgar said and hesitated. "I've known her for forty years."

"Forty?"

"Yep. She was always around the Cattleman's Hotel when I was a kid. And then she left Tucson when she got married and I didn't see her again till she come back after her husband was killed in the war, 1918 or 1919."

Joshua stared at him. "You mean she's older than me?"

Edgar looked at him quizzically. "Well, I think she's 'bout fifty-three, year younger 'n me. I thought you said this mornin that you'd been with her Saturday night?"

Joshua nodded. "I thought I was."

Edgar shook his head slowly. "I reckon if it was her you'd remember. She's been drunk for about the last twenty years and it shows on her. Last time I saw her I couldn't believe how bad she looked. I see her ever' now and then on the reservation. She pays one a the young bucks to come home and sleep with her. Drives over there in her Caddy convertible weavin and jerkin, drunk as a skunk."

Joshua turned to leave.

"What's goin on with you, boy? Ya look plum strange."

"I don't know exactly," Joshua mumbled. He turned back to Edgar. "Can you tell me how to get to the Lukises' house?"

"Yeah, sure. Go through downtown and turn left on Grant to the Oracle Highway, then north about five, six miles to Orange Grove Road, then left past Desert Treasures to the first road on your right. But I sure wouldn't go out there without a invitation."

Joshua nodded. "Thanks, Edgar." He went back to his car and drove home.

Magdalena had made Papago fry bread and chili colorado. She and Hanna and Adam were sitting at the table in the kitchen eating when Joshua came in.

"Hey, Dad," Hanna called out, "you gotta try this red stuff. It'll set you on fire."

Joshua slowed himself down and made himself smile. He went up to the table. "Well, I've got just a little more work to do this evening, and I've got to go out for a couple of hours. I'll be back by eight. You kids don't hog it all, and I'll have some when I come back."

Adam took a bite and clutched his throat like he was gagging and took a big drink of water. He smiled broadly at Joshua. "We'll save you plenty, Dad. Don't worry."

~~~~~~~~~

He found the Lukis house easily. All the cars were in the garage and the exotic sports car was parked out front. Joshua went to the front door and knocked. An old Mexican woman opened it, looked at him, and closed it again. A couple of minutes later she opened the door wide, gestured for Joshua to come in, and pointed down the hallway toward the music room.

The doors to the music room were open. Joshua walked in. Sitting on the satin sofa was Steve Lukis. He looked to Joshua like he'd been drinking, and as he got nearer he could smell the alcohol.

"I want to see your father."

"You don't barge in here telling me you want to see my father. You call his office in the post office for an appointment."

Joshua stepped directly in front of him. "Look, you low-life filth," he said quietly, "I want to see your father now."

Steve reached up to the end table, withdrew a small pile of five-by-seven photographs, and spread them on the couch next to him. There were about a dozen grainy, poorly lit photos of Joshua lying in bed with Nona Ponsay.

"I especially like this one," Steve pointed, "with your tongue like a bloodhound six inches up her pussy." He smiled viciously. "This one ain't half bad either. Look at her sucking away like a baby with a nipple in her mouth. And this one too, with you doggie fucking her. Looks like you might have had your prick right up her ass."

Joshua stared at the photographs. "This is what it was all for, Saturday night?"

Steven Lukis nodded, his sluggish eyelid twitching wildly. "There's a shitload of minerals in that mine tunnel. We aim to get it."

"You think I give a damn about these pictures?" Joshua's voice was very soft, just above a whisper.

"I think you will, when we give a set of these to your son and daughter and Edgar Hendly and Father Hausner. And of course, Buford will have to take a set over to the sheriff. You know, that kind of sex is against the law in Arizona—'infamous crime against nature' the nice folks call it. You eastern shyster bastards are always fucking each other in the ass, but we only go in for polite fucking in these parts." He snickered. "That other stuff is for perverts. We lock people like you up." His look turned savage.

Joshua's right fist caught him square on his nose and crushed it. This is the day for right crosses, Joshua thought inanely. Try the hook this time. He caught Lukis just under his chin this time and snapped his head back. Steve fell over on his side and blood poured from his smashed nose onto the bone-colored satin couch. Lukis gasped and sputtered for breath.

Joshua heard footsteps running down the hall. Buford Richards burst into the room. He wasn't in uniform, but he had a revolver in his hand. He stood still watching Joshua and listening to Steve gasp for breath. He came slowly toward Joshua, holding the gun down to his side.

"I heard about the little ruckus downtown," he said casually. "Got a call just a half hour ago, figured it had to be you. I thought I'd best get out here right away. Figured you might not take it too well." He looked down at the bleeding, unconscious man. "He's sure messin up that fancy couch." He looked up at Joshua. "You plannin to kill him?" he asked matter-of-factly.

Joshua looked back at him silently, unmoving.

"Pity you had to run into Nona this afternoon. We sure didn't plan it that way." He shook his head and shrugged. "Just another day or two and we'd have had our mineral rights contract, huh?" He looked gravely at Joshua. "Then we wouldn't have been forced to use any of this nasty shit." He nodded toward the photographs. "Pity."

"If you ever come near my family, I'll kill you," Joshua said in a low, hard voice, "and I'll kill the senator and this pile of garbage." Joshua walked past Richards, brushing hard against his shoulder, and left the house.

CHAPTER SIX

He awoke with a start to the sound of chickens screeching. He glanced at his watch, with the luminous hands glowing. It was a little after midnight. He had just gone to bed an hour ago. The chickens were ordinarily very quiet at night. He got up from bed and looked out the bedroom window and saw nothing. The chickens were on the opposite side of the house. He pulled on his pants and his sneakers and walked out of the house.

As soon as he opened the front door, he saw the leaping flames to the right of the chicken coop. He ran toward them. The pile of old hay had caught fire and flames were leaping high.

Joshua turned on the spigot near the coop and trained the water hose on the fire. The whitish smoke turned to thick gray billows. It took almost a half hour to douse the fire and soak the hay sufficiently to stop it from smoldering.

How could the fire have started? The sky was clear, so it couldn't have been a lightning strike. He didn't think that it would spontaneously combust. Someone must have started it. He felt chilled to the bone. It was so easy to burn the pile of hay, just throw a match on it. But the adobe house would be much harder to burn, he felt certain. Mud brick shouldn't be flammable. Of course the wooden porch would go up in flames in two minutes. The roof of the house? He didn't know what it was made of. He'd check tomorrow.

Suddenly he felt fearful, vulnerable. It was dark now, the chickens had quieted. It was very still. He thought he heard footsteps behind him and whirled around. Nothing, just darkness. He walked quietly into the house and locked the door. The living room window was slid up a couple of inches on the bottom to allow air circulation for the evaporative cooler. He locked the window and also the one in the kitchen.

What did he have for self-defense, to protect his family? Nothing. He looked in the kitchen closet. A broom, a mop, a metal pail. He'd have to buy a gun. What would that cost? He had no idea. Maybe fifty dollars for a new revolver or pistol. Less for a used one, say twenty-five. But he didn't have the money. He had thirty dollars for food for the next ten days until he got paid. What with federal withholding and the other deductions, his paycheck would probably only be about fifty dollars. Then out of that would have to come the money to pay for the clothes at Porter's. That would leave less than ten dollars.

He opened Adam's door a crack. Adam was sleeping soundly. He tiptoed into the room and pushed down the window and locked it. He shut the door softly behind him.

He opened the door to Hanna's bedroom and it creaked slightly. Magdalena was sleeping on a quilt on the floor. Her nightshirt was a long T-shirt, and it had hiked up around her waist. Moonlight through the window glinted off her smooth skin. Joshua felt a little guilty, like a voyeur, but he walked into the room and slid the window down as softly as he could and latched it. He tiptoed around the girl sleeping on the floor and tried not to look at her, but his eyes couldn't help themselves. She was very pretty. He closed the door silently and sat down on the couch.

So what the hell was he going to do about a gun, money? He rubbed his eyes and sighed deeply. Damn, what a mess, he thought. I'd better check first thing on taking the bar examination as soon as possible so I can take private clients. I'm about to get fired anyway. But in the meanwhile—

The door to Hanna's bedroom opened slowly. Magdalena came out and sat down on the couch next to him.

"I heard the chickens and smelled the smoke," she whispered. "Someone set fire to the hay?"

He nodded.

"You are in very big trouble, Mr. Rabb." She took his hand gently and held it with both of hers in her lap.

"My cousin Henry came here at six this evening, when you were gone. Gossip travels like wildfire on the reservation. He told me that he had heard that the Lukises had tricked you, that you were in big trouble with them."

Joshua smiled softly at her. "At six it wasn't as big as it was at eight. Tomorrow you'll hear even worse stories."

She nodded. "Yes, and it will keep getting worse until you do exactly as they say. They are very bad people."

Joshua grimaced.

Magdalena leaned over and kissed him on the cheek. It was a daughter's kiss, an affectionate family kiss.

She got up and went silently into the bedroom and came out a moment later with something in her hand. She sat next to him on the edge of the couch and handed it to him. It was a small revolver.

"I didn't want to give this to you in front of your children earlier, when you came home. I didn't want to frighten them. It's my grandfather's. I went to him after Henry came by tonight. I told him you had troubles. He knows too. He had also heard about it. He believes that you are a good man. He gave this to me for you. No other BIA man has ever stood up to the Lukises."

Joshua shook his head. His face was grim. "I don't know if I can stand up to them," he whispered. "They play very rough."

She said nothing, just leaned over and kissed him again on the cheek and then looked at him with her gentle eyes. "Good night, Mr. Rabb." She got up and went back into the bedroom and closed the door.

He stared into dark space for a long time. He pressed open

the cylinder lock with his thumb and snapped the cylinder out with his middle finger. He shook out the cartridges into his lap. They were all live rounds. He replaced them in the cylinder, went into his bedroom, put the gun on the nightstand, and went restlessly to sleep.

~~~~~~~~

When Joshua walked into the bureau the next morning, Frances Hendly was sitting behind the smudged glass partition in the reception booth. She pointed down the hallway toward her husband's office. She looked like a disciplinarian Sunday school teacher. Now he was certain that he was either getting arrested or fired or both. He walked into Edgar's office and sat down in front of the desk. He hoped that the sound of his heart squishing in his ears couldn't be heard across the desk. Edgar was engrossed in a group of photographs on the desk under his staring eyes. He looked up at Joshua, unsmiling, and stared again at the photos, slowly from one to the other, studying them all.

"Looks like you in these pitchers," he drawled.

Joshua nodded.

"You posed for these?" Edgar sounded a little shocked.

"No," Joshua said.

"You mean they're all phony?"

"No, I just said I didn't pose for them." Joshua held out his hand. "Can I see them."

Edgar handed them across the desk. Joshua took them and peered at them closely.

"No. They're not phony," Joshua said, trying to act tougher than he felt. He studied one of the photos. "I remember this." He slid it toward Edgar. He studied another one, turning it upside down and appraising it thoughtfully. "Yeah, I remember this, too." He handed it to Edgar.

Edgar looked closely at the snapshots, pulled a pair of bifocals out of the jacket pocket of his rumpled brown wool suit, and held them in front of his eyes, the earpieces still folded. He scrutinized the photos intently. Then he put the glasses back in his pocket, nodded his head, and let out a long breathy sigh.

"Sure wish I coulda been there with ya. This one here's my favorite," he said, holding up one of the pictures and clucking appreciatively. "Coulda lost a couple of pounds with that much exercise." He laughed heartily and patted his belly. "That there's Nona Ponsay, but I 'magine you know that by now."

Joshua nodded.

"I reckon that's the Jennifer you thought was the senator's daughter?"

Joshua nodded.

"Woulda been better if ya just stuck with Penny like I suggested."

"Penny?"

"Yeah, that visitin nurse over at Indin Health Services."

"Oh, her," Joshua said. "Well, she didn't seem very interested."

"Leastways not quite as interested as good ol' Nona." Edgar snorted.

Joshua gritted his teeth and said nothing.

"They kinda set you up like a hamstrung lamb bein prepared for the butcher, huh, boy?"

Joshua felt hot blood rush to his cheeks and ears.

Edgar shook his head gravely. "Didn't take you more 'n a couple days to rile up these Lukises somethin fierce," he said. "You're 'bout like Superman, faster 'n a speedin bullet."

Joshua shrugged and breathed deeply. "So what happens now?" He forced his voice to be calm and steady despite the fact that he could hear his heart pounding in his ears.

"Buford come in this mornin to drop these off. Says Stevie's in the hospital. Seems you broke his nose or somethin."

Joshua nodded slowly.

"Well, I reckon old Buford'll be droppin a set a these on Sheriff Dunphy's desk." Edgar looked at his wristwatch. "Right about now." He stared hard at Joshua and frowned. "I could see if you was married this'd be one hell of a firecracker, yessir, a doozy. But thisaway, you bein single and all, why I reckon you could take this bunch a pitchers down to the Esquire Bar by the bus station and auction em off for a buck apiece!" He smiled at Joshua and chuckled.

Joshua began feeling relieved. "And the sheriff?"

"Aw, shit! Don't worry none about old Patrick Dunphy. Why hell, he knocks off a piece a Nona Ponsay hisself about once a week down at the Catalina. He's prob'ly just gonna keep these pitchers in his desk drawer, and ever' now and then why he'll open it up just a crack and check in on em!" He laughed and smiled at Joshua. Then he shook his head slowly.

"But a course," he drawled, "that ain't gonna solve our real problem, and that's the contract old Senator Jacob wants. And I'd say from the looks a things," Edgar's voice became serious, "he wants it awful damn bad, bad enough to go to a hell of a lot a trouble to make it happen."

Joshua nodded. "So what do we do?"

Edgar shook his head. "That I dunno, my friend. It ain't a good situation, not a good situation at all."

Joshua breathed deeply. "I'm square with you?"

Edgar nodded. "You're square with me. When Buford brought these here pitchers in this mornin, I glanced at em and asked him if they was clean enough for me to touch, since I figured old Stevie'd been jerkin hisself off over em all night, got pecker tracks all over em. Buford said it just wasn't that funny, said the senator would have my ass and yours both." He stared hard at Joshua. "I told him to fuck off and get outta my office."

Joshua smiled a grateful smile. "I can't tell you how much I appreciate it. And I'm really sorry about all the trouble."

"Listen, boy," Edgar said, "the trouble ain't your makin alone, it's just part a the whole thing with the Sand and Gravel Company. They done found somethin down there under the riverbed that's makin em all crazy as a bunch a two-dicked mules. I don't know what, and old Jacob ain't about to tell me. And the problem ain't gonna go away so easy for us. But I ain't gonna order you to do nothin, leastways not as long as the tribal council won't agree to it. Otherwise we're gonna have a gott damn *gen-u-ine* Indin uprisin on our hands. So we're just gonna have to take this one step at a time, see if maybe we can both live through it."

He stood up and extended his hand to Joshua. Joshua shook it solemnly.

"The council is meetin at three o'clock this afternoon in Sells," Edgar said, walking Joshua to the door. "You better come with me. And bring yer toothbrush. If the meetin goes into dark, we'll have to stay over for the night. That road's too damn rough to take in the dark. We'll leave here at noon. It'll take the better part a three hours to get there."

Joshua wrinkled his brow. "I hate to leave my kids alone at night. I'm kind of worried about the whole situation."

"Don't worry," Edgar said, patting Joshua on the back. "Magdalena'll take care of em just fine. She's a heck of a good girl. And you tell em if they hear any noises or get scared or anything, just come on down to our house. Frances will be happy to put em up for the night."

~~~

Francisco Romero sat at the center of the long table. On each side of him were five old men. It was the first time Joshua had ever seen Papago Indian men without their hats. Most of them, despite their years, had long thick black hair. A few were graying. Chief Romero's hair was like luxurious white ermine fur. They all wore the de rigueur uniform of plaid shirt, Levi's, and boots.

They each shook hands with Edgar Hendly, cool but not hostile. They shook Joshua's hand firmly but with hooded eyes, not revealing anything. The BIA men sat across the broad Formica-topped table from the Indians.

The three o'clock meeting began a few minutes after four. "We're on Indin time now," Edgar muttered to Joshua.

"We are disturbed that no progress seem to be made dealing with contract with company," Chief Romero said.

"We're also disturbed, Chief," Edgar said. "It certainly ain't from lack of tryin, that I can assure you and the council."

"What you going to do about it? Tribe need money. We got two hundred people with tuberculosis here in sanitarium." The chief stared accusingly at Edgar. "Need money or got to close down sanitarium, send them all to Tucson."

"Now listen, Francisco," Edgar said with an edge to his voice, "I'm doin my best and you all know it."

"You told us last council meeting you get us federal money for sanitarium. You get us money?"

"I'm still tryin, Chief. I applied for it, but it takes time to run up the ladder to the man who signs the checks. I'll get it for you."

Francisco Romero stared angrily at Edgar. He spoke in Papago with the man next to him. Several others joined in. A heated conversation went on for almost fifteen minutes.

"We got no water for crops. All stole by Lukis. We get no money for minerals. All stole by Lukis. What is it you suppose do for us?"

"Listen, Francisco, *gott* dammit," Edgar slammed his fist down angrily on the table, "I didn't come here to be scolded by you for things I have no control over! I told you fifty times that the pumpin station was approved by the BIA in Washington, way over my head. There wasn't nothin I could do about it. And the Sand and Gravel Company? Lukis's old man got a contract on that land from Territorial Governor L. C. Hanley back in 1894, before the government had even put clear boundaries on the San Xavier Reservation. The company's always been restricted to the surface materials only, the sand and the ABC. But right now they ain't satisfied with that. Suddenly they want the underground rights too. I damn well know we have a problem. I'd have to be a *gott* damn deaf mute not to know it." He glared angrily at the chief. "Mr. Rabb here's the one who's takin the lion's share a shit on this thing. But by God, we're still workin for your best interests!"

Chief Romero directed his stare to Joshua, but his features softened almost to a look of compassion. "We hear that you have big problem with the senator. We hear about fire at *Schuchulik*."

"Choo choo what?" Joshua asked.

"*Schuchulik*," the chief said, articulating slowly. "Is what we call your house: the 'place of the chickens.' " A smile flirted briefly with his eyes.

Joshua nodded and chuckled.

"You had a fire over there?" Edgar asked.

"Yeah, last night. Somebody set fire to the haystack out beside the coop."

"Shit!" Edgar said. "Them gott damn people're gettin plum crazy!"

It was stiflingly hot in the small room. There was no air conditioner or cooler, but the Indians didn't seem to perspire much. Edgar was dripping wet, his suit soaked through under the arms and across the shoulders. Joshua was wearing a dark blue suit, so the patches of wet didn't show as obviously.

"How we can be sure you don't double-cross us again?" Francisco Romero stared at Edgar.

Edgar's face blanched and his jaw muscles tightened. He leaned across the table and impaled the chief with a pugnacious scowl. "Listen, you big-mouthed bastard. I never double-crossed any a you people. I'm not the one livin like a oriental potentate with a harem. The army surplus food goes to the mission for distribution, because that's what *you* wanted. The 'common areas construction funds' go to this council, because that's the way *you* wanted it. But when we came past the Baboquivari Mountains this afternoon, the box culvert and the bridge down by Coyote Creek is still washed out, been that way for nine months now. None a the roadwork has been done that was needed after the flood last October. And yet the council received thirty-seven thousand dollars in common area funds to do the work. I know, I checked on it. Don't talk to me about *me* stealin yer money!"

Edgar stopped shouting and looked directly at the gold wristwatch worn by the old man next to Chief Romero. The man slowly withdrew his hands from the tabletop and folded them in his lap.

"A few dollars fall off the wagon," the chief said quietly, "because we got no other way to pay the council. Our 1937 constitution says we divided into eleven districts on all Papago reservations and each district elect two representatives to council, and each council member get paid, just like U.S. congressman get paid. But we got no money. So we only elect eleven representatives. And we gotta pay a little, so we pay them out of common area funds, and then rest goes to support TB sanitarium because we not get our public health funds."

"Well, I told you I'm tryin to do something about that, Chief." Edgar's tone became conciliatory. "And in the meantime, we're tryin to resolve this thing with the senator so nobody gets hurt. As tough and determined as old Senator Jacob is, he's liable to bypass us all and bully some rule change through the BIA in Washington or push a new law through Congress that gives him what he's after. The only problem with that is it'll take months and maybe years, and he's obviously too anxious to wait that long. But right now, we're at a standoff, and we've got to see what happens next."

The Indians spoke together for fifteen minutes, looking sullen and tired. It was almost six o'clock, and they weren't finished yet.

"We do not want you to sign any contract with Lukis without bringing it to council."

"We understand that, Chief," Edgar said. "We're goin to do our damnedest on that one. Now listen, I asked you last time about sendin a delegation to our Independence Day picnic down at the bureau this Thursday. You know, like you did last year. That group of Indian warrior dancers and the tom-tom players. We'd sure love to have em."

"It's *your* independence which you celebrate, not ours," Chief Romero said, his voice caustic.

"Come on, Francisco, it's good for your people too. Shows the tourists that you're all proud of your heritage and that the BIA honors it. Whattaya say?"

A short conversation took place among the council members.

"We must discuss it later among ourselves," the chief said, "after supper." He stood up and nodded brusquely to Edgar and Joshua.

Joshua stood up and followed Edgar out of the room into the open air. It was actually cooler outside than it had been inside, probably only ninety-five degrees with a slight breeze blowing, and it cooled Joshua's wet face and neck.

"Well," Edgar said, looking at his watch, "too late to go back to Tucson. Reckon we'd best bed down in the visitors' quarters over at the BIA office."

They walked down the rough wooden plank sidewalk a block and a half to a small redbrick building. The painted sign on the window read FEDERAL GOVERNMENT: BIA, OLM, IHS. Edgar unlocked the front door with a key on his key ring. The small anteroom was hot and close.

"Gotta turn on the cooler, get the dead air outta here," Edgar said.

Joshua followed him through the door into a large office and Edgar switched on two wall switches. The evaporative cooler clattered to life, and hot air blew from the vents.

"Take a couple a minutes for the pads to get soaked, then the air will cool off," Edgar said. "This here is a foldout sleeper couch. You can have it. I always sleep on the trundle bed in the storeroom."

Joshua threw his Dopp kit on the couch. He took off his soaked jacket and tie and hung them over a chair. He stood in front of the cooler vent to dry off.

"Is there somewhere to eat?" Joshua asked.

"Sure. Sam's Cafe is just down half a block. Great food. Fry bread and chili, steaks, tamales, enchiladas."

"Is there anything to do around here at night?"

Edgar laughed. "Get drunk and howl at the moon. Otherwise, eatin and sleepin's just about it. The whole town is what you saw out there, two blocks long. Period."

"How soon can we get out of here?"

"Soon as it starts gettin light, about four o'clock."

"I sure hope nothing happens with my kids," Joshua said. "Wish I could call them."

"Well, there's only two problems about that. First, you ain't got no phone in your house, and second, there ain't no phone in Sells that works since the lines got knocked out in the big storm last October. But take it easy, nothin's gonna happen to em. The Lukises ain't all *that* gott damn crazy."

When Joshua had told Magdalena that he probably wouldn't be home that night but not to worry, she immediately began to worry. Last night someone had burned the haystack. Tonight the chicken coops? The house? She didn't think that Vittorio Ponsay had died by accident. It was a warning to Joshua about Adam, just like Sister Martha said. Over the years, Magdalena had seen three drowned Indians dragged from the ditch and the reservoir. They all had pinkish foam coming out of their mouths and nostrils. Their eyes had been open and the pupils were big and dilated. Their tongues were hugely swollen and pushed out of their mouths. But not Vittorio. Mouth wide open, tongue swallowed, eyes rolled back white, and no foam at all from his mouth and nostrils. Vittorio was already dead when he was thrown into the water. She was sure of it.

Adam was off somewhere as always with Jimmy, either racing frogs down at the reservoir or playing cowboys and Indians on Lourdes Hill or chasing Grandma's cows around the pasture. Hanna was home with Magdalena, helping with the housework, listening to her stories about life on the reservation and at the Phoenix Indian School ("Boys used to sneak through the dormitory windows and try to steal our panties"). Magdalena had also told her all about the yearly pilgrimage her family and many others always took down to Magdalena, Mexico, for two weeks late in September and early in October, when there was a huge Papago fiesta, the high point of which was that they got to kiss the life-size wooden statue of their patron saint, St. Francis of Assisi, which was enshrined in the church there. Like the mardi gras, Magdalena said. She'd read about the big carnival in New Orleans. A little bit of piety and a whole lot of drinking and dancing and carnival.

"You know, I've been thinking," she said. "Since your dad probably won't come back tonight, why don't we all go over to the reservation? You can sleep in my house."

"Really?" Hanna said. She wrinkled her brow. "Well, what if Dad *does* come back? He'll be worried that we're not here."

"I'll leave him a note that you're staying with me. It'll be okay."

"Okay," Hanna said hesitantly. "But we're really not supposed to go on the reservation. Dad might be really mad."

"Well, I think this is a special situation. Don't be scared, my family won't hurt you. They're really very nice, I promise."

Hanna blushed. "I—I didn't mean to insult you."

"I know," Magdalena said. "Come on, let's go find Adam."

They locked the house and walked to the reservoir, but no one was there. They walked back to the house. Adam hadn't come home, and they crossed the ditch onto the reservation. They walked past the mission and up to the top of Lourdes Hill. There were the boys and Charger on the riverbank. Jimmy was making a pass at the "buffalo" while Adam waited at the end of the thin strip of pasture.

"I'll go get him," Hanna said, looking apologetically at Magdalena.

Hanna didn't have to go far before Adam saw her and started running toward Lourdes Hill. Jimmy also saw her, and Magdalena standing on the hill, and cantered Charger toward the irrigation ditch.

"I didn't do anything," Adam said as he came up to his sister. "I was only watching."

"You can't keep chasing Mrs. Antone's cows," Hanna scolded.

He hung his head and looked very abashed. "Is Magdalena mad at me?"

"I bet she is."

"Well, I'll tell her I'm sorry."

"That doesn't always make everything better, you know."

They walked up the rocky slope of the hill to the path where Magdalena was waiting.

"I'm sorry," Adam said in a low voice, not looking at her.

"Let's not tell Grandma what you were doing, or she's liable to cut off your tunies and boil them."

"What?" Adam asked, looking at her fearfully.

"Tunies are the little round fruits of the prickly pear cactus." Magdalena looked at him sternly.

It took Adam a moment to make the connection. Then a look

of horror crossed his face. Hanna burst into laughter and put her hands over her mouth to suppress it. Adam stared at his sister and began to get mad. He clenched his jaw.

"Come on, you two," Magdalena said. "Let's go get some food for supper."

"What are we going to have?" Hanna asked.

"A real traditional Papago meal," Magdalena answered. "Nopalitos, tunies"—she glanced at Adam and he looked away, a little embarrassed—"and you can grind some corn in the metate and I'll make corn bread."

"What's the nopa—, nopal—, whatever you said first?" Hanna asked.

"You'll see." Magdalena smiled at her.

They walked into the village of small grass houses and came to a large square house with walls of saguaro cactus ribs laid horizontally and mortared with adobe mud. The roof was supported at the corners by mesquite wood posts.

Magdalena stopped outside and held Adam's and Hanna's hands. "This is my grandparents' house. We built it when Grandpa was the chief. I live in the *olas kih* over there." She inclined her head toward the igloo-shaped bear grass and mud house to the right of the much larger square structure.

"Come on," Magdalena said.

They walked to her *olas kih* and she knelt down in front of the small entryway. Magdalena pushed aside the heavy beaded canvas square that covered the entry and crawled inside. The children followed her on hands and knees. Inside, the floor consisted of a foot-thick layer of yellow straw. Most of it was covered by a heavy wool rug woven with a geometric design of black and gray. It was surprisingly spacious. The sun showed through myriad fenestrations in the grass walls of the house, and it was much cooler inside than out.

"Okay, let's go get dinner," Magdalena said. She rummaged through some clothes and things in a bright turquoise-painted orange crate and came out with a heavy pair of leather gloves. She crawled out of the *olas kih* followed by the children.

She picked up a small wicker basket outside and walked toward the large flat hill to the southwest of the village. "That's

Black Mountain," she pointed. "I go up there often at night and sit and listen to the birds and think."

At the foot of the hill was a broad expanse of cholla cactus. Magdalena put on the leather gloves and broke off a few of the cholla pads with clusters of bright red fruit on them.

"These are nopalitos." She pointed at the cactus pads. "We'll roast them in a little lard and they'll taste just like eggplant. And we'll peel the skin off the prickly pears. They're sweet as sugar."

"Wow, look at all these wildflowers," Hanna said. "This lavender one smells like Wrigley's Spearmint gum." She held it to her nostrils.

"That's hyssop. We crush the leaves and use the oil as perfume."

Hanna took a few leaves in her hands and crushed them and sniffed the oily fluid. "Ummm."

"It's food made just for bumblebees. See, the petals are lavender and they fold outward flat. Bumblebees need a place to perch when they gather pollen, so they always feed on these open flat flowers. Now look here." Magdalena pointed to a four-foot-high stem clustered around with flowers that resembled long narrow tubes with petals slightly flared on the end. "This is scarlet penstemon, and these flowers were made just for hummingbirds. Birds can see red and bumblebees can't, so the bees don't even see them. And hummingbirds don't need to perch anywhere, they just hover in the air and stick their long bills in the tubes and feed on the pollen."

Magdalena walked up the hill to a small ridge and sat down. Hanna and Adam sat beside her. About thirty yards away was a small cave, blackened by the soot of a thousand campfires.

"Did you ever hear about Ho'ok?" Magdalena asked.

The children shook their heads.

"She was a witch that used to live in a cave in the Baboquivari Mountains and eat little children. And when she would run out over there, she'd come here."

Adam's eyes widened. "A witch?"

Magdalena nodded. "She had the mouth of a pig and eagle claws for hands and feet. The people who lived in the nearest village went to their hero I'itoi, who was Ho'ok's uncle, and begged him to protect them from her, so he devised a plan. He invited her to the village for festive eating and dancing, and he put a special sleeping medicine in a cigarette. After four days of dancing and smoking, she fell into a deep sleep, and I'itoi carried her back to her cave. The people of the village followed with armloads of firewood and covered over the entrance of the cave and lit a great bonfire. Ho'ok awoke and jumped up and hit her head on the ceiling and cracked the top of the cave open. I'itoi put his foot over the crack and sealed it up and Ho'ok died. The village was saved."

Adam stared at Magdalena suspiciously. "That's just a story, isn't it?"

"Of course, silly," Hanna chided.

Magdalena laughed. "But when I was little, I believed it. When I was bad, my grandfather used to point up at this cave and tell me Ho'ok was waiting to get me."

They walked back into the village. Between Magdalena's *olas kih* and her grandparents' house was the cooking area, a large stone metate, a brick oven three feet high, and pots and pans and baskets stacked on a wooden shelf, all under a lean-to covered with ocotillo staves and bear grass.

Magdalena put some wood from a pile into the stove and lit it with kindling. She went into her grandparents' house and came out a moment later with a four-inch chunk of fatback in one hand and a pitcher in the other. Her grandmother followed her to the oven, her squinted eyes studying Adam and Hanna. The old woman stepped up to Adam and pinched his cheek softly, smiled, and said something in Papago.

"You know what Grandma said?" Magdalena asked, looking from Adam to Hanna.

"Yeah, I think so," Hanna answered. "My grandma back home used to do the same thing. She'd pinch our cheeks and say, '*Shaineh poonim.*' What a pretty face."

Magdalena nodded and smiled. "Actually, Grandma was checking to see if Adam was tender enough to put in the skillet along with the nopalitos." She looked at Adam, and his cheeks turned bright red.

"Tell her I'm sorry, and I won't chase her cows anymore," he murmured.

"You can tell her yourself, Adam. She understands."

He looked at her with red-rimmed eyes. "I won't do it again."

Magdalena said something in Papago to the old woman and they both laughed.

"Okay, you forgiven," the old woman said in a husky voice. She smiled broadly and patted him on the shoulder.

Magdalena put the fatback into the heating skillet and it began to sizzle. Her grandmother began peeling the skin off the cholla pads and laid them in the skillet. Magdalena handed Adam the basket with the prickly pears in it and the leather gloves and told him to get a knife off the shelf and strip the outer skin off. Then she picked up two handfuls of corn from a large burlap bag and put them in the metate. She showed Hanna how to crush the corn into flour with the stone pestle and watched her do it.

Suddenly Hanna didn't feel so strange here. It wasn't like going to a foreign country where everybody was dirty and smelled bad and lived like pigs in cardboard shacks between puddles of their own sewage. Hanna had seen pictures like that, of people starving to death in Africa, of squalid slums in South America. But this wasn't like that at all. When she'd heard Mr. Hendly describe it, she pictured a bunch of drunken ogres who beat up little children just for fun and caught desert mice and devoured them raw. But that wasn't what was going on over here. Not at all.

Adam had been lost in thought for several minutes. He cocked his head a little and studied Magdalena. "Did you bring us here because you're worried about us staying in our house without Daddy, because something bad might happen?"

Magdalena didn't want to scare him, but it was not a time for lying. Hanna was also studying her, waiting for an answer.

"Yes," Magdalena said, "I do think that there could be trouble over there with us there alone. There's some bad things happening, but we'll be safe here."

Adam frowned. "I knew it. Daddy always writes in a black book when he's upset, and he's been writing a lot lately."

Hanna nodded.

"What's he write in the book?" Magdalena asked.

"We don't know," Hanna said.

"Maybe it's a diary," Magdalena said.

"What's that?" Adam asked.

"It's just a book where someone writes down whatever happened that day, so they can go back later and read it over and remind themselves what went on."

"Could be," Adam said and shrugged.

"Is someone trying to hurt us and our dad?" Hanna asked.

Magdalena furrowed her brow. "I don't know. But it's sure better to be safe than sorry."

Hanna nodded.

CHAPTER SEVEN

The rubicund sun rose at about four-fifteen in the morning as it had yesterday and the day before, and it disappeared from the aubergine night sky behind Black Mountain in a blush at about seven-thirty, as it also had yesterday and the day before. And Joshua marked each passing uneventful day as a lull before the inevitable tempest. He feared for the safety of his children. But at least Magdalena was always with them, and she always carried the Smith & Wesson .38 when they were outside. Joshua knew that she wouldn't be too timid to point it at anyone and pull the trigger, if it came to that. God willing, it wouldn't.

Independence Day arrived. At seven in the morning, two Indians slaughtered a three-hundred-pound pig and gutted it. They hauled it over to the picnic grounds, a huge empty lot next to the BIA, where another Indian had already got a fire started in the barbecue pit. When the mesquite wood had burned down to coals, they filled the pig's belly with garlic and carrots and celery and onions and laid it in the bottom of the pit, covered it with more mesquite, and then pushed dirt over the top of the pit. At the six brick ovens around the pit several Indian women made stacks of fry bread and great cauldrons of red and green chili. By ten o'clock, when the people from town began gathering for the picnic, the savory scent of the food covered the whole area.

Many Mexicans and Indians had come to the picnic, and they looked very much alike to Joshua, except that they were immediately distinguishable by their languages. Papago sounded like a monotonal stream of guttural grunts.

Joshua sat with Edgar under a bright yellow canopy which Frances Hendly had set up near the barbecue pit for the BIA people. Out of the corner of his eye, Joshua kept track of his children. Vendors from Tucson had set up various booths, balloons, ring toss, duck shoot, candy, and there was a popcorn wagon and a cotton candy stand. He had given Adam and Hanna each fifty cents to spend, and by the looks of their pink chins and noses they had spent most of it on cotton candy.

The Indian warriors and the tom-tom players from the big reservation arrived at about one o'clock in the bed of an old Army "deuce and a half" stake truck. They danced bare-chested in deerskin masks with colorfully beaded tassles bouncing and eagle feather headdresses, some in loincloths and others in buckskin pants, and they carried tomahawks of wood and stone and small shields of gaily painted leather stretched over wooden frames.

They danced for an hour, while the tourists from Tucson and wherever snapped their Kodaks and clapped. And then the Indian minding the barbecue pit announced that lunch was ready and shoveled the dirt off the succulent roasted pig. Two Papagos lifted it up by the hooves and hung it crosswise from a wooden stand. The skin pulled off of it in several broad pieces, revealing gleaming steaming roast pork. Long lines formed and everybody got a big chunk of pork and fry bread and all the chili they could eat.

A cloud of dust billowed up on Indian Agency Road, and Joshua watched it approach. The Security Police car parked on the road by the picnic lot, and Buford Richards and Senator Lukis and his son walked toward the BIA canopy. Steve had a metal splint held over his nose with long strips of adhesive tape.

All around his eyes the skin was black. He had a large scab in the corner of his mouth.

"Good afternoon, Mrs. Hendly, how lovely you look today." The senator touched his hand to his straw cowboy hat. He was wearing a cream silk Western suit, a plaid cowboy shirt with a bolo tie, and shiny black cowboy boots. Steve was in Levi's and a polo shirt and Buford wore his uniform.

Buford doffed his cowboy hat and pressed it to his chest. "Howdy, ma'am. Edgar, nice to see you."

"Well, Mr. Rabb," the senator said affably, "are you enjoying your first Independence Day picnic with all our friends here?"

"I surely am, Senator. Thank you for asking."

The senator gave Joshua a fatherly look. "Come on, son, let's you and me take a walk over to that Coca-Cola stand over there and get us a cool one."

He started walking without waiting for Joshua to respond. Joshua got up and limped after him. His new loafers were stiff and tight, and his lame foot was very sore. He had unfortunately left his cane at home. Senator Lukis reached the stand and looked back, waiting for Joshua to catch up.

The senator handed two nickels to the vendor and pulled two bottles of Coca-Cola out of the watery ice wagon. He opened them both and handed one to Joshua. He lifted his bottle in a toast and drank a sip. "Sure do love a Coke in the hot weather," he said, smacking his lips.

Joshua said nothing.

The senator moved a few yards away from the wagon. He turned to Joshua and smiled affectionately. "I'm really sorry for what happened, Mr. Rabb." His voice was low, confidential. "Steve started out just having a little fun, and unfortunately he went too far. I didn't know anything about the pictures. I certainly wouldn't have condoned something so sordid."

Joshua made his face show no emotion, and his voice was nonchalant. "But the whore was okay? Is that what you mean? You tried to sucker me into signing your contract, but it was just a harmless prank?"

"Believe me, son, I wouldn't have let it all get carried too far. I feel too fond of you for that."

Joshua just stared at him. You rotten old bastard, he thought. What's up your sleeve now?

"Why don't you let me try to make it up to you?" the senator said. "I'm having a few old friends for lunch at the M.O. Club tomorrow, then we'll probably have a couple of Jack Daniel's shooters and play a few hands of stud. These are some really good old boys for you to meet, businessmen, ranchers. I think you'd really impress them, probably do miracles for your private law practice."

"I don't think so, Senator. Got too much work piling up on my desk. Thanks for the Coke." Joshua walked away and laid the empty bottle on the wagon.

"You shouldn't turn your back on me so fast, son. I can do you a lot of good."

Joshua turned and stared at him. "You already have, Senator. You already have."

"Now you ought not talk to me like that, boy." The old man's lips were twitching, his voice hoarse and biting.

"How do I have to talk to you, Senator? Do I have to call you 'massah' or 'boss'? Is that it?" He limped back directly in front of the old man. "Or do I just say 'yes, sir' and sign any piece of paper that you put in front of me? That's the way the Nazis did it with prisoners of war, tortured them and then had them sign confessions to war crimes. Is that what's going on here, Senator, you torture me and my family until I beg to sign anything you want?"

The senator's face lost its color. His lower lip trembled. "You two-bit scum. You call *me* a Nazi? I'm a United States senator! I don't have to deal with scum like you! I'll piss on you like a cockroach in the dirt!" He was out of breath from anger and he bent over with a coughing spasm.

Steve came up next to his father and took his arm. "You okay, Dad?"

The old man straightened up slowly, hawked up a wad of phlegm, and spat it toward Joshua's shoe. It fell short. Steve stared sullenly at Joshua but made no move toward him.

"Love your new nose," Joshua said, not smiling.

"You have made a big mistake," the old man whispered hoarsely. "You have made a very big mistake."

"Good day, Senator Lukis," Joshua said.

He walked back toward the bright yellow canopy. Father Hausner had come onto the picnic grounds accompanied by Brother Boniface, the monk who had been with Hausner in the mission sacristy. Joshua stopped and watched them. Hausner was walking slowly among the Mexicans and Indians. They quickly knelt before him and crossed themselves and kissed the back of his outstretched hand. Boniface walked slowly behind like a servant or courtier. As each person knelt servilely before him, the priest made the sign of the cross and mumbled, "*In nomine patris . . . , In nomine patris . . . , In nomine patris . . .*"

Joshua watched the scene in fascination. Forgive me, Father, for I have sinned, he thought. I have just taken the name of Jacob Lukis in vain. If it were only that simple, just kneel in front of this priest, and he'll dispel all evil from me and my family.

There was a whooping and hollering of children to his left, and Joshua turned to see the reason. At least ten boys and girls had gathered around Sister Martha, and she was throwing peppermint sticks in the air for them to jump for. They howled with delight. She held up empty hands and strode toward Joshua, her black skirt billowing, her big head covering jumping up and down.

"Well now, Mr. Rabb," she said, stopping directly in front of him. "What new inducements has the good senator brought to you today? Surely his appearance in full regalia at this picnic must herald a major new effort to pervert your soul or injure your body." She spoke softly so that no one else would hear.

"Whatever makes you think that, Sister? The senator's here because he's a true patriot."

Sister Martha laughed.

"He did offer me a position with his firm, of course, and I've given him legal title to the mission."

He said it with a straight face, and she frowned and tilted

her head and studied him. He allowed himself a grin, and then she burst out laughing. She wagged her finger at him to chide him. "Well, I just think I'll go give him a piece of my mind. The nerve of that man to treat my people—good people—with such disdain. May God have mercy on his soul."

She strode off, skirts flying, wimple bouncing, and he watched her charge up to the senator, shake her finger at him, and put her hands on her hips in defiance. Steve stood menacingly next to his father, but the old man just doffed his hat and bowed slightly and walked away with her still jabbing her finger at him and yammering away.

Shoot the bastard, Sister. Just pull a gun out of your pocket and blow his brains out. Don't worry, I'll get you off. I'll have fifty Indian eyewitnesses testify that he and his son attacked you and he was about to crush your skull with a rock. Why just fifty? I can get the whole damn reservation to testify! He smiled at the thought.

"Hello there, Mr. Rabb, hello there," Father Hausner said. He didn't extend his hand toward Joshua.

"Hello, Father, nice to see you again."

"Fine group of people here today, eh, Mr. Rabb? By the way, I don't think I had the chance to introduce you to Brother Boniface. He's a monk from a monastery just south of Seattle."

"Yes, you introduced us at the mission the other day." Joshua held out his hand automatically. The monk didn't reach for it. His hands were inside the large sleeves of his robe, crossed over his chest. The cowl was over his head, and he didn't even look at Joshua, just stood blankly behind the priest.

"He's taken a vow of silence and service to the Church," Hausner said. "Never says anything at all."

Joshua shrugged. The monk was at least fifty years old, tall and stocky. Joshua had never seen a real honest-to-God monk before, well, except Friar Tuck in *Robin Hood*. But that was just a movie monk. This guy was the genuine article.

"Well, we'll be off and get a little of that pork before it all gets gobbled up," the priest said. "Good day, Mr. Rabb."

"Good day."

The senator was gone. Joshua looked over at the BIA canopy and Edgar and Frances were gone. He spotted Magdalena and Hanna by the cotton candy stand burying their faces in pink fluff.

He walked up to them. "Hi. Where's Adam?"

"He went with Jimmy Hendly to swim in the reservoir. A whole bunch of guys went," Hanna said.

Joshua glanced at his watch. A little after three-thirty. It should be all right. "I'm going on home," he said. "You can hang around here if you want, but come home by five."

"Okay, Dad."

He limped slowly away from the picnic, down Indian Agency Road to his house. As he stepped onto the front porch, he saw it. Someone had torn one of the chickens apart and smeared blood and its entrails all over the door. The remains of the chicken lay in a pool of blood on the WELCOME doormat. The stink was nauseating.

Joshua walked off the porch and picked up the water hose by the coop. He turned it on full blast and pulled it in front of the door and sprayed the door and the porch for five minutes.

His mind was roiling with hatred for the people who had done this. He could picture Steve Lukis ripping the chicken apart gleefully while Buford and the senator sat in the car lamenting the fact that Joshua Rabb just wasn't becoming one of the team. Suddenly he became frightened for Hanna and Adam. He walked back to the picnic area quickly and waved Hanna and Magdalena over to him.

Hanna was unhappy about leaving so early. There was a softball game starting, and the tall blond boy swinging the two bats, whom Hanna had been talking to a few minutes ago, had asked her to stay and watch the game.

"Sorry, honey," Joshua said, "but I really do have a reason for wanting you home right now. Look, honey, I'll go over and find out his name and where he lives and maybe we can invite him to dinner. He looks like a nice kid."

"Oh *God*, Dad, you *wouldn't*. Oh, I'd be so *embarrassed* if my *father* talked to him. He'd think I was a baby."

"Okay, honey, I'm sorry I ever even thought of it. What a humiliation. Why don't you run over and tell him you've got to leave?"

"But, *Daa-aad*, I just *couldn't* do that, go right up to him with all those *other* boys around."

"Listen here, sweetie pie, you're driving me nuts! Now go back to the house with Magdalena."

Hanna pouted.

"Now!"

"*Okay*, Dad, I'm *going*."

They got to the house before Joshua, and he came in a few minutes later.

"Why's the front door all wet, Dad?"

He looked at her annoyedly and wrinkled his nose. "A bald eagle flew over and peed on it."

"*Daa-aad*." She giggled.

"Magdalena, would you please go down to the reservoir and get Adam? I can't walk any more on this foot."

"Sure, I'll be right back."

"So what are we supposed to do that's so special?" Hanna's voice was whiney.

"Listen to the radio!" Joshua said. He walked into his bedroom and slammed the door behind him.

Jesus, man, take it easy. Calm down, you're acting crazy, not thinking. Cool off. He sat down on the edge of the bed and breathed deeply. Got to get out of this place before they hurt my kids. Got to get out of here right now. How? I don't even have enough money to rent an outhouse for a week.

The front door slammed, and he heard Adam say something to Hanna. Then she said, just loud enough to be heard by Joshua, "Better leave Dad alone. He's got a cockroach up his pants."

Joshua sat on the edge of the bed, and his breath came easier. Well, there was nothing to do today about anything. Too late to look for somewhere to move to. Tomorrow morning he'd look for a new job, somewhere to live, maybe call the bar association in Phoenix, see if they had a job service. No wonder that other lawyer, Henry Carboneau, just up and left one day. The BIA in Tucson was one hell of a dangerous place to work.

Maybe I'd better write Mom and Dad tomorrow and ask them to wire me a hundred dollars. Maybe even go back to New York. Dying of bronchitis in Brooklyn beats getting murdered in Tucson. Damn! What a mess . . .

He sat unmoving as darkness gathered in the window, and soon he was looking at his own reflection. Drawn, worried, a little haggard. Scared? Was that there too? Yes. Scared.

~~~~~

Joshua jerked his head up off the pillow. The siren sounded like it was right in front of the house. His luminous watch hands pointed to two-fifteen. It was pitch-black outside and overcast. The siren stopped. He got out of bed and dressed.

He opened his bedroom door, and Magdalena had just come into the living room followed by Hanna. Adam came out of his room rubbing his eyes.

"What's happening, Dad?" Hanna asked.

"I don't know, honey."

They heard loud voices in front of the house. Joshua went to the door and opened it a crack. Several people with flashlights were standing by two sheriff's cars and shining the lights into the irrigation ditch.

"You stay here," Joshua said. He walked over to the men by the ditch. "What's up?" he said to the deputy.

The deputy sheriff shined his light down to the bottom of the ditch. "One of the nuns from the mission," he said.

There was a sharp crack of lightning and then the crashing of thunder, but no rain. Two other deputies lifted the body. The nun's white scarf fell off into the mud. They carried the body up and laid it on the embankment and shone their flashlights on it. Joshua gasped.

"You know her?" asked one of the deputies, shining his light in Joshua's face.

Joshua shaded his eyes with his arm. "Yes, Martha Robinette."

Hanna and Adam and Magdalena tiptoed up behind Joshua. Magdalena gasped and let out a cry and ran to the nun. She knelt beside her and cradled her head.

"Get back in the house," Joshua said to Hanna.

She shook her head. She held tightly to Adam's hand.

Behind her came the lights of another car. It parked, lights on, and Buford Richards came toward the group. "I just got a call from the dispatcher, says you got a murder here." He wasn't in uniform and looked like an elderly cowboy, Levi's, a plaid shirt, and cowboy boots.

"Howdy, Buford," said one of the deputies, coming up to him. They shook hands.

"What's cookin, Marty?" Richards asked. "That sure looks like Sister Martha." He shook his head gravely. "This town sure ain't gonna take too kindly to no Indian murderin a nun."

"We got an anonymous call an hour ago about a dead nun. When we verified it, I had dispatch get you. You know we ain't got no jurisdiction on the res. But you sort of do, I reckon, since the company's located over there."

Richards nodded. "You want me to see if anyone's hangin around that shouldn't be?"

"You never know." The deputy shrugged.

Richards turned around and stopped, as though he had noticed Joshua and the children for the first time. "Oh, evenin, Mr. Rabb. Terrible thing, ain't it?" He shook his head sadly. "Better take them kids back into the house. This ain't nothin for them young eyes to see. And it's about to blow up a real thunderstorm. Better get inside under cover." He walked quickly to his car and drove away.

Edgar Hendly walked up beside Joshua. "Holy Jesus," he muttered. "Second drownin in a week."

Joshua looked grimly at him. "They say murder this time."

"Who the hell would murder a nun?"

Joshua shrugged. Magdalena knelt next to the nun, cradling the dead woman in her lap. Martha had close-cropped brown hair, and her eyes were wide open, eerie, rolled back and all veiny on the whites. A deputy walked over and closed her eyelids. The three other deputies were walking slowly beside the irrigation ditch, scrutinizing the ground in the light of their flashlights.

"Nothing on this side," one of the men said.

"Let's go across and check out the other side," said a second deputy.

"Not our territory," the first deputy said.

"Shit!" the deputy named Marty said. He climbed down the side and splashed across the bottom. He shone his light on the other side of the ditch. "Here's the drag marks," he called out.

He climbed onto the other bank and studied the ground intently. "I got more drag marks over here." He walked slowly into the barren cotton field and stopped. "There's fresh tire tracks in the field here. It looks like the body was pushed out of a car door and dragged over to the bank and rolled into the ditch."

"One of you guys bring the forensic evidence case over here. It's in my trunk," Marty called out.

"Come on, Marty. We got no place here. We gotta call the Indian police in Sells on this one."

"Shit!" Marty yelled. "The phone's out, and by the time they get here, all the signs will be washed out by a thunderstorm. Bring me the freakin F.E. kit, dammit. I'm going to make a mold of these tire tracks. Maybe I can find some footprints, too."

There was another menacing clap of thunder and the wind picked up. A deputy crossed the ditch carrying a big box. He joined Marty about twenty feet into the field. They busied themselves mixing molding plaster in a glass jug. While Marty poured the plaster into the tire tracks, the other deputy examined the ground for footprints.

"Here, I got some," he called out, about ten feet from Marty. "Looks like pointy cowboy boots. Bring me some of that plaster."

Joshua saw headlights moving slowly along Mission Road, in front of the mission. It must be Buford Richards, he thought. Then the car stopped for a minute, and he could hear doors slamming, and then the car made a U-turn and sped out of sight.

A few minutes later the car came down Indian Agency Road and parked by the ditch. Richards got out and walked to the passenger side and opened the door. He pulled a man out of the car. The man's hands were cuffed behind his back. Richards pushed him forward, and he fell at Joshua's and Edgar's feet.

"I got him," Richards said. "The son of a bitch was sleeping off a drunk on the edge of the field. Didn't even bother to zip up his pants."

One of the deputies shone a flashlight on the man. He stirred and struggled to his knees with difficulty. He stank of alcohol.

"Ignacio?" Magdalena gasped, disbelieving. She stood and walked up beside Joshua. "That's my brother, Ignacio," she said, her voice breaking.

Ignacio was too drunk to take notice. He swayed back and forth dizzily.

"Ignacio hasn't been on the reservation in a year," Magdalena said to Buford Richards. "He lives in a shack downtown near the railroad switchyards. He never comes around here, because my grandfather kicked him out of the house."

"Well, I don't know about all that crap," Richards said angrily. "Alls I know I caught him sleepin on the edge of the field with his pecker still hangin out of his pants."

"But we don't even know if the nun was raped," Joshua said.

Richards pulled the Indian to his feet. Ignacio was wearing sneakers with no laces, and one of them fell off. He didn't seem to notice.

The sound of the deputies' voices came from the field. Richards looked over to them, startled, and his jaw gaped open. "Hey, what are you boys doing on the res?"

"Making some plaster casts," Marty called back.

Joshua watched Buford Richards's eyes narrow and his face become contorted.

"Now you come back out of there, hear. You got no business on the res. Sheriff Dunphy's gonna be plenty pissed about this."

"Yeah, Buford, we're just about finished," came the response from Marty.

Richards stood there fidgeting, nervously combing his thick white hair with his hands. There was a ferocious crash of thunder, and a thin rain started. Then it began raining harder.

"Damn," Marty said. "There go all the signs."

The two deputies folded the F.E. box and came trotting back

through the ditch. An ambulance arrived, and the attendants placed the nun's body in the back of the van and rode off. Marty pushed Ignacio into the back of his car, and all of the deputies drove off.

"I told you if you stayed out here you'd be gettin caught in a storm," Buford Richards said to Joshua. He got back in his car and drove away.

"I reckon the girl's right about Ignacio," Edgar said, his face drawn. "I ain't seen him around the reservation in a coon's age." He turned and walked down Indian Agency Road.

It was pouring now. Joshua and Magdalena and Hanna and Adam ran into their house. The children went into their bedrooms. Magdalena lingered in the living room with Joshua.

"I'm sorry I didn't tell you about Ignacio. I was ashamed," Magdalena whispered. "He sometimes gets drunk. But I haven't seen him like that in a long time."

Joshua nodded. "But he never hurt anyone, right?"

She shook her head vigorously. "Absolutely not. Ignacio's a gentle man. But he and my grandfather had an argument a couple of years ago, and my grandfather make him leave his house. I felt very bad for Ignacio, but there was nothing I could do. I think that sometimes a sadness comes over him, and then he has to drink to dull the pain." She sniffed and swallowed down her tears. "But he would never do anything to harm anyone, certainly not Sister Martha." Tears fell from her eyes and she went into the bathroom and closed the door. Joshua heard her muted weeping through the thin door.

CHAPTER EIGHT

J oshua lay wide awake in bed, listening to the rain pelting the roof. It died down after about twenty minutes and then subsided completely after another half hour. The swamp cooler didn't cool at all in wet weather, and the air coming out of the vent was humid and hot. He got up and went into the living room and turned off the two switches. Magdalena was sitting fully dressed on the couch.

"What's wrong?" he whispered.

"I was just waiting for the rain to stop. I'm going over to talk to Grandpa about Ignacio." She got up and opened the front door. "I'll be back in a little bit."

It was already almost sunrise. He went into the kitchen and poured coffee, which Magdalena had made. He opened the front door facing the reservation and latched the screen door. The air was cooler outside than inside and he felt a little refreshed. He sat down on the couch, and the fabric felt clammy against his bare legs and back. He was wearing the gym shorts he always wore to bed.

The sunrise came quickly, as it always did out here. It got dark very slowly at night and light very rapidly in the morning. By six o'clock, the sun was well over Martinez Hill to the east. The sun burned the moisture out of the ground like steam, and it formed a huge vividly colored iridescent rainbow over the mission. Joshua was hardly in a romantic mood, but he still couldn't shut out his growing sense of the beauty of this place. It grew quickly on you, this stark desert the color of sun-bleached bones, studded with cactus and bear grass and mesquite, with red wildflowers that reached to your waist and white flowering thistles that grabbed like fire ants at your ankles.

He walked to the screen door, sipping his last cup of coffee, and stood watching the dawn. The clusters of greenery at the edge of the porch that looked pathetic in the evening, like straggly droopy shrubs, now strutted up, erect and vibrant, sporting peacock blue morning glories open widely to the sun. Bees bustled hungrily around the flowers. A couple of gophers ran across the front yard, fast, stood up every twenty feet or so, looked around, and then ran some more. One came out of the ditch and ran to the house with a little baby field mouse two inches long hanging limply out of its mouth. The gopher scurried under the porch with its prize. A two-foot-long skinny brown snake, with shiny yellow beads on its back in a succession of diamonds, slid slowly over the bank of the irrigation ditch, came into the front yard of the house to look around for a moment, and then slithered back into the ditch.

~~~~~~~~

Macario Antone sat slumped at the little wooden kitchen table. He felt like he was back in a muddy trench in the Ardennes forest, ducking German bullets. He stared vacantly at his gnarled and roughened hands, their skin made saurian from years of picking crops and planting with a stick and a hoe. He had five acres of vegetables a mile down the river, tomatoes, onions, carrots, a few eggplants and jalapeño peppers, and they had to be pampered continually. It had become his only useful pastime since he had retired as chief of the tribe.

Ernestina came out of the bedroom scratching her big belly through her gingham nightdress. Her gray hair fell loosely to her shoulders.

"You feed the pigs?" she asked in Papago. In their own home, nothing but Papago was ever spoken.

Every morning she practically had to pry Macario out of the chair to go feed the pigs. His feet hurt him, his legs hurt, everything hurt. It took time—longer and longer, it seemed—for him to get the juices flowing and massage the aches away.

Macario stood up stiffly and yawned. "The pigs eat better than I do," he said. "I don't want any damn oatmeal again this morning. I want bacon and eggs."

"Until your bowels start working again like they're supposed to, you'll eat oatmeal." Ernestina gave him a sour look. "You aren't the rooster you think you are, old man."

"And you aren't the dainty little lamb I married," he muttered.

He pulled the suspenders on his baggy Levi's over his shoulders and flexed his right elbow gingerly. "I'm going into Tucson later, Ronstadt's Hardware, to pick up some insecticide for the onions. I found some aphids yesterday. You need anything?"

"Yeah, a new back. It's breaking from bending over this oven."

He swatted her expansive behind. "Your back looks in pretty good shape to me," he said.

She straightened up quickly and shook her finger at him. "You keep your hands off of me, you old billy goat. First thing you know I'll get pregnant again."

"*Chihuahua!*" he laughed. "You're a horny old bitch."

"Sweet talker," she said. She bent over again to pull a baking pan out of the coal oven. Macario walked out of the house and picked up the bucket of slops from supper last night. He looked up toward the mission and saw Magdalena walking toward him. She had a very purposeful, long stride. How pretty she is, he thought. Why is she here so early? Trouble with the BIA lawyer? He's a handsome man, young. Did he try to touch her?

"*Shah p a'i masma, ni-woji?*" [How are you, Grandpa?] she said, coming up to him and kissing his cheek.

He studied the sadness in her face. "*Ani sha'i sapu. Nap shoak?*" [I'm okay. And you, have you been crying?]

"He'u ni-woji." [Yes, Grandpa.] "I guess you haven't heard what happened last night?"

He shook his head.

"Sister Martha was murdered and thrown into the ditch."

"Ai, Madre de dios," he mumbled. He crossed himself.

"And they've arrested Ignacio. They think he did it. He was lying drunk, over there in the field." She pointed.

Macario's mouth fell open. "Ignacio, our Ignacio? What was he doing there?"

"I don't know, Grandpa."

He stared at her, trying to make sense of what she was saying. "He would not do such a thing," he said slowly.

"Of course not, Grandpa."

He put down the pail of pig slops. "Come," he said, "let's talk to Grandma."

They walked into the little adobe house, and Ernestina looked up from kneading dough on the kitchen table. "What's wrong?" she asked, appraising the troubled looks on their faces.

Magdalena told her grandmother what she had just told Macario. The old woman's reaction was the same as her husband's. She crossed herself and murmured, "Oh, Mother of God, what will we do?"

Macario sat down heavily at the table. "I knew there would be trouble from him," he said.

"Don't say that, Grandpa. Ignacio is a good boy."

He stared at her and shook his head. "Fucking *maricón*, he's a fucking *maricón*." He swallowed noisily, showing his distaste for the word. "I knew when the army turned him down he would bring great shame on us." His black eyes glistened with tears.

"That's not true, Grandfather," Magdalena said. "I've told you a hundred times it was the sickness. You are a stubborn old man."

He stared morosely at her and then sighed deeply and rubbed his eyes. "But he would never kill a nun," he mumbled. "That I know. He would never kill anybody."

Magdalena sat down at the table. "We've got to get him a lawyer."

Macario snorted. "Yeah? Who's going to defend one of us for killing a nun? And anyway how would we pay?"

"Joshua Rabb," Magdalena said.

Ernestina looked at her oddly. "Your acculturation man?"

Magdalena nodded.

"You're crazy," Macario said.

"No, I'm not." She looked at him earnestly. "I have lived with them for a week now. He's a very good man. I can see it. I can see how he is with his son and daughter. And he is a sad man. His wife died in an accident. But I think it's even deeper than that. Something that happened in the war. He sits sometimes and stares and thinks and looks very unhappy. There is just something about him I cannot explain, but he will help us. I know he will."

"You are a little girl, you don't know these white people. They have no use for any of us," Macario said. "We are dogshit under their heels."

"Not him, Grandpa. He's not like that."

"They're all like that."

"Just ask him. Please ask him to help Ignacio."

Macario shook his head and frowned. He shrugged his shoulders with the pointlessness of such a request. He looked from his wife to his granddaughter. Ernestina reached into a pottery bowl on the counter by the oven. She pulled out a wad of crumpled bills and handed them to her husband.

He counted the money deliberately, his face sour. "Eighty-four dollars. I didn't know we were so rich." He smiled wryly. Again he studied Ernestina and Magdalena. "I can't do this without talking to Francisco Romero. Ignacio being arrested for murder affects the whole tribe. And Francisco may want to talk to some of the others."

He got up and left the house. Magdalena heard the pickup start and pull away.

~~~~~~

Joshua heard the sound of a car engine coming down Indian Agency Road. It parked in front of his house. He looked out the living room window. It was a fairly new Ford pickup truck, and four elderly Papago men climbed out of the bed. Macario Antone got out of the driver's side. Francisco Romero and Magdalena Antone got out of the passenger side. The girl led the men up to the porch.

Joshua stepped onto the porch and closed the front door. He put his finger to his lips. "Quietly, please, my kids are still sleeping."

"My grandfather wishes to speak to you, Mr. Rabb," Magdalena said.

Joshua nodded.

"*Tt wo hikin k wo cheggia,*" the old man said.

Joshua listened to the grunts and then looked at Magdalena.

"He says we have to fight," Magdalena said.

"Sure," Joshua said. "Then we'll all end up one by one in the ditch like Sister Martha."

Macario shook his head sadly. "Do you know what Sister Martha used to tell us?"

Joshua stared at the old man surprised, then looked quizzically at Magdalena. "What are you, a ventriloquist?"

She smiled and translated into Papago. The men laughed.

"I spent twenty-three years in the United States Army, Mr. Rabb," Macario Antone said. "Started on the border here with the cavalry, ended up in France with the Fortieth Division, One-fifty-eighth Infantry. I was the division sergeant major. F company was all Indians, mostly Papagos and Pimas. Francisco was in France with F company for two years, a corporal. I got out in 1921." He spoke perfectly fluent English with hardly a trace of accent.

"How come you hide your English?" Joshua asked.

Macario shrugged. "White men talk around me since they think I can't understand. I hear of lot of things that I otherwise wouldn't."

"Your secret's safe with me, Chief. I'm getting the hell out of here."

The old man stared blankly at him.

"All right, so you were going to tell me what Sister Martha used to say."

"She called it Saint Barton's ode: 'I am hurt, but I am not

slain; I will lie me down and bleed awhile; then I will rise up and try again.' "

Joshua shook his head slowly. "Well, Chief, it sure didn't work out that way for her."

Macario looked hurt. "She is in rapture now, Mr. Rabb. She is where all mysteries are revealed and there is only love."

"Listen, if believing that gives you strength or solace or whatever, then I'm happy for you. But I'm not ready to have anyone send my kids or me to that kind of rapture."

The men murmured together in Papago for a moment.

"We need your help for Ignacio," Macario Antone said, his voice a little less steady and resolute. "We need you to represent him. You are all we have."

Joshua stared at him in surprise. "What are you, nuts? He's way beyond *my* help. He's a dead man!"

"He didn't hurt Sister Martha. Whatever kind of man he may be, Mr. Rabb, he's not a killer. He wouldn't have hurt Sister Martha or anyone else."

"Jesus, Chief! You don't seem to get it. This has nothing to do with whether he *did* a damn thing! He was in the field. He got arrested at the scene of a murder. He's a Papago Indian and a drunk to boot. What the hell do you think I can do for him, except maybe get strung up next to him and accompany him to the promised land?" He looked disbelievingly at Macario.

"Are you really so cynical, Mr. Rabb?" The old man spoke softly. "Have you really so little faith in your own system of justice? Is a court of law in Tucson no better than a vigilante's rope over the limb of a mesquite tree?"

Joshua gritted his teeth and breathed deeply. "I didn't know that you knew all those big English words, Chief." He frowned at Macario. "But you can't convince me. I'm not going to risk getting my children killed over something this hopeless."

Macario nodded and mumbled, *"Koi a mea g ban."*

Joshua looked at Magdalena.

She looked down apologetically. "He said he didn't know that you haven't yet killed a coyote."

"What's that mean?"

"We have four stages of becoming a man," she said quietly,

hesitantly. "The first stage is when a boy kills his first coyote." Her voice trailed off, and she looked away.

Joshua flared with anger. Stop it, he scolded himself. Don't get suckered into this meaningless fight. But why do I feel so low, why do I feel like a chickenshit coward? Who cares? Who cares for two whole seconds what happens to a bunch of Papagos in this little hole at the end of the world? Just pack the kids up and get the hell out of here. Go where it's safe.

Safe. Where? Where is it safe? Where *is* there no Senator Jacob Lukis?

Suddenly he was back in Germany, staring in paralyzed horror at the helpless living dead inmates of the concentration camp that his unit had stumbled into. And behind the barracks were obscene heaps of bodies, mounds of putrid starved flesh and bones, too many for the SS to bury before they fled from the advancing American army. And who had done this? Just people, Germans, led by scum like Jacob Lukis, Steve Lukis, Buford Richards. Did running away from them and ignoring them avoid the conflagration of World War Two? No. Did it avert the Holocaust? No, only fighting back worked. You cannot hide from evil, you must destroy it. But wait a minute, he chided himself, this isn't World War Two. Quit overdramatizing it! This is just a petty pissing match over mineral rights in the middle of nowhere.

But where do you make your stand?

But where is it written that a man must suffer for someone else's misfortune? Where is it written that you risk your kids' lives for a bunch of Indians?

Damn it all! What are you doing standing here in front of a couple of Indian chiefs and some warriors and Pocahontas? Get the hell inside and pack up your son and daughter.

But he didn't move. His feet were leaden on the porch.

Francisco Romero turned to Macario. *"Pegih neh! Ai att heg t-gahgi!"*

It startled Joshua out of his reverie. He looked at Magdalena.

"He said that we've achieved what we came for." Her voice was gentle. "He can read it in your face."

Joshua swallowed hard, said nothing. Oh God, please! Don't let me do this.

Macario Antone reached into his pocket and pulled out a wad of crumpled bills. He handed it to Joshua. "We are not beggars, Mr. Rabb," he said. "Here is money to hire you to defend Ignacio. What they're trying to do to him is wrong, Mr. Rabb. He's not a killer. He's a good man."

Joshua reached out and took the bills. Don't do this. Walk away. Walk away. Don't be a fool.

"There is one hundred and thirty-seven dollars. We have collected it from our people. Tomorrow I'll go to Sells, I'll get you more."

Joshua stared at the money and felt his eyes moistening. God help me! What am I doing?

The men turned and went to the pickup truck. Magdalena passed close to him and went into the house, leaving the door open for him to follow.

He went inside and closed the door. Magdalena was already in the kitchen preparing breakfast. He went into his bedroom and slumped wearily on the edge of the bed. He stared glumly at the wall, and suddenly he saw the concentration camp in front of him.

There were four ramshackle wooden barracks in which were huddled perhaps five hundred starved and diseased human beings. They were covered with suppurating stinking sores and thriving lice and were but vacant-eyed remnants of what had once been real people. Most of them were obviously dying. And behind the barracks were heaps of decaying, stinking cadavers, toothless protruding mouths gaping open, eyes rolled back white, sixty- or seventy-pound skin bags of putrid flesh. They all had filthy yellow Mogen Davids stitched on their striped pants.

That had been their crime.

I and many of my men had doubled over and vomited convulsively, embarrassed to look at each other, frightened to look at the still barely alive inmates. But they couldn't simply be ignored. They needed help, at least those few who weren't obviously going to die.

The fourth barrack was different from the rest. A sign on the front said FELDHÜREN, *and instead of rows of wooden bunks reaching to the ceiling, this one had thirty small enclosed cubicles off a central corridor like a squalid flophouse. This was the military whorehouse. I opened the door to each cubicle. Several of the inmates, who had been used as prostitutes for the German troops, were lying on the beds dead from bullet wounds. They were all better dressed and fed and cleaner than their fellow inmates in the other barracks. I opened the door of the next to last cubicle. A naked girl lay on the bed staring vacantly at the ceiling. She was no more than eleven or twelve years old, but precocious, with small buds of breasts and rounding hips and a few wisps of blond pubic hair on her vulva. Her face was very much like Hanna's. At her feet lay a naked little boy, probably seven or eight. He was beautiful, with curly brown hair and alabaster skin. His eyelids were shut. A bullet hole in his temple was crusted over with blood. On the floor beside the bed was another boy, also naked and also dead, with a bloody hole above his ear. He was no more than six years old.*

I couldn't hold back my tears. I wrapped the girl in a thin gray wool German army blanket and carried her into the open air compound. I laid her on one of the stretchers outside the first barrack, where medics were attending to the dying inmates.

I looked down at her, and she stared upward, her eyelids never moving, her gray eyes not flickering. She began to sob, thin, hollow, lingering wails like an injured cat. But no tears came, and her eyes didn't close. A medic knelt by her and pulled her left arm out of the blanket. He attached a blood pressure cuff and pumped it up and listened through a stethoscope. Then he put his hand on her forehead. He stood up and turned to me.

"Nothing physically wrong, Major. But like a lot of them, they just seem to want to die."

"Ask Captain Goldberg to come over here, Doc," I said.

The medic walked into the first barrack. Dr. Goldberg was a short, stocky man. He came out a moment later and walked up to me. "Can you believe this place?" he mumbled.

I shook my head. "Check this girl out, will you, Joe?"

"Sure." Dr. Goldberg knelt down and examined her.

"It isn't physical, Josh," he said, standing up. He shook his head resignedly and walked back into the barrack.

I was reluctant to leave her. Every time I looked at her I saw Hanna, and it made me shudder with irrational fear. But I couldn't do anything for her. I went into the small cement-block administration building and set up my headquarters, and I could still hear the girl's sobbing across the eerily silent compound. I put my hands to my ears, but I couldn't block it out.

Two days later, Joe Goldberg came into my office and told me that the girl had died. I began to tremble and couldn't speak. The doctor left, and I began to cry. I sat staring out the window into the bright spring sunshine of Czechoslovakia and wept for Hanna and Adam.

———

"Yer gonna do *what?*" Edgar stared at Joshua across the broad desk.

"I'm going to defend Ignacio Antone."

Edgar sat back in his chair and studied Joshua. "Yer puttin me on, right? You don't think a cup a coffee in the mornin is enough of a waker upper for me." He pointed at his coffee cup on the desk. "So you're trying to jump start me, huh?" He smiled.

Joshua shook his head, his face solemn.

"Sweet Jesus! What are you, outta your gott damn mind? The senator will call the air force base and have em drop a five-hundred-pounder right here on the BIA. You suicidal, or what?"

"I have to defend him. He's been unjustly accused."

The look that Edgar gave him defied singular description. It was shock, annoyance, disbelief, horror, fear. "By God, you're serious."

Joshua nodded.

"*Unjustly accused,*" Edgar said slowly, mouthing each word articulately. "This is the gott damn Papago Indin reservation, not the Supreme Court a the United States! You ain't gonna get your pitcher on the front a the *New York Times,* you're just gonna get your brains smeared all over the front door a your house, and your kids are gonna end up in the bottom a the ditch."

Edgar shook his head. "Look, pal, you got a big pair a balls, I grant you that, but they ain't big enough for what yer talkin about takin on here. This whole town says that drunk Indin murdered a beloved Poor Clare nun." He held up the morning newspaper with the headline NUN KILLED—DERELICT ARRESTED and slid the newspaper toward Joshua. There was a photograph of a sheriff's deputy leading Ignacio into the Pima County Jail.

"He didn't do it, Edgar. Buford Richards or Steve Lukis or somebody working for them did. You know that."

"I don't know shit!" Edgar exploded. "Alls I know is I'd like to have this job tomorrow and the next day! I been workin at it for fourteen years, and suddenly some gott damn Brooklyn"—he caught himself, held his breath, didn't say what he was going to say—"some New York *dude* comes out here and spiffs up in a Western belt and a cowboy hat and turns into the gott damn Statue a Liberty in about three days flat! 'Gimme your poor, your hungry . . .' You must be drinkin too much tequila!"

"Don't you think somebody has to stand up to these people and say 'no more'?" Joshua said wearily.

"Not us, pal! Not me! That's precisely what Sister Martha done, and look where it got her."

Joshua nodded. "I know," he said quietly.

"I don't know what's suddenly got into you. What happened? You get too close to Sister Martha last night when they hauled her into the meat wagon? You catch her virus or somethin?"

Joshua shook his head. "It's just that we have to take a stand against people like the Lukises. This is America, not Germany. There's justice here. We can't be paralyzed by fear."

"Better to be paralyzed by fear than just plain paralyzed," Edgar said grimly. "Look, I'm gonna end your misery on all this shit. Today we're signin the senator's contract for mineral rights and it ends right there. We won't even see the old fart for another three years, and he'll prob'ly be long dead by the time it comes up for renewal."

Joshua shook his head slowly.

"What the hell is that? You got Parkinson's disease or somethin, can't stop your head from shakin?"

"I won't sign it."

"The hell you won't! I'm orderin you to sign it!"

"You have no authority. You can give me orders as to the BIA, but as to the Office of Land Management, I'm the independent agent here."

Edgar gritted his teeth. "I can't let you do that. We got to settle this thing or we'll have no end a problems."

Joshua shook his head.

"Look, you don't get it. For some damn reason you just don't get it. I ain't got no nobility, I can't afford it. I got a wife and kid and a little house and a job that I can do. What do I do if I get tossed outta here? I only got through the tenth grade, I ain't got no trade or skills. What the hell do I do?"

Joshua sat silently.

"You're a handsome guy, a lawyer. You'll hang around here just long enough to drum up a few clients. Then you'll quit and move into Tucson and buy a ranch-style house on the east side and get your pitcher in the paper every now and again for presidin over the food campaign for hungry kids or for raisin money for the Home a the Good Shepherd where they look after poor girls that get knocked up. None a this'll mean jackshit to you this time next year. But me? This is it! This is my life! It's all I got! And if I keep buckin the senator over a few lousy rocks that don't even belong to me, then I got nothin. Then I got shit!"

Joshua frowned resignedly. "I'm sorry, Edgar. I'm not real happy either. But sometimes a man just has to do what he thinks is right."

Edgar stared angrily at Joshua. "A man gotta do what a man gotta do," he said, his voice bitter. "That's crap! That's just cheap hero talk outta dime novels."

Joshua frowned. He felt emotionally drained, empty.

Edgar sat back and appraised him. "You are a seriously confused man," he said. "You don't know which way is up. I'm firin you for yer own good."

Joshua stood up. "You have that authority, Edgar. Sorry things didn't work out." He turned and walked out of the office, out of the bureau, and limped painfully home.

~~~~~~~

Joshua drove down to the courthouse and parked in the lot opposite the coroner's office. The smell inside the office was a mixture of formaldehyde and something organic and awful. The office was small with nowhere to sit. He pressed the buzzer on the jamb by the inner door. He stood there for five minutes, pressing the buzzer now and then in increasing frustration. Finally the door opened. It was the coroner's deputy, whom he had talked to when Vittorio's body was recovered. A lighted cigar hung out of his mouth.

"Remember me?"

"Yeah, yeah. You're Mr. Rabb from the BIA."

"Right. I'd like to talk to the coroner."

"Well, Dr. Wolfe is doing an autopsy now. Just started. It's going to take a couple hours."

"Is it Sister Martha Robinette?"

The deputy nodded.

"I'm going to be defending Ignacio Antone, the Indian they arrested for her murder. Could you ask Dr. Wolfe if I could observe the autopsy?"

"Defend Antone?" The deputy's eyes widened.

Joshua nodded.

"Hold on."

Several more minutes passed and the door opened wide. "Come on," the deputy said. "You ever see an autopsy?"

Joshua shook his head.

"Who's your next of kin? I'll be notifying them in about ten minutes." The deputy laughed.

The autopsy room was painted shiny white. The floor was cement which sloped on all sides toward a central drainpipe a foot in diameter which was directly under the surgical table.

"I'm Stan Wolfe," said the green-robed man standing over the body. He had a soft, round, pink face in a small pudgy body.

"Joshua Rabb."

The nun lay on her back on the table. Her belly had been slit open from the sternum to the mons pubis. The sternum itself had been cut in two, probably with the big pair of scissors that looked like poultry shears and lay covered in blood on the instrument table. The doctor had just pulled the left lung through the hole and quickly excised it with the shears.

Joshua had seen enough death, bloody violent death, not to fall into a dead faint. But enclosed in this little room, the smell of the body was overwhelming. The doctor jutted his chin toward the deputy. "Better give him one."

The deputy opened a drawer in a white metal wall cabinet and took a cigar out. "Here, I'll light you up," he said, handing the cigar to Joshua.

The aroma of the cigar smoke right under his nose was literally therapeutic. He puffed eagerly for a few moments to cloud the air around him. The doctor had sliced open the lung and was holding it up to the intense overhead light and scrutinizing it.

"Did she drown?" Joshua asked.

"I don't think so," said the doctor slowly. "There's no mucous froth in the lung tissue. I'd expect to find at least some invasion of ditch water in the lung which would mix into a froth in the alveoli. But this is a normal lung. I've still got to check the bronchii."

He threw the lung into a pail under the table. Then he reached into the chest cavity and pulled out the tube from which he had excised the lung. He pulled a little water hose down from its winding spindle overhead and sprayed the bronchus. He leaned over and examined it closely.

"Nope, no mucous froth," he said. "No distension."

"What's that mean?" Joshua asked.

"Well, for the moment it means she's dead and she didn't drown, but I don't know why she died." He looked up at Joshua and shrugged.

He took a scalpel off the table and cut into the nun's neck beside the windpipe. Again he leaned over and studied it closely.

"She was strangled," he said slowly, straightening up. "Someone wrapped both hands around her neck from behind and strangled her."

"How can you tell?"

"Come here, but don't vomit on my cadaver."

Joshua stepped up slowly to the table, puffing steadily on the cigar.

"You see these almost black bruises on the side of the neck, both sides, about three inches long, the size of four fingertips, and there are two small thumb-size bruises on the nape of the neck. If it's just postmortem hypostasis, which means normal settling of the blood in the body after death, which also causes this kind of lividity, then there wouldn't be any blood around the blood vessels where I made my incision." He pointed, and Joshua looked closely.

"But in violent bruising, the vessels are injured or crushed and the blood spills out into the surrounding tissue. That's what we have here. Also, see all the burst blood vessels in the skin on the tops of the cheeks and these broken capillaries all over the whites of the eye." He opened the left eyelid so that Joshua could see. "These are called petechiae. They're hemorrhages of certain groups of blood vessels specific to strangulation."

Joshua looked closely at the various signs of violence. "Vittorio Ponsay had the same burst blood vessels on his cheeks and in his eyes," Joshua said.

The doctor looked surprised. "What do you care about him for?"

"Everybody thought he drowned. But maybe he died the same way."

"So what?" The doctor's voice was hard.

"Did you do an autopsy on him?"

"Man, you are really begging for trouble."

Joshua stared blandly at the doctor.

The doctor hesitated a moment, then nodded his chin toward the deputy, who walked over to the metal cabinet, pulled out a file drawer, located a manila file folder, and brought it to Joshua. The tab said, "Ponsay, Vittorio, June 30, 1946." Inside were two handwritten pages. The first page was a description of the boy and a superficial examination and a recitation of the various incisions and techniques used in the autopsy. The last paragraph on the second page read, *"Clinical Impression:* The anal orifice is funnel shaped and has the appearance of dilatation. There is epithelialization of the puckered mucosa, and the presence of semen is noted."

Joshua read it silently and couldn't understand it. He read it out loud to the doctor. "What's that mean?"

"It means that some giant of humanity had just sodomized him."

Joshua nodded. He read the next sentence aloud. "There is severe extravasation around the superficial blood vessels of the throat in two livid areas approximately five centimeters in length, and petechiae are noted in expected distribution." Joshua looked up at the doctor. "Strangled just like the sister?"

The doctor nodded. "Except I can't be certain it was from behind. The body had lain on its back a long time so there was too much hypostasis and I couldn't find marks on the nape. Something else, too." He pointed to her lower body. "She's been forcibly raped, but not in the vaginal orifice."

Joshua nodded. "Some giant of humanity?"

"Yes," the doctor said, his face grim for the first time. "Looks like two leaves off the same branch to me."

"Can you tell if the rapes were committed before or after death?"

"The answer with the nun is that she was already dead. There was only minimal bleeding around the fresh tears in the anal sphincter. When the heart stops, it stops pumping, so you don't see much postmortem bleeding from small blood vessels. But I couldn't tell with the boy. He had no open fissures. It wasn't his first time."

Joshua looked at the autopsy report on the boy. "It says here 'nonsecretor.' What's that mean?"

"I tried to type the semen. About eighty percent of the population secretes what we call A and B properties in saliva and sweat and semen which can be typed the same as blood. But as to the other twenty percent, there are no typable secretions. We don't know why, except that it's a genetic trait. Anyway, I couldn't type the semen."

"How about the nun?"

"I didn't type it yet. Call me later."

"There was another Indian found in the ditch a few days before Vittorio, a thirteen-year-old Papago girl named Norma Enriquez. Did you do an autopsy on her?"

"No, she wasn't brought here."

"Isn't that unusual?"

"Not at all, not for the Papagos. I don't have jurisdiction over the reservation. If the sheriff brings the body here, I look at it. But usually the Indian's family won't let it come here. They just want to do the funeral right away. It's up to them."

Joshua nodded. "Thanks, Dr. Wolfe, I really appreciate your help."

"You'll need more than *my* help if you're defending this nun's killer. You're probably going to get yourself lynched."

"How about if he didn't do it?"

The doctor smirked and swept his arm around. "You think any of those good folks out there are going to listen long enough to find out? Hell, they saw the Indian's picture in the paper in handcuffs this morning. That gives them all the evidence *they* need."

Joshua thought for a moment. "Is there any way of testing Ignacio Antone to see if he's a secretor?"

The doctor nodded slowly. "Deputy Hoskins here went over to the jail three hours ago and got a test tube of your friend's saliva. I checked it. He's not a secretor."

Joshua shrugged.

"There is one other thing. I almost forgot," the doctor said. He walked over to a table in the corner. He picked up the black habit and held it toward him. "You see those crusted stains? There's quite a lot of bloodstaining on the front of her habit. But it's type AB. It's not hers, she's an O."

"Her assailant bled all over her?"

"Sure looks that way. Pretty severe cut. She must have bitten him or cut him with something."

"Ignacio Antone?"

"Nope. No cuts or abrasions."

Joshua screwed up his face in thought. "Who has type AB blood?"

"What do you mean?" the doctor asked.

"Well, I don't know, are there certain blood types for women, others for men, others for negroes and Chinese and Italians?"

The doctor shrugged. "I can't imagine that there is, but the truth is it beats the hell out of me. I don't even know if any studies have been done on that."

"Who might know?"

Again the doctor shrugged. He thought for a moment. "My best guess would be Dr. Howard Falconer in the anthropology department over at the university. He's a physical anthropologist, does a lot of work reconstructing skeletons, differentiating between animal species, stuff like that. We use him when we find a decomposed body in the desert. He can tell you whether it was man, woman, approximate age, so forth. He might know something about blood types."

"Okay, thanks."

Dr. Wolfe nodded. Joshua left the coroner's office. He threw the cigar stub on the ground outside and breathed in the fresh air deeply. It was almost eleven o'clock and already close to one hundred degrees. He walked around to the Pima County Jail. Inside was the same deputy he'd had the encounter with over "Jennifer."

"Hey, Shit for Brains. I didn't think I'd see you around here again. Nona's back at the Catalina Hotel."

"I'm here to see Ignacio Antone."

"What the hell for?"

"I'm his lawyer."

The big man's mouth fell open and he gaped at Joshua. "Holy shit, boy, when I found out who you was a couple a days ago, I figured you for a stupid bastard, getting yourself into a fix like that, but now I think you're downright crazy as a coot!"

"May I see Mr. Antone, please?"

"No you may not, asshole!" the deputy shot back. "County attorney's office just picked him up for his initial appearance before Judge Rooks."

"Is he the federal judge?"

"Hell no, he ain't no federal judge. Judge Rooks has to work for a living! He's the Pima County superior court judge."

Joshua looked surprised. "He hasn't got any jurisdiction over a crime on an Indian reservation."

"Hey, don't give me any a that bullshit. I don't give a flaming dog turd *who* hangs the bastard, just so the job gets done!"

"Where's the courtroom?"

"Out here, turn right, through the portico and up the stairs. Right on top of us." He pointed to the ceiling. "But I'd take it mighty slow with old Judge Rooks. He ain't gonna believe this shit! You gonna catch your lunch, Shit for Brains."

At the top of the stairway were wooden benches on each side of a large wooden door going into the courtroom. Three haggard-looking ladies of the evening sat handcuffed together on one bench. Joshua looked through the foot-square window on the door and saw Ignacio standing with another man before the judge.

Joshua opened the door and walked down the center aisle. The judge had a moon-shaped sallow face and closely cropped salt-and-pepper hair. He looked up annoyedly as Joshua opened the short wooden gate which separated the spectator area from the front of the courtroom.

"What is it?"

"Your honor, my name is Joshua Rabb. I've been retained to represent Mr. Antone."

The judge slowly removed his glasses and laid them on the desk. "I've heard your name mentioned, Mr. Rabb," the judge drawled. "Are you a member of the bar of the State of Arizona?"

"No, your honor, not yet. I've been a member of the New York bar for eleven years, but I've just arrived here in Tucson."

"Well, you won't be representing Mr. Antone until you're admitted to the bar, Mr. Rabb. Our little hicktown rules are no different than New York. If you're not admitted to the bar, you can't practice in court."

"Yes, your honor, of course that's true in state court, but this is a federal matter. I can be admitted just on motion to the federal bar, at least for one case. I suppose that's the same out here too, isn't it, Judge?"

"Mr. Rabb, you aren't in federal court now. You're in *my* court, and I just told you that you can't practice here."

"Your honor, with all due respect, I believe that this court does not have jurisdiction over a crime on a federal reservation. Now if your honor will assure me that I'm wrong about that, I'll most certainly leave this courtroom immediately."

The judge sat back slowly into his big black leather chair. "You say 'with all due respect,' but I have the unpleasant sensation that you don't mean it, Mr. Rabb. I think what you're really saying is 'Kiss my ass, you hick son of a bitch.' "

"It hadn't even crossed my mind, your honor."

The judge gritted his teeth. "If I was a man who became insulted easily, I think I'd just have to put you in jail for contempt of court."

Joshua was silent.

"But I'm not a volatile man, Mr. Rabb, so I'll give you five seconds to be out of my sight."

Joshua turned on his heels and quickly left the courtroom. No sense getting cited for contempt and spending a day in jail or worse. Outside in the corridor he asked one of the women on the bench where the federal courthouse was.

"I dunno. Never been arrested federal."

One of the other two pointed east with her free arm. "Two blocks down, Scott and Broadway. It's on the second floor of the post office."

Joshua hurried to the post office. He was happy that he had his cane with him. He climbed the stairs in the post office and came into a long hallway with a smoked glass door to an office at the far end. He walked past the double doors of the courtroom. The sign on the smoked glass door of the end office read, PRIVATE: JUDGE BUCHANAN. He knocked and walked in. An old woman in a tight gray bun and rimless glasses sat at a small metal desk facing the door.

"Yes, sir?" she said.

"Is the judge in?"

"Yes. Who are you?"

"I'm Joshua Rabb. I'm an attorney with the Bureau of Indian Affairs."

"One moment, sir." She walked through a side door and closed it softly. Three or four minutes later she returned to her desk. "The judge will see you."

Joshua walked into a walnut-paneled office with heavy furniture and walls lined with bookshelves. The nameplate on the desk said, ROBERT BUCHANAN. Another plate next to it read, THE BUCK STOPS HERE.

"How do you do, Judge Buchanan. I'm Joshua Rabb with the BIA."

The judge stood up and extended his hand. "Call me Buck. Everybody calls me Buck." He was about sixty years old, slight of build, had a rich shock of graying brown hair and very tired-looking blue eyes. "Have a seat."

Joshua sat in front of the desk. The judge shook a Camel out of a pack and lit it with a lighter, then gestured with the pack toward Joshua.

"No, thank you, sir. I came here because I have a problem. I've been retained to represent a Papago Indian who was arrested last night for the murder of a nun on San Xavier Del Bac Reservation. I've just been in Judge Rooks's courtroom, and he declined to give up jurisdiction. I'm here for a writ of habeas corpus."

"I read about the case this morning," the judge said, pointing at the newspaper on the desk. "I've been hearing quite a lot about you for only being in Tucson such a short time. Senator Jacob said you are a fast-moving young man, and he wasn't whistling Dixie. He was mentioning you just last night at the M.O. Club."

Joshua felt deflated. Was everybody in this town bought and paid for? "You know the senator?"

"Son, didn't you go to school the day they taught how federal judges are born? We don't come from storks, we come from senators. I was Jacob's lawyer for twenty years. He recommended me, and President Roosevelt appointed me to the bench two years ago."

Joshua nodded. Nothing is going to work out right in this damn town. Nothing. He got up to leave.

"Where you going? I thought you needed a writ?"

Joshua looked quizzically at the judge. "You mean you'll grant me a writ?"

"Damn right I will! I'm not Jacob's lawyer anymore. I'm the federal judge here. That means something to me. I took a solemn oath to uphold the Constitution, and that's damn well what I intend to do. That prick Fran Rooks doesn't have any more sense than a pack mule. All he cares about is that the great unwashed who foolishly elected him twice will foolishly elect him again. I don't have that problem. I got appointed for life." He smiled. "The only problem I have is that you're probably not a member of the Arizona bar, right?"

"Yes, sir."

The judge reached to the telephone on the desk and dialed. "Wally? Buck here. Listen, Wally, I got a young lawyer here name of Joshua Rabb—yes, yes, the one and only, old Jake's favorite guy—well, anyway, he needs to be admitted on motion for a case in my court. Can you come on over for about a minute and a half so I can ordain him? Fine, fine, thanks."

The judge hung up the telephone. "My former partner, Walter Chandler. He'll be here in two shakes. His office is right across the street on Scott."

"I really appreciate your doing this for me, Judge. The senator probably isn't going to be very thrilled about this."

The judge shrugged. "He was my client. He's not my iron lung. Old Jake can be an irascible bastard—he's had a hell of a lot of power all of his life—but believe me he isn't a bad man. Getting a little cranky in his old age, I guess, but down bottom he's a decent man." He held up his hand in a halt gesture. "Now I know what you're going to say, all about the contract bullshit that's been going on over there for a couple of months, but that's politics and money, son, dirty politics and dirty money, and I suppose old Jake is a master at that game. Why hell, I'll tell you about the time that he and I and Buford drove up to the state legislature in Phoenix, that's when Jacob was a state senator, probably back in 'thirty, 'thirty-one—"

There was a knock on the door and it opened. A rotund, completely bald man came in. He was wearing a droopy seersucker suit and brown military shoes. The judge stood up and shook his hand.

"Walter Chandler, this is Joshua Rabb. I was just telling him about that trip we all took up to Phoenix when Senator Jacob wanted to force the state to build an aqueduct on his property so he could drain off the water and irrigate his orange trees. Never saw anything like old Jake when he went after something he *really* wanted."

"Nice to meet you," Chandler said, shaking hands with Joshua.

"Joshua here is going to represent the Indian accused of killing the nun last night," the judge said.

Chandler gave Joshua a wry smile. "I'd be doing you a favor if I marched out of here and refused to move your admission."

Joshua shrugged.

"Well, it's your ass," Chandler said. "At least you won't be around very long to give me any legal competition. Folks around here will have you strung up in about four or five days."

"Yeah, I'm beginning to get the impression that defending Mr. Antone won't make me very popular."

"That's putting it mildly," Chandler said.

"Come on, let's go out in the courtroom, make this official," the judge said.

They walked into the outer office, the secretary joined them, and they walked down a narrow corridor into the courtroom through a door marked JUDGE'S ENTRANCE. The judge took the bench, Joshua and Walter Chandler stood in front of it, and the secretary sat down at the court reporter's desk.

"Court is in session," Judge Buchanan intoned. "The court recognizes the distinguished Walter Chandler, Esquire. Have you business for the court, sir?"

"I do, your honor. I have the pleasure to introduce before the bar Joshua Rabb, Esquire, a member in good standing of the bar of the State of—"

"New York," Joshua whispered.

"—New York, and who has practiced with distinction before the state and federal benches for—"

"Eleven years," Joshua whispered.

"—for eleven years and who should be admitted to the bar of this court for the"—he looked at Joshua, and Joshua whispered—"Ignacio Antone."

"—for the defense of Ignacio Antone."

The judge rapped his gavel. "Granted." He looked down at his secretary. "Mrs. Hawkes, please prepare a writ of habeas corpus to Sheriff Dunphy ordering the release of Ignacio Antone to the federal marshal. You can use the same one we did in the Castellano case last year. Send Marshal Friedkind over with it, and I'll call my friend Fran Rooks and tell him the good news." He looked at Joshua. "The marshal will have your client in custody on the first floor of this building, west wing, in an hour. I'll have the initial appearance up here at one o'clock." He banged the gavel and walked off the bench and through the back door to his office.

For the first time in days, Joshua felt as though he had finally achieved something beneficial, positive.

"Come with me, Mr. Rabb," the secretary said. "I'll type up your writ and you can bring it over to Marshal Friedkind's office."

It took about fifteen minutes to have the writ typed and another twenty minutes to find the U.S. marshal eating fried chicken at Woolworth's counter. He wore Western clothes and a felt cowboy hat, even while eating, and was less than cheery about cutting his lunch hour short to pick up an Indian, especially this Indian. But when Joshua told him the judge expected the prisoner in his courtroom at one o'clock, the marshal got up grumblingly and walked off to the county jail. It was twenty minutes to one.

Joshua went back to the post office, but the marshal's office was locked for lunch. He wouldn't have time to interview Ignacio before one o'clock anyhow. He went up to the courtroom on the second floor and sat down. Ten minutes later, a man walked in. He was thin and medium height, around Joshua's

age, with pleasant features, brown hair and eyes, and a deep
tan.

"You Joshua Rabb?" he said.

"Right."

"I'm Tim Essert, the assistant United States attorney."

They shook hands.

"I just saw the note from the judge's secretary that you're
going to be representing the nun killer."

"Alleged."

"Yeah, right, alleged nun killer."

"His family retained me."

"This your first case in Tucson?"

Joshua nodded.

"One hell of a way to break in," Essert said, shaking his head.
"I guess you believe in starting with a bang."

"He's entitled to representation just like anyone. He's entitled
to a defense."

Essert drew back his head and scowled. "Defense? Don't tell
me you're going to plead this dirtbag not guilty."

"Of course."

Essert shook his head slowly and fixed Joshua with a baleful
stare. "This guy didn't kill another Papago drunk or a Mex.
Why hell, that's a misdemeanor around here, a 'Meyer Street
misdemeanor' we call it. Those drunks over on Meyer Street
cut each other's throats for a swallow of Gallo muscatel. But
this dirtbag killed a *nun*. That's kind of a different thing around
here altogether."

"Well, Mr. Essert, that's about the third or fourth time I've
heard that same speech today, but nobody's told me yet why
it's okay to suspend the Constitution of the United States when
an *Indian* is accused of murdering a white person."

Essert pursed his lips and sucked in his breath. "Boy, you
really are a foreigner. She wasn't just a white person, she was
a child of God, a real saint." He made the sign of the cross.
"She was on the board of directors of St. Mary's Hospital, she
was the chairwoman of Casita de los Niños, Tucson's orphanage.
My wife was on that board with her, loved her like family."

Joshua said nothing.

"The bar association doesn't need people like you. We got nine lawyers in Tucson, and we think we got a pretty good group of boys, look out for each other, you know, sensitive to what this town needs to be a good place to live and raise your kids, and we don't need any—"

The wooden door creaked open and Ignacio Antone walked through it followed by Marshal Friedkind. The stink of Ignacio's filthy clothing billowed around him. He had lost his other sneaker and was barefoot. The marshal pushed him in front of the railing and he stumbled. His hands were cuffed behind him, and he stood up with difficulty and looked around with a blank stare.

"Hey, Timmy," the marshal said, "I can't stand the stink of this maggot. I'm gonna take him down to holding and hose him off and give him a jail uniform. Tell Buck we'll be back in fifteen minutes." He pulled Ignacio by the arm and they walked out of the courtroom.

Essert followed them out. Joshua waited ten minutes, fifteen minutes, and the secretary came into the courtroom and sat down at the court reporter's desk. A moment later Ignacio and the marshal came in again. Ignacio was dressed in a faded blue air force jumpsuit and black half-boots without laces. His hair was combed straight back and glistened under the chandeliers in the courtroom.

The judge came through the door of his private corridor followed by Tim Essert. Joshua walked past the wooden railing and stood next to his client.

"Time for the initial appearance in United States versus Ignacio Antone," the judge said. "The prosecutor is Assistant U.S. Attorney Tim Essert, and Joshua Rabb is for the defendant. Can you understand me, Ignacio?"

Ignacio nodded.

"Let's hear you say something so I'm sure."

"I understand," the Indian mumbled.

"Okay, you're being held on charges of rape and murder, Ignacio. The United States attorney has issued what we call a criminal complaint." The judge held up a sheet of paper and displayed it, then laid it on the desk. "And the government's charging that you raped and murdered Sister Martha Robinette with malice aforethought. Now this gentleman here"—he pointed at Joshua—"is going to be your lawyer."

Ignacio looked at Joshua for the first time.

"You getting all this, Ignacio?" the judge asked.

The Indian nodded.

"All right, I'm setting your *preliminary hearing* for Monday at ten o'clock. You know what a 'preliminary hearing' is, Ignacio?"

He shook his head. He was thin, average height, and had the same delicate features as his sister. He looked bewildered and frightened, and his eyes darted around the courtroom as though he were trying to find something familiar to focus on.

"Well, the complaint which the government filed that charges you with rape and murder doesn't mean anything unless either a grand jury *indicts* you or I hold a preliminary hearing and find *probable cause* that you committed the crimes. Then you have to stand trial. Otherwise we just release you and you're a free man. Are you following me?"

"Yessir."

"So in your case, since you have an attorney, I'm going to let you have a preliminary hearing in my courtroom here instead of letting Mr. Essert assemble thirteen citizens in a room down the hall and have them secretly hear the evidence that he presents against you and return an *indictment* and make you stand trial. Understand?"

Ignacio nodded.

"That means that next week we're going to have a sort of trial, a real short one, but there won't be a jury, just me. And after everybody testifies, I'll decide whether you actually have to stand trial in front of a jury or whether I can just set you free. You still following me?"

Ignacio nodded soberly.

"Good boy," Judge Buchanan said. "In the meantime you'll be held without bail at the federal detention center on Mount Lemmon. Anything else, gentlemen?"

"No, your honor," Essert said.

"Your honor," Joshua said, "isn't Mount Lemmon what they call the top of the Catalina Mountains?"

"A for geography, Mr. Rabb."

"Well, may it please the court, I have to prepare Mr. Antone's defense, and I've never even talked to him before. Can he be kept here in the marshal's office till the preliminary?"

The judge shook his head. "The federal government has no detention center in Tucson, Mr. Rabb, only on Mount Lemmon or in Florence. Mount Lemmon's only about forty miles from here, Florence is seventy-five. I'm doing you a favor. All Marshal Friedkind has here is a holding pen, no water, no toilet, no food, nobody to watch him over the weekend. I'm afraid I have no choice, Mr. Rabb."

"Then is it possible for me to interview him right now before he's taken?"

"Well now, Ollie," the judge said to the marshal, "what do you think about that?"

"I don't think too much of it, Judge. It's one-thirty now, it'll take me at least four hours to bring him up there 'n get back by six o'clock for Marian's birthday party. I'd just catch some serious hell if I was late for that."

"You heard it, Mr. Rabb. He's going to have to leave with your client right away. Of course, they have visiting hours up there two to four on the weekends." The judge banged his gavel and walked off the bench.

Joshua gritted his teeth. Damn! He walked slowly back toward the door to leave the courtroom. A small middle-aged woman with a kindly face and stark dyed-brown hair in a stiff wavy 1930s hairdo got up from a spectator's seat and waited in the aisle.

"Mr. Rabb, I'm J. T. Sellner with the *Arizona Daily Star*. May I talk to you for a minute?"

"Yes, of course," Joshua said.

"I talked with Edgar Hendly a little while ago—I've known him ever since high school—and he says he had to fire you this morning for insubordination."

Joshua shrugged wearily. "I guess that covers it."

"You wouldn't take certain actions required of you with respect to contracts with the Indians."

"*A contract* between the tribe and Senator Lukis."

She wrote quickly on a stenographer's pad. "And how did you get into *this*, Mr. Rabb?"

"I was hired by the young man's grandfather."

She nodded and wrote. "Are you intending to plead him not guilty?"

"Well, he hasn't been formally charged with anything yet, but assuming that he's bound over on a murder charge next Monday after the preliminary hearing, yes, he'll plead not guilty."

"Do you have any evidence to prove his innocence?"

"Well, Mrs. Sellner—"

"Miss."

"Excuse me, *Miss* Sellner, he doesn't have to prove his innocence, the government has the burden of proving him guilty. And I don't think they can. I think that he was brought by someone to the field next to the mission and dumped there in a dead drunk. There were tire tracks and cowboy boot impressions in the field where the nun's body appeared to have been dumped out of a car and dragged to the irrigation ditch and rolled into it. Mr. Antone had no car and was wearing sneakers."

J. T. Sellner wrote furiously, sucking on her lower lip. "Can you prove any of that?"

"Let me repeat, Miss Sellner, it's the *government* that has to prove something, not the defense, but I wouldn't say it if I didn't think I could. I was there last night when they found the body. I don't think Ignacio Antone did a thing."

"Then who did, Mr. Rabb? Any ideas?"

"Not a clue, Miss Sellner, not a clue."

"Just for the sake of curiosity, Mr. Rabb, and please don't take offense, but how did that happen?" She inclined her head toward his missing arm.

"Well, I too don't wish for you to take offense, Miss Sellner. But I simply don't like talking about it." He walked out of the courtroom.

When he got home no one was there. There was a note on the kitchen table in Magdalena's careful hand that they had gone up to the reservoir to go swimming. It was a little after two o'clock. There was a knock on the front door.

"I saw your car raisin up a dust storm down the road," Edgar said. "I'd like to talk to ya fer a minute."

"Come in," Joshua said, opening the door wide and stepping aside.

Edgar sat down heavily on the couch. "Hell of a day, huh? Must be a hunnerd 'n five."

"Sure is hot," Joshua said.

"Jimmy's madder 'n a hornet."

"Oh yeah? What's the problem?"

"He says he and Adam are pals, and he don't want Adam to leave."

"I'm sure Adam won't be overjoyed either. But some things can't be helped."

"Well, maybe this one can."

Joshua sat down on the chair and said nothing.

Edgar fidgeted with the frayed arm of the couch. "I'm sorry about what happened this mornin'."

"Which part?"

"The firin part."

Joshua studied Edgar. "What are you trying to tell me?"

"I'm tryin to tell ya that ya ain't fired."

Joshua wrinkled his forehead and squinted at Edgar. "I don't get it," he said slowly. "Nothing has changed since ten o'clock. I'm still not going to double-cross all those Papago Indians just for the sake of old Jake." He smiled thinly. "Has a nice ring, huh? For the sake of old Jake."

Edgar nodded. "I know that. And I ain't either."

Joshua pursed his lips in surprise. "What's gotten into you? The senator and his boys will have your ass. Like the pig at the barbecue."

"That's a hell of a thought," Edgar said with a grimace. "Good eatin too, huh?"

Both men laughed.

"You're serious about this? You've thought about it?"

"Yes," Edgar said. "Plenny. I got no choice." He shook his head grimly. "I'm fifty-four years old and I been Jacob's cocker spaniel for thirty-five a them years. I just reckon by anybody's honest calculatin that I done plenny for the old boy, and he done for me too, that's for sure. And I can't believe he's to blame for all the dirty business goin on, what with bodies floatin around in ditch water every four or five days. This is kind of a new wrinkle out here. Maybe it's Steve's doin—that ain't so hard to believe—or Buford thinkin he's doin what the old man wants. Could even be one a the priests for all I know. But whatever it is, I ain't never been scared before, not since my ma died, and now all of a sudden I'm scared. I'm scared for my boy. I'm scared for my wife and myself. And it's my own damn fault." Edgar paused and pursed his lips sourly. "I feel like I'm rope dancin."

"What's that, some Papago ritual?"

"No, no, it ain't no ritual. Leastways not a nice one. I hadda go up to Utah State Prison six years ago to be a witness at a hangin. They hung some piece a shit white trash for murderin two a my Indin kids who was up there in Salt Lake City. You ever see a hangin?"

Joshua shook his head.

"Well, they dance, danglin from that rope. They just hang there a coupla feet off the ground and shimmy and jerk and reach down crazy like with their legs tryin to get a foothold. It's somethin to see." He rubbed his chin and mouth and swallowed hard. "Ever since then I always kinda felt like a rope dancer whenever old Jacob was around, like he was a danglin me and watchin me kick and laughin like a som bitch." Edgar shook his head dolefully at Joshua. "But instead a plantin my feet and tellin them Lukises to quit sprayin piss around *my* territory like a bunch a scruffy alley cats, I just dangled and squirmed and peed my pants while them Lukises laughed and clapped." He looked morosely at Joshua and shook his head. "But you didn't. No sir, you reared back and got mean. That's also a new wrinkle out here."

THE DIVIDING LINE 159

Joshua shook his head. "Don't be misled, Edgar. They've got me damn scared."

"I ain't misled. I know it. But you ain't doin no rope dancin and you ain't peed your pants. You just plum reared up and started kickin ass and takin names. I never seen nothin like it in my life, leastways not outside a John Wayne movies."

A smile spread on Joshua's face. "Edgar, I'll be damned! Let's get married and live happily ever after. Nobody's ever whispered sweet nothings like *that* in my ear."

Edgar grunted a short laugh and then looked solemnly at Joshua. "I don't want to marry you. I just want some a your guts."

Joshua swallowed, embarrassed. Edgar was serious. Joshua suddenly felt an onerous and painful weight descend on him. This morning he'd been the Lone Ranger, crusading alone. Now all of a sudden he had unexpectedly and very unwantedly acquired the burden of Edgar's conscience. Suddenly he felt querulous, less easy, less sure.

Edgar got up and walked to Joshua, his hand outstretched. They shook hands. Edgar left, and Joshua remained sitting motionlessly in the chair. Beads of nervous perspiration rolled down his forehead.

He heard the voices of children coming toward the house, and a moment later they all came inside. The half-mile walk in the heat had dried them off, but they had mud splattered all over the bottoms of their legs. Jimmy Hendly was with them, and he looked sorrowfully at Joshua.

"Sorry you have to move, Mr. Rabb."

"We're not moving, Jimmy. We're staying right here."

"Oh wow!" Adam said. "Honest, Dad?"

"Honest." He looked at Hanna and Magdalena and smiled. "Honest Injun."

"Can me and Adam go ridin'?" asked a newly enthused Jimmy.

"Sure. But first you better hose off that mud. Come on."

They went outside and Joshua turned on the hose, and they all stood on the porch and washed the mud off their legs.

"Use the big towel hanging in the bathroom," Magdalena said.

The three children went inside. Magdalena waited until the door slammed. "What happened?"

"Well, Edgar decided I wasn't fired. I guess he's developing a conscience over all the garbage the Lukises have been trying to get away with. And as for your brother, I haven't even had a chance to talk to him yet. I got him over to federal court—he'll have a lot better chance there—but then they took him off to the detention center on Mount Lemmon. So I guess tomorrow I'll have to drive up there and talk to him."

She nodded. "What do you think will happen?"

"I don't know, I really don't. But what's going to happen first is that he's going to have a preliminary hearing. It's not a trial. It's the procedure that the judge uses to decide whether there's enough evidence to make Ignacio stand trial. It's like a mini trial except there's no jury, just the judge. And the prosecutor will present witnesses to show that Ignacio probably committed the murder. And I'll present witnesses to try to show that he didn't. And then the judge will decide whether to drop the charges against Ignacio or to bind him over to stand trial in front of a jury. I think he'll get a fair deal with Judge Buchanan, but if Buchanan binds him over to stand trial, it's going to be up to a jury. And from what I see and hear, that won't be so easy."

She breathed deeply. "Tomorrow morning is the funeral for Sister Martha."

"Where?"

"At the mission. There'll be a mass at seven o'clock in the morning, then the burial. I'd like to go."

"Of course. I'll go with you."

She smiled at him. "You ready for lunch?"

"Sure."

She went into the house, and he followed.

CHAPTER NINE

E ach of the two towers of the mission had four bells. But only one bell was being rung, a single gong about every ten seconds, and the result was a pervasive aura of mournful desolation. Hundreds of Indians over-flowed the church, standing silently, the men with their hats in their hands, the women nervously fingering rosaries, as Father Gerhard Hausner began the mass.

Joshua stood in the rear of the church with Magdalena. When communion came, she joined the long line up to Father Hausner in front of the casket in the transept. The priest then sprinkled the dead nun in the open pine box with holy water, and an Indian acolyte lighted a censer and the priest swung the smoking vessel back and forth over the body.

Six Indians placed the top loosely on the casket and carried it outside to Macario Antone's pickup truck. The monk, Brother Boniface, removed Father Hausner's white chasuble and alb as the church emptied. Over Hausner's brown cassock the monk placed a white stole. The priest went outside and led the congregation in a slow walk be-hind the pickup truck to the cemetery a quarter of a mile away. On either side of the truck, two men held aloft six-foot-high whitewashed wooden crosses.

The cemetery was full of the same kind of crosses, mostly much shorter and faded to gray and cracked. They were the rickety headstones in the front of the mounded graves. Some were blank. Some had hand-painted names. In the entire cemetery of hundreds of mounds, only a half dozen had engraved granite or marble headstones.

Father Hausner blessed the grave with holy water, and then the top was taken off the casket and he sprinkled more water on the nun. Four Indians held a colorfully woven wool blanket over the casket as a canopy, and everyone passed by for one last look at Sister Martha. It must have been obvious when Joshua passed by that he was shocked.

"It's the old Papago way," Magdalena whispered. They stood back from the open grave. "They painted her face with red clay called *heht* and blackened her eyelids with *mots*, like mascara. They'll put her blanket and her pillow in the grave with her so she'll be comfortable as she sleeps."

The priest walked away, back toward the mission. The pallbearers laid the lid on the coffin and lowered it into a shallow grave. Many men passed by and shoveled earth on the coffin. When the grave was mounded over with dirt, the people walked silently away.

Joshua stood there rigidly, his eyes tightly shut, and he saw the long mounds at the concentration camp near Medzibiez. What good was all the praying? he thought. Did it bring anyone back to life? Did it augur a gentle eternity for the soul?

An old man comes to my office in the administration building. He is tiny and shriveled and thin like a dehydrated apricot on toothpicks. He has no hair, not even eyelashes or eyebrows, and his skin is etched with a million fine wrinkles like the parchment of a Torah scroll, and just as white. He has lost all of his hair from fear, he tells me in a quavering voice, but God has saved him from the ovens.

I look at him oddly and can't help asking him why God hadn't seen fit to save him from the concentration camp altogether, and why He had overlooked the hundreds of tortured and starved human beings who were being buried by my men under mounds of dirt in long mass graves at the edge of the forest. And the old man looks earnestly at me with watery brown eyes and says that there is no knowing what horrible evil might have befallen the Jews if God had not intervened to protect them. I can only stare at him with a mixture of incredulity and grudging admiration that so powerful a faith could still exist in a man like this in a place like this where evidence of God's love could not easily be imagined let alone discovered.

We must have a memorial service for the dead, the old man says, we must have a yiskor *service to usher their souls into the eternal peace of heaven. I feel like crying and laughing at the same time. I feel as though the messenger of Mephistopheles is standing in front of me, mocking me, throwing a finger at God and smirking over the ultimate victory of Satan.*

But the old man is clearly not joking or mocking. He is serious. He tells me that he is a Chassidic rabbi from a tiny village near Berdichev, descended from a three-hundred-year-old dynasty of rabbis, and he will hold a yiskor *service. They must extol the greatness of God, they must honor the souls of the dead.*

I cannot say no. How often I had gone with my father to the little shul *on Brighton Beach Avenue, even when there was nothing to be thankful for, even when there was too little bread and too much sickness and not enough money for rent. And my father would wrap himself in his prayer shawl and rock back and forth in deep passion while he recited the ancient words of prayer.*

So I tell the rabbi that he can hold his service, and the next day the tiny trembling rabbi stands with a hundred hollow-eyed survivors at the edge of the forest before the long mass graves of the hundreds who had been buried in the last few days, and they chant the Hebrew words of the memorial service which I had so often heard my father recite: "And now, O great and benevolent God, what shall we say, how can we speak to Thee? Our needs are so great, our knowledge so small. Shame overwhelms us each time the remembrance of all Thy love for us rises up in our minds . . ."

But I feel no shame. No God of love and compassion and benevolence could have let this happen to His people. Why are they all standing in front of the graves of so many murdered human beings, singing words of gratitude and praise? Gratitude for what? Praise for whom?

And then the rabbi's tinny weak words change from Hebrew to Yiddish, and he raises his emaciated arms to the Heavens and begins to scream at God, "Ribbono shel oylum, How could you do this, O Lord of all that is and was and will be? How could you spill the blood of so many of your faithful servants upon the earth like water, like urine, to be ground like excrement into the dust? Tell us, O Lord our God, tell us how we have sinned and why you have punished us." And then the little rabbi begins to weep and beat his chest with all his strength.

And I walk away. I go to my office and take out a bottle of Steinhäger left behind by the SS commandant, and I drink from the bottle in long gulps to anesthetize my mind. I look through the window with tear-filled eyes at the little rabbi, who is now lying prostrate on the dirt mound of one of the mass graves and is beating it with his fists.

The road up Mount Lemmon began at the foot of the Catalina Mountains and wound precipitously upward seven thousand feet to the tiny town of Summerhaven, elevation eighty-six hundred feet. The population varied from four hundred in the summer when it was eighty degrees up here and one hundred and five in Tucson, to fifty in the winter when it was fifteen degrees up here and sixty-five in Tucson. The town consisted of a lodge with a restaurant, a grocery store, the Six Shooter Saloon, and about a dozen log cabins. There were another fifty cabins scattered through the pine forest.

Joshua asked at the lodge where the detention center was, and he was told to go back about five miles to the ranger station and take a right on the lumber mill road.

The mill road was really a rutted dirt path, probably impassable in a rainstorm, and Joshua drove the old De Soto as carefully as he could over the bumps. He came to a sawmill where business was booming, men in blue jumpsuits running all the machinery, driving trucks, stacking timber. Tan uniformed guards with shotguns were sitting in ten-foot-high guard stands ringing the mill.

He drove past it another half mile to three army barracks behind a chain link fence with a four-strand topping of barbed wire. In front of the fence gate was a guard shack, actually a small barrack as well. Joshua drove up beside it. A man dressed in a tan uniform and logger's boots came out of the barrack holding a pump shotgun in both hands. He came around to the driver's door.

"What are you up to, buddy?"

"I'm a lawyer for one of your inmates. I was told visiting hours are two to four."

"Yeah, I reckon they are." He glanced at his watch. "Just that nobody ever comes up here for a visit. Shit, most of what we got up here's Mexican wetbacks and Papagos serving time for drunk and disorderly. Don't get many visitors. All right, park your car over there by that clearing and come on in the shack."

Joshua backed up and drove to the clearing on the west side of the fence. He walked back to the guardhouse.

"What's your boy's name?"

"Ignacio Antone."

"Antone, Antone," he mouthed as he looked down the list. "Oh yeah. I remember now. I reckon that's the boy had the fight last night, damn near got beaten to death. Some of the inmates heard he was in here for killing a nun. They didn't take too kindly to it. Beat him pretty bad before we could stop it. We had to take him over to the ranger station. They got a clinic we use in emergencies. Actually, it's for the locals that live in the cabins up in Summerhaven and the tourists and the skiers, but we have to use it every now and then."

"So he's there now?"

"He's either there or he escaped!" He laughed. Seeing no humor in Joshua's face, the guard's demeanor quickly sobered. "Yeah, he's there. We got a guard over there with him."

Joshua went back to his car and drove to the ranger station. *The poor bastard hasn't got a chance in court or in jail either,* Joshua thought. *Hell of a place.* A separate entrance to the rear of the long log building said, CLINIC. He parked and tried the door. It was locked. He banged on it. A small square opened in the middle, and a pale blue eye looked out at him.

"I'm Joshua Rabb, an attorney from Tucson. I came up here to talk to my client, Ignacio Antone, and I was told he's being held here."

The small square closed, he heard a bolt slide, and the door opened. A woman came outside and closed the door behind her. Her long blond hair was loose about her shoulders. She was wearing Levi's and logger's boots and a baggy plaid wool long-sleeved shirt.

He stared at her in pleased surprise. "You're the nurse from the Indian Health Services Clinic."

She nodded, a small smile playing about her lips. "The only one Ignacio Antone can talk to right now is himself. I just gave him another hip full of joy juice. I think he has a broken jaw, so I don't think he's going to be particularly talkative when he wakes up."

"How long till he wakes up?"

"Maybe tonight, maybe tomorrow. Depends on whether he has serious internal injuries."

"Well, he's got a hearing Monday at ten. I've got to talk to him before then."

"I hate to ruin your plans, Mr. Lawyer, but your client will be lucky to have his senses back by Monday. But it sure won't be before then."

"Jesus Christ," he muttered.

"Don't look so crestfallen. You're up here at the top of the world in a gorgeous pine forest, it's seventy-five degrees, and I bet it's hot as hell back in Tucson. Enjoy! Go to the lodge, drink a beer."

"You live up here?"

"Sure do. I got a cabin right back here on federal land." She pointed through the woods. "Free rent, birds, chipmunks, and all I have to do is give a few tetanus shots and splint sprained ankles and give cough medicine to kids with bronchitis."

He smiled. "Nice place to hide."

"I'm not hiding from anything or anybody. I just love to sit and listen to birds and Beethoven and I have a pet fawn. Straight out of a Walt Disney movie." Her eyes sparkled, and she smiled at him, a warm, open smile.

"That accent of yours isn't Tucson," he said. "How'd you ever find this place?"

"Federal Department of the Interior advertised for it. I was passing through Tucson on my way to Los Angeles, stopped at a hotel for a couple of days, and I saw the listing in the newspaper. Simple as that." She snapped her fingers. "I do a clinic for the Papagos every two weeks, and the rest of the time I live up here in paradise."

"You from back east, New York?"

"Matawan, New Jersey, near Rutgers. My father taught at Rutgers."

"Really. My dad taught German in Brooklyn. What did yours teach?"

"Classics," she said. "Listen, Mr.—, I'm sorry I didn't catch your name."

"Rabb."

"Listen, Mr. Rabb, I've got to get back inside with Mr. Antone. He could hurt himself in his sleep." She walked quickly into the clinic and he heard the bolt slide.

He drove down the mountain and stopped at a gas station. While the attendant was filling up the De Soto, Joshua went to the Coke machine and put a nickel in. The newspaper in the rack next to the Coke machine caught his eye: BIA LAWYER DEFENDS NUN'S KILLER. He picked up the newspaper and started reading:

by J. T. Sellner

Joshua Rabb hadn't been in Tucson for more than a week as the BIA's new lawyer before BIA Superintendent Edgar Hendly was forced to fire him for insubordination. Rabb had refused to approve the renewal of a contract for excavation on Papago property for Mission Sand and Gravel. Mission has been part of the Lukis family holdings since Senator Lukis's father founded it in 1894, and the Lukis family has held the contract since that time. "All of a sudden he just balked," said Mr. Hendly of Rabb's refusal.

Not more than an hour later, Rabb had manipulated his temporary appointment as a lawyer authorized to practice in federal court, despite the fact that he is not a member of the state bar of Arizona. All these machinations had the apparent intent of permitting him to defend Ignacio Antone, the derelict San Xavier Papago Indian arrested early Friday morning near the body of Sister Martha Robinette. The nun had been raped and murdered.

Joshua's jaw tightened as he read. He read three more paragraphs of saccharine biography about Sister Martha's work with orphans and the hospital and the Indians, whom she treated as if they were her own children. Then he read:

In the Manuel Castellano case last October, we saw some of the same things that are happening with Antone. Castellano is a Papago Indian who was a notorious drunken troublemaker. He had served a three-year term in Arizona State Prison for armed robbery and had just been released on parole. He was arrested for the murder of three tourists who had been visiting San Xavier Mission, two seventy-one-year-old women and a man of seventy-four. Castellano robbed them of $3.92 so he could buy whiskey. After he was arraigned before County Judge Fran Rooks, Federal Judge Robert Buchanan issued a writ of habeas corpus which took Castellano out of state jurisdiction and brought him into the federal court. And shortly thereafter Judge Buchanan committed Castellano to the State Mental Hospital in Phoenix, ruling that he was permanently brain-damaged from chronic alcoholism and could not properly be tried for murder! Can the same distortion of justice happen again?

Joshua's chest felt constricted. He gritted his teeth. J. T. Sellner was obviously out to crucify the judge, and Ignacio Antone would inevitably get caught in the middle. He shook his head grimly and read on:

And there's more. Mr. Rabb told this reporter that he could prove the innocence of Ignacio Antone. If that is true, then we all would welcome it as proof that ours is the finest legal system in the world. But if all that Mr. Rabb has in mind is a long and highly publicized trial, in which the sordid details of a nun's murder by a drunk Papago derelict are trashed around in open court day by day, then the public will indeed be ill-served and justice can only be tarnished.

Mr. Rabb came to Tucson with his two children after his wife died in an accident in Brooklyn. He apparently was injured in the same accident and lost his left arm. He was hired to work for the BIA. He was fired for misconduct after just one week, and immediately was hired to represent Ignacio Antone. It would be a tragedy indeed for our system of justice if taking on such a high-profile case as Sister Martha's murder should be employed as a device to stimulate Mr. Rabb's legal career. As Assistant U.S. Attorney Tim Essert remarked, "It looks like that's exactly what he's after, and the Bar doesn't need people like him."

"Hey, pal, you wanna read the paper, it costs you a nickel." The gasoline attendant held out his hand.

"How much is the gas?" Joshua mumbled. His voice sounded a little distant, like someone else's.

"Two-seventy."

"Here's three dollars," Joshua said.

"Hey, thanks, pal."

Joshua's jaw ached from gritting his teeth. He breathed deeply to calm himself. He felt a little woozy, as though he had been kicked in the face by this vicious newspaper reporter. Newspapers make money by selling controversy, but this was far more than that. It was as though she were intentionally trying to get him killed. And the slant toward the federal judge was something else which Joshua hadn't expected. When a cause célèbre became entwined in a controversy between a newspaper and a judge, it never took long for the judge to begin making damn sure that his actions played well with the public. Lifetime appointee or not, a judge needed either anonymity or the broad support of the public so that he could function properly without fear. This kind of public finger-pointing would make Judge Buchanan cautious and conservative. Now he'd bend over backward to go hard on Ignacio Antone and prove what a tough law-and-order man he really was.

Joshua felt nauseous. He got into the car and sat still, staring morosely ahead.

~~~~~~

They had eaten late and left the dishes on the table so that they could listen to the radio. "Amos 'n Andy" and "Blondie" and "Skippy Hollywood Theatre" were on, and they laughed and laughed as they raptly listened. Joshua got tired of the nonstop comedy and went into his bedroom. He bunched up the pillow on his bed and lay back and picked up *A Bell for Adano*, John Hersey's Pulitzer Prize–winner about a little town in Italy under American occupation right after the war. But he had trouble finding anything amusing about the war or anything endearing about people who sided with the Nazis.

He was reading page 37 for the second time when he heard several automobiles drive up outside. It was almost nine-thirty, and he got out of bed wearily. Everything happens in the middle of the damn night around here, he grumbled.

Magdalena had the curtain pulled back slightly from the window.

"Who is it?" Hanna asked.

"Shhh!" Magdalena whispered, and gestured with her hand for Hanna and Adam to stay on the floor by the radio.

"What's going on?" Joshua asked, coming out of his bedroom.

"I don't know," Magdalena whispered.

Joshua saw the fearful look in Magdalena's face and drew back the curtain slightly from the front window. There were two cars and a pickup parked in the front yard. In front of them stood ten or twelve people, visible only as dark figures by the light of burning torches held by two of the people.

"Oh my God," Joshua breathed. "They weren't kidding. There are some real unhappy folks out there."

Hanna and Adam crawled to the window and peeked out.

"What are we going to do, Mr. Rabb?" Magdalena asked in a thin voice.

Joshua squinted into the darkness, waiting for the torches to be thrown. Nothing happened. It looked like some of the people in the front were passing a bottle around.

"Get the gun," Joshua said.

Magdalena ran into her and Hanna's room and came out with it. Hanna and Adam stared at it in surprise and fear. She held the gun down at her side.

"If anything happens out there," Joshua said quietly to Magdalena, "don't let anything happen to any of you."

Magdalena nodded.

"Don't go out, Daddy," Adam whimpered.

"I have to, Adam. Please don't worry. We'll all be okay."

He opened the front door and screen and stepped onto the porch, pulling the door closed behind him. He went to the edge of the porch and stood there, looking around at the group ten feet in front of him. He could make out most of their faces now, but he didn't recognize any of them. Just hardworking farmers and ranchers in overalls and Levi's and work boots. One of them tossed a bottle to the side, and it hit the ground and shattered.

"Evening, folks," Joshua said, trying to appear nonchalant, fighting to keep his breathing steady so his voice wouldn't quiver. "Little late for a housewarming party. How's about coming back tomorrow noon, we'll make lemonade and hot dogs."

Someone laughed. Another swore in a low voice, and the laughter stopped abruptly.

"Reckon you're Mr. Rabb, the BIA lawyer. Za right?"

"Yes sir, I am."

"Done been readin about ya, Mr. Rabb, me 'n some a my friends. We don't much cotton to nun killers round these parts."

"Well sir, I don't much cotton to em either, not around any parts," Joshua drawled, trying to sound like one of the boys with a Western accent, fearful that he was actually sounding like he was making fun of them.

"That ain't what we been readin'," said one of the other men.

"Listen, folks, I'm tellin ya that I just don't think that Indian hurt the nun. I think someone else did and tried to pin it on the Indian."

There was an undercurrent of grumbling. "Listen up here, asshole," said one of the two men with the torches. He was a middle-aged man, tall, thin, with a gaunt furrowed face and unruly grizzled hair. He wore dirty overalls over a dirtier T-shirt. "We ain't gonna let no shit happen this time as happened last October. Fuckin drunk Indin walked away from three murders like as he was some kinda fuckin prince. That God damn communist bastard judge done walked him free right outta the courthouse. We ain't a-lettin that happen no more. We got our families to worry over, our wimmin 'n kids. We just cain't have that shit."

He walked toward Joshua and stopped three feet away. The rest of the group edged forward. "We also hear as yer livin with a Indin slut in there," he tipped his torch toward the house. "Folks say she's a pretty li'l girl. But we don't cotton too highly to mixin a the races out here, Mr. Rabb. We don't think God intended that."

Joshua put his hand in his pocket, trying to appear casual despite his fear. Six of the men were carrying rifles or shotguns, and this man had a gun in a holster belted around his waist.

"Ya get yer brood out here, Mr. Rabb. I'll give ya a minute. We don't wanna burn them along with yer house. We ain't up to doin nothin criminal, just convincin ya to mosey on down the highway a few hunnerd miles."

The door opened and the screen door creaked behind Joshua, startling him. He jerked around. Hanna came onto the porch and walked right up to one of the group. Joshua was almost blinded by the torch a few feet from him, and he squinted to see.

"Hanna! Go back inside."

She ignored him. She stood in front of a tall, gangling boy, shaggy-haired. Suddenly Joshua recognized him. It was the boy Hanna had been talking to at the Fourth of July picnic.

"Hi," she said pleasantly, "sorry I couldn't stay and watch you play baseball. I really wanted to, but Dad wanted me to do some chores. Dad was going to invite you for dinner the next time we saw you."

"You live here?" The boy's voice was tentative, surprised.

"Yes, sure do. That's my dad."

The boy looked from her to Joshua and back again. "I'm sorry about this, I didn't want to come," he said softly. "Pa," he said louder, "come on now, we done made our point. Mr. Rabb, he knows how we feel now. Come on, let's go back to the house."

He walked up to the man holding the torch who had been talking to Joshua. He reached for the torch, and his father stumbled backward and almost fell.

"Come on, Pa, maybe you hit a little too much of that jug tonight, huh? Lemme have that there light before someone gets hurt."

The man stared searchingly at Hanna and then guiltily at his son. His son took him by the arm and held him firmly. Then he turned his father around and they walked toward the pickup truck. The father threw the torch on the ground. The others slowly got into the vehicles and drove away.

Joshua stood still. His knees felt weak. Hanna came to him and hooked her arm in his and said gently, "Come on, Dad, let's go listen to 'The Lone Ranger.' " Her voice was shaking.

They went inside and sat down on the couch. Adam sat cross-legged on the floor, crying. Magdalena sat down next to him.

"It's okay now," Joshua soothed. "I don't think it will happen again. They got it out of their system."

"What's going on, Dad?" Hanna asked.

"There was kind of a rough story in the newspaper about me defending Magdalena's brother for the murder of the nun. Some people are very upset."

"But he's innocent, Dad." Hanna's voice broke and she began to cry. Everything had suddenly caught up to her.

Joshua hugged her. "We know that, honey. I've just got to prove it to them out there." He looked at her. "You were very brave, honey. I'm proud of you."

She sobbed harder and choked out, "I wasn't brave, I was scared."

"That's what real bravery is, honey. Doing something decent even when you're scared."

They sat for a few minutes and the crying stopped. "I want you two to let Magdalena know where you are from now on if you leave the house, okay? And I don't want you off alone, okay?" He looked at Adam and Adam nodded. "Just for a few days, until this all goes away."

Hanna and Adam nodded. Magdalena sat on the floor next to Adam, and she hugged him.

"What do you say we go to bed and get a good rest?" Joshua said.

They all nodded and went into their bedrooms.

~~~~~~~

Joshua couldn't sleep. He kept seeing in front of him the men and the torches. He saw their hatred and his fear, and he knew what would happen next time, tomorrow night, the night after, the flames on the porch, the chickens screeching, the roof on fire. He heard a rustling sound outside his window, like someone walking around, and he leapt out of bed and rushed to the window and stood beside it pressed back against the wall, afraid to move the curtain and look out lest there really be someone there, looking at him, pointing a gun at him. And then he knew that he had heard nothing but his own heart, his own breathing, his own fear, and he flopped down on the bed and closed his eyes and tried to sleep.

He heard the noise again and jumped out of bed. He took the revolver off the nightstand and went into the living room. Magdalena was just closing the front door, coming inside.

"My cousin Henry saw the torches. He came over to look around, make sure everything is okay," she whispered.

"Jesus! He scared the hell out of me," Joshua breathed.

"It's all right, Mr. Rabb," she whispered. "He'll be out there. Nothing more will happen." She came to him and laid her head against his chest and hugged him.

He could feel her body through the thinness of her night T-shirt, and the scent of her was tangy, spearminty. He kissed the top of her head. He felt himself get hard, and he pulled back from her.

"We can't do this," he whispered.

"I'm a woman, I'm not a girl. And I'm not a virgin."

He shook his head. "I can't take advantage of you."

"You're not taking advantage," she whispered.

He wanted to. Oh, how he wanted to. But somewhere a voice said that you didn't do this with your daughter's friend, that you didn't take the responsibility of being a teacher to a pretty twenty-year-old girl and then take her to your bed. Even if you weren't her first, even if she wanted to go. And he chided himself for all his morality or inhibitions or fears or whatever they were. But he felt guilty already, and he could not take the next step.

"You are lovely," he whispered hoarsely, "and I know you're a woman. But we can't do this."

She stepped close to him and kissed him lightly on the lips. She lingered just an instant, reluctant to leave, and then went into Hanna's bedroom and closed the door.

Joshua went into his bedroom and sat down on the edge of the bed. He looked at the bulge in his gym shorts and felt an ache for her. I could put you out of your misery, he thought, and pointed the .38 at his erection and closed one eye and sighted down the barrel. He put the gun on the nightstand and lay back in bed and stared vacantly into the darkness and wondered why he didn't have the courage to have Magdalena here with him, touching him. There should be a limit to all this nobility bullshit.

He got out of bed Sunday morning unrefreshed. He took a shower and shaved, just to wake himself up, and then he heard the kids stirring. Adam came out of the bedroom and turned on the radio. It was "The Great Gildersleeve," his favorite program. He sat down in front of the radio and stared at it.

Joshua went outside and filled the chickens' water pails with the hose. He threw a couple of handfuls of corn through the wire, and they scrambled for them, fluttering their wings and squabbling raucously. He stood idly and watched them for a few minutes. Jimmy came down Indian Agency Road on Charger and plodded up to Joshua.

"Mornin', Mr. Rabb."

"Hi, Jimmy."

"Can Adam come out and play?"

"Sure, just as soon as he's had his breakfast. Just stay away from Mrs. Antone's cows."

"Yes, sir."

"Come on in, you want some breakfast?"

"Well, I just had. I reckon I'll go down to the reservoir and see if any a the guys are there. Be back in a few minutes."

"Okay, Jimmy."

"Breakfast," Magdalena called from the door.

Joshua went into the kitchen and sat down. Magdalena's ebony eyes sparkled, and she gave him a sweet smile. "Cereal or eggs?"

"Eggs."

"Omelet?"

"Sure."

Hanna and Adam joined him at the table. Hanna looked miserable.

"What's wrong, honey?" Joshua asked.

"Nothing."

"That's a mighty painful-looking nothing. Didn't you sleep well?"

"Yeah, all right. But I guess we won't be having him over for dinner, huh?"

Joshua couldn't help laughing. "Honey, they almost had *us* for dinner."

She frowned and then nodded. "Yeah."

Magdalena dished out portions of cheese omelet from the frying pan and then sat down at the table. They all ate, subdued and quiet.

"What are you two going to do today?" Joshua asked.

"I'm going over to Magdalena's house," Hanna said. "We're finishing up a basket. It's really neat."

"Good, just be sure and be back by one o'clock."

"I will, Dad."

"Adam, you go over and stay with Jimmy today. Be back for lunch by one, okay?"

Adam nodded.

Joshua went outside and got into the De Soto. He didn't know where he was going, but he started the engine and drove slowly down Indian Agency Road. He just felt like driving, anywhere, spreading his wings and flying, free and careless as an eagle. He drove downtown. It was deserted and quiet, and he turned east on Speedway Boulevard, finding himself twenty minutes later on the Catalina Highway. He drove more quickly. There were very few other cars on the road.

What am I doing here? he thought. I'm going to see Ignacio Antone. No, you're not. You're just saying that. Okay, I'm just saying that. I'm really going up to see the blonde with the powder-blue eyes and the cute little nose. What the hell for? She sure didn't seem very interested. Because I'm lonely.

He banged hard on the clinic door at the ranger station, but there was no answer. He got back into his car and followed the well-worn tire-rutted trail about a hundred yards through the fragrant pine forest. He came to a large log cabin with a cedar-shingle peaked roof surrounded by a flagstone walkway and well-tended groups of wildflowers. There was a broad garden in front that looked like neat rows of budding vegetables. The enchanted cottage from a Walt Disney movie. A shiny black Chevrolet roadster with an open rumble seat was parked beside the cabin. He walked up on the cedar-plank porch and knocked on the doorjamb. He saw the curtain rustle on the picture window next to the door.

She opened the door about three inches, as far as the chain would allow, and peeked out at him. "You lost?"

"I wanted to talk to you about Ignacio Antone."

"You think I snuck him into my bedroom?"

Joshua was embarrassed. Being treated like a horny schoolboy was getting on his nerves. Then again, how else would you describe it?

"No, of course not. I just wanted to know what his condition is."

She squinted at him and wrinkled her nose. "I think you came to visit *me*."

He shrugged embarrassedly and felt the blood hot in his cheeks.

"You married?" she asked.

"No."

"You wouldn't believe how many married men come up here to get away from their wives and come sniffing around here like bloodhounds."

"I'm not married."

"You look married."

"I was married. I got kids."

"What kind?"

He pursed his lips and thought for a moment. "Well, they're both human," he said seriously.

She stared at him and then laughed. The door closed, the chain clinked, and then she opened the door wide. "Come in, Mr. Lawyer. Sorry, I forgot your name."

"Joshua, Joshua Rabb."

"I'm Penny Chesser."

She was in bare feet in a pair of tan shorts like Hanna wore and a blouse tied just under her ample breasts. Her hair was in a ponytail that she had wound around the top of her head and pinned loosely. She was very pretty.

"Sit." She pointed to the chintz couch. "You want a cup of coffee?"

"If it wouldn't be too much trouble." He was very much out of training for courting behavior, and he felt awkward and stiff.

"Just made a pot." She went into the kitchen and came back with two steaming china cups on saucers with real silver spoons.

"Pretty fancy for a cabin in the woods," he said.

"A gift from my grandmother," she said. "So how old are your children?"

"A daughter fourteen and a son eleven."

"What brings you to Tucson?" She sat down on the edge of the couch and sipped her coffee.

"Got sick of Manhattan. Just had to get out. And I got a

part-time job with the Bureau of Indian Affairs down by the Papago reservation."

"That's why you want to talk to Antone?"

"No, his grandfather hired me to defend him. He's charged with murdering a nun last Thursday night."

"Oh yes," she said. "I did hear something about that on the radio. But I didn't catch his name. I'm not so good with names, you may have noticed. But they said he raped her too."

Joshua nodded.

"Well, I don't think it's Antone."

He looked at her oddly. "What do you mean?"

"I mean I listened to his heart, checked him over when they brought him in. He's got a very severe rheumatic heart, a serious murmur. Probably from scarlet fever or the mumps. I'd be very surprised if he isn't impotent."

Joshua sat bolt upright on the couch. "That's fantastic! Are you a real nurse?"

"Yes. Real."

Joshua stood up excitedly. "I'm going to get him off!"

"Good," she said, smiling at his enthusiasm. "I'm glad you're happy."

"I'm a lot more than just happy!"

She laughed.

"Will you testify?"

"Oh no!" she said. "I'm not qualified for that. But any doctor you get to examine him will tell you the same thing."

"You know any doctors?"

"Sure. A couple of them come up here to ski. Paul Krampis, he's an internist. Murray Robertson, he's probably your best bet. He's a very distinguished-looking surgeon, gray hair. He'd make a great witness."

"God, you're fantastic!"

"I didn't do anything," she said.

"You ever come down from the mountain other than for the clinic at the reservation?"

She shrugged. "Once in a while. I go shopping for clothes, or for tools I can't buy up here."

"You going shopping soon?"

She smiled at him. "I was thinking next Saturday. I'll probably go to Goldberg's at noon."

"Can I buy you lunch?"

She nodded and smiled. "I'd love it."

"I've got to go," said Joshua. "I've got to get to Dr. Robertson this afternoon. I'm really glad I came."

"I'm glad, too," she said quietly.

He left and walked as quickly as he could down the path. She stood sipping her coffee on the porch and watching him until he disappeared into the trees. She went back into the house, into her bedroom, and took the little bottle of Chanel No. 5 perfume off her dresser. She pulled out the stopper, put her forefinger over the end, shook the bottle, and touched the perfume to both sides of her neck. She scrutinized her reflection in the mirror, tilting her head this way and that, and then she began to smile.

Why am I smiling? she thought. She scolded her reflection in the mirror. You lied to the poor fellow. Actually you haven't been "down from the mountain"—as he put it—for almost six months. Don't need any clothes up here. And you've got a shed full of tools. So who needs to leave this place? But I had to lie a little. Am I supposed to start gushing and wringing my hands and say, oh please, please, please, take me out? I'm lonely. I haven't gone out with a man in six months. The last one was married and promised to get a divorce, and—well, you've heard it all before. She walked out on the porch and sat down on the swing chair.

She heard the engine of a car whine, and a mud-splattered Ford came slowly up the car trail toward the cabin. There was some sign on the driver's door, but the car parked seventy-five feet away, and from this angle she couldn't read it. The driver remained in the car and was obscured by the glare of light off the windshield. The passenger got out and walked slowly toward her.

She stopped swinging in the chair and stiffened. It was very rare that anyone drove up the trail to her cabin. Most people didn't know about this cabin.

"Good morning, miss," the man said. He had washed-out green eyes and a veiny alcoholic's nose. He stood a few feet in front of the porch and took his straw hat off and held it over his chest. With the other hand he held up a badge wallet. "I'm Special Agent Delahanty with the Federal Bureau of Investigation."

"Yes?" What in the world could he want from me?

"I hear as you had a patient up here a few days ago, a Indian boy from the camp."

"That's right."

"Could you tell me what was wrong with him?"

She shrugged. "He got into a fight, had a broken jaw, some internal injuries."

"You mind if I come up on the porch, ma'am? I hate to have to be yellin like this."

He didn't wait for a response. He walked up the steps and sat down on a wooden rocker across from her. "Mighty cool and comfortable up here," he said smiling. "Damn sight nicer than Tucson."

She said nothing. He smiled at her, and she felt uncomfortable. He studied her too closely and too long. Sweat had dried in brown stained patches on the underarms of his rumpled tan linen suit, and he exuded an unpleasant body odor.

"You been visited by a lawyer from Tucson, name of Rabb?" he asked, but it sounded almost like an accusation. "We seen him down the road a mite, just as we was comin up."

She looked at him steadily. "I'm afraid I'm missing the point of this visit, Mr. Delahanty."

He wrinkled up his cheeks and forehead in what he must have thought passed for an engaging smile. "Don't you worry none about the reason I'm here, ma'am. It certainly has nothin to do with you. Just doin my job, you know. A nun got murdered and sodomized down the hill by that Indian boy Antone, and I've got a job to do investigatin the matter."

"Well, I've told you everything I know."

"Well now, ma'am"—he shook his head and wagged his forefinger at her—"that ain't exactly so. I asked you if you been visited by this Rabb fella."

"I have, Mr. Delahanty. But I can't imagine that Mr. Rabb visiting me could be viewed by the FBI as official business."

"You leave that decision to me."

His tone was now unmistakably accusatory. Penny stood up and walked to the door. "I'm getting a little chilly. I'm going inside."

"Why yes, ma'am," he said, standing. "I only got a few more questions for you about Antone. I'll just come in for a minute."

"No, Mr. Delahanty. I don't want you in my house."

His forced smile turned to a vengeful glare. "I didn't come up here to socialize, lady. This is official business."

She was deeply fearful, and she felt that he was about to turn from words to physical abuse. His eyes were frightening, flat and cold. She put on her best scowl and strengthened her voice. "Listen, mister. Whatever business the FBI has with me doesn't have to be done on Sunday in my cabin. This is my day off. I'm just a nurse who treated an Indian for a broken jaw. And that's all I talked to Mr. Rabb about. Now excuse me. If you want to talk to me again, come see me at the Indian Health Services Clinic in Tucson."

She opened the door and went inside. He stepped up to the door and she quickly slid the inner bolt closed. He tried the knob, then banged on the door. She stood back against it, her heart beating fast and hard. This was no official visit. This guy was very scary, dangerous. She heard his steps off the porch and peeked out the window next to the door.

He walked quickly toward the car. The driver got out of the car and waited for him. He was an elderly man, tall and stocky, dressed like a cowboy, with a rich shock of pure white hair. She watched them stand and talk animatedly for a moment. Then they both got into the car and it backed slowly down the trail and disappeared into the trees. She kept watching for five minutes, making sure that the car didn't return and that neither of them came back by foot. She had lived alone up here for over a year, and she had never felt this frightened. It was his eyes. Sick eyes. FBI man or not, he was very scary.

She went up the stairs to the dormer bedroom and rummaged in the closet for the .22 rifle she had bought a few months ago.

It was after a couple of the skiers got drunk and one of them broke his wrist. They had come to the clinic, and she had splinted the wrist, and both of them had come on to her like God's gifts to women. She got rid of them, but later that evening, when it got dark, the uninjured one had come to the cabin, still drunk, and banged on the door for an hour, refusing to leave. He had finally left without hurting her, but it had scared her, and she had bought the .22 rifle. It was a simple bolt action. She had shot it a few times into a tree trunk just for practice. Then she had felt foolish, like a bloodless old maid worrying about losing her virginity, and she had put the gun in the back of the closet and forgotten about it.

Now she took it out, carried it downstairs, and stood it up next to the door.

Back in Tucson, Joshua stopped at a little grocery store that had a phone booth outside. He looked up Dr. Murray Robertson, didn't find him in the residential listings, and looked him up in the business pages. He telephoned, but there was no answer. Damn, he thought. In Brooklyn the doctors all practiced out of their homes. But not here. Their home phones are unlisted. Have to wait till tomorrow.

The disappointment brought him down from his high. He drove back home thinking about tomorrow. Get to the doctor's office early tomorrow morning, have him examine Ignacio, testify for five minutes in court, and Ignacio will be a free man.

When he got home, no one was there. It was almost one-thirty. He saw Hanna and Magdalena walking across the cotton field toward him and figured that they must have waited to come home until they saw the dust from his car. Where was Adam? He got back into the car and waved at the girls. He drove to the reservoir and there were a few Indian boys playing with frogs. He drove anxiously back to the house. He saw Adam walking home on Indian Agency Road. He parked in front of the house.

"Hi, Adam. Why are you late? I told you to be right on time for the next few days."

"I know, Dad, but I was at Sunday school. I couldn't leave till Jimmy's mom picked us up." He held up a book.

"What's this?"

"It's the *Jesus Coloring Book*. I got it at church. Isn't it neat?" He was very excited and handed the book to his father.

The girls came across the ditch and joined them.

"What's that?" Hanna asked.

"It's the *Jesus Coloring Book* Adam got at Sunday school with Jimmy," Joshua said.

"Sunday school?" she said. She turned to her brother. "Where'd you go?"

"First Southern Baptist Church. It was neat. We watched a movie about how our missionaries are converting these natives in Africa—they run around naked and drink cow blood and milk—and then we got cake and candy, and then they handed out these coloring books and we got to color for a whole hour. See, Dad?" Adam took the book from his father and thumbed the pages. "See here, this is Jesus feeding lambs, and this is him at the Sermon on the Mount. Did you know that the Jews could have saved him, but they chose a thief instead? His name was Barber or Barbus or something."

"Well, Adam, you're a real fountain of information today. And after just *one* day at Sunday school. My, my, I wonder how you'd be after a few more weeks."

The sarcasm was lost on Adam, but Hanna began giggling.

"Yeah, Dad," he gushed, "I can win a whole bag of candy if I color *this* one the best." He flipped a few pages to Jesus on the cross.

"Well, I think that maybe it's time to see if there's a Hebrew school in Tucson. You're so interested in religion, it might as well be your own."

"Aw, Dad! I'm just interested in the bag of candy," Adam groaned. "Do I have to go to Hebrew school again?"

"Yes, I think you do. If there is one. Otherwise you and I will have to sit down on Sunday mornings and do a little learning together."

Adam frowned and walked dejectedly into the house. "I knew I shouldn't have said nothin'," he grumbled.

CHAPTER TEN

J oshua drove to the doctor's office at eight o'clock
Monday morning. The door was locked. He sat in
his car waiting until the office finally opened at a few
minutes before nine. The nurse told Joshua that "Doctor"
always did rounds at the two hospitals in the mornings,
and that was why he didn't come in until after nine. Joshua
sat in the waiting room for another fifteen minutes until
the doctor arrived. The nurse showed him into "Doctor's"
office, and he was just as Penny had described him: at-
tractive, suave, impressive. Joshua explained why he was
there.

"Sure," he said. "I testify in court regularly as an expert,
but I'm not a philanthropist."

"We can pay."

"Let's see, a complete exam will be seven dollars and
the semen analysis will be four dollars and I charge twenty
dollars for going to court." He looked searchingly at
Joshua.

"No problem."

"I don't have the time to do it today," Dr. Robertson
said, looking at his calendar.

"But it's critical that we have the examination before noon and that you testify today at the preliminary hearing."

"Impossible, Mr. Rabb. I've got a full load this morning." He counted names in his appointment book. "Fourteen people from nine-thirty to twelve. Let's see, that's at least ninety-eight dollars. I'm not a rich man."

"All right. Assuming I can get the hearing put off, what day are you available?"

"I don't have office visits on Wednesdays."

"Okay, I'll try to make it happen." Joshua stood up and shook the doctor's hand.

There were a couple of hundred spectators crowded into the courtroom. J. T. Sellner was sitting right behind the railing with a steno notebook in her hand. She looked coldly at Joshua. The prosecutor was already sitting at his table. Joshua walked up to him.

"Let's go back to chambers and talk to the judge," Joshua said. "I need a continuance."

"What for?" Tim Essert asked, looking extremely annoyed.

"I've got to have my client medically examined, and the doctor can't do it till Wednesday."

"No way," Essert said. "I been through that shit one time too many. You can make your motion in open court, and we'll see how the judge takes it."

Marshal Friedkind brought Ignacio Antone into the courtroom in hand and ankle cuffs. The marshal led him to the jury box and told him to sit. Ignacio looked around the courtroom fearfully.

The judge's secretary came in followed by the judge. He sat down at the bench and opened the file before him. "Time set for the preliminary hearing in U.S. versus Antone. Announce your appearances."

"Tim Essert for the Government, your honor," the assistant United States attorney said, standing up at his table.

Joshua stood up. "Joshua Rabb for Mr. Antone. Your honor, I have a motion for continuance."

Judge Buchanan looked sternly at him. "What's the problem, Mr. Rabb?"

"Your honor, I've got to have the defendant examined by a physician. I believe I will be able to show lack of capacity to commit a rape."

Out of the corner of his eye, Joshua could see Ignacio Antone's face turn toward him. J. T. Sellner's pen made audible sounds on the steno pad as she wrote furiously just behind him.

The judge drummed his fingers on the bench for a moment. "How would that impact probable cause for the murder?"

"Well, he's not only charged with murder, Judge. He's also charged with rape."

Judge Buchanan shrugged. "Could have been done by two of them, couldn't it, Mr. Rabb? One rapes, the other murders." His eyes flicked to the newspaper reporter and back again.

Joshua was becoming angry. "But that's not the charge, your honor. He's charged with both crimes."

"Just settle down, son," the judge said evenly. "The complaint that's been filed isn't final, you know that. Only this preliminary hearing can result in formal charges. And I'm the one who says whether there's probable cause that he committed this or that crime. I don't think there's any pressing need to delay the hearing."

"Your honor," Joshua said, his voice rising, "this is a capital crime. Surely a three-day delay in the interest of justice is not too much to ask."

Again the judge's eyes wandered to J. T. Sellner, as though he were seeking approval. "Justice delayed is justice denied, Mr. Rabb. Let's get on with it."

"But, your honor—"

Judge Buchanan leaned forward over the bench and fixed Joshua with a stern glare. "When this court says get on with it, Mr. Rabb, that's what you'll do."

Joshua sat down and gritted his teeth. He breathed deeply and clenched his hand in his lap to keep it from shaking.

"We call Martin Hankins," Tim Essert said.

Marshal Friedkind left the courtroom and came back a moment later. The sheriff's deputy followed him into the courtroom. He walked up to the bench, the judge swore him to tell the truth, and he took the stand.

"Tell us your name and occupation," Tim Essert said.

"I'm Marty Hankins, deputy with the Pima County sheriff's office."

"You arrested this man?" Essert pointed to Ignacio Antone.

"I did."

"Tell us the facts and circumstances."

"Well, I was on midnights last week and got a dispatcher call about one-thirty in the morning about a possible murder victim found in the irrigation ditch on the north edge of San Xavier Reservation. I responded out there and drove down the bank of the ditch starting from Indian Agency Road toward the west. I spotted the body about fifty feet west of the road."

"What did you do then?"

"I exited my vehicle and took my flashlight and went down into the ditch. It was a nun, and she was lying facedown in a couple of inches of water. I pulled her out of the water and checked her pulse. She was dead. I went back to my car and called for backup and the coroner's ambulance. I also told dispatch to call the resident FBI agent, you know, Tom Delahanty."

"Did you contact the Indian police in Sells?"

"Well, there wasn't any use trying that. Their telephone lines out there have been down since the big flood last September, October, whenever it was. So the only way to get them is to ride out there. Takes almost three hours to get there, so there was no use to it."

"All right, continue with the story, Deputy."

"I also asked dispatch to try to locate Buford Richards. He's the head of security for the Sand and Gravel Company out there, and he knows the reservation real good. The sheriff's office don't have jurisdiction out there, not even to investigate, so when we get a call of trouble out there, Buford generally gets brought in."

"How was the defendant found?"

"Well now, Buford said that—"

"Objection your honor, hearsay," Joshua said.

"Yes. Sustained," the judge said. "Don't tell us what Buford told you, Marty, just what you saw and did."

"Well, I didn't see him find the defendant."

"All right, Deputy, you actually arrested Antone, is that correct?"

"Yes, sir."

"Describe him at that time."

"He was drunk and he stunk to high heaven. I put him in my car and had to keep all the windows wide open."

"Were his pants open?"

"Yeah, the buttons on his Levi's were undone."

Essert sat down at his table.

"Mr. Rabb," the judge said.

"Thank you, your honor," Joshua said. "You did in fact do some investigation of the crime scene, didn't you, Deputy Hankins?"

"Yes, I did."

"Why did you do that?"

"Because there was a thunderstorm brewing and I wanted to collect all the evidence I could before it got washed away."

"What did you find?"

"Well, actually it wasn't just me. There were three other deputies out there with me, they came about ten minutes after I got there."

"Tell the court what *you* found."

"Well sir, I found drag marks over on the reservation side of the ditch, and I found a spot where it looked like there were tire tracks and a body had been pushed out of a car door or taken out of a trunk and laid on the ground. And there were fresh boot prints all around."

"What kind of boot prints?"

"Looked like cowboy boots, you know, narrow heels, pointed toes."

"What was the defendant wearing on his feet?"

Marty screwed up his mouth and eyes in thought. "Near as I remember, he had on sneakers. In fact, I think he only had one sneaker."

"Did Mr. Antone have an automobile?"

"No, least not that I saw."

"Thank you."

"You're excused," the judge said.

The deputy walked off the stand.

"The Government calls Diego Sabrosas to testify," Tim Essert said.

A nervous, slightly built middle-aged Mexican man took the stand.

"Where are you employed, Mr. Sabrosas?" Essert asked.

"I'm the night weekday bartender at the La Paloma bar in South Tucson."

"Have you ever seen Ignacio Antone?" Essert pointed at the Indian sitting in the jury box.

"Yes, sir, I know Ignacio. I known him for years."

"When did you last see him?"

"He came into the La Paloma last Thursday night, maybe nine or ten."

"How did he look?"

"Like he looks now."

"Did he have anything to drink?"

"Not at first. He didn't have no money, so I couldn't give him nothing. He was mad."

"Did he meet anyone at the bar?"

"Yeah. He sat down next to another Papago, a guy named Juan, Juan something. I never seen him before, and I don't know his last name."

"Did it appear to you that Mr. Antone knew this Juan?"

"Yeah, sure. They shook hands, real friendly."

"How do you know that Juan is a Papago Indian?"

Sabrosas looked oddly at the U.S. attorney. "What do you mean, how'd I know? I lived down there around Papagos all my life. And they were talking Papago." He shrugged.

"All right. Did they leave together?"

"Yeah, Juan bought two pints of Four Roses. They went out together, drove off in Juan's car."

Essert sat down. "Thank you, no further questions."

"You may cross-examine, Mr. Rabb," Judge Buchanan said.

"Thank you, your honor." Joshua remained seated and pointed at Ignacio. "Are you sure it was this man you saw?"

"Sure. Like I said, I known him for years."

"Please tell the court how you could possibly see that they left in an automobile?" Joshua thought that the bartender looked like a cartoon coyote, dark and pointy-faced and sneaky-eyed. He knew he was lying.

"The two front doors were open, always are in the summer. Gets real hot in there. I saw them get into a car. It was parked right out front, an old jalopy."

"How did you find out about this hearing, Mr. Sabrosas? How did you get here to testify?" Joshua stared harshly at him. Who paid you off, he thought, you low-life lying bastard?

"I saw Ignacio's picture in the paper, Friday I think it was. I called the sheriff's department to tell them what I knew."

"Just a public-spirited citizen?" Joshua asked, his voice sarcastic.

"Objection, your honor. Argumentative," Tim Essert said.

"Yes, sustained," the judge said.

Joshua nodded, his face sour. The man was going to stick to his story, no matter what. "Nothing further at this time," Joshua said.

The witness left the stand and walked out of the courtroom.

"Call Buford Richards," Tim Essert said.

The elderly white-haired man who looked like everybody's favorite uncle took the stand. The preliminaries lasted only a minute.

"Now, Buford, please tell the court how you came to be on the reservation in the early morning hours last Friday."

"I was called at home by the Pima County sheriff's office dispatcher and asked to lend a hand in a murder investigation."

"Is that common?"

"Yes, when a white person is found on the reservation, particularly at night, when they can't reach the tribal police or the FBI."

"What did you do?"

"I drove around to the road into the reservation off the No-gales Highway and followed it around to the road in front of the mission. Behind the mission is the old cotton field that stretches maybe a half mile, three quarters, down to the irrigation ditch. I drove slow along the road and saw someone on the ground a few feet into the field."

"Do you see that person here?"

"Yes, sir, it's Ignacio Antone over there." He pointed to the jury box.

"In what state was he when you found him?"

"He was dead drunk, passed out. I rolled him over with my foot, and he had his pants open, no underwear. I pulled him up and he came to. I cuffed him and put him in my car and brought him back so Marty could arrest him."

"Thank you, Mr. Richards." Essert sat down.

Buford got up to leave, and Joshua stood up and said, "Not quite yet, Mr. Richards." A few of the spectators snickered as the witness reluctantly sat down again.

"How long have you known Ignacio Antone?"

"Oh, I reckon I've known him since he was a little boy. I've been chief of security for Evelyn Enterprises for about twenty-one years now, and Ignacio's maybe just a little older than that."

"Have you ever known him to be violent, particularly sexually violent?"

"Objection, your honor," Tim Essert said, standing up at his table. "It's irrelevant."

"It isn't irrelevant in a rape case, your honor," Joshua said. "Proclivity to commit a sex crime is admissible."

The judge nodded. "Overruled. Answer the question, Buford."

"I forgot the question, Judge."

Several spectators laughed. The judge grinned. Joshua asked the question again.

"No, I can't say I ever heard about him being violent or anything like that," Buford said.

"What were you wearing that night?"

Buford stared at Joshua. "Who, me?"

"Yes."

"Regular clothes, I guess, can't remember exactly."

"Cowboy hat?"

"Yeah, I reckon."

"Levi's?"

"Reckon so." He shrugged.

"Cowboy boots?"

"Sounds like me," he said and smiled like a good old boy.

"Nothing further," Joshua said.

Buford Richards left the stand.

"Call Dr. Stanley Wolfe," Tim Essert said.

The Pima County coroner took the stand and was sworn in.

"Did you perform an autopsy on Sister Martha Robinette?" the assistant U.S. attorney asked.

"Yes, I did."

"When and where?"

"Last Friday morning at the coroner's office."

"What were your findings, Dr. Wolfe?"

"She died of strangulation."

"Had she been stabbed or cut?"

"No sir. Her habit was heavily stained on the front with blood, but it wasn't her blood. It was type AB, her blood is O."

"Did you type Ignacio Antone's blood?"

"Yes, I drew blood from him at the jail."

"What's his blood type?"

"He's also an O, like the sister."

"Did your examination of the nun reveal any particular injuries to her other than from the strangulation?"

"Yes. She had been anally raped after death."

Several of the spectators gasped. J. T. Sellner wrote rapidly and scratchily on her pad. The judge grimaced and stared at the witness. A hush fell over the courtroom, and Essert sat down slowly and said nothing, milking the shock.

"Dr. Wolfe," Joshua said, standing up at his table, "did you find semen in the anal orifice?"

"Yes, I did."

"Did you test it?"

"Yes, I did."

"What were the results?"

"I found it to be from a fertile nonsecretor."

"What do you mean by fertile?"

"I mean that the sperm count was in the millions."

"Have you at any period of time preceding the nun's murder seen a body which exhibited the same characteristics, namely strangulation from behind and anal rape?"

Tim Essert looked at Joshua. The judge glared at Joshua and then back at the witness.

"Yes, an Indian boy was brought in just five days earlier. He was found in the same ditch, and it appeared to be murder by the same modus operandi. But although he was strangled, I cannot be certain that it was from behind."

"Did you test the semen?"

"Yes. It was also from a fertile nonsecretor."

The judge turned annoyedly toward Joshua. "Maybe you wouldn't mind telling the court just why you're so anxious to get this testimony into the record, Mr. Rabb? Do you want Mr. Essert here to file additional rape and murder charges against your client?"

"Of course not, your honor. But this testimony about 'fertile' semen is critical to the defense. That's why it is so necessary that we continue this hearing for a short time to enable Mr. Antone to be examined by Dr. Murray Robertson." Gotcha, you prick, thought Joshua, looking victoriously at Tim Essert.

The judge pursed his lips and wrinkled his brow. "Mr. Essert, what's the Government's position on this?"

"It's just a smoke screen, Judge. This whole thing about medical testing doesn't have a thing to do with the murder of Sister Martha."

The judge looked at him and rubbed his chin and yanked his nose and drummed on the desk. "You have any redirect, Mr. Essert?"

"Yes, sir. Dr. Wolfe, you used the term 'nonsecretor.' What's that mean?"

"About twenty percent of the population do not have certain components in their bodily fluids other than blood that can be typed like the blood can."

Essert nodded, letting this sink in.

"Did you test the defendant to determine whether he is a nonsecretor?"

Damn, thought Joshua. The dumb son of a bitch stumbled all by accident on a vein of gold.

"Yes. I tested his saliva. He's a nonsecretor."

Essert smiled and sat down.

Joshua stood up at his table. "Does being a secretor or not have any effect whatsoever on sperm counts or the fertility of the semen?"

"No, not at all," the doctor said.

Joshua sat down and watched the judge closely. Judge Buchanan looked at his pocket watch, wound it, and opened and closed the hunting case a few times. He twisted up his mouth, chewed on his cheek, and cast a resentful glance at Joshua.

"Gentlemen, it's lunchtime already, and Mr. Rabb hasn't even had a chance to present any evidence to the court." He flipped a few pages on the desk. "My calendar appears to be loaded up for the next few days. I guess I'm going to have to put the rest of this hearing over till Wednesday of next week at ten o'clock."

"Your honor," Joshua said, "I need to have a court order bringing the defendant back to Tucson for a medical examination by Dr. Robertson this coming Wednesday."

The judge's eyes flicked around the courtroom for a moment, rested on J. T. Sellner, and came again to Joshua. "No sir, the court sees no purpose in that, Mr. Rabb. We know that there were two Indians out there in that field, and we know the other one had a car. Even if the other man committed both the rape and the murder, Ignacio Antone is still guilty as an accessory under the felony murder rule, at least as far as this preliminary hearing is concerned. I'm not here right now to convict him, Mr. Rabb, just to determine if there's *probable cause* to bind him over for trial before a jury. So I just don't know what relevant evidence a medical exam of your client is going to produce. But of course I won't prevent you from having him examined, but you'll have to make arrangements to do it up at Mount Lemmon if you really think it's necessary. Mrs. Hawkes will prepare a minute entry ordering the superintendent up at the detention center to give you access to your client for that purpose this Wednesday at the ranger station clinic, ten in the morning." He rapped his gavel and left the bench.

Well, thought Joshua, at least he gave me half a loaf. And then it occurred to him that it would give him an opportunity to go see Penny, and he felt better. All he had to do was talk Dr. Robertson into a drive up to Mount Lemmon.

"Mr. Rabb, could I speak to you for a moment?" J. T. Sellner asked, walking up to him.

"No," Joshua said, and left the courtroom.

Marshal Friedkind was standing down the hallway with Ignacio. He signaled Joshua to come over. "We won't be leaving for Mount Lemmon until about one or one-thirty," said the marshal. "You can talk to him down in the holding cell."

"I really appreciate this," Joshua said.

They walked down the rear corridor to a narrow stairway and down to the marshal's office on the first floor. Friedkind locked both of them in the cell. "I'll go over to Woolworth's and get you some fried chicken for lunch, okay, boy?"

Ignacio nodded. He and Joshua sat down carefully on the floor between reeking piles of dried excrement and vomit. The stink was horrendous. There was no bed, no bench, no chairs, just a bare eight-foot-square cell with a claustrophobically low ceiling only about seven feet high. An overhead light was recessed into the center of the ceiling and covered with two steel bars.

"Your sister and grandparents send their love to you."

Ignacio nodded. "I appreciate it that they hired you to defend me. I did not kill Sister Martha." His voice was sonorous and deep, and his English was fluent and unaccented. He looked earnestly at Joshua.

"I believe that. I want you to tell me everything you remember about that night, Ignacio."

He rubbed his face hard with his hand and ran his hand through his thick straight black hair. He screwed up his cheeks in thought. "I can't remember much about that night. But I do remember it was Independence Day, and it was once a big holiday with us. Grandpa was in the army many years and always July Fourth was a big day for us with firecrackers and games and a picnic. I wanted a drink, but all the stores were closed. I waited all day down by the switchmen's sheds at the yard, but nobody had anything to drink. So I walked to South Tucson, the Mexicans don't close their bars for American holidays, and I saw Juan Carlos at the La Paloma bar in South Tucson. I've known him a long time. He's from Cowlic on the Big Reservation near Sells. My sister and I went to school there, and I've known him for many years. So he says to me we'll buy a bottle and go to San Xavier, sing Indian songs like the old times. I didn't have any money, so he bought two bottles of Four Roses. He told me he'd been working highway construction down by Carmen, making big money. He had a car, an old car but okay, and we drove to San Xavier."

Joshua was silenced, surprised. There goes my theory about Buford picking him up downtown and planting him there. God damn it! It was a good theory. Now what the hell do I do? He sat and stared at the opposite wall, churning ideas over and over. The stench of the cell was insufferable. He began to get a headache. Could I have been dead wrong about this, about Ignacio? Joshua stared at the Papago and let out his breath slowly, like an inner tube losing all its air. The judge was right. Two of them. One of them murders her, the other rapes her. Or Juan Carlos does both with Ignacio there. Still first-degree murder for Ignacio. This case was turning into a nightmare.

Marshal Friedkind came into the cell corridor and handed a brown paper bag through the bars. Joshua took it. There were several pieces of greasy fried chicken inside. He had no appetite. He tossed the bag to Ignacio, and the Indian took out a drumstick and nibbled at it distractedly.

"What did you do when you got to the reservation?"

"Rode around a little. Then he parked in the field and we got out of the car and drank."

"Did he drink with you?"

"Yah."

"Did he leave soon or stay around awhile?"

"I don't know. I passed out. Soon. He was gone later when Buford came."

"What do you mean, 'when Buford came'?"

"You know, he came and arrested me, put me in his car."

Joshua frowned. "You know where Juan Carlos lives?"

Ignacio shook his head. "I just know he said he was working a construction job on the highway down by Carmen, thirty-five, forty miles south of here."

"Is that his whole name, Juan Carlos?"

"Yah, I'm pretty sure."

"Well," Joshua said, "I guess I'm going to have to try to find him. I'm also going to have a doctor go up to Mount Lemmon this Wednesday to examine you."

A look of hostility clouded Ignacio's eyes. "I heard you saying in court 'fertile,' 'not fertile,' and talking about 'capacity' "— he mouthed the word carefully—" 'to do rape.' What were you talking about?"

"Well, the nurse who examined you up on the mountain this last weekend said she thought you had a rheumatic heart, and that's usually an indication of mumps or scarlet fever, either one of which is likely to leave you unable to commit a rape."

Ignacio's eyes flared angrily. "You can't say that! You can't say to all those people that I'm not a real man."

Joshua stared at him, again surprised. It had never occurred to him that Ignacio would balk at any kind of defense as long as he could get out from behind these bars. In a first-degree murder case, you take whatever you can get and run like hell with it.

"What are you telling me, Ignacio?"

"I'm telling you not to bring a doctor to me. You're not going to tell all those people that Ignacio Antone is not anything. Better to be a *maricón*."

"I don't know what that means."

"It mean a man goat with a cock that doesn't work except for other men and a big asshole for making love."

Joshua shook his head vigorously. "I'm not saying anything like that."

"Why do you think my grandpa threw me out of his house? I was in my third year at the University of Arizona when the

Japs attacked Pearl Harbor. I dropped out of school and went to join the army, and Grandpa was real proud. But they turned me down, said my heart was no good. And Grandpa called me a *maricón* and didn't want to see me. He was ashamed. And there had been plenty of talk that I didn't go out with girls because I couldn't get hard with them, only with boys. But that's not true. I couldn't get hard with anyone. Never. But I was afraid to admit that. Better to be a *maricón* than to be without sex at all."

There were tears in Ignacio's eyes, and Joshua didn't know what to say. He felt completely deflated.

"I never went back to the university. I had nowhere to live, no money. So I got a job as a switchman down at the Southern Pacific yard, and sometimes I drink too much. So what?"

"Listen, Ignacio," Joshua said gently, "this is not just a little humiliation that could happen here. You will be executed if they find you guilty of murdering Sister Martha. You have to defend yourself, and that means using the medical defense. It's the best evidence you have. Don't tie my hands on this."

"I'm tying your hands, mister." Ignacio was sullen, resolute. "Listen, I don't want to die. Don't think I'm just a crazy drunk Indian. I want to live just like everybody else. But if you take my manhood from me, I can never look anyone in the face again. My life will be over. Better they should think I fucked a nun."

Joshua shook his head in disbelief. He stared at Ignacio, but he could see that nothing would convince him now. "Look, Ignacio, I promise I'll try every other way to defend you without using this information. But I won't be able to use it at all, under any circumstances, unless I get you examined by a doctor. I'm going to do my best to get a doctor up there this Wednesday—"

Marshal Friedkind came down the corridor. "Let's go, Ignacio, they're waiting down at the car."

The Indian stood up as the marshal unlocked the cell.

"Just let him examine you, that's all I ask. At least we'll have the testimony ready if we absolutely have to use it."

Ignacio walked out of the office with the marshal. Joshua stared glumly after him.

~~~~~~

Tuesday. Joshua sat in his office at the BIA and stared out the window. He'd spent two hours drafting the proposed contracts for the repair of the flood damage on the Big Reservation, repairing the culvert and the bridge at Coyote Creek, putting up twenty-three new telephone poles, a few other odds and ends. It was four o'clock in the afternoon, the hottest time of the day, and the heat radiated through the window. How does anybody work on summer afternoons around here? thought Joshua. He could see Adam and Jimmy in the field across Indian Agency Road. Now that their buffalo-hunting days had ended, they were into some sort of engineering project in the field. Adam was dragging a dead mesquite branch toward Jimmy, who was pointing to the spot to put it.

There was a loud knock on his doorjamb, and Joshua swiveled around in his chair.

"Hi, I'm Tom Delahanty," said the tall, burly man, coming into the office. "I'm the resident special agent with the Federal Bureau of Investigation." He sat down without being asked, as though he were accustomed to doing exactly as he pleased.

"Yes, I've heard your name," Joshua said. "What can I do for you?"

"Well now, that's sure the kind of thing I like to hear, yes sir, I don't often hear folks being quite so cordial." He smiled broadly.

Joshua said nothing, just smiled back amiably.

The FBI agent had a bumpy veiny nose which he rubbed repeatedly, as though it itched. "Yeah, I've been looking into this terrible thing with the sister." He shook his head sadly. "Got just a couple a loose ends I need to tie up."

Joshua nodded.

Tom Delahanty reached into the pocket of his rumpled tan linen suit and pulled out a gold pocket watch and chain. He laid it on the desk in front of Joshua. Joshua looked at it and flinched. He sat back in his chair.

"Marty Hankins brought this over to me last week. He said the coroner's deputy found it in Vittorio's pocket. But I guess ya know that," he said, staring at Joshua.

Joshua said nothing. He rocked slowly back and forth in the chair.

"I didn't think much about it at the time, ya know, just a Indian kid who done the faggots down at the Catalina Hotel. But then the weird writing inside this hunting case kind of intrigued me, ya know what I mean?"

He picked up the watch, opened the hunting case, and displayed the inside to Joshua. "So I went over to the languages department at the university, and someone said he thought it was Hebrew." Delahanty pronounced it *Heee-brew*, a little distastefully. "So I went over to Rabbi Bilgray's house this afternoon, and sure enough he said it was Hebrew. A name." Delahanty reached into his shirt pocket and pulled out a little spiral notebook and flipped a few pages. "*Yehoshua ben-Aryeh-Lev*," he said slowly and distinctly. "Rabbi Bilgray says that *Yehoshua* is the Bible name for Joshua." He put the little notebook back in his pocket and stared at Joshua.

"It's my watch."

Delahanty nodded. "Well, now, I figured that much out all by myself. But what I cain't quite figure is how it got in Vittorio's pocket the night the coroner says he was strangled and fucked in the ass."

Joshua swallowed. "His sister stole it from me and gave it to him."

The FBI agent nodded soberly. "Yeah, unfortunately that's what Billy Don Racker said. He's the county jail deputy who popped ya one. He heard Nona tell you that. And she admitted it when I talked to her." He frowned. "Pity I cain't throw yer ass in jail. Billy Don'd love t' see ya again." He chuckled maliciously and tossed the pocket watch and chain on the desk in front of Joshua.

"Now about these pictures you and Nona made down at the Catalina." He took a packet of photos out of his inner jacket pocket and spread them on the desk. "Looks to me like you go in for some pretty kinky sex. Like this one," he pointed. "Looks like you're fuckin her in the ass."

Joshua shook his head. "No, I wasn't. And I didn't know these photos were being taken, and it wasn't at the Catalina Hotel, it was in Senator Lukis's guesthouse, right beside his home. I was set up by the senator and his son and Richards." He stared hard at Delahanty.

The agent raised his eyebrows and wrinkled his forehead. He rubbed his nose and sniffed. "Ya got a real attitude there, boy. Buford was right about you. Said ya'd be makin up dirty stories. Said yer a genuine hard case, got a hard-on for the senator for no damn reason. Just a real attitude." Delahanty shook his head unhappily and shuffled the pictures together and put them back into his jacket pocket. "Yer sweatin like a stuck pig, boy," he muttered. "I'll be seein ya again, Yehoshua. I sure will." He stood up abruptly and walked out.

Joshua sat back in his chair and listened to his heart flailing at his chest wall. His head ached as the blood pounded up in him.

~~~~~~

Wednesday morning was brutally hot. By eight-thirty, when Joshua picked Murray Robertson up at his office, it was already at least one hundred degrees. They both bemoaned the weather and settled uncomfortably into the De Soto's sticky leather seats for the two-hour ride up to Mount Lemmon. Robertson had been born and grew up in Detroit, and he and Joshua reminisced fondly about big city life. The farther you got from it and the longer you stayed away, the better it looked, said the doctor. But living there was out of the question.

Joshua couldn't agree more, although he wasn't sure he'd be staying in Tucson too long. "Kind of a tough place to break in a new law practice," he mused.

The doctor laughed. "Yeah, well particularly if the first case you get is defending a Papago drunk for murdering a nun!"

Joshua rolled his eyes. How many times did he need to have people scoff at his apparent naiveté? The simple fact was that he was doing what he believed was right. But that wasn't something you said to anybody. It was more comfortable to let them think that you hadn't exactly known what you were getting into, that you kind of got roped into it and were now stuck. And that was *partly* true anyway. At least he hadn't fully understood that the Indians out here occupied the hapless, dismal position reserved in most other places for negroes. Since there weren't many negroes here, at least that he had seen, the Papagos therefore enjoyed the lowly distinction of being at the bottom of the social heap.

It was pleasant driving up the mountain, feeling the air get cooler, seeing the change in the plants on the mountain, creosote bushes and saguaro cactus and desert broom at the bottom and manzanita and cedar trees in the middle and Douglas fir and juniper and pine beginning sparsely at about six thousand feet and becoming a thick forest toward the top.

He parked in front of the clinic at the ranger station. Penny Chesser opened the door even before Joshua knocked, and he and Robertson went inside. Penny and the doctor exchanged pleasantries. She was even prettier than Joshua remembered, and this time she was wearing a kelly green skirt and pale celery blouse and her figure was lovely, slender, long-legged.

"You look beautiful today. Why are you all dressed up?" Joshua asked.

She smiled up at him. "Because the superintendent at the center called yesterday and told me he'd just gotten a court order for an examination. He sounded very unhappy. He said some pushy two-bit shyster would be coming over here at ten o'clock this morning."

"And naturally you knew right away it was me."

She laughed.

They were in a small anteroom, and she opened the door to the inner clinic. It was a well-supplied doctor's examining room.

A moment later, Ignacio Antone came into the clinic in handcuffs followed by a guard. The guard unlocked the cuffs. Joshua shook the Indian's hand.

"They treating you okay?" Joshua asked.

Ignacio shrugged. "That the doctor?" He jutted his chin toward Murray Robertson, standing in the inner clinic.

"Right. He's a nice guy, Ignacio. Please cooperate. I told you, I won't use any of this unless we absolutely have no choice. But we have to be ready with it."

Ignacio breathed deeply and chewed his lower lip. His jaw was still swollen, and the skin on his cheek was deeply bruised. He walked slowly into the inner clinic.

Penny came out and closed the door to the examining room. The guard sat down on a chair in the anteroom to wait. Penny and Joshua left the clinic.

"Murray said to give him a half hour," she said.

They walked to the cabin. Joshua sat down on the chintz couch, and Penny went into the kitchen. She was back a minute later. She sat down on the couch next to him and kicked off her flats.

"The coffee will be ready in a few minutes."

She was close enough to him that he could smell her perfume. He turned to her and leaned over and kissed her earlobe. Her face turned toward his, and she looked at him searchingly. "Are you sure you're not married?" she whispered.

He nodded.

She kissed him lightly on the nose, and then on both cheeks and his forehead, and then she kissed his mouth, tentatively. He felt the erection that was always lurking around down there, waiting to pop up, like a dachshund lying beside the dinner table ready to leap up instantly to get any scrap that might just fall out of someone's plate.

"You're not getting into my knickers until I meet your family and look under the bed and the couch," she whispered.

He pulled back in mock hurt. "How come you don't trust me?"

She looked at him soberly. Her voice was soft. "Because I lost my husband in the war and I've had a long run of bad luck, and suddenly you show up at my door, and I don't want to just roll around with you and then wonder why you don't come back again. I don't like sitting by the phone and waiting for it to ring while some jerk tells stories about me down at the bar."

"I didn't promise to marry you. I didn't think we were that far along." He grinned at her.

"I'm not looking for promises. I'm just looking for honesty, no sneaking around hiding from anybody."

"Okay, this Saturday we meet at the department store at noon and you're coming home with me for dinner."

She nodded and smiled. "I'd love it. I really would."

She went into the kitchen and came back with two mugs of coffee and handed him one. She sat down again.

"So what happened to your husband?"

"Normandy. The second day. He was an insurance salesman in Matawan, made a nice living, but suddenly he decided he was a coward for staying home. He wanted to be a hero and have medals on his chest and travel around the country with showgirls and Lana Turner and raise money for war bonds, like those war heroes they paraded around every few months. So he up and enlists one morning just like that," she snapped her fingers. "That was all."

"I'm sorry," Joshua mumbled.

"I'm sorry too," she said. Blood pinked her cheeks, and her eyes were just a bit bloodshot. "But it's long over, long long over. Two years."

He nodded and sipped his coffee. They sat silently for a few minutes.

"How about you? You get that limp in the war?"

He nodded. "I thought I was hiding it pretty well."

"Pretty well," she said and smiled. "And the arm too?"

He nodded.

She leaned over and took his mug and brushed his lips with hers. "We'd better get back," she said. She brought the mugs into the kitchen.

They walked arm in arm back toward the ranger station. At the edge of the woods she pulled away.

Ignacio Antone and the guard had already left when they got to the clinic. The doctor was wiping his hands on a towel at the sink. "Okay, I'm done here," he said.

Penny looked at Joshua and smiled, a smokey smile. "See ya."

He nodded.

He and the doctor drove a few miles in self-absorbed silence.

"I didn't realize you and Penny had something going," Murray Robertson said, looking slyly at Joshua.

Joshua shrugged. "Well, we really don't. Not yet anyway. I'd sure like to. I didn't know it showed."

"Oh yeah! The sparks almost exploded the oxygen bottle in the clinic," Robertson said, laughing.

They drove on in silence. At the bottom of the mountain, Robertson roused himself from his reverie. "Ignacio Antone didn't rape the nun," he said.

Joshua turned toward him, attentive.

"His prostate is literally destroyed by some disease process I can't be certain of, and I couldn't even get a smear. There is certainly no seminal productivity. He can't engage in any sexual activity. There's no doubt about it."

Late that afternoon, Edgar came into Joshua's office. He asked Joshua about the storm damage contract, and they spoke briefly about letting out bids for it.

"You heard from the senator lately?" Edgar asked.

Joshua shook his head. "You?"

"Not even a belch or a fart," Edgar said.

Joshua laughed.

"Frances said Tom Delahanty was in to see you yesterday," Edgar said. "What's that alcohol-soaked tub a piss want?"

"He wanted to talk about dirty pictures and why I murdered Vittorio Ponsay."

"Yeah, I heard about the watch," Edgar said. He grimaced. "But I see ya got it back." He nodded toward the gold chain hooked into Joshua's vest.

"Yes. Poor Delahanty just couldn't get enough folks to lie for him. Even good ol' Nona managed to tell the truth for once."

"You read today's paper?"

Joshua shook his head. "J. T. Sellner still out to get me lynched?"

"Yep. You and the judge both. Man, I known Jane for years, never knowed she had such a hate for Buck Buchanan. Looks to me like as there's more to it than meets the eye. You know, 'Heaven hath no greater wrath than a woman scorned.' "

"Well, I'm sure pleased I could accommodate her and jump into the middle of their personal problems."

"Anyway, what I come for is to tell you that Chief Romero and his boys want another council with us."

"Sells again?"

"Naw, I told Francisco I ain't up to Sells twice in one week. We'll meet em right here. He pissed and moaned, but he said they'd come in tomorrow mornin about ten."

"Indian time?"

"You're catchin on!" Edgar smiled. "Yep, it'll start right about noon. I'll have em in my office, even have a couple a the ladies on the res fix us up some fry bread and chili. We'll have a regular lunch meetin just like the big boys, you know, Ford and GM and orderin lunch from Howard's Beanery."

"What do they want to talk about?"

"Same gott damn thing, I reckon. They wanna peek in old Jacob's mine tunnel and see what he's stealin from em."

"What chance is there of that?"

"Oh, plenny," Edgar said, nodding enthusiastically. "Just so long as the senator and Steve and Buford all die a the black plague tomorrow mornin. Then we'll have no problem at all."

Joshua laughed. "I sure do look forward to meeting the boys again." His voice was bland.

"Yeah, me too," Edgar drawled.

"By the way," Joshua said, "I heard there's some construction going on down on the Nogales Highway near a place called Carmen. You ever hear of it?"

"Sure. Right this side a Tumacacori mission. That's another Papago mission down about forty miles from here. But it was never finished like San Xavier was. It's just adobe ruins."

"There's supposed to be a whole crew of men down there working on the highway."

"Yeah, I reckon there is. There's a labor camp set up down past Kingsley's ranch, just a bunch a shacks and a few trailers. Been there for four or five months now. Work on the highway's real slow. They ain't got enough earth-movin machinery." He looked quizzically at Joshua. "What's up?"

"Ignacio Antone says that he was with a guy named Juan Carlos the night of the murder. He's working on the construction job in Carmen. I've got to go down there and talk to him."

"Ya'd best take a machine gun with ya. He's damn sure not gonna be happy about you gettin 'im mixed up in this shit."

Joshua shrugged. "I've got no choice. Right now it's the only lead I have."

Edgar shook his head grimly and left the office.

CHAPTER ELEVEN

As Joshua drove south of Tucson through the Santa
Rita Mountains on the east and the Sierritas on
the west, it was easy to imagine that the small
wisps of clouds were smoke signals, and the saguaros were
warriors gathered along the mountain ridges on both sides
of the road. But this was cattle-ranching country now, the
descendants of the hardtack white settlers who had refused
to be run off the land by Indians, who had lost family and
friends in raids, who had been burned out and had come
back to begin again, whose grandfathers now sat in rocking
chairs in the living rooms and told the kids stories of the
old days, when every time you saw an Indian you reached
for your gun, when every Indian wanted the white man
dead, when the only good Indian was a dead Indian.

Just sixty years ago, traveling the land south of Tucson
had been extremely dangerous. It was peopled by the many
tribes of the legendary Chiricahua Apaches. Unlike the
peaceful Papagos and Pimas who had farmed the land for
ten centuries by the time the itinerant Apaches migrated
into Arizona in the 1500s, the Apaches' way of life was to

ravage farmers' crops and ranchers' cattle and sheep to provide their sustenance.

In the 1860s and early 1870s, the great Chiricahua chief Cochise had been the master of southeastern Arizona. From his stronghold in the Dragoon Mountains he sent forth warriors to ambush the Overland stage riders and the wagon trains headed for Tucson. When Cochise signed a peace treaty with the United States, some of the chiefs refused to go to the reservations and went instead into the mountains of New Mexico and southern Arizona and the Sierra Madres of Mexico. The most fearsome of these renegades was the Bedonkohe Chiricahua named Geronimo. But the Apache wars came to an end as cavalry troops swarmed over southern Arizona after the Civil War, killing or capturing the renegades. And when Geronimo was captured in 1886 and incarcerated on a reservation like all the other Indians, the Old West died.

It was astounding to Joshua how much the times had changed. The Indians now lived in poverty on the poorest of the land, and the only thing fearsome about them was their despair. But the stories of the old days still were told by the white grandfathers, and the stories became enhanced and romantic, and then they became legends. And the Indians today were so far from the stuff of legends that they engendered no respect in comparison, and they were almost totally forgotten. They had become part of the landscape like the creosote bushes and the bear grass and the desert broom, and just as easily ignored and trampled. The distinction between peaceful Indians and savage warriors had long since died, and no white man could tell the difference between a Papago and an Apache. And few people now cared.

It was beautiful country down here, high hilly desert, lush with mesquite trees and palo verdes and prickly pear cactus and a great colorful kaleidoscope of wildflowers. Occasionally Joshua saw a coyote or gray wolf, and he knew why the settlers had come to displace the Indians from this spectacular land, and why they had stayed and clung to it through every peril.

Kingsley's ranch wasn't a ranch at all, at least not this part. It was a restaurant just off the highway. It looked like one of those Old West saloons from the movies, with a hitching rail running along the front of the wooden building and stag horns and steer horns nailed to every available inch of space on the outer wall. Across the highway from it was a faded old sign that read, KINGSLEY'S LAKE, TROUT AND CATFISH. The "lake" was a cattle-watering pond a couple of hundred feet in diameter, ringed by cottonwood trees.

Joshua went into the restaurant, and a waitress wearing a "saloon girl" dress told him that the work camp was up by Carmen just a few miles on the right, can't miss it. A few men were sitting at a long bar nursing drinks, even at eight-thirty in the morning.

He drove through Carmen, a town of a dozen low square stucco houses and a gas station, and then passed the adobe ruins of Tumacacori mission. The asphalt ended, and several Caterpillars were grading the dirt road. He pulled off the highway by the camp. A crew of men was shoveling pea gravel from a huge mound into wheelbarrows. They were all Mexicans and Indians.

"Do you know a man named Juan Carlos?" Joshua asked one of the workmen.

"*No hablo Inglés,*" he said and kept shoveling.

Joshua asked three other men and got the same shrugged response. The fourth man said he didn't know him but to ask the foreman, Jesus Armijo, over there by the stake truck. Joshua walked over to him.

"Mr. Armijo?"

"Yes." He looked Joshua over from head to foot, as though it were the first time that he had ever seen a man in a suit and tie.

"You gonna get dirty out here, mister."

"Yes, I know." Joshua smiled pleasantly. "Do you have a man named Juan Carlos working for you?"

"Why? You from Immigration, FBI?"

"No, I just want to talk to him."

"About what?"

Joshua stared at the man and weighed what to do. Under normal circumstances he would have told him it was none of his business. He might even have emphasized that by grabbing him by the shirt and lifting him onto his toes and looking mean. But there were fifty men with shovels and rakes and hoes standing around watching them, and this was no place for pressing your luck.

"I'm a lawyer in Tucson. I'm defending a Papago Indian on a murder charge. I want to talk to Juan Carlos, to see if he might know something."

Jesus Armijo's scowl turned blank. He studied Joshua's face. "He's working right over that hill." He pointed across the road. "On the shovel crew."

Joshua walked across the highway and up the small knoll. On the other side, a half-dozen men were shoveling sand from a pit into wheelbarrows and loading it on a dump truck.

"Juan Carlos," Joshua called out.

One man looked up abruptly, then went back to shoveling. Joshua walked up to him. "I want to talk to you about Ignacio Antone."

His black eyes flickered with an unmistakable look of fear. Then the short gaunt man made his face bland and stared at Joshua.

"I'm Ignacio's lawyer. I'm trying to help him."

Still the man just stared. He wasn't more than twenty-five years old, but the skin of his face was as brown and cracked as a dried mud puddle in the sun, and his hands gripped around the shovel were so calloused and thick that it looked at first glance as though he were wearing gloves. There was a long fresh scab on the back of his left hand. It was probably ninety degrees already, but he wasn't even sweating.

"He needs your help, Mr. Carlos."

"What you think I can do?" His accent was thick Papago.

"He says you were with him, that you drove him to the mission and you were both drinking there the night the nun got killed."

"So what?"

"He remembers how he got to the field. He saw you at the La Paloma, and you bought a couple of bottles of whiskey and drove out to San Xavier."

The Indian stared malevolently at him. His eyes narrowed. "You not gonna tell nobody that, mister."

Joshua wasn't sure whether it was a threat or a question. The Indian's grip tightened on the shovel. Joshua backed up a step.

"That's a real bad cut you got on the back of your hand, Mr. Carlos."

"So what business is it to you, mister? I didn't do nothin to no nun," Juan Carlos hissed. He glared at Joshua.

"I didn't accuse you of anything, Mr. Carlos." Joshua was aware that the other men had stopped working and were staring at him. He was afraid to look around, afraid to take his eyes off Juan Carlos's shovel. He backed up another step.

"I ain't going near that courtroom. Those people up there" —he jerked his chin toward Tucson—"be very happy hang me next to Ignacio. Ignacio kill their favorite nun."

"Are you saying that you saw Ignacio kill her?"

"No, no, no. He no kill her. He drunk, pass out. But they say he kill her." Again he jutted his chin toward Tucson. "Nothing else matter. They string him up."

"Listen, Mr. Carlos, I'm trying to make sure that doesn't happen. His sister, Magdalena, lives with me and my two children; his grandfather, Macario, asked me to help Ignacio."

The mention of the familiar names had a visible effect on Juan Carlos. He relaxed his grip on the shovel and his shoulders lowered. He shook his head slowly. "We got to the field by the mission, then got out and drank. Ignacio was gone, real quick. Can't hold it. Take him three swallows to get drunk, and that pint bottle put him on his back. I never see no nun."

Joshua studied his eyes and nodded slowly. "When did you leave him?"

"I dunno. Got no watch. Maybe eleven, twelve."

"You left him lying in the field."

"Sure." He shrugged. "Out cold."

"You didn't see anything?"

He shook his head. But Joshua saw his eyes narrow. "You did see something." He stared hard at the Indian. "Tell me."

Juan Carlos walked close to Joshua and lowered his voice. "I see a priest come out of *convento.*"

"*Convento?*"

"Yes, yes, where the sisters live."

Joshua let it sink in. "When did you see that?"

"Late, just before I leave."

"How do you know it was a priest?"

"Well, was big man, was wear one of them robes, you know, with big hood, come all the way to ground like a dress."

"You sure that's what you saw?"

The Indian nodded.

"Did you recognize the priest?"

"No, too dark. Too far away."

"What did he do?"

"I dunno. I lost sight of him in the darkness."

It was time to go before he got himself killed. "Okay, thank you, Mr. Carlos."

"Don't come back here, mister." The Indian looked at him steadily and spoke softly. "You come back here, I put you in that truck under the sand. You be part of cement footing for that bridge." He gestured with his thumb over his shoulder toward the highway.

Joshua believed him. He backed up until he was out of shovel range and then turned around and walked quickly to his car. So what the hell did he know now that he didn't know yesterday? That Juan Carlos had a badly cut hand and almost certainly committed the rape and murder? But that sure as hell wasn't going to help Ignacio. It was still felony murder.

When he got back to the bureau, the tribal council had just arrived. They were milling about in the reception area, and Frances Hendly had the look of a rancher's wife fearful for her virtue and her scalp. The look wasn't much relieved by seeing Joshua. She pointed down the hallway toward her husband's office.

Joshua went first to his own office and took the big black three-ring binder off his desk. He limped down the hallway to Edgar's office. The stroll up and down the hill this morning hadn't done much for his foot other than make it hurt like hell. Going to have to use the cane again, he thought.

The Indians were sitting on metal folding chairs at four card tables that had been pushed together to make one long table in Edgar's office. In the middle was a stack of fry bread, a big metal stockpot of chili, tin plates, and spoons, and an elderly woman dishing it all out to the men. They ate quietly and quickly. Edgar sat at one end of the long table and Joshua at the other. The woman walked around picking up plates and spoons and putting them in a basket. Another woman carried the stockpot out.

"Okay, Chief, what's so important?" Edgar said to Francisco Romero.

"We want to see inside the mine tunnel of the Sand and Gravel Company."

Edgar rolled his eyes. "I keep tellin you boys that I ain't got no power over that. You gotta go talk to the senator or Buford. I ain't got no authority to let you in there. Shit! I can't even get in myself!"

"We know he stealing minerals from us."

Edgar was exasperated. "Now dammit all to hell, Francisco, we been over this road a dozen times, and I keep tellin you I can't do a thing about what the senator does on his own property."

"But it not his own property. The tunnel go into the riverbank on our land," Francisco said. He raised his arms to encompass the men around him. "Is our property."

Edgar stared dejectedly at the Indians.

"I think the chief has a good point there, Edgar," Joshua said.

Edgar shot an annoyed glance at him.

Joshua opened the notebook and laid it on the table in front of him. He folded out a plat map of the Santa Cruz River bed where the company was located and the adjacent west bank and the fields up to Lourdes Hill. Yesterday he had sketched in red lines to show the boundaries of the area licensed to Mission Sand and Gravel. A small red X marked the entrance to the mine tunnel in the riverbank.

He picked up the plat map and displayed it so that everyone could see. "The tunnel is right into the bank where the company land ends, and it continues underground onto Indian land, how far or exactly what direction we just don't know. But there's no question that it's outside the company's licensed property."

Romero spoke in Papago for a moment. The men watched Joshua and his map intently.

"There are two ways into the tunnel. Through here." Joshua pointed with his pen at the red X. "But we can't get through the fence and the gate and the private army they have out there. The other way is through here." He pointed to a red spot on the map on the riverbank a couple of inches from the X.

"You mean bore into the tunnel from the top?" Edgar asked. Joshua nodded.

A look of extreme exasperation wrinkled Edgar's cheeks and lips. "You got some serious brain disease, boy. You got a whole passel a worse ideas in one week than any twenny of us has had collectively in the last fourteen years." He sat still and watched Joshua intently.

Joshua flipped the pages of the notebook and ran his finger down a list. "I'm showing in my inventory that the Office of Land Management has a backhoe and flatbed transport."

Francisco nodded. "It's down by Coyote Creek. We been trenching out the rock so the culvert can be replace."

"Well, I think we ought to bring the backhoe over to the bank and start digging a five- or six-foot-deep trench right about here." Joshua pointed to the red dot on the plat map southwest of the mine tunnel entrance. "Then we'll continue cutting the trench north until we bisect the tunnel." He traced the imaginary trench on the map. "It's all on reservation property, a full forty feet from the edge of the bank where Lukis's contract land starts."

Francisco and several of the men spoke in Papago for five minutes. Edgar sat at the end of the table staring incredulously at Joshua and the map and the tribal council.

"Somebody gonna get killed," Edgar mumbled. The men quieted down and looked at him. "Somebody gonna get his balls shot off," he said louder, looking around at the men. "That what it's gonna take to make you boys happy?"

The men spoke quietly together for several minutes. Their voices were subdued. Silence settled over them, and Francisco

Romero spoke soberly. "We will bring the backhoe here to-morrow morning, Mr. Rabb. You do not have to take part in this. You have done enough for us."

"When the backhoe is in place on the riverbank, please come here for me," Joshua said. "We will do this together. Maybe with me there, we will be able to avert trouble. But there's something we must do now. We must go to the Sand and Gravel Company office and ask to see inside the shaft. This will give them fair warning."

"Now we go?" Francisco asked.

Joshua nodded.

"You come with me in truck," Francisco said.

They got up from the tables and walked out of Edgar's office, leaving him sitting, drumming on the table with nervous fingers, staring gloomily at the wall.

Macario Antone was sitting in the reception area. When he saw Joshua he got up and walked to meet him. "How is it with my grandson?"

The other men went outside and waited while Joshua spoke quietly with the old man. He told him of Ignacio's impotency. Macario's eyes filled with tears and he wept quietly.

"I was ignorant," the old man said hoarsely. "I did not know that he had been so sick as a boy. He lived then with my daughter and son-in-law in Pisinimo on the Big Reservation, seventy-five miles from here. And when they both died and Ignacio came to live with me, he never told me he was so sick. All I ever heard was talk, gossip, about him not being like the other boys, and I believed it. I am very ashamed."

They stood together for a few minutes until the old man's tears had stopped. "I must go to see him," Macario said. "I must tell him that it is my fault, I should have been a better father for him. He must save himself from this thing."

"I don't know if they'll let you see him, Chief."

"You must make them let me see him." He looked implor-ingly at Joshua.

"I will," Joshua said. "Visiting hours are Sunday. I'll go with you and make sure you get in."

Macario nodded. "You are very good man, Mr. Rabb."

They walked slowly outside to the waiting trucks. "You coming with us, Chief?"

He shook his head. "No, I am too old for all of this. I told Francisco I only have enough strength for one fight now, for Ignacio."

Joshua got into the cab of the old black pickup next to Francisco Romero. The three pickups drove slowly down Indian Agency Road. They drove to the Nogales Highway, then south to the access road to Mission Sand and Gravel. Clouds of trailing dust announced their arrival at the front gate.

A young man in a tan uniform carrying a shotgun came over to Francisco Romero in the lead pickup.

"You here for a delivery?" he asked the chief.

"We here to go inside mine tunnel," Francisco said.

"You got permission from Mr. Richards?"

"We don't need permission. Is on our land."

"Well, hold on a minute, uncle. I don't know nothin about none a this. I gotta call Mr. Richards, get permission." He walked away to a small guard shack next to the locked gate.

Two cement mixer trucks came from the plant and drove up to the gate. The guard let them out. A huge dump truck lumbered up to the gate, loaded high with sand. The guard opened the gate and let it out.

They sat in the three pickup trucks and waited silently. Ten minutes. Twenty minutes. A car approached from Nogales Highway. It came up to the gate beside Romero's pickup. Buford Richards got out of the driver's seat. Steve Lukis got out of the passenger side.

"Howdy, Francisco," Buford said, walking up to the driver's side. He took off his straw cowboy hat and wiped the headband with a soiled handkerchief. "Hot as hell, ain't it? Sure wish the monsoons would start, take some of the burn out of the air."

The chief stared at him and said nothing. Lukis stood stiffly by the Evelyn Enterprises Security Police car.

"You get lost, take the wrong road?" Richards asked, putting his hat back on.

"We want to see inside mine tunnel. It is on our land. We want to see what you are mining there."

"Sorry about that, Chief. But we got a contract in the making for that tunnel. Just ask Mr. Rabb here, he'll tell you. Few more days Edgar and him will sign the contract. Perfectly legal, Chief."

"Nobody sign your contract, mister. Is our land. We want to see."

Steve Lukis reached into the car and pulled out a sawed-off pump shotgun. He walked up to the driver's window beside Buford.

"Now you don't want to make any more trouble here, uncle," Lukis said. "You want to drive this thing out of here and take your girlfriend with you." He jutted his chin at Joshua. "Otherwise, I'm going to blow your fucking brains all over the inside of that fancy limousine of yours."

The splint was off his nose, but he still had raccoon rings around his eyes, which intensified his lupine snarl. His eyelid twitched weirdly.

"Let's go, Francisco," Joshua said quietly. "They've had their chance."

The chief started the engine and turned slowly in front of the gate. The others also started their trucks and followed behind.

Joshua jumped at the sound of a shotgun blast. He looked through the rear window and saw Lukis pointing the gun high in the air, and he heard another blast. Then Lukis whooped, "Eeee-ha, Eeee-ha," like a rodeo cowboy who had just ridden the full ten seconds on a bucking bull.

What in the world am I doing here? thought Joshua. Some lunatic with a shotgun is going to put a dozen double-ought buckshot right through my face, and nothing will ever happen to him because he's the son of a United States senator! Edgar's right about this place, "the Wild West." And I'm the eastern rube who got in the middle of the whole mess. But I can't leave. These Papagos need me. And I need them too. I need them to need me. For the first time in a long time, I finally feel like I'm worth something to somebody.

Damn! As Edgar would say, "There's all that noble bullshit squirting outta yer brains again. Ya got a serious problem there, boy!"

"What's going on?" Joshua asked as he came into the kitchen.

Magdalena took another fry bread out of the skillet and placed it on a high stack.

"We feeding the seventh cavalry tonight?" he asked.

"No," she answered and smiled. "Just a few of my friends."

"What's up?"

"There's going to be a processional tonight by the mission. Then my cousin Henry and a few of his friends will camp out in the yard until Sunday afternoon." She didn't look at him.

"You heard about Steve Lukis and his shotgun?"

She nodded.

"Are we in that much trouble?"

She nodded again.

"Where are the kids?"

"With my grandmother. I'll go get them in an hour."

"Okay, I'll be back in a bit. I'm going to the market and get a newspaper, see what they have to say about me today."

But he didn't drive to the market. He drove downtown to Congress Street and parked right in front of the Fox Theater. Next to it was a small store only about ten feet wide, with a window just barely large enough to paint a few words: PAWN SHOP—GUNS, JEWELRY, CAMERAS—BOUGHT AND SOLD.

"I need a large-caliber handgun," he said to the man behind the counter. "Used."

"Well, I got this Smith and Wesson Model Twenty-five. It takes a Long Colt forty-five." He reached under the counter and brought out the revolver. "Six-inch barrel." He reached under the counter and brought up another revolver and laid it beside the .45. "This is a Colt Single Action Army caliber forty-four." He looked at the empty sleeve of Joshua's suit jacket. "Of course, it's kind of hard to load this one with only one arm. Better stick with the Smith and Wesson. It's got a swing-out cylinder."

Joshua studied it. "How much?" He realized instantly that he should have changed out of his suit before coming here. This was a time and place for overalls and work boots.

"Fifty dollars," said the man.

"Thirty and throw in a box of cartridges."

"No, no, no. I can't do that. I'll lose money."

Joshua turned to walk away. The man held up his hands.

"Forty," said the man.

"Thirty-five and two boxes of cartridges," Joshua said.

"Cash?"

Joshua pulled a wad of bills out of his pocket. He counted thirty-five dollars and laid it on the counter. The man put two boxes of cartridges in a small paper bag. Joshua picked up the revolver and tucked it under his belt. He took the bag of shells and left the store. He drove to the Army-Navy Surplus—Used Clothes Store a couple of blocks away. Time to blend into the landscape and look like a native. He bought two pair of used Levi's, a not-too-worn pair of army boots, and three faded blue chambray work shirts. He changed clothes in the little dressing room.

When he walked into the house, Adam's face lit up with excitement. "Wow, can I touch it?"

Joshua sat down on the couch. "Get the girls."

Adam went into the kitchen. A few seconds later Hanna and Magdalena came into the living room. Adam sat down on the couch, next to the handgun lying beside Joshua.

"This is a high-powered revolver," Joshua said, "and it is not a toy."

Adam was staring with wide hungry eyes at the gun, his mouth open slightly.

"It's unloaded now, and I want each one of you to hold it and see how it feels and get all of your curiosity out of your system. Adam."

Adam picked it up and hefted it like a treasure.

"Hanna."

She took it gingerly from Adam and held it in front of her. She handed it back to Joshua.

"Okay, you understand how it works?"

All three of them nodded.

"It's not a toy."

They nodded solemnly.

"I want you to watch carefully while I load it."

He opened one of the boxes and shook six cartridges into his lap. He depressed the cylinder lock, snapped it open, and loaded it. "Okay." He held it up. "Now I've got all the bullets in it. It's ready to fire. All you do is aim it and pull the trigger. Understand?"

They nodded.

"I'm putting this in my bedroom, and I never want you to touch it unless there's trouble." Joshua looked at them sternly. "But if there is any trouble, you must not be afraid of using it. Okay?"

They all nodded.

The muffled sound of guitars came from outside. Magdalena went to the window and opened the curtains. "That's the processional, Mr. Rabb."

There were at least two hundred Indians, in a long file four or five abreast, walking very slowly across the field from the mission toward the irrigation ditch in front of the house. The front row consisted of three guitar players and a man playing a simple squeeze box. Another man in front carried a white wooden cross about four feet high and two feet wide. In front of them all, leading the procession, was an Indian dressed in black trousers and a black shirt, reading from a missal and holding a long heavy rosary in one hand.

Joshua carried the revolver and cartridges into the bedroom. He put the gun on the nightstand and the boxes of shells beside it.

They all walked outside on the porch and watched.

"Why are they doing this?" Hanna asked.

"It's for your father. It is to honor him," Magdalena said.

Joshua turned toward her. "Are you kidding? What the hell have I accomplished?"

"It isn't what you've accomplished, Mr. Rabb," she said. "It's what you're trying to do for us. No white man ever tried so much. There has never been a processional for a white man."

Joshua felt guilty. These people were so trusting, so eager to show their appreciation. And he had nothing to give them in return. Not their minerals, not their water, not their brother who awaited the hangman on Mount Lemmon. He felt like jumping up and shouting, "Don't expect so much! I can't give you what you need!" But instead he could only stand and watch. Too heavy was the burden of their faith, the innocence of their affection. And far too real was his inability to help them.

The Indians reached the irrigation ditch. All of them stood abreast on the other bank, the musicians in the middle. They sang in Spanish.

"They are singing a prayer for you, Mr. Rabb," Magdalena said. "Please go into the yard and wave to them. Otherwise they will feel bad."

Joshua walked off the porch up to the side of the ditch. He felt embarrassed and very much alone. He bowed toward them. The man holding the cross bowed toward him. Then the entire group got into a long file again and marched back toward the mission.

"They'll go to the mission and say mass for you," said Magdalena, coming up beside him.

Joshua felt like hiding from everybody. Tears welled in his eyes, and he was ashamed that they might see him cry. He knew that he would never be able to live up to their expectations. Hanna came up to him and put her arm around Joshua's waist, and they stood silently. He rubbed his eyes with his hand as though he had gotten dust in them.

From the back of the group of Indians, five men turned around and returned to the ditch. There was a little water in the bottom and they splashed through. Two of them carried duffel bags slung over their shoulders. They all walked up to Magdalena.

"This is my cousin Henry," Magdalena said, introducing a tall, heavyset man of twenty-five or thirty. "And these are our friends Tomas, Samuel, Husi, and Jimmy." They all shook hands with Joshua. "They're going to camp out in the yard here, if it's okay with you, Mr. Rabb."

Joshua nodded. "Yes, sure. I'm happy to have you guys here."

"They were all in the Hundred-and-first Airborne together," said Magdalena. "So they think they're tough guys. Especially Samuel. He thinks he's real macho."

The taunted one was medium height and weight and in his early twenties. He had short, straight black hair and a ruggedly handsome face. He frowned at Magdalena, and Joshua could instantly see and feel the chemistry between them.

"Hey, Magda, where's the food you promised us?" Henry asked. He was built as though he had never voluntarily missed a meal.

"It's all ready, don't worry. You don't look like you're going to starve."

"Why don't you guys put your stuff on the porch out of the sun?" Joshua said. "Come in, we've got a ton of fry bread and chili."

"Naw, we'll just stay out on the porch, Mr. Rabb," Henry said. "You ain't got no room in that little place for all of us. Magda can bring it out."

It was almost seven o'clock. The sun was sliding toward Black Mountain. Magdalena brought the kettle of chili and the fry bread and laid them on the porch. Joshua went inside.

"I'll eat out here," Magdalena called from the porch.

"Can I eat out there with them too, Dad?" Adam asked. He lowered his voice, like he was telling a secret. "Did you see that big guy, he's wearing a knife on his belt?"

"Yes. We'll all eat out on the porch," Joshua said. He left the front door open so some of the cooler air from inside would blow out on the porch.

The Indians sat in a circle around the food, and Adam sat with them. Magdalena and Hanna sat on the porch steps, and Joshua sat back against the doorjamb keeping as cool as possible. The sun slithered behind Black Mountain and left a yellow-and-orange-and-vermillion outline on the crenellated horizon that faded after about ten minutes. It began to get dark.

"Better get some wood," Henry said.

Husi and Samuel got up and gathered some driftwood from the irrigation ditch. They put it in a small pile a few feet from the porch steps. Samuel lit some small twigs with a lighter, and soon the fire was going strongly. Darkness came quickly.

"So, Mr. Rabb," Henry said, "I hear you were in the Battle of the Bulge."

"Right. Down in Luxembourg. Were you guys there?"

"Me and Samuel were, we parachuted into Belgium. Husi and Jimmy came later, by taxi." He laughed.

"Hey, man, that stake truck wasn't no damn taxi," Husi said.

Henry said something quickly to him in Papago.

"I'm sorry about swearing," Husi mumbled. "I forgot we have children here."

"I'm no kid," Adam said.

"Yeah, we came up with Patton," Jimmy said. "It was so cold, some of the guys made fires in the backs of the trucks. Below zero for weeks. I never been so cold, almost got frostbite in both feet."

The word *frostbite* made Joshua flinch, and his foot began to ache.

"You get wounded there?" Henry asked.

"Dad never talks about the war," Adam said. "He didn't like it."

"Yes, I got wounded and taken up to a hospital in Antwerp," Joshua said.

"Antwerp," Jimmy said. "Antwerp." His voice had a dreamy tone. "I was there for two months after the fighting was over. The girls were very grateful." He chuckled with his memories.

"Were they grateful to you too, Samuel?" Magdalena asked.

"No, I was over there as an army priest," Samuel said with a smile. "I just prayed all the time." It was obviously time to tease Magdalena.

"Right, *Father* Samuel," Henry said. "How come I only ever saw you wearing corporal's stripes and carrying a thirty-caliber carbine?"

"I was incognito," Samuel said. "There was a nun that looked like you, Magda. When she wasn't praying, her job was to keep Father Samuel warm."

"How did she do?" Magdalena asked, playing the game.

"I didn't get frostbite."

Henry mumbled something in Papago and snickered.

The other Indian men laughed. Magdalena looked just a little angry. Joshua decided to change the subject before the teasing got too strong.

"What do you guys do now?" he asked.

"I got a hundred-acre farm just south of Black Mountain," Henry said. "I got some pecans, some onions, and carrots."

"We work for the post office, me and Husi," Jimmy said. "We deliver way over on the Big Reservation."

Joshua looked at Samuel.

"I'm going to school at the University of Arizona. I'm getting a master's degree."

"Yeah, he's got brains," Henry said, his voice carrying none of the earlier sarcasm. "He got a *scholarship*." He said the word importantly. "He's gonna go on and become a professor. He's even got an apartment over by the university."

Samuel nodded, looking a little embarrassed at the attention. "I hope," he said.

"Hey, Dad, is 'Sergeant Preston of the Yukon' on yet?" Adam asked.

Joshua looked at his watch. "It's just ending. 'The Green Hornet' and 'The Scarlet Pimpernel' will be."

Adam went into the house and turned on the radio.

"You guys want to come in and listen to the radio?" Joshua asked.

"No thanks, Mr. Rabb. We'll stay out here," Henry said.

Joshua got up.

"I'm gonna sleep in front of the door here, Mr. Rabb," Henry said. "Two of the guys will sleep behind the house and two out front in the yard. You won't have any trouble tonight. We gotta go back to work in the morning, so we'll be gone early. But we'll be back again tomorrow night."

"Thank you, Henry. I'm really grateful."

"We are the ones who are grateful, Mr. Rabb."

Joshua went inside, and Hanna and Magdalena followed.

CHAPTER TWELVE

Adam walked with his father to the bureau the next morning. Joshua carried the Smith & Wesson .45 tucked into the waist of his trousers. When Adam asked why, his dad just said he was going to clean it. It was a monsoon day, overcast with billowing slate gray cumulus clouds, hot and humid already. Adam pointed at one of the clouds which looked like a great whale with its mouth open wide and flopping its tail.

Jimmy was sitting on Charger in the big mesquite field across the road from the bureau. He was getting a bird's-eye view of their new fortress. Adam walked up beside the horse.

"I think we gotta build up that far side in case we get attacked from the south." Jimmy pointed at the low back wall of the eight-foot-square fort.

"Then how we gonna get into the fort?" asked Adam.

"We gotta put a door in. Right here in front."

"Where we gonna get a door?"

"There's a old adobe shack on the reservation way down the riverbank. I bet there's a old door there."

"That'd be stealing," Adam said.

"Heck no it ain't. There ain't nobody livin there for as long as I know. Whatever's there has just been left."

"How are we gonna get it back if there is one?"

"I got a piece a rope." Jimmy held it up. "I can drag it behind Charger."

"Well, if you say."

"Okay, let's first get the doorway made." Jimmy climbed down from Charger, and the boys began rearranging the dead branches comprising the walls of their fortress. They removed branches from a three-foot area along the west wall and piled them on the south wall to build it up. After an hour they had all the walls up about four feet, to where they could just look over the tops to see who was attacking.

An old pickup stirred up the dust on Indian Agency Road and parked in front of the bureau. A white-haired Indian got out and went into the building and came out a moment later with Adam's father. They got in the pickup and were quickly obscured by their trail of dust as they drove off. Adam watched idly and then went back to his construction task.

"Let's go now and get the door," Jimmy said.

Adam gave him a boost up on Charger, and they walked through the field, crossed the irrigation ditch, and walked down the Santa Cruz River bank. As they passed Lourdes Hill a hundred yards to their right, they could see a bunch of people and a big truck and some kind of tractor about a half mile in front of them on the bank at the bend in the river near the Sand and Gravel Company.

"What's goin on up there?" Jimmy asked.

Adam shrugged.

As they got closer, Adam saw that the tractor was actually some kind of earth digger that had a big Ferris wheel contraption on the back which was cutting a two-foot-wide trench in the ground. Several Indians were watching, and Adam's dad was with them, looking kind of out of place in his gray suit. The company chain link fence ran for about thirty yards down the riverbank, six feet from the edge. Several men in tan uniforms came up onto the bank behind the fence and stood holding shotguns.

Then Buford Richards and Steve Lukis came up on the bank. The boys were about a hundred feet away, and nobody had seemed to notice them yet. Jimmy climbed down from Charger.

"What's happening?" Adam whispered.

"Looks like everybody's mad," Jimmy answered. "Let's get closer. I can't hear nothin'."

They walked closer to the trench and the men. Adam's father had his back to them. They could hear the voices clearly now.

"What're you assholes doin over there?" Buford called out.

No one answered. The trenching machine was forty or fifty feet from the company fence.

"Hey, I'm talking to you," Buford hollered. "What are you doin?"

No one answered.

Steve Lukis took a shotgun from one of the uniformed guards. He pointed it skyward and the blast echoed over the pasture.

"Jesus!" Jimmy said. "There's gonna be a war!"

Adam was frightened. His father looked so terribly out of place. In a suit, no gun. The Indian on the trenching machine got off and stood behind it, shielded. The other men also edged behind it.

Joshua walked about ten feet closer to the fence. "This is reservation land," he called out. "They can do anything they want here."

"You can't dig a trench over there," Lukis bellowed. "You get that backhoe out of here!"

Joshua walked back to the black pickup truck. He pulled the .45 revolver out through the passenger window. Adam watched him walk back up to the fence, cock the hammer, and aim the gun directly at Lukis's head, five feet away.

"You're crazy," Lukis said.

Joshua said nothing.

"Shoot him," Steve Lukis said to the guard next to him and handed him the shotgun.

The guard drew back. "I ain't gonna shoot him, Mr. Lukis, that's the BIA lawyer."

"I know who the fuck he is," Lukis snarled. "He's trying to destroy my property! Shoot him!"

The guard shook his head slowly.

"You're fired, you piece a shit. Get off my land," Lukis screamed.

Buford Richards put his hand on Lukis's shoulder. "Cool down, Steve. We can't just shoot a white man like he was a Indian. Just cool down. We'll get a injunction."

"Don't I have anybody out here with a pair of balls?" Lukis screamed, looking around at the seven armed security guards standing behind the fence. One of the guards slowly unsnapped the strap on his holster.

His father must have seen the movement out of the corner of his eye, because Adam heard him say, "Tell him if that gun comes out of his holster, I'll put a bullet between your eyes."

Adam was terrified. He had to protect his father. He cocked his BB gun and started running toward him. Joshua turned at the sound and movement and his eyes opened wide in shock. The revolver came down.

"Get out of here! Go home!" he bellowed at Adam.

Adam ran up to him. The guard pulled his gun out of his holster and pointed it at Joshua. Buford Richards wheeled and struck the guard a savage backhand blow to the face, knocking him to the ground.

"No guns," Buford yelled. "We hurt a white boy we got serious trouble! Get back to the plant!"

The guard stood up, wiping blood from his nose. He reached for the revolver and Buford kicked it away. "Get outta here, Sandy, goddamn it! Take the men with you back to the plant!"

The guard wiped more blood off and stared at his hand. He walked shakily down the riverbank toward the plant below. The other guards followed. Steve Lukis looked like his eyes would explode out of his head. His face was deep red.

Father Hausner ran up to the group, the cowl of his cassock bouncing around his shoulders, the wide sleeves bunched back around his elbows. The sleeves fell back down his arms as he came to a stop in front of Joshua. Brother Boniface, as always, was close behind. The bald crown of his head was glistening with sweat. He had a fringe of gray-blond hair and a thick, meaty face and blue eyes.

"You put that gun away!" Hausner yelled at Joshua. "No more shooting!"

"It's not me shooting, Father. It's your pal Lukis."

The priest looked confused, worried. He shook his finger at Joshua. "Until you started causing trouble, there's never been any need for anyone to shoot a gun around here. You are defiling the holy mission of Saint Francis and endangering my people." The priest was so angry that he was sputtering.

"Get your hand out of my face or I'll rip your fingers off," Joshua growled.

"Go into town and get a injunction from Buck Buchanan," Buford said to Lukis. It was not a suggestion, it was an order. "I'll stay here and keep an eye on this."

Lukis stood still for a moment, then turned around and walked down the bank.

Joshua turned to Adam. "Get in that damn pickup truck and don't you move a muscle or I'll give you a beating you'll never forget."

Adam started crying. His dad had never sworn at him before. He had never been spanked by his father. He ran to the pickup truck and got inside.

Edgar Hendly came running toward them. He had parked on the mission road a hundred yards away. He ran up soaked with sweat, puffing heavily.

"What happened? I heard a shot!"

"It's all over, Edgar. Just Steve Lukis trying to make a point."

"Anybody hurt?"

"No."

Edgar looked around, and his jaw dropped. "What the hell is Jimmy doin over there?"

Jimmy was standing behind Charger, trying his best to hide.

Edgar ran to him. Jimmy was sobbing loudly. His father lifted him like a sack of onions and put him on Charger's back. Edgar swatted the horse's rump hard. The horse loped away toward the irrigation ditch.

Edgar walked back toward Joshua, but Father Hausner intercepted him, shaking his finger in his face. "You get rid of that Jew," he snarled. "He is sent by the Devil. He will cause us irreparable harm. I heard about his watch being in Vittorio's pocket."

Edgar looked him over with a bitter frown. "I'll tell you what I'm a gonna do for you, Padre. I'm gonna let *you* take care a sayin mass and swipin nickels from these poor folks, and *I'm* gonna take care a the BIA. Thataway we might just keep on gettin along."

The priest scowled and his face reddened. He turned and strode back toward the mission, Brother Boniface shuffling behind him. Edgar walked up beside Joshua, and they stood watching the backhoe dig the ditch northward. A half hour, forty-five minutes.

"Here it is!" called out the Indian operating the backhoe.

The half-dozen Indians and the two white men gathered around the trench. The hoe had broken through timber braces about four feet underground, and a hole went down into the darkness of a mine tunnel. One of the Indians widened the top of the hole with a shovel, sat down with his legs hanging into it, and jumped into the tunnel. A moment later he threw out some stones.

Francisco Romero picked up two of them and studied them closely. He murmured in Papago to the others, and they nodded.

"Gold," he said to Joshua, handing him one of the rocks.

It didn't look like gold to Joshua, just a dull greenish-yellow network of capillaries in gray rock.

Two Indians hauled the man up out of the mine shaft. He walked up to Francisco. "Huge vein down there, Chief. Very high quality."

"Are you sure?" Joshua asked.

The Indian nodded. "I been working mines forty years—silver, gold, copper. I know gold."

"Hey you, Mr. Rabb," came a voice from beyond the fence.

Joshua looked over. It was the United States marshal, Oliver Friedkind, standing next to Buford Richards. Joshua walked over to him.

"Got a temporary restraining order here for you and an OSC." He handed the folded pages through the fence to Joshua.

"When's the Order to Show Cause?" Joshua asked.

"One o'clock."

"Today?"

"Yes, sir. Old Judge Buck looked like a giant tarantula bit him on the ass. Don't see him like that too often."

Joshua looked at his watch. It was a little after eleven. "Terrific," he mumbled, "only an hour and a half to prepare."

"Let's see what happens now, asshole," Buford said.

Joshua walked over to the backhoe. "All right, shut it down," he called out. "I've got to go to federal court. No more digging for the time being."

~~~~~~~

"Well now, Mr. Rabb," Judge Buchanan said, looking dourly down from the bench at Joshua, "I've sure been seeing a lot of you lately."

"The pleasure is all mine, your honor," Joshua said.

The judge looked sternly at him. "Don't be flippant to the court. There's been a serious accusation made against you."

"I apologize, your honor. I meant no disrespect to the court." Better watch my mouth, Joshua thought, or good ol' Judge Buck is going to have me for lunch.

Walter Chandler sat at plaintiff's table with Steve Lukis and Buford Richards. They were all obviously enjoying watching the display. Joshua heard Chandler whisper, "Now we'll watch the judge rip him a new asshole."

"Mr. Chandler here tells me that you destroyed a mine tunnel owned by his client, Mission Sand and Gravel." The judge glared at Joshua through spectacles perched on the end of his nose.

Chandler nodded his head at his former partner.

"Now what do you have to say about that, Mr. Rabb?"

"The tunnel is on reservation land, your honor. The company is mining gold. Mission Sand and Gravel not only doesn't have subsoil rights on its holdings, but it also has no authority to trespass on Papago land."

The judge wrote quickly on the pad in front of him. "Mr. Chandler?"

"Thank you, your honor." Chandler arose from his chair and stood behind the table. "Mr. Rabb is confused as to the law of mineral rights, your honor. Gold is not considered part of the subsoil. It is open for the taking by anyone who has a right to the surface on which it's found. This principle was established in the leading case of *Hopson versus Dumire*." He raised a leather-bound volume off the desk and read from it. " 'Mineral rights, denoting the rights to excavate and extricate below the loose surface soil, are applicable only to those minerals which are fixed in place and which do not freely meander or flow. In the case of the latter, principally gold, diamonds and emeralds in loose form, and other freestanding gems, they are not proprietary to the subsoil from whence they come, but are subject only to the law of surface rights.' Your honor, Evelyn Enterprises has the absolute right to that gold." He sat down.

"Mr. Rabb," the judge said.

"Thank you, your honor." Chandler had just done a sophisticated job of misstating the holding in the *Hopson* case. Joshua opened one of the two books he had brought to a place marked by a folded corner. "This is from *Prentiss versus Garheim*. 'Nothing in our previous decision of *Hopson versus Dumire* should be construed to mean that we exclude all minerals, that have a freestanding form, from being protected by subsoil rights in those frequent instances where they are fixed beneath the surface of the land. Placer gold, for example, panned in streams by the forty-niners, is clearly free-standing and free for the taking. However, when gold is found in fixed form as a vein in the deep earth, subsoil rights apply.' Your honor, this case is on all fours with the case at hand."

Joshua opened a brown paper bag and took out two rocks. "This is fixed into the mine tunnel, your honor. It only becomes free-standing when Mr. Lukis's employees go in there with jackhammers and drill it out of the walls." He walked to the bench and laid the rocks before the judge.

"Let me see that case, Mr. Rabb," the judge said.

Joshua handed him the open volume. The judge read for a few moments. He handed the book back to Joshua, took the spectacles off his nose, and settled back in his chair. He took the pocket watch out of his vest pocket, fiddled with it, wound it, and put it back in his pocket.

"Well, give me something to hang my hat on so I can rule in your favor, Wally," he said to his former partner. "Otherwise the Papagos are just going to appeal, and the Ninth Circuit Court of Appeals is going to give me a swift kick in the butt."

Walter Chandler stood up looking like a bloodhound with a sore foot. "Your honor, I just don't know how much more evidence I can present the court other than to say that Senator Lukis and his father before him have had rights to that ground for over half a century, and suddenly this lawyer from New York comes in and tries to turn us all topsy-turvy. His conduct is absolutely without justification. I ask the court to issue an injunction against the tribe interfering with our operations for at least six weeks so we can all try to settle this mess, and set a hearing for that time to determine whether the injunction will be made permanent."

"Well now, Mr. Rabb," the judge drawled, "I think old Wally's got a mighty sensible suggestion there. What do you say?"

"I say that in six weeks they'll steal another million dollars worth of Indian gold. I say that it's wrong, just plain wrong. The injunction must not be issued. This court would be committing a travesty of justice."

The judge glared at him. He toyed again with his watch for a full minute. Then he hunched over the bench and said, "The temporary restraining order is dissolved." He banged his gavel and left the bench.

It took a moment for Joshua to realize what had happened. He was stunned. He turned around slowly toward Francisco Romero sitting behind the railing and smiled and nodded. Romero's eyebrows raised, and he broke into a broad grin. Joshua looked at Chandler. The elderly lawyer had a dumbstruck look. Steven Lukis's eyes bulged inside the raccoon rings. He glowered at Joshua. Then he pointed his hand toward Joshua, forefinger out like the barrel of a gun, thumb up like a cocked hammer, and he bent his thumb forward twice. He got up from the table and walked out of the courtroom, Walter Chandler and Buford Richards silently following him.

Chief Romero and Joshua drove back to the reservation and parked again by the backhoe. Romero gave instructions to the operator, and the backhoe lumbered next to the fence. The four other Indians went in the flatbed truck to Black Mountain to collect large rocks. By the time they returned, the backhoe had exposed the mine tunnel to within six feet of its mouth in the riverbank. Joshua watched from the truck. He was exhausted.

His foot needed exercise or his hip would soon start aching. He got out of the truck, waved to Romero, and walked toward his house a mile and a half away. He forced himself not to favor his foot and to walk evenly. By the time he crossed the irrigation ditch, his gait was almost limp-free and he felt much better. He was also starving.

As he entered the yard, he could hear the radio playing. When he came up on the porch, the radio went off, and when he unlocked the front door, he heard Adam's bedroom door slam. He went inside and called through Adam's door, "You stay in there, no radio. The only reason you can come out is to go to the bathroom."

Hanna and Magdalena weren't home. He opened the icebox and took out the pot of leftover chili from last night. He put it on the stove to warm. He struggled out of his coat and necktie, slung them over a chair, and slumped into another chair. Three o'clock, he thought. A little time to rest. There won't be another murder till midnight.

~~~~~~~~

Hanna and Magdalena came back an hour later. They had walked to the market a couple of miles away on Valencia Road and bought pinto beans and marinated jalapeño peppers and Mexican white cheese and onions. Hanna sat with her father at the kitchen table while Magdalena prepared the refried beans.

"You know who I just saw over at the store?"

"No, honey, I sure don't," Joshua said.

"That boy, the tall blond boy."

Joshua wrinkled his brow. "You don't mean the boy who paid us a visit with his father and friends the other night?"

She nodded.

"Well, that's very nice, dear."

"*Daa-aad.* Don't be so sarcastic."

"Oh, scuse me for being unkind."

"*Daa-aad*. He's really very nice. He said he was sorry for what happened. He said they all were. The people around here aren't that way. It's just that they're real upset over all the murders."

"We're all upset, honey."

She looked at him earnestly. "He said he wanted to take me to the movies."

Joshua gritted his teeth. "Of course you told him to drop dead?"

She shook her head.

"You're not going out on a date with that boy."

"It's not a date, Dad. I just want to meet him at the Lyric tomorrow. *Beau Geste* is playing."

"No."

"*Daa-aad*, I'm old enough to go out on a date."

"Not with that trash, you're not. And you're only fourteen."

"I'll be fifteen in three months." She was getting whiney, and he was getting angry. "*Pleeease*, Dad."

"No."

She sat pouting in the chair.

"You and your brother are getting a little crazy. I guess it's all this wide-open space out here. But it's going to stop."

Magdalena was stirring the beans on the stove, and she kept her back to Joshua. "What if I go along, Mr. Rabb? And we just sort of run into him?" she said. "I'll be there all the time."

His eyes narrowed and he fixed Hanna with a stare. "No. That's final. We'll talk about it again in five years."

He got up and walked into the living room and slumped down on the couch. Why me, God? he thought. What the hell did I ever do to deserve all of this? Hanna came to the couch and sat down beside him.

"We've always talked things over, Daddy. You always said that I can talk to you about anything." Her voice was sober, adult.

"I lied." Now we're into the "Daddy" stage, he thought. What happened to "*Daa-aad*"?

"You can't get out of it that easily."

"Please, honey, don't be ridiculous. You're talking a lot of nonsense. There are a zillion other boys in the world. This one is trash."

"He is *not*. He's the captain of the baseball team at Tucson High and he's going to run for senior class president."

"And his father is the president of the goddamn Ku Klux Klan!"

"Daddy," she said chidingly. She gave him a slightly shocked look. Rachel used to do exactly that, thought Joshua. She'd get that same little hurt look in her eyes and begin to pout and then she'd sound a little indignant and lecture him about his temper and talking dirty.

"You shouldn't talk that way, Daddy, it just isn't nice," Hanna said indignantly. "You're just letting your temper get away with you, and you're not thinking rationally."

"How would you like a punch in the nose?"

"Well, Daddy, I think I'd like that very much." She looked at him with big innocent eyes. "I guess you're in a really bad mood, huh?"

"Today has been a real tough one. There was a little trouble."

She looked alarmed. "What happened?"

"Another run-in with the Lukis clan."

"Where's Adam? Is he okay?"

"He's okay. He's in his bedroom. He's being punished. You leave him alone. Go stir the beans."

She nodded. "I'll help Magdalena." She got up and walked into the kitchen. Now was definitely not the time to be fooling around with her father.

Adam slunk out of his bedroom and went into the bathroom. He started to pee.

"I didn't hear the toilet seat go up," Joshua called out.

The peeing stopped. The toilet seat banged against the water tank, and the peeing resumed. The toilet flushed.

"Come here," Joshua said.

Adam slunk over. He stood in front of his father not looking at him.

"What the hell did you think you were doing today? You could have gotten badly hurt."

Adam started crying.

"Come here." His father held out his arm.

The boy crawled into his father's lap, sobbing and shaking.

~~~~~~~

Night fell, and as the horizon purpled and the morning glories at the edge of the porch folded their petals inwardly, Henry, Samuel, Tomas, Husi, and Jimmy came across the irrigation ditch. They had left the duffel bags with their sleeping bags on the porch, but they carried their rifles and shotguns with them.

They sat on the porch and ate the refritos and tortillas that Magdalena and Hanna had made. Adam sat with them, subdued. The door was open allowing the cooler air onto the porch, and Joshua had fallen asleep on the couch. Magdalena hushed them all and told them not to make noise, because Mr. Rabb had had a hard day.

When Joshua woke up, it was almost eleven. He'd slept for over four hours. He was stiff from the lumpy confinement of the couch. He got up slowly and went to the window. Two of the Indians were sleeping in their bags in the front yard, illuminated only by the tepid light of a quarter moon. It was quiet. He went into the bedroom and undressed and stretched out on the bed, and he waited for the inevitable gunshots or explosions or whatever. But nothing happened. He lay there and slept fitfully while the night remained silent and undisturbed.

CHAPTER THIRTEEN

J oshua lay in bed a long time on Saturday morning. There was nothing to do if he got up. He wasn't in a social mood and didn't want to chat with anyone. So he lay there and read *A Bell for Adano*. It wasn't so bad, he decided. Italians weren't Nazis, they didn't run concentration camps, and they were portrayed as innocent, loving people. He read almost a hundred pages and finally put it down at eight-thirty. He showered and shaved and dressed in a cowboy shirt and Western pants and loafers. By then he could smell food cooking in the kitchen, and he went in and sat down at the table. Hanna and Adam came into the kitchen, drawn by the aroma. They sat down and Magdalena gave them each a plate of hash brown potatoes and eggs.

"I'm going to be gone until probably three or four," Joshua said. "I want all of you staying around the house today. Don't leave the yard, okay?"

Both children nodded.

"And I'm bringing a guest for dinner. It's the nurse who took care of Ignacio Antone up at Mount Lemmon."

His children didn't say anything. They were busy eating.

"Okay, I'll see you later," Joshua said, standing up from the table.

He had one loose end to tie up before the preliminary hearing started again on Wednesday: Dr. Howard Falconer, at the university. The coroner, Dr. Wolfe, had said that Falconer might know something about blood types. It was a long shot, searching for a pin in the dark, but what else was there? Ignacio didn't rape Sister Martha—that was a certainty. And he wasn't the one who got cut and bled all over her habit—that also was certain. But someone did. Someone named Juan Carlos, Joshua was dead sure. But that didn't help a bit. Ignacio had been there, and he was as culpable of first-degree murder as the actual killer under the felony murder rule, unless of course he could prove to Judge Buchanan that Ignacio didn't know anything about the killing and rape and didn't take part. But how could he prove that? No way.

He drove to the university, and it took him half an hour of asking around to locate Professor Falconer's office in the basement of the Arizona State Museum. Joshua found the door marked FORENSIC PHYSICAL ANTHROPOLOGY and went into a large room filled with tables upon which were piled bones of every description. The formaldehyde smell was almost choking. An old man wearing a jeweler's loupe and a green visor over thin gray hair was peering closely at something on his desk. He looked up startled, annoyed. "What is it?" he demanded.

"Professor Falconer?" Joshua asked.

~~~~~~

Magdalena had an oddly distant look. She was washing the breakfast dishes. Hanna and Adam were drying.

"What's wrong?" Hanna asked.

"Today is the day my parents died," Magdalena said.

"When did it happen?" Hanna asked.

"When I was ten."

"Both on the same day?" Adam asked.

"Yes. They got some terrible sickness in an epidemic, we called it *chuk wihosig*, black vomit. It took three days and they were gone. My grandfather wouldn't let me stay with them. He said it was contagious."

"Our mom died too," Adam said. "In an accident."

"Yes, I know."

They finished the dishes.

"I'd like to go to mass at ten-thirty this morning at the mission, but I can't leave you here alone. Your dad wanted me to watch you till he came home."

"We'll be okay," Adam said. "He just thinks we're kids."

"Well, I can't leave you alone."

"We could come with you," Hanna said.

"Is that okay, Adam?" Magdalena looked at him.

"Sure," he said. "But I'd rather hunt buffalo with Jimmy." He grinned.

"So would I," Magdalena said.

She got her rosary and missal out of her room, and they walked across the ditch to the reservation. Masses were said every day at eight and ten-thirty in the morning, and the eight bells ringing in the two towers had become a familiar sound to them. Indians—mostly women, except for Sundays when some of the men also would come—could be seen walking from the village area to the mission. Most of them wore faded black dresses to their ankles and long drab gray or black scarves covering their heads, and those who had the extra money to spend wore laced shoes and black stockings instead of sandals.

They walked into the mission. Magdalena touched the holy water and crossed herself. Hanna and Adam followed meekly behind, a little daunted by the ornate, stately church. There were about thirty women. Magdalena knelt behind several rows of them near the transept. Adam and Hanna knelt beside her. To the front on their left, on a bench set crosswise in the apse, sat three nuns in full habits and wimples.

Father Hausner came out of the sacristy and conducted the mass. Brother Boniface assisted him. It was all in Latin until the Gospel reading.

Then Father Hausner faced the congregation and said, "I will depart today in our reading of the Holy Gospel to read to you from chapter eleven of the Gospel of Saint John." He turned back to the altar and opened the Bible on it. Brother Boniface knelt beside him.

" 'Now a certain man was sick named Lazarus, of Bethany, the town of Mary and her sister Martha. Now Jesus loved Martha and her sister and Lazarus. When he had heard that Lazarus was sick, he saith to his disciples, Let us go into Judea again. And his disciples saith unto him, Master, the Jews have lately sought to stone thee, why goest thou there again? And Jesus saith unto them, Our friend Lazarus sleepeth, but I go that I may awake him. Then said Jesus unto them plainly, Lazarus is dead. When Jesus went to Bethany, he found that Lazarus had lain already four days in his grave. Then Martha, as soon as she heard that Jesus was come, ran out to greet him. And Jesus saith: I am the resurrection and the life; he that believeth in me, though he were dead, yet shall he live, and whosoever believeth in me shall never die. Dost thou believe? And Martha saith unto him: Yea, Lord, I believe that thou art the Christ. And Jesus lifted up his eyes and he cried with a loud voice, Lazarus, come forth. And he that was dead came forth. Now many of the Jews who had come to Mary and Martha and had seen the things which Jesus did, believed in him. But some of them went their ways to the Pharisees and told them what things Jesus had done. Then the chief priests and Pharisees gathered a council together and said, What do we do? For this man doth many miracles. And from that day forth they took counsel together to put him to death. Jesus therefore walked no more openly among the Jews.' "

Father Hausner closed the Bible and bent over and kissed it. He turned toward the congregation.

"I speak to you today of things which burden my heart," he said. "We have lost our dear Sister Martha, and she is now in the eternal keeping of our Lord and Savior Jesus of Nazareth. But the horror of her death still angers our souls, and the evil of her murderer and his defender defile this holy mission. For her murderer came from among you, and his defender comes from those very Jews who knew not the one and eternal Christ."

Magdalena gasped and clutched her chest as though she were

having a heart attack. Hanna was frightened by the solemn pronouncements of the priest, which she barely understood— but just enough to know that it was her father and Ignacio Antone who were being excoriated by him. The look of shock on Magdalena's face frightened her even more. Adam was looking at them both in perplexity, not having understood a word of what the priest said.

"And they who conspired to murder the holy Son of God now conspire to protect the murderer of his dear friend Martha." Father Hausner's voice was stentorian. He had worked himself into a passion. "May God strike down these spawns of Satan! May God blot them out from our midst, they are a defilement to us!"

Magdalena stood up. Hanna and Adam also stood. They walked out of the church. Well over half of the congregation also left. Most of them stood silently in the patio courtyard of the church and stared at each other in melancholy silence. They began slowly to drift away to their homes. Magdalena stood weeping and quivering. Hanna and Adam held on to her arms.

A nun came out of the church and walked up to Magdalena, shaking her finger. She was young, not more than twenty-two or twenty-three, and except for the look of revulsion in her eyes and blanched cheeks she would have been quite pretty. "May God have mercy on your soul, girl. You should not be living in that evil household. And these must be his issue. How dare you bring the son and daughter of such a father into God's holy temple?" She crossed herself. "Sister Agatha always told me you would come to no good, but I used to say, 'Agatha, you are too hard on our young Papago charges, they are really just unkempt children in need of a good mother.' And I have always tried to be that mother. But Agatha is right. Once the corruption is in you, it is like a fouled stream, and none of our good works—"

Magdalena slapped the nun so hard that her wimple flew off, leaving only the white scarf over her hair. Blood trickled from her nose. Magdalena had stopped crying, and her lips were curled in anger.

"We are good Catholics, Sister Mary Rose, better than many of you who come to minister to our souls. It is you who need the ministry."

The nun looked frightened. She tenderly fingered the bright red bruise on her cheek. She stepped back and made the sign of the cross.

"I'm not a vampire, Sister. I'm not so easy to get rid of."

"Steve Lukis was right about you all," the nun said in a shocked, thin voice. "He said you were a generation of vipers sent here to test our souls, to tempt us in the way of the Devil. He said you wanted to take away our money for the school and our government food. You shall not succeed in your evil mission." She picked up her wimple and walked unsteadily back into the church.

"I don't believe what just happened," Hanna said.

"Neither do I," Magdalena said. "Sometimes the nuns are a little mean, but I've never seen anybody like her before. She's been here two years, but I guess she doesn't like the Papagos very much."

"Or us neither," Adam said.

"Well, she probably didn't have a very happy childhood," Hanna said.

"Yeah," Magdalena said. "Come on, let's go for a walk to Black Mountain. It's very peaceful there. I don't want to go back and get cooped up in the house yet."

They all joined hands, Magdalena in the middle, and walked to Black Mountain. There was an old cement cistern about a hundred feet up the slope that was used to collect rain. It was hidden behind some rocks and jutted out so that people could stand under it and fill water buckets from two spigots. The crest of the shallow hill was four hundred feet above it. They walked up the steep grade and sat down on the crest against a large boulder.

They could hear the bells of the church pealing, and they watched the last of the parishioners walk to their homes. A few minutes later they saw one of the priests come out of the church and walk this way. He got to the bottom of the hill and they could see it was Brother Boniface. He had his cowl down, and his tonsured bald spot gleamed in the sun. They lost sight of him as he walked under an outcropping.

Hanna was mortified by Father Hausner's words and haunted by the nun's hateful look. "Is what my daddy is doing right?" She looked searchingly at Magdalena.

"Yes. I believe it is," Magdalena said.

"But how can it be?" Adam said. "Most everybody hates him for it."

"What I'm going to say may sound dumb," Magdalena said, "but I think it's very hard to do what's right when a lot of people are against you. But you still just have to do it."

"But how do you know what's right?" Hanna said. "Especially when so many people disagree?"

Magdalena shook her head. "I don't know how, but men like your father know, they just somehow know. Your father just automatically takes it upon himself to do right, because that's the kind of man he is. It's as simple as that."

They sat quietly for a half hour, absorbed in their own thoughts.

"You about ready for lunch?" Magdalena asked.

They both nodded. They walked slowly down the hill. As the cistern came into view, they heard what sounded like weeping. They passed by the cistern, some forty feet away, and Brother Boniface was under the trickle of water from one of the faucets, standing nude, his back to them, whipping his back with a faggot of thorny mesquite branches. He was crying out painfully with each self-delivered scourge. Blood rolled down his back in rivulets.

He seemed in a trance, and he didn't act as though he was aware of them. They ran down the hill to the bottom.

"My God," Magdalena gasped, crossing herself. "That was perverted."

"Boy, did you see that?" Adam said, out of breath. "That's the scariest thing I ever saw in my whole life." He took hold of Magdalena's hand for protection and glanced back fearfully to be sure they weren't being pursued.

Hanna looked like she had been bitten by a wasp. "He must be crazy," she said.

"This has been a heck of a day," Magdalena said. She shook her head and frowned bitterly. "Please don't tell your father about all this. He'll shoot me for bringing you here."

〰〰〰

By the time Joshua parked in the lot beside Goldberg's department store it was almost twelve-thirty. He went inside, and Penny was not there, or she had already left. He was upset with himself for being so late, but it couldn't be helped. He looked around the men's shoe department, which was near the door, trying to act nonchalant. He studied the same pair of Johnson and Murphy brogans for ten minutes, and the salesman stood nearby and eyed him suspiciously.

"Hi," Penny said, coming up behind him.

Her blond hair fell loosely around her shoulders, and she was wearing a pale red jersey dress that clung closely to her figure and dimpled at her navel. She was lovely.

"Sorry I was late," he said.

"Oh, that's okay. I've been over in the dress department trying on a few things. I came over to look for you a couple of times."

"You hungry?" he asked.

"Starved."

"What do you like?"

"Everything."

"Well, we can go downstairs right here."

"Let's go."

They went down to the restaurant.

They gave their orders to a Western-clad waitress and the food came quickly. A department store restaurant wasn't designed for long casual dining, but for fast turnaround calculated to get the customers back on the sales floor to spend their money.

"So how did you get the name Penny?" Joshua asked.

"My dad and mom gave it to me."

He laughed. "I assumed that. What's it short for, Penelope?"

"No, Peninah. My father taught classics at Rutgers. Peninah's from the Bible."

"Yes, I know. She was one of the two wives of Elkanah."

Penny raised her eyebrows in surprise. "You study in a yeshiva?"

He shook his head. "No, I was hospitalized in Belgium for three months, and the only things in English to read were *The Collected Short Stories of O. Henry* and the Bible. After I read O. Henry six times, I couldn't handle it again. So I started on the Bible."

They ate slowly, talking, finding out about each other, and then they walked to the parking lot. They each got into their own car, and Penny followed Joshua home and parked behind the De Soto across from the irrigation ditch.

Adam was on the floor in front of the radio doing a jigsaw puzzle. Hanna was sitting on the couch half-reading a Nancy Drew book, half listening to "I Love a Mystery" on the radio. Magdalena sat in the upholstered chair knitting a red wool sweater.

Joshua and Penny walked into the house, and Hanna stared at her, Magdalena opened her eyes wide, and Adam glanced up, then went back to his puzzle.

"I'd like to introduce Penny Chesser. This is Hanna, my daughter, our friend, Magdalena, and my son, Adam."

"Nice to meet you all," Penny said.

Magdalena smiled and said, "Hello." Hanna and Adam just stared at her.

"Don't you two have any manners?" Joshua asked, disconcerted by the shocked look on his children's faces.

"Hello," Hanna mumbled, staring. "Won't you sit down?"

"Hello," Adam said, not looking at her and concentrating on the puzzle.

Magdalena walked into the kitchen.

Penny sat down. Joshua followed Magdalena into the kitchen.

"What the heck's got into them?" he whispered.

She turned to him. "I guess they didn't think she'd be so pretty," she whispered.

Joshua studied Magdalena. "Oh, I see." He nodded soberly as it dawned on him. "I'm sorry, I didn't realize."

She was already busy at the stove, her back turned to him.

"She said your brother's doing fine. No permanent effects of the beating he took."

Magdalena turned around to him and smiled gratefully. "I'll be out in a minute. I just have to start soaking the lima beans. And tell her 'thank you' for Ignacio." She turned back to the stove.

Well, thought Joshua, I didn't expect all of this. She's the first woman the kids have seen me with since their mother died, and I should have been more sensitive. Damn, I've been too self-absorbed, I just didn't think about this. He walked into the living room.

"Bathroom?" Penny asked.

Joshua pointed, and she went into it. Joshua stood in the middle of the floor and looked at his children.

"Please be polite to her," he whispered. "She's very nice."

"We didn't think she'd be so pretty," Adam said. "She's a nurse."

"Some nurses are pretty."

"Is this a date?" Hanna looked hard at her father.

He nodded. "Yes, I guess so."

"We didn't know it was going to be a date."

"I'm sorry I didn't explain it to you as well as I should have. I met her because she was treating Ignacio Antone, and I like her a lot."

"You loved Mommy, didn't you?" Adam said, looking with round eyes at his father.

Joshua got down on his knees on the floor. "Yes, I did," he whispered. "We all did. But Mommy's been dead a long time, and I'm lonesome sometimes. Nobody will ever take Mommy's place, but it's okay for us to treat Penny nicely. That won't hurt Mommy."

The toilet flushed.

"Please," Joshua implored, looking from Adam to Hanna.

Penny came out and said, "Well, I'm going to have to be going. I like to get back up the mountain before it gets dark."

Hanna bit her lip and swallowed. She got up and walked over to Penny and took her hand in both of hers. "Please stay. We really didn't mean to be rude."

Magdalena came out of the kitchen carrying a plate. "Here is a whole bunch of oatmeal cookies I made this morning. I hope they're good."

They each took a cookie and made a big show of chewing and smiling approvingly. Penny sat down on the upholstered chair. Hanna and Magdalena sat on the couch.

"What are you knitting?" Penny asked.

"Oh, it's just a sweater for a friend," Magdalena said.

"It's really a pretty color," Penny said. Her smile was genuine and disarming. The atmosphere softened.

"You live on Mount Lemmon?" Adam asked.

She nodded.

"Dad said it's really neat up there, and cool," Adam said.

"Yes, it's a forest, and it's never more than seventy-five or eighty degrees. I love it there."

"We're from back East," Adam said.

"I know." She smiled. "Your dad told me."

"We came out here 'cause Dad didn't like to take the subway," Adam said.

"Do you like it here?"

He nodded. "Yeah, it's neat. It's like in the Western movies. Except the Indians look a lot different. You know, they don't wear war paint and go around in loincloths. Except at the Fourth of July picnic."

"You like it here, Hanna?"

She shrugged. "Not so much. I had to leave my friends. And Dad won't let me go out on dates. He thinks everybody wants to attack me." Her voice was a little petulant.

Joshua stared at her and narrowed his eyes.

"Honey, as pretty as you are, I don't blame your dad for being very careful." Penny looked earnestly at Hanna.

Hanna looked surprised. A smile gradually took over from her frown.

They heard footsteps on the porch and voices in Papago.

"Those are some friends of ours from the reservation," Joshua said. He got up and opened the door. "Nice to see you guys," he called out.

"Good afternoon, Mr. Rabb," Henry said. "We heard some

rumors, so we thought we'd come over a little earlier today."

Joshua looked at his watch. Only four o'clock. He stepped out on the porch and closed the door behind him. "What's up?" he asked in a low voice.

Henry shrugged and answered in an equally low voice. "Just heavy rumors. The guard, Sandy, who got his nose broken yesterday was in a bar shooting his mouth off, about how he's going to kill you, going to get your daughter."

"Just booze talking," Joshua said.

"Let's hope so. We also hear that Steve Lukis and Buford Richards bought a whole load of dynamite from the copper company down at Sahuarita."

Joshua shook his head. "What's next, they're going to blow up the BIA?"

Henry shrugged. "Don't know, Mr. Rabb. But nothing is going to happen to your family."

Joshua nodded. His face was drawn. He went back into the living room, and Magdalena looked at him oddly.

"Trouble?" she asked.

He glanced apologetically at Penny, sorry for having to say anything in front of her that would be upsetting, but it was unfair not to be honest with Magdalena and the children. "Henry says there's a rumor that there might be some more trouble tonight."

Penny looked around at the long faces. "Is something wrong?"

"Maybe. I've been having a little dispute with the Sand and Gravel Company about how much they can encroach on reservation land. Senator Lukis owns the company, and they've drilled a pirate tunnel into Indian land. They've got a few hotheads over there who might try to make a little trouble. But nothing will happen to us. There are some young men outside from the reservation who'll see to that."

"What kind of trouble?" Penny asked.

He shrugged. "Guns. Explosives."

"Oh," she said, sitting forward stiffly, her forehead wrinkled with concern. "And who's protecting the fort outside?"

"Five Indians with rifles."

She stared at him, her mouth open a little.

"Maybe you'd best go on home," he said apologetically.

"No," she said slowly, "I don't think so."

"But this is really very dang—"

"You need any help with dinner, Magdalena?" Penny asked. "Come on, Hanna. Let's help Magdalena rustle up some grub for the menfolk." She sounded like she was trying to do an imitation of Dale Evans.

Hanna walked with her into the kitchen.

Joshua sat down on the couch and watched Adam put pieces into the jigsaw puzzle. Big-band music was playing on the radio, some orchestra and singer from the ballroom of the Waldorf-Astoria.

"Is she gonna be our new mom?" Adam asked quietly, looking searchingly at his father.

"I don't know, Adam. I haven't thought about it."

Two more pieces in the puzzle.

"She's real pretty," Adam said.

Three more pieces in the puzzle.

"Mom was real pretty, too, wasn't she, Dad?" He looked at his father with sad eyes.

Joshua got down on the floor and fitted two more pieces in the puzzle. "Yes," he said quietly.

≈≈≈

Penny got up to leave at eight-thirty. At her car, in the darkness, she kissed Joshua long and deeply and held him.

There was no moon, no light. It was an overcast night. Joshua watched her drive away and walked back to the porch and sat down on the step. Henry was sitting against the wall of the house smoking a cigar, and the aroma was good.

"She's beautiful," Henry said.

"Yeah," Joshua said.

The smoke curled around them and hung like a wispy cirrus cloud in the breezeless humid air.

"Where are the rest of the boys?" Joshua asked.

"Scattered around."

"I didn't even see them."

"That's the point."

Joshua nodded. He began to stand up. The roar of an enormous explosion startled him and jolted him back down. He saw a ball of flame shoot skyward near the dim night lights of the Sand and Gravel Company a mile and a half away.

Henry was on his feet. "There it is," he said.

The other four Indians came running to the front yard, carrying their rifles. Hanna and Magdalena and Adam came out on the porch.

"I think they blew up the mine," Joshua said. "Adam, bring me the gun. Magdalena, you have the thirty-eight?"

She nodded.

"Okay. You four guys stay here. Henry, come with me over to the reservation." He took the revolver from Adam.

Joshua drove around to the reservation entrance off the Nogales Highway, drove down Mission Road, and turned into the pasture where the mine tunnel was located. He parked beside the rubble of what was now a crater sixty feet in diameter. The backhoe was a huge lump of twisted steel. The flatbed truck had no bed at all and was toppled onto its crushed roof. The priests and nuns from the mission were standing at the edge of the field. Several Indians were already standing by the pit. Macario Antone drove up in his pickup.

They stood silently surveying the blast area.

"Macario, who has a phone?" Joshua asked.

"Only in the mission office and the rectory."

"Henry, take the car and go over to the mission and call Tom Delahanty, the FBI man." He handed Henry the keys.

Francisco Romero drove up. "Now we got a open pit mine," he said ruefully, walking up beside Joshua and Macario.

They stood quietly for ten minutes. Henry drove up. He walked over to Joshua and handed him the keys. "He sounded drunk. I told him about the explosion, to come right over. He said maybe."

Buford Richards and two company guards came walking up the riverbank. Fifty feet of the fence had been obliterated. They walked up to Joshua and the three Indians.

"Big hole, huh?" Buford said, shaking his head.

Nobody responded.

"Just like alchemy," Buford said. "Turned all that gold into dust." He chortled.

"You wouldn't know who the alchemist was, would you, Buford?"

"Why no, Mr. Rabb, I sure wouldn't, no sir. Looks to me like you had a methane gas buildup, done exploded on you. Minin is a dangerous occupation, you can bet on that. Not somethin for amateurs."

Three of the Indians were searching in the pit with flashlights. One of them walked up to Chief Romero and handed him what looked like a piece of shredded red wax paper.

"Dynamite," Romero said, handing the shred of paper to Joshua.

A car lumbered through the field and parked nearby. Tom Delahanty got out and walked up to the men. His shirt was half out of his trousers and he smelled of alcohol. But he wasn't drunk.

"Howdy, Tom," Buford said.

"What's going on here?" the FBI agent asked.

"Had a methane explosion in their mine tunnel, Tom. Blew the son of a bitch to kingdom come."

Joshua handed Delahanty the red wax paper. "Dynamite," he said.

The agent peered at it closely and put it in his shirt pocket.

"Methane gas, Buford?" Delahanty asked.

"Yep, sure as hell. They done closed up the tunnel with rock yesterday mornin, not a smart thing to do, particular in the middle of the summer, it bein so hot and all. Boom!"

"You don't believe that bullshit, do you?" Joshua said to the agent.

"You got a attitude, boy," Delahanty said, shaking his head. "You got a real shitty attitude."

"Give me that piece of paper back," Joshua said. "I'll take it to the sheriff's office, see what they think it is."

"Don't be gettin too far out of line, boy. This is federal jurisdiction here; ain't no business of the sheriff. I'll take care of the evidence."

"Look, you corrupt bastard," Joshua growled, looking hard at Delahanty. "There'd better be a real investigation of this explosion, or I'll call the FBI headquarters in Washington."

The agent reached behind his back and pulled out a snub-nosed revolver. He stepped to Joshua and held the revolver an inch from Joshua's nose. "You keep it up, boy, you gonna be honkin lead snot outta your nose."

"In front of fifty witnesses?" Joshua said, not moving.

Delahanty looked around, stepped slowly back, stared with hatred at him, and replaced the revolver in the holster at the small of his back. He walked back to his car and drove off.

"You gonna go a little too far one a these days," Buford said. "Then somebody's gonna hand you your nuts." He turned and walked away, followed by the two guards. Everyone slowly dispersed.

Edgar Hendly was standing in the yard with the other four Indians when Joshua and Henry drove up. "Reckon Steve and his boys blew up the mine tunnel?"

Joshua nodded.

"This shit ever gonna end?"

Joshua shrugged. Edgar walked back up Indian Agency Road. Joshua walked into the house, into his bedroom, and slammed the door shut.

~~~~~~

It was impossible to sleep. Joshua rolled over on his side, his back, his stomach. Every position was uncomfortable. He was obsessed with the desire to take the Smith & Wesson .45 and push the barrel into Tom Delahanty's or Steve Lukis's or Buford Richards's mouth and pull the trigger. Splatter their brains around. Rid the world of filth.

He dozed on and off restlessly, alternating with clutching the sheets and staring into the impenetrable blackness. He woke up with a start at some real or imagined noise, but he knew that with five Indians outside, there was really nothing to fear. But it wasn't sleep that he needed. He got up at the first light of dawn, a little after four, brushed his teeth and shaved and showered and dressed quietly. He went outside, and Henry jerked awake.

"I'll be back by nine o'clock," Joshua whispered. "Please don't leave until I get back."

"Don't worry, Mr. Rabb, we'll take care of them. We're going to be able to stay until about four o'clock this afternoon. Then we've got to get back. I got crops going in. Jimmy and Husi have to get back to Sells."

"That's fine," Joshua said. "I don't think there'll be any more trouble. I'm really grateful for what you've done."

It was a fresh morning, probably seventy degrees, and the skies were still overcast. Joshua drove to the Catalina Highway, and as he ascended toward Mount Lemmon it became much cooler. By six-fifteen, when he reached the ranger station, it was only fifty-five or sixty degrees and semidark because of the overcast and thick tall trees. He drove down the narrow lane to Penny's cabin and parked behind the shiny roadster.

She opened the door as he climbed up onto the porch. She was wearing a thin cotton nightshirt that clung enticingly to her puckered nipples. "Oh God, I was so frightened," she gasped and hugged him closely.

"What happened?"

"Someone was prowling around the cabin last night. I was scared to death."

"You sure it wasn't an animal?"

She nodded. "Animals don't make the kind of sounds in the leaves that this guy did."

"Do you have any idea who it was?"

She shook her head. "I took a shot into the trees from the dormer window. I heard running in the woods and then he was gone." She pointed at the .22 rifle leaning against the wall by the door. "I have that for courage."

His intense, grave look disconcerted her. "What's going on?" she asked, searching his face.

Joshua sat down on the couch. "I'm not sure. But there have been three deaths on the reservation in the last couple of weeks, and at least two of them weren't accidental. They may have something to do with the problem I told you about that I'm having with Senator Lukis's rock and sand company stealing the Indians' minerals. And there was an explosion in the mine tunnel last night after you left."

She sat down next to him. "You don't really think that a United States senator is having people killed because of a mine?" Her tone was incredulous.

He shrugged and looked back at her with troubled eyes. "But anyway, I had no idea that anyone knew anything about you."

"You really think that someone's"—she searched for the right word—"*stalking* me?"

"I just don't know. I really can't figure this whole thing. But I think it's dangerous for you to stay here alone, at least for right now. You should come into Tucson for a while."

She pulled back from him and studied his eyes again. "I just can't leave here like that, quit my job. I need it. I need the money. Don't you think that as long as I have that twenty-two rifle handy, I'll be okay?"

He shook his head slowly. "I don't know. I think we're dealing with some crazy man, a real lunatic. I'm afraid for your safety."

She looked into his tired eyes. "You look real tired, like you haven't slept all night," she said.

"You kept me awake all night." He gave her a wry smile.

"Well, then I'd better get you to bed right now to make amends."

She took the .22 rifle and walked up the stairs to the dormer bedroom. She laid the rifle beside the bed. The peak of the roof was directly over the middle of the bed. Joshua had to hunch over to keep from hitting his head on the sharply angled knotty pine ceiling.

He watched Penny undress, and she was gorgeous. Big round dark pink areolas and pouting nipples on creamy big breasts. Slender and long-waisted with a plum-shaped behind and a luxuriant blond triangle. He sat on the edge of the bed unmoving, watching, and she came to him and unsnapped his cowboy shirt and undid his belt buckle and unzipped his pants. He kicked off his loafers, stood up and pulled off his pants and underwear. They stood next to the bed and kissed, and his head literally swam with the pleasure of being with her.

Penny got in bed and pulled the quilt up to her chin. "Brrrrr!" she said. She watched him undress, and he watched her watch him. He felt oddly unembarrassed about the puckered stump of his arm. He struggled his shirt off and dropped it on the floor.

There were two skylights in the steep ceiling, and he could see the tops of swaying pines and Douglas firs and aspens. She rubbed his arm and chest to warm him up. Her hand crawled delicately down his chest, his stomach, and she touched him. She put her hand around him and held him. He felt a little light-headed. Incredible what a woman's hand on that little devil will do to a man, he thought. Like holding the throttle of a fighter airplane, complete fingertip control. The image flashed instantly before his mind's eye, but he didn't feel flippant about her love, about her sharing herself with him.

He turned his face toward hers and kissed her lips. He touched the butter soft skin of her belly and her thighs. She sighed with pleasure.

Then he lay back and she ran her tongue down his chest and kissed his belly button. She sat on him and he entered her, and they stared at each other as they rocked slowly, then faster, faster, and she let out a groan and he gasped and they pressed hard to each other.

She dozed lightly with her face nestled in his chest. The room had become warm from their lovemaking, and the covers were off of them. Joshua felt comfortable and safe. He hadn't felt like this for years. But he knew he wasn't safe; neither of them was. He listened to her soft breathing of untroubled sleep, and he turned his face to her and kissed her forehead softly. She awoke slowly and snuggled closer against him.

"I think you should come stay in Tucson for a week or two. It could have been anything last night, but we can't take a chance that it's related to the killings. Do you have any girlfriends in Tucson, anywhere you could stay?"

"No, no one."

"Well, this time of year, there aren't any vacationers there. Too hot. I bet the Cattleman's Hotel is practically empty. They've probably got very low rates, maybe even a weekly rate."

She turned her face up into his. He kissed the tip of her nose. "I only have a few dollars," she said.

"I'll help. Can you take the time off?"

She shrugged. "Well, I have a week of vacation coming, and there's nothing much happening up here. I only get busy during the winter, ski accidents mostly. I'll go into Summerhaven and see the chief ranger and ask him if I can take my vacation now. I don't see why not."

"Okay, I'll go down and check the Cattleman's, maybe some others. I'm coming back up here at two o'clock with Macario Antone. He's going to visit his grandson. I'll come by here for you a little after that."

"You sure you're not just scaring me so you can lure me into Tucson and have your way with me?" She smiled and propped herself on one elbow, looking at him askance.

"I'm not sure at all," he said. "Especially when you rub me there."

"Ooooh, goody!" she giggled.

Despite Joshua's apprehensions, Macario and he had no trouble with the guards at the detention center. When Macario first saw his grandson, his leathery-jowled, furrowed face broke into a smile of astonishing power. And Ignacio, seeing this warmth for the first time in years, was rendered speechless, like a little boy luxuriating in much-needed love, his face beaming. They embraced, and a guard gruffly called over that they weren't permitted to touch. Then they sat across from each other on benches around a redwood picnic table within a chain link enclosure, which constituted the visitors' area, and they spoke quietly in Papago.

Joshua told Macario that he'd pick him up in an hour. He drove to Penny's cabin and parked next to it. The roadster wasn't there, and he had an odd sensation that something was wrong. He walked up the stairs of the porch and there was a folded piece of notepaper thumbtacked to the front door: *Joshua—I went into Summerhaven to talk to the chief ranger. Be right back.*

It was written in black ink in a neat hand. Below it was scribbled in pencil *Don't count on it.*

Joshua was immediately chilled. He had been right this morning: Penny was in danger.

He ran to his car and backed down the trail to the clearing in front of the ranger station. He spun the car around and skidded over the loose dirt and pebbles onto the highway to Summerhaven. Where would he look? He didn't know. But Summerhaven was tiny, and the chief ranger must live in one of the cabins scattered around the town in the woods. A shiny black Chevy roadster wouldn't be hard to find. He had a hollow feeling in his stomach. He was afraid to think about what the bastard would do if he actually got to Penny. No, that wasn't true. He knew what the bastard would do. Delahanty? Lukis? Richards?

The roadster was parked beside the little general store. Joshua skidded to a stop alongside of it in a billow of dirt and flying gravel. He ran inside the store.

"Penny Chesser?" he gasped to the clerk, a huge young woman wearing a great cotton housedress that looked like a burlap bag. She had black roots for an inch under golden hair hanging to the middle of her back. A three-hundred-pound Rapunzel.

"Up the hill, sweetie," she said, pointing her thumb over her shoulder. Her blue eyes sparkled atop round pink cheeks. "Up at the ranger's. But you'll get a better roll with me than with that chocolate-covered steel wool pad." Her voice was soft and sultry. She let out a huge laugh.

Joshua ran out of the store and almost knocked Penny over. She looked at him strangely. "What's with you?"

He gaped at her, deeply relieved that she was safe. He handed her the note.

She read it and a quizzical look clouded her eyes. "Maybe it's just someone who came to visit me playing a joke," she offered.

"I hope so," Joshua said.

"Did I tell you that an FBI agent named Delahanty came up here to talk to me about Ignacio Antone a few days ago? He's a really scary guy."

Joshua gritted his teeth. "It's a good thing that you're coming down to Tucson with me. That son of a bitch is dangerous."

"I've got a week of vacation," she said. "You think you can protect me that long?"

"Damn right, even if I have to stay with you twenty-four hours a day."

They both smiled.

"The Cattleman's is only twenty-six dollars a week."

"Well, I have about forty saved," she said.

"Mrs. Midas." He laughed. "I'll follow you over to the cabin and help you load your stuff."

"I'm just taking a couple of small suitcases."

"Fine. Then you can follow me to the detention center while I pick up Macario Antone."

The gigantic Rapunzel came out of the little store. "Hey, Penny," she called out, "you never told me about this one. No fair keeping him all for yourself." She laughed and her mammoth chest jiggled.

"You'd be too much for him to handle, Adrienne," Penny said with a smile. "He's just a beginner. I'll get him in shape for you."

Adam sat on the bank of the irrigation ditch absently throwing rocks into the shallow water. Hanna came up next to him and sat down. The sun was low on the horizon, and their father had just left to meet Penny downtown.

"Do you remember Mommy?" Adam asked, not looking up.

"Yes," Hanna said.

"I kind of forget sometimes what she looked like," Adam said hesitatingly.

Hanna was still for a few minutes. "She was real pretty," she said softly.

Adam skimmed a flat stone across the placid water. "Did Daddy love her?"

Again Hanna was still, engrossed in thought. "Yeah, a whole lot."

"How could you tell?"

"Whenever they were together. You could just tell."

Another stone went skipping over the water from Adam's hand.

They sat squinting morosely at the roseate evening sun flirting with the serrated crest of Black Mountain, enveloping it in layers of lavender and orange and purple.

CHAPTER FOURTEEN

Joshua got to his office at a little after nine o'clock on Monday morning. There was a folded sheet of paper on his chair. He picked it up and spread it open on the desk. It was three-ring-binder lined school paper. The handwriting was in pencil, in careful block printing:

MR. RABB:
    WE BELIEVE IT IS NESESARY TO WARN YOU THAT PENNY CHESTER IS NOT A NICE WOMAN. SHE HAS A HUSBAND WHO SHE JUST LEFT AND WENT AWAY. AND IT ISNT NICE FOR YOU BE WITH HER.
                               YOUR FRIENDS

He slumped into his chair, staring at the letter, and tears sprang to his eyes. He rubbed his eyes hard. Damn, damn, damn, he thought. I've been acting like a lovestruck jackass. Hanna and Adam think that I've forgotten all about their mother. I have to talk to them, explain to them. They must be hurting very badly. He felt as though he had double-crossed them, failed them. He had become selfish, more interested in himself than in Hanna and Adam. He had uprooted them and plunked them down in a place so harsh and hostile that day by day he did not know whether they would be in mortal danger. And maybe worse, he had been blind to their undiminished love for their mother, unfeeling of their pain when he brought a new woman home. He felt very guilty.

He folded the sheet of notebook paper and put it in his jacket pocket.

~~~~~~

Joshua pulled up to the Cattleman's Hotel entrance almost exactly at noon. Penny had been standing by the door waiting, and she came out to the car as soon as he parked. He pulled awkwardly away from the curb, having a little trouble with just his one hand guiding the car into the noontime traffic.

He looked over at her and grinned sheepishly. "Sometimes I think things would be easier with two arms."

"I never doubted it for a minute," she said.

"Let's go to that fancy-looking place on South Sixth Avenue for lunch, you know, the new Italian restaurant."

"Sounds great."

They rode awhile in silence. "Have you ever thought about a prosthetic arm?" she asked.

He shrugged. "I played around with one at the VA in Brooklyn. But it hurt like hell to put it on."

"Well, you're a lot better healed now. I think you ought to try it again."

"Where at?"

"Over at the VA there on the Nogales Highway. It's just a mile or so from where we're going to eat."

He raised his eyebrows. "Why all of a sudden are you so worried about my arm? I get along pretty well."

She looked at him. "It's not all of a sudden," she said soothingly. "I think it will give you more freedom, probably make you feel better. There's nothing to be ashamed about getting a prosthetic device."

They drove in silence. "Captain Hook," he drawled.

She laughed.

The elderly woman who seated them at the Napoli Cafe had

stark black dyed hair in a tight bun framing her swarthy withered face. She is the mother, she told them, her son is the chef in the kitchen, her daughter-in-law is usually the waitress, but she is about to have a baby, my first grandchild. The old woman smiled contentedly and little tears of joy came to her eyes. She brought them menus mimeographed almost illegibly on single sheets of typing paper. She talked so fast, it seemed as though she felt a need to recite her entire family history to every new patron.

Joshua and Penny managed to give her their orders during the breath she took between a passionate diatribe over how Mussolini had commandeered her home near Florence for the army, and how her husband was killed in Ethiopia, and a tearful description of his burial place near his tiny home village of Montevecchio.

When she brought the food to them, she hovered over the table like a hungry buzzard, smiling, looking alternately worried and victorious, wringing her hands nervously as she awaited honeyed words of praise. They ate quickly, anxious to escape. Luckily, another couple came into the restaurant, and the woman transferred her attention to the new victims.

Penny sighed with relief. "I got exhausted just watching her writhe," she whispered.

Joshua laughed. "But the food really is terrific," he said.

The old woman came back, bobbing and weaving around the table like a skillful boxer. Joshua laid two dollars on the table and they fled quickly.

"Wow, that was a close call!" said Joshua. "I felt safer in a foxhole in Luxembourg."

Penny laughed.

Joshua sat behind the steering wheel holding the key poised like an orchestra conductor's baton. "You really think this VA thing is worth doing?"

She nodded vigorously. "It's sure worth a try."

He drove to the hospital, and at the front desk he showed his U.S. Army veteran's benefits I.D. card. He asked to see a prosthetician.

"Yes, Major," purred the nurse, a young pretty brunette in

a snug white uniform. "Please go down the hallway to C-2 and have a seat. Mr. Kirschner will be down there in a minute."

They walked down the long corridor. *"Yes, Major,"* Penny mimicked in a falsetto, fluttering her eyelashes.

"This place is growing on me already," Joshua said.

"Keep it in your pants, G.I.," Penny said, holding tightly to his arm. "I don't want you coming here without me to protect you."

Hanna and Magdalena were in the kitchen preparing supper. Joshua sat at the table watching absently. Adam was in his usual spot in front of the radio playing with several little toy cars. There was a knock on the front door just as they all sat down at the kitchen table.

Magdalena answered the door and came back into the kitchen. "Samuel Santos came to visit me," she said a little shyly. "Can I ask him to stay for supper, Mr. Rabb?"

"Of course," Joshua said. "This is your house, too."

Samuel sat down at the table and murmured hellos. He looked around sheepishly. He appeared embarrassed and obviously felt out of place. Joshua and the children traded small talk and ate casually. Magdalena and Samuel were silent, glancing at each other furtively with hungry eyes.

After dinner, Samuel and Magdalena went for a walk. She was wearing Levi's and a red tube top which she had borrowed from Hanna. Samuel couldn't take his eyes off of her sylphlike figure. They walked across the irrigation ditch and strolled slowly through the barren cotton field.

"You want to go up on Black Mountain?" he asked.

"Sure," she said.

It was still ninety degrees and humid, and they were both perspiring by the time they reached the foot of the mountain.

"Let's go under the cistern, like we used to," he said.

She turned to him. "We're not going to do that."

"Why not?" He studied her gorgeous face in the light of the full moon and felt an aching for her.

She shrugged. "You didn't look at me for a whole year since

you came home from the war. Now all of a sudden you're interested again?"

"Come on, Magda. I've been going to school, living in a shack way over near the university. I have to work thirty-five hours a week besides school, and I don't have a car. What do you want from me?"

"I want more than to be ignored," she said quietly. "Four years ago it was you and me, all the time, everywhere. Now, you just show up a couple of weeks ago and I'm supposed to jump into your arms?"

He toed the ground, embarrassed. "Well, I wasn't sure you were interested in me anymore."

She took his hand and squeezed it. "I've been in love with you since I was sixteen," she said. "Do you think it ends so easy?"

They walked up the hill to the cistern. Samuel tried the spigot and water poured out. The cistern was obviously full from the recent monsoon rains. He took off his shirt and Levi's and underwear and shoes and put them out of the way so they wouldn't get wet. He faced away from her and stepped under the spigot and turned it on, and the water glistened over his lean back and legs.

They had come here many times before Sam had left for the army. She was in love with him then, madly, schoolgirlishly head over heels infatuated with him. He was handsome, one of the only college graduates on the reservation, and he was going to be somebody. A doctor, maybe. A lawyer, a professor. Maybe even chief of the tribe someday. And she would be his wife. But when he had come back from Europe a year ago he was different, taciturn and morose. They went out together, but his softness was gone, his tenderness, and he had almost torn off her shirt and pants. That was the last time. She had run away from him, and after that he'd gone back to the university and was gone most of the time. She'd seen him again for the first time just several days ago, when he had been a guard at the Rabb house. And he was changed, back much more to his old self, the way he'd been before the war. And there was still something strong between them.

She pulled the tube top off and kicked her sandals off. She laid her Levi's on the rocks next to his. She turned on the spigot on the other side of the cistern, two feet from Samuel, and the water cooled her and puckered her nipples. Samuel turned toward her, and he was hard and erect, big, and she remembered. He stepped to her and kissed her and kissed her breasts. She hugged him and spread her legs slightly, and he pressed her to him and his erection was between her legs. She rocked her hips lightly back and forth and rubbed herself on it.

He turned off both water faucets and took her hand and led her to a flat rock a few feet away. She lay back on it, and his head was framed by the pale moon as he lowered himself on top of her. He pushed himself into her and she gasped with the pleasure of it. He rocked on her, in her, and she opened herself to him and lost herself in him. They rolled apart after several moments and lay comfortably in the moonlight.

Suddenly she heard a rustling below them. She squinted to see what it was. Someone in a robe with the hood up was below them on the hill about fifty feet away.

"What is it?" whispered Samuel.

"Someone's down there. One of the priests, I think."

He rolled over and squinted down the hill. "I'd better go look." He pulled on his clothing and shoes and walked slowly down the hill.

She lost sight of him as he reached the bottom of the hill where there was very little moonlight. Suddenly she heard a gasp and then a groan. She heard someone running, then someone else. She was terrified. She dressed quickly and began running down the hill. She heard a yell and squinted toward the sound. It came from near the irrigation ditch. She began running toward it. As she neared it, she saw the silhouette of someone in a hooded robe. The figure ran down into the ditch, up the other side, and disappeared into the darkness.

She ran toward the place where it had been and tripped over something. She fell to the ground on her hands and knees and scrambled around to see what it was. It was Samuel. His face was covered with blood and he was motionless. She couldn't hear him breathing. She doubled over and vomited. She got up shakily and ran toward her grandparents' house.

⁓⁓⁓

Joshua was sitting on the couch absently listening to the radio. Hanna flopped down on the big upholstered chair.

"Wonder why Adam's late?" she said.

Joshua hadn't noticed. He glanced at his watch. It was almost nine-thirty.

"Well, why don't you go down to Jimmy's house and bring him home," he said. "Adam's not so good with being on time."

Ten minutes later, Hanna and Edgar Hendly both came through the rear door.

"They went off with Charger to the reservoir at about seven-thirty, said they'd be back by nine," Edgar said.

"Well, let's go find them," Joshua said. "You stay in the house," he said to Hanna.

Joshua drove quickly beside the irrigation ditch. The moonlight was weak. As they reached the end of the ditch, they could see Charger standing at the edge of a copse of cottonwood trees past the reservoir.

"There they are," Edgar said.

Joshua stopped the car and left the lights on. They got out and Edgar hollered, "Jimmy, get over here."

A form emerged from behind a cottonwood tree beyond the reservoir. It ran toward the car.

"Daddy, Daddy," Jimmy sobbed. He ran into his father's outstretched arms.

"What happened?" Joshua asked in a terrified voice.

"Adam, he's out there," Jimmy gasped. "Somebody wearing a big dress dragged him off." He pointed toward the field.

"Oh God, no!" Joshua cried. He ran a little way down to where the reservoir joined with the irrigation ditch and splashed through the mud to the other bank. Adam's limp body lay twisted on the ground. His lower body was nude. A strangled scream came from Joshua's throat. He knelt beside Adam and cradled his son's head. The boy groaned.

"Joshua," Edgar called out, "is he all right?"

"He's still alive," Joshua yelled. "Bring the car around. I can't carry him that far."

"I'll be there in a couple of minutes."

It seemed more like hours to Joshua, kneeling helplessly with his son's bloody head in his lap. Each of Adam's labored breaths sounded like an old man's death rattle.

Joshua wept softly, muttering over and over, "Please, God, don't let him die."

The De Soto rumbled jerkily over the field. Edgar and Joshua lifted Adam's slack body and Joshua got in the backseat. Edgar laid Adam down with his head in his father's lap. The boy's face was bloody and his nose was bent to one side. He was unconscious, breathing through his mouth with shallow wheezes. Edgar drove in silence to Mission Road and followed it to the Nogales Highway.

"What did you mean, 'a big dress'?" Edgar asked Jimmy.

"You know, it's long and has a big bunched-up collar."

"You mean like what the priests wear?"

"Yeah, like that."

"When did it happen?"

"Right before you came. The car scared him away."

Edgar drove down Indian Agency Road and dropped Jimmy off in front of the BIA. He watched the boy run off to the house. Then Edgar sped back up Indian Agency Road.

"It's gotta be one a the priests," Edgar said. "The way Jimmy described it, it must be one a them priest's cassocks."

"Just a little longer," Joshua muttered to his unconscious son.

Edgar pulled into the parking lot of St. Mary's Hospital, in front of the red neon EMERGENCY sign which cast a bloody puddle of light on the parking lot. Joshua carried his son through two swinging glass doors that Edgar held open. A nurse behind a counter immediately picked up a telephone, and they heard her voice over a booming intercom: "Dr. Martinelli to Emergency, Dr. Martinelli to Emergency."

The nurse came out from behind the counter and wheeled a gurney up to Joshua. He laid Adam gently on it. A moment later, a young man in what looked like white pajamas ran up.

Without a word, he pulled the gurney into a room up the corridor. Joshua followed.

"Please wait," said the nurse, pointing to a wooden bench in the waiting room.

"But he's my son," Joshua blurted.

"You can't do him any good in there. You wait here," she said sternly. She went into the room with Adam and the doctor and pulled a long curtain closed over the wide entrance.

"I'm callin the sheriff," Edgar said.

Joshua was pacing, totally preoccupied and frightened. He grunted.

Edgar used the nurse's phone and dialed the emergency number for the sheriff's department in the phone book. He talked for a moment. Then he pressed down the cradle, waited for a dial tone, and called his wife, Frances. He told her to go over and get Hanna and bring her to their house until they got back from the hospital. Then he hung up and walked over and sat down on the bench.

Twenty minutes later a deputy came in. "One a you guys called the sheriff?" he said.

"Yes, I did," Edgar said, standing up and walking to him. "Mr. Rabb's son was attacked on the Indian reservation. My son says the attacker was wearing a big dress, you know, a robe like them priests wear."

The deputy looked very tired and exasperated. He closed the spiral notebook that he had just opened and put it and the pencil back in his shirt pocket.

"Well, that's not my backyard, mister. You're gonna have to contact the FBI and the Indian police over in Sells."

"Everything that happens in this *gott* damn town is somebody else's jurisdiction," Edgar snarled at him. "I've never seen so many asses and elbows runnin the other way. Why don't *you* get on that phone and call em. We got a hurt little boy in there." He pointed down the hallway.

"Now you settle down, fuckhead," the deputy said. "I cain't go on the reservation. I get my ass bounced right outta the goddamn department I go bangin on doors at the rectory at midnight."

Edgar put his hands on his hips and glared at the deputy. "I'm Edgar Hendly, superintendent of the Bureau of Indian Affairs. You get on that phone and call Sheriff Dunphy, now."

Joshua had never heard that tone in Edgar's voice. He thought Edgar was about to attack the deputy.

"Take it easy, mister." The deputy backed up. "Just take it easy now. I gotta call dispatch. I just cain't call the sheriff in the middle a the night." He went to the nurse's station and telephoned.

A half hour passed with hardly a sound. A man who looked a little like Edgar, balding, short, heavy, sweating in a too-tight tan uniform, came striding through the double glass doors.

"Edgar, what in blazes is goin on?" he said, walking up to him. They shook hands.

"Pat, Joshua Rabb's boy was attacked over by the reservoir at the end of the irrigation ditch off a Indian Agency Road. My son, Jimmy, says it was a man dressed in a robe like the friars wear out there."

"Is he okay?" the sheriff asked.

"Well, he's alive. Don't know anythin else right now."

Dunphy looked over at Joshua on the bench. "You Rabb?"

Joshua nodded.

Dunphy walked up to him and stretched out his hand. Joshua shook it.

"I done heard plenny 'bout you, son. Yes sir! You 'pear to have a pair a balls the size a pomegranates." He studied Joshua's face. "Served a plate full a mouse turds to old Judge Rooks." He shook his head. "You better be wearin a cast-iron jockstrap the next time you wander into *his* courtroom." He pursed his lips. "Now what was yer boy doin out there?"

"Well, I guess he and Jimmy went down there to play with the bullfrogs like they always do."

"Did the attack happen on the res?"

Joshua shrugged.

Dunphy looked at him and then at Edgar and frowned. He crooked his finger at the deputy. "Scotty, you take statements here and make sure they get on Fraker's desk tomorrow morning." Dunphy turned to Joshua and explained, "Billy Fraker's our top investigator."

"Aw shit, Chief, I'm off shift in less 'n fifteen minutes."

Dunphy fixed him with a hard look. "Yer workin overtime tonight, Scotty. Ya hear me talkin'?"

"Yes, sir."

"Thataboy."

Edgar started pacing. The sheriff's deputy made a telephone call and then sat down on the bench next to Joshua and resentfully began to take his statement. Dunphy walked over to the double glass doors, clasped his hands behind his back, and stared stolidly into the night.

Curtain rings skidded on the rod. The doctor came into the lobby. "Who belongs to the boy?"

"I do," Joshua said, sitting up stiffly, bracing himself for whatever the doctor had to say.

"He's going to be fine," the doctor said.

"Oh, thank God, thank God." Tears filled Joshua's eyes.

"I stitched up a couple of lacerations on his forehead." The doctor lowered his voice. "He wasn't penetrated, but he's got a pretty bad concussion, so I've got to keep an eye on him for a couple of days. He's sleeping soundly now, and you'll be able to take him home Thursday or Friday."

The doctor turned to the deputy sitting next to Joshua. "You making the report?"

Scotty nodded.

"Come on over to the counter," the doctor said, walking into the nurse's station and sitting down.

Joshua stood up, looking lost. "I want to go kill somebody," he mumbled.

Sheriff Dunphy frowned. "Yeah? Who?"

"One of those pervert priests is killing people."

"Now listen here, boy," Dunphy said, "let's not be jumpin off half-cocked."

A sheriff's deputy came quickly through the glass entry doors and walked up to Sheriff Dunphy. "We got another floater in the irrigation ditch on the res."

"Whattaya talkin about?"

"I just been out there, Chief. Some Indian boy with his brains half stove outta his head. A girl was with him, but she wasn't hurt. They're both on their way over here."

Joshua walked over to the deputy. "Who are they?" he asked.

"Dunno, pal. Just a couple a greasers."

An ambulance drove up under the Emergency canopy outside and two attendants wheeled a gurney through the lobby. Magdalena, looking terrified, followed it in. Samuel's face was covered with blood. The doctor came from the nurse's station and ran down the hallway to the emergency treatment room. Joshua gasped when he saw them. He put his arm around Magdalena's shoulders, and she began to weep hysterically. He led her to the wooden bench and sat down with her.

Sheriff Dunphy walked up to Edgar and whispered, "Does he know her?"

"Yeah, she's his acculturation girl," Edgar whispered.

Dunphy pursed his lips and raised his eyebrows and nodded. "Damn good looker fer a greaser."

CHAPTER FIFTEEN

J oshua and Hanna went to the hospital early Tuesday morning. Adam looked very unhappy and cried intermittently, but they sat quietly with him for two hours and he seemed to feel much better. A nurse came in and gave him a shot and asked them to leave.

They looked in on Samuel in the intensive care unit. Magdalena was sleeping in a chair next to the bed. Samuel was in a coma, the nurse told them.

～～～～

Wednesday morning. Ignacio Antone's preliminary hearing would start at ten. Joshua decided not to tell Ignacio about what had happened to his sister and Samuel until after the preliminary hearing. He wanted to make sure that Ignacio was emotionally strong enough to make it through the morning. There was nothing about it in the morning newspaper, just a short story about Adam's being assaulted. Whatever happened to Papagos apparently wasn't newsworthy.

Joshua got to the courtroom in the federal building a few minutes before ten o'clock. It was crowded with mur-

muring spectators. At least a hundred Papagos sat in the rear rows. Another hundred people were up front. Macario and Hanna sat beside Chief Romero.

Tim Essert sat at the prosecution table, his thumbs hooked in the pockets of his beige linen waistcoat. He glanced at Joshua but made no gesture of greeting.

Joshua looked around the courtroom and found his second witness, Dr. Robertson. He nodded to him. But his first witness wasn't here yet. He had not wanted Murray Robertson to have to testify first, if at all.

Marshal Friedkind brought Ignacio into the courtroom in ankle and handcuffs and a belly chain. Ignacio looked healthy, albeit drawn and thinner. He sat down at the table next to Joshua.

"You okay?" Joshua whispered.

"I'm okay," he answered somberly.

"We're going to do fine this morning, Ignacio. Just take it easy."

The Indian looked intently at Joshua and nodded. "Okay, Mr. Rabb."

Ignacio turned around and looked at the faces of so many people he knew from the reservation, and Joshua could see that he felt mortified, as though he were a human monkey cavorting to an organ grinder's tune. Tears of humiliation fogged Ignacio's vision and he brusquely rubbed his eyes.

The court reporter came in and sat down at her table. The bailiff banged the gavel, and the judge took the bench. He looked around at the crowd of silent spectators and then at Joshua Rabb and Tim Essert.

"All right, gentlemen. This is the time set for the continuation of the preliminary hearing in U.S. versus Antone. Counsel are present, Mr. Antone is at counsel table. Let's go. Who's up?"

"The Government rests, your honor," Essert said.

"Very well. Mr. Rabb, do you have evidence for the defendant?"

"Yes, your honor. My first witness hasn't come yet, so I'll start with Dr. Murray Robertson." Damn, thought Joshua, I didn't want to have to do this.

The doctor came forward, was sworn, and took the stand. Ignacio stirred uneasily in his chair. He looked angrily at Joshua. "I told you not this. I told you not to talk about my manhood," he hissed.

Joshua put his hand on Ignacio's arm. "Listen, Ignacio," he whispered, "I didn't want to have to do this. But I don't know if my other witness is coming. He may not have been able to come up with the evidence I asked him to look for. This may be your only chance to survive this thing. Just take it easy."

He turned toward the witness. "You are Dr. Murray Robertson, a physician here in Tucson?"

"Correct."

"At my request, did you accompany me to the Mount Lemmon Detention Center last Wednesday for the purpose of examining Ignacio Antone?"

"Yes, sir."

"Did your examination have any specific element that I asked you to determine?"

"Yes, it did."

"Tell the court what that was."

"Well, based on the findings of the Pima County coroner that Sister Martha Robinette and Vittorio Ponsay were anally raped by a fertile individual, you asked me to attempt to determine two things: first, was Mr. Antone capable of an erection and ejaculation, and second, was his semen fertile."

Ignacio stood up at the defense table and smashed his handcuffed wrists down on it. "No! You can't do this, you can't do this!" he screamed.

"Sit down!" the judge bellowed.

"God damn you! God damn you!" Ignacio screamed, turning toward Joshua.

Joshua stood up and put his arm around the Indian, but Ignacio wrenched himself free and knocked Joshua to the floor. The bailiff and Marshal Friedkind ran to the table and grabbed Antone by the arms and pulled, dragged, struggled him out of the courtroom. Joshua stood up slowly.

The judge riveted Joshua with a harsh frown. "We'll let your client cool his heels in the holding cell, Mr. Rabb. Right now we'll take a five-minute recess to compose ourselves, and then you will resume and bring this hearing to an end. I've had just about all that my patience can bear."

Joshua sat at the defense table and stared at his hands. Dr. Robertson sat still in the witness chair, looking very unhappy. There was a dull, sullen murmur from the spectators.

Dr. Howard Falconer walked up the aisle to the defense table. "Sorry I'm late," he said quietly. "Car trouble."

Joshua jolted up straight in his chair, surprised, and suddenly felt hopeful. "Did you get the information you thought might be available?"

"Yes, I finally found it," said the professor. "That's why I didn't have a chance to get hold of you. I just found it last night. You have no phone." He opened the book he was carrying and showed Joshua. Joshua quickly scanned several pages.

"Jesus!" he said under his breath. "Fantastic. I'm going to put you on as soon as the hearing resumes, in a minute or two."

Joshua walked up to Murray Robertson and told him that he would excuse him as a witness as soon as the judge came back. The doctor nodded, relieved.

The judge came back to the bench. Joshua was standing by the table with Dr. Falconer.

"Go ahead, Mr. Rabb."

"Your honor, at this time I would ask the court to excuse Dr. Robertson. I will not be questioning him further."

"Mr. Essert?" the judge asked.

Tim Essert shrugged.

"All right, Dr. Robertson, you're excused." The doctor left the stand. "You have another witness, Mr. Rabb?"

"Yes, your honor. We call Professor Howard Falconer."

The small gray-haired man walked with a slight stoop to the bailiff as though he knew his way around courtrooms. He raised his right hand and was sworn and took his seat in the witness stand.

Joshua stood at the defense table. "Tell the court your name, please."

"Howard Falconer."

"What is your occupation?"

"Professor of physical anthropology at the University of Arizona."

"Would you tell us your schooling, please?"

"I received my doctor of philosophy degree from Harvard in 1913, in anthropology. I spent two postgraduate years studying in the pathology department of Yale University Medical Center."

"What is your teaching background?"

"I taught at Harvard until 1937. I developed a bronchial condition and was told to come to Arizona for my health. I have been a professor here since that time."

"Do you have a specialty, Dr. Falconer?"

"Yes. The identification and differentiation of human remains."

"Are you considered an expert in that field?"

"Well, that's for others to say, Mr. Rabb. But I've published widely in the field, and I am often called upon by law enforcement agencies to study remains."

"Did I contact you some days ago and ask you to review certain reports and certain literature having to do with this case?"

"Yes, you did. Saturday morning, I believe it was. You gave me these reports for my review." He held up a manila folder. Joshua came forward and took them from his hand and looked at the papers inside.

"Did you review these, Dr. Falconer?"

"I did."

Joshua handed the file to the judge and waited while he quickly scanned the sheets and then gave the file back to Joshua. He handed it to Tim Essert, who glanced casually at the documents and gave them back to Joshua. Joshua handed them to the witness and went back to his table.

"Now could you tell us what information you gleaned from those reports?"

"Yes. They are reports of Stan Wolfe, the Pima County coroner. He typed the blood of Sister Martha Robinette as O, the blood of Ignacio Antone as O, and the bloodstains on Sister Martha's habit as AB, apparently her murderer's blood type."

"Dr. Falconer, could you tell us in lay terms what these blood types mean?"

"Part of the genetic makeup of every human being is the makeup of his blood. If you think of blood as a cocktail, you immediately realize that the same glass may hold a mixture of gin and dry vermouth—we call this a martini; it may hold bourbon and sweet vermouth—we call this a Manhattan; it may hold straight bourbon, it may hold straight scotch, and so on. All of them are cocktails in a container, but they have different components. Blood is precisely the same. Every person is a container with blood, but that blood differs from person to person by the nature of its components. Roughly there are four types of components. We call them O, A, B, and AB. And in a laboratory we can tell them apart distinctly."

"Okay, Doctor, are there any particular things we should know in general about the different types of blood?"

Professor Falconer opened the book he had brought with him. Some of the spectators shifted in their seats. The judge looked particularly bored. He rested his head back against his big brown leather chair cushion. Dr. Falconer took a pair of glasses out of his coat pocket and put them on. He flipped the pages of the book.

"Yes, here it is," he said. "Numerous studies by Hirschfield, Slough, Fisher, Vaughan, Ikin, and others between 1919 and 1946 have determined that type O blood is the dominant blood type of virtually all racial and ethnic groups in North and South America, Africa and most of Asia. In Japan, type B is most common. In contrast, Type A predominates among most racial and ethnic groups in Europe."

"What can you tell us about AB blood, Professor Falconer?"

"Well, it's by far the least common blood group in the entire world. Only 4.7 percent of American whites possess it, and some 3.7 percent of American negroes, and we believe that no native North American Indians such as Sioux and Bloods and no South American and Mexican Indians of Mayan and Aztec racial origin possess AB type."

The judge stiffened visibly in his chair. His head came forward from the cushion, and he stared at the professor. The shifting in the spectator seats stopped. Joshua waited until he could have heard a pin drop.

"Do we have Indians of Aztec racial origin in southern Arizona, Dr. Falconer?"

"Leading anthropologists believe that we do. Although we cannot be certain, the Papago and Pima Indians are most likely an Aztecan migration from many centuries ago. Their language is part of the Uto-Aztecan family of languages, extending from tribes of Nicaragua all the way north to the Paiutes of Washington. In all of the studies that I have seen which were done by the Indian health services on the Papago reservations, no apparently pure-blood Papago has ever been tested with AB blood."

"*Could* it happen?" Joshua asked.

"It appears to me that among pure-blood Papagos, it would be as unlikely as finding a blond, blue-eyed, alabaster-skinned offspring of a native couple from Kenya."

"In other words, Doctor, you would not expect a pure-blood Papago to bleed AB."

"That's correct."

"Well, what about intermarriage? Could that affect blood types?"

"Yes. In studies done among highly intermarried Cherokees, 2.4 percent were found to be AB. Among highly intermarried Blackfeet, 1.8 percent. While studies have not been done with children of Papago/white, or Papago/black marriages, such intermarriage is exceedingly rare and almost never occurs with Papagos from San Xavier and the Big Reservation. As for the much more frequent Papago/Mexican marriages, which have occurred for centuries, you must keep in mind that virtually all of the Mexicans around the Papagueria—the Papago lands in southern Arizona and Sonora—are themselves predominantly descendants of Indians and show virtually no incidence of AB blood."

"What is the likelihood that a Papago Indian bled AB blood on Sister Martha Robinette's habit?"

"Terribly unlikely, Mr. Rabb. Only a very small statistical possibility."

Joshua sat down.

The judge rubbed his chin and pulled on his nose a few times. He wrinkled his brow, pursed his lips, and turned to the assistant U.S. attorney. "Well, Mr. Essert, what do you have to say to that?"

Tim Essert sat back in his chair, a sour look on his face. He folded his hands in his lap and shook his head slowly.

"I guess you're done now, Mr. Rabb?" the judge asked, peering over his spectacles at Joshua.

"I am, your honor. Defense rests."

"All right, bailiff, go get Marshal Friedkind and help him bring Mr. Antone to the courtroom. The defendant's entitled to hear the court's decision."

The bailiff left. The courtroom remained silent. The judge lay back against his chair cushion and drummed idly on his desk blotter. He toyed with his pocket watch. Joshua doodled nervously on the pad in front of him.

Ignacio Antone shuffled through the door of the courtroom, Ollie Friedkind behind him. The Indian took mincing steps, restrained by the ankle cuffs and belly chain attached to his shackled wrists. He stood sullen-faced at the defense table with the marshal beside him.

"Sit," the marshal said.

"Take the chains off," Ignacio growled.

"Can't do that, boy. I done had enough trouble with you. Sit!"

Ignacio sat down stiffly in the chair next to Joshua. "Take it easy," Joshua whispered. "The judge is going to give his decision. Don't make any demonstration, no matter what happens."

Judge Buchanan looked the people in the courtroom into silence. "I want all of you folks to listen carefully to what I say," he said, glaring around slowly at the white faces in the front rows. "It is my judgment that there is no evidence that a Papago Indian, not Ignacio Antone or Juan so-and-so, had anything to do with the death of Sister Martha Robinette."

A querulous muttering arose from the spectators. The judge stared hard at them and rapped his gavel for silence. A brooding stillness fell over the courtroom.

"There is no reason in the world for any one of you to feel that this man"—the judge pointed at Ignacio—"has escaped justice because of some legal hocus-pocus. There is simply a total lack of evidence to force him to stand trial. Is that clear?"

It was not a question anyone was expected to answer. Several of the white spectators cast the judge rancorous looks. Buchanan stared back at them sternly.

"There's been plenty enough rabble-rousing in the newspaper and grousing around town about this case," the judge continued. "This man is innocent, and that's the end of it. I want every one of you to hold your ire in check until the real murderer is found and justice can be done. Hear?" He surveyed the white faces again and narrowed his heavy-browed eyes cautioningly. He sat there for a moment, and then he banged his gavel and walked off the bench.

Ollie Friedkind unlocked the handcuffs, belly chain, and ankle cuffs. He slid them off the rigidly still Indian and walked out of the courtroom. The white spectators slowly, silently left the courtroom, as though they were in shock.

Tears rolled down Ignacio's cheeks. He sat immobile, staring straight ahead, and the tears gradually subsided. Joshua remained sitting beside him, waiting until Ignacio was ready to get up. After a few moments, Ignacio stretched his hand toward him.

"Thank you, Mr. Rabb," he said in a thin, cracking voice. "God bless you for what you did."

Joshua smiled and shook his hand. They both stood up and turned around. None of the Indians had left the courtroom. Macario walked through the railing gate and hugged his grandson.

Joshua walked down the aisle and the Papagos began to clap. He walked out of the courtroom and leaned against the wall in the hallway, catching his breath, letting the anxiety of weeks flow out of him. Hanna came up beside him and kissed his cheek. They walked slowly down the stairs and out of the courthouse into the bright, burning sunshine.

Penny had come into the courtroom shortly after the hearing began, and she had left as soon as the judge had rendered his verdict. She wanted desperately to run to Joshua and hug him and tell him how proud she was of him. But she didn't want to hurt Hanna, to alienate her further. So she simply left.

She strolled down Congress Street toward the Cattleman's Hotel. McClellan's window had a sign advertising the lunch special: BARBECUE RIBS AND FRENCH FRIES, CHOICE OF COKE OR COFFEE, 45¢. It reminded her that she was hungry, and she went inside. It was twelve-thirty and very busy, and she had to wait fifteen minutes for a free stool at the counter. The waitress took her order and brought the plate of ribs and fries in less than a minute. She ate slowly, having nowhere to go and nothing in particular to do, and the food was surprisingly good. As it neared one o'clock, the customers at the counter thinned out considerably. The two stools next to her were empty.

Two men and a woman came in. One of the men and the woman sat down next to Penny. The other man stood behind them waiting for the stool next to them to become free. He cast Penny an angry glance, like she was intentionally trying to deprive him of food. She watched the three of them in the mirror behind the counter. The man standing looked like a winter-starved bobcat, short cropped blond hair and brown eyes set in gaunt hollows, pale skin and a lanky bony body in faded overalls and a dirty tan work shirt which smelled of sweat and hay and goats. The two on the stools were of the same make, with enough of a resemblance to be related, except that the man was brown-haired like a coyote and the woman had a pinched face and red hair like a vixen.

"Don't that just beat all," the coyote at the counter grumbled. His voice was incongruously high-pitched. "Instead a swingin that greaser like he oughta, he marches him out a there like a crown prince and then lectures us like we's a bunch a low-life scum. Somebody oughta string that commie bastard Buchanan up by his *cojónes*."

The vixen next to him chuckled. The bobcat standing behind them guffawed, then got a mean look. "Can you 'magine that prick lettin a killer go like that?" He shook his head in shocked disbelief. "I was talkin to Cap Hadley just the other day about Buchanan. Cap thinks we oughta teach him a lesson or two. And that Jewboy lawyer too."

"Ol' Henry Bowers tried it with the lawyer," said the coyote. "Didn't work out too good."

"Well," the bobcat drawled, "whattaya expect from ol' Henry? But a few good men could do the job."

Penny looked over at the man next to her, then at the one standing. Whatever was in her look silenced them.

"We'll talk about it later," the vixen said, looking cautioningly at the two men.

Penny put down a half-dollar on the counter and left. She didn't feel like listening to these redneck filth vent their venom.

The day was another one of those that was a Tucson specialty during the summer. Very hot, maybe as much as 105, but the humidity couldn't be more than 6 or 8 percent. Not at all the oppressive humid heat of New Jersey. The sky was so clear and bright it was almost colorless. Penny strolled down Congress Street feeling clean and alive, as though the heat purified her and gave her new life. No wonder all the Indians who lived so close to the earth and so unprotected from the sun worshipped the sun as a god, the purifier, the giver of life. You could feel the sun god work on you on a day like today.

She ambled languorously down Congress Street and onto the bridge over the Santa Cruz River. There was hardly a trickle of water in its hundred-foot-wide rutted bed. She leaned over the railing and stared placidly down. How many times she and her father had walked by the Hudson River, when he would visit her. She was in nursing school at Columbia then, and he would meet her now and then after school at five o'clock outside the Presbyterian Hospital, and they'd walk along the river up to Fort Washington Park and buy kosher hot dogs with lots of mustard and relish and walk up on the George Washington Bridge and watch the sailboats and the yachts and the barges and the tugs in the water below.

A far cry from the Congress Street Bridge over the Santa Cruz River. She chuckled. She wasn't married when she was in nursing school, and she had met a fellow whom she really liked. He sold insurance back in her hometown, Matawan, really a cute guy, and he drove a flashy Cadillac convertible. He threw money around when she was with him, and she wasn't used to being treated so lavishly. Her father taught Old Testament Hebrew and New Testament Koine Greek in the classics department at Rutgers, but his salary was modest.

Mark was very good-looking and charming, and his father had taken him into his insurance business, and Mark was making big money. He had taken Penny and her parents to dinner at a fancy restaurant in Matawan, and Penny was sure that her parents liked him. But then her father came up to New York to see her a week later, and they strolled by the Hudson and got the hot dogs and stood on the bridge, and he told her that he thought that Mark was a *putz*.

Do you know what a really good man is? he'd said to her. She had shrugged. And he recited to her a line from the *Ethics of the Fathers* in the Talmud: *U'vamakom she'ayn anashim, hish-tadayl l'hiot ish.* "In a place where there are no men, strive to be a man."

She had said to him indulgently, because she really was too old for these schoolgirl lectures (but after all, he was her father and she loved him), what does that mean, Daddy? And he had said that a man wasn't a flashy car and a hairdo and a sweet-talking tongue and a few dollars. A man was someone with common decency, *menshlichkeit*, intelligence, *saychel*, and inner strength and courage, *koyach*. A man didn't just display his qualities in front of others to impress them. A man was the same even when he was all alone, when there were no other men around, in the dark, in his own room, whether people were watching or not. A man's true worth was deep inside, intrinsic, the essence of him—we call it his "soul." Penny had smiled and thanked her father for his advice and forgotten about it in the length of time that it took her to finish her hot dog.

Her father hadn't been happy when she married Mark, but it was her choice and her life and he wouldn't interfere. And slowly, painfully, she had come to the realization that her father was wiser and more perceptive than she had realized. Mark had found it impossible to limit his great gifts to just one wife, when there were so many abandoned wives around whose husbands were off sunning themselves in the jungles of New Guinea and on the beaches of North Africa.

All that Penny wanted out of life was to have someone she really loved and who really loved her. Like Clark Gable and Carol Lombard. Couldn't she have a Gable/Lombard love just once in her life? Was that too much to ask? Please, God, please make Joshua Rabb love me. I need him. I love him so much it makes my teeth hurt just thinking about him. I will take care of him and make him better with me than he is without me. And I will take care of his children and love them. I promise. Please make this happen. I'll never ask for another single thing the whole rest of my life, I swear.

She walked slowly back to the Cattleman's Hotel. There was a note there from Joshua. She felt a stab of pain that she had missed him, but at least she'd see him tonight. Joshua Rabb, she thought, I want you to meet my father. Oh God, that would be so wonderful! Daddy would sit with Joshua, and they would talk, and then Daddy would take her aside and kiss her on the cheek and his eyes would be brimming over like they did when he was happy, and he would say to her, "In a place where there are no men, strive to be a man."

～～～～～～

Joshua had stopped by the Cattleman's Hotel to see Penny at two o'clock that afternoon, but she wasn't in her room. He was crestfallen. He needed her, just to see her, to be with her. He wrote her a note, asking her to come to the house at seven-thirty that night, sealed the note in a hotel envelope, and had the clerk put it in Mrs. Chesser's box.

He drove to the hospital and sat with Adam for three hours. Adam was feeling better, and they played checkers and old maid. The pleasure that he felt over Ignacio's freedom was perforated by the knowledge that there was still a killer out there, and Adam and Samuel could easily have been murdered. It was only by some miracle that they had survived. A man in a robe had attacked both of them. One of the priests? Yes, it had to be. The same one who sodomized Vittorio in the mission that night. But which one?

———

When Joshua came home at five o'clock, he admired the cake that Hanna and Magdalena had baked. They had spent the entire afternoon making a chocolate cake and a huge batch of chocolate chip cookies. They had decorated the cake with fudge frosting, and Hanna had painstakingly written on the top, GET WELL SOON, SAMUEL AND AD. Joshua wondered about the SAMUEL AND AD, and Hanna was a little abashed and told him that she had run out of white icing. Joshua laughed and hugged her.

Penny came over at about seven-thirty. Hanna was cool toward her, but it was more because of her preoccupation over Adam and Samuel than anything else. They all left for the hospital, and Adam was asleep when they arrived at eight o'clock. The doctor came into the room and whispered to Joshua that the concussion seemed to be improving, but that he had been a little dizzy and disoriented earlier in the evening. The doctor had heavily sedated him so that he would sleep. They stood around his bed for a half hour, silent, brooding, shuffling their feet.

Then they went down the hall to the intensive care unit. Samuel had suffered a setback of some kind, but the nurse wouldn't explain, and his attending physician wasn't there to speak with them. They watched him lying still in his bed, wires and tubes attached to him from the various blinking machines. A bladder in a cylindrical glass tube in a ventilator hissed and sucked rhythmically. The room looked like Frankenstein's laboratory.

They left the hospital more gloomy than they had come. Hanna cried softly, and Magdalena hugged her in the backseat. Hanna and Magdalena went to bed at nine-thirty, emotionally exhausted.

Joshua and Penny sat on the couch listening to the radio. At a little after ten-thirty, Joshua switched off the radio. The house was very still. They sat silently for another fifteen minutes, and then he turned off the lamp on the living room table. They tiptoed into his bedroom, and he locked the door. They lay down on the bed. She snuggled up against him and her perfume was intoxicating. She was wearing a loose cotton shirtwaist, and he discovered to his great pleasure that she had nothing on underneath. He felt a little nervous about doing this with Hanna and Magdalena in the house, but he needed Penny desperately, and he felt almost no control.

If their lovemaking had been a little groping and exploratory and physical the first time and the second and the third, they were now really making love, so that neither was holding anything back from the other. Their tentativeness was gone. And their only self-consciousness was to keep their sounds low. She held her hand over her mouth for a whole minute, and only when both of their bodies relaxed did she dare remove it.

CHAPTER SIXTEEN

Thursday was a day of thanksgiving for Ignacio Antone, strongly tempered by shock over the attacks on Adam and Samuel. Fear hung palpably over the San Xavier Reservation. There would therefore be only a small family celebration for Ignacio that evening.

The day started with a huge thunderstorm that lasted for less than an hour, dropping at least two inches of rain and muddying everything. It had one benefit: the irrigation ditch flowed with three feet of water, and Hanna and Jimmy and fifteen or twenty of the Papago boys and girls swam all day. Magdalena had gone to her grandparents' house at seven in the morning to help them prepare the celebration.

Joshua sat on the couch under the cooler vent in the living room and tried to read *A Bell for Adano*. He fell asleep at about three-thirty and didn't awaken until five o'clock. By then, the water was down in the ditch, and the swimming had ended.

In the midst of the enormous relief that had grown in Joshua since Ignacio was freed yesterday, now in the emptiness of the little house with everyone outside, he felt desperately alone. He thought about Adam with deep anguish and unsuppressable anger. Then he thought of Magdalena, and he felt visceral grief for her. Why had Samuel been hurt, and Adam? Over what? Over a few gold pieces in a mine shaft? Over an affront to a United States senator? Could these terrible murders and injuries really be for reasons that banal, that meaningless? No, it can't be. It had to be one of the priests. That weird monk Boniface . . .

He heard the hose running outside, and then Hanna came in and went into her bedroom to change out of her bathing suit. She came into the living room a few minutes later and flopped down on the couch next to her father. "You ever going to finish that book?"

"I keep falling asleep."

"It's your age, Dad. Your body's changing."

"Oh, yeah?"

"Yeah. We learned about it in health. When you get old you need a lot more rest just like you did when you were a kid, you know, so your body has time to recuperate and build up."

Joshua nodded thoughtfully. "You think I'm at that point, huh?"

She looked at him and suddenly realized that he looked a little crestfallen. "Well, I didn't mean you were *old* exactly, you know, not like Grandpa. I just meant that as you get *older* you need more naps."

"Thank you for the medical advice, honey."

"Maybe you ought to get some of that Geritol that they always advertise on the radio for perking you up. They say it cures *iron deficiency anemia*." She said the words carefully.

"What's that?"

"Well, I'm not sure, but it has something to do with having tired blood when you get older." She looked at him earnestly.

"Maybe I'll try that, honey."

"We'd better head on over to the barbecue," Hanna said. She went into her bedroom to put on her squaw boots.

I didn't think I was quite that old, Joshua thought. He looked himself over, sitting on the couch. He pinched the little spare tire around his waist. Well, maybe I better go on a diet.

He went into his bedroom and changed into Levi's, a Western shirt, and his tan loafers. As he came back into the living room, Hanna was just opening the front door for Penny. Hanna smiled at her, but Joshua could see that it was forced, exaggerated.

Penny was wearing a pair of wide-legged light green linen shorts, revealing her gorgeous legs. A white silk blouse was knotted around her midriff. Her hair was down, long on the shoulders, and Joshua hadn't noticed before that it wasn't just blond, it was richly maize-colored, wavy and shiny. He smiled at her, and he saw that she was basking in the look that he gave her.

Joshua had talked to Hanna earlier that day about Penny, trying to make her understand that she wasn't trying to hurt Hanna and Adam or make them forget their mother. They had sat on the porch steps and talked for an hour. But Hanna was still a little subdued.

They drove to the reservation and parked on the road across from Black Mountain. They walked up to where others had already gathered. The celebration for Ignacio was very simple. There was no brass band, no Marine Corps honor guard for the colors, no tomahawk and tom-tom dancers. There were just Ignacio, Magdalena, their grandparents, their cousin Henry and Henry's wife, Maria, with their three young children, a half-dozen family friends, Penny, and the Rabbs—except for Adam. The barbecue was done in a pit like the one at the July Fourth picnic. Ernestina Antone and Magdalena had slaughtered a kid early that morning and put it in the pit at seven o'clock to roast all day. They removed it after ten hours of roasting and stripped the succulent goat meat off the carcass, shredded it, and simmered it in a cauldron filled with red salsa and garlic and onions. The resulting *birria* was a rare delicacy among the Papagos.

Macario and Ernestina and Magdalena had spent most of the day boiling saguaro fruits to make the much-treasured saguaro wine. The making of the wine was generally reserved for religious celebrations, and particularly the *Wihgita*, a fertility festival which took place every August in the town of Quitovac, Mexico, and which ended with the men consuming as much wine as they could hold. But tonight was an auspicious occasion, and no grandiose sign of their happiness would be spared.

The strangeness of it all was wearing off for Joshua and Hanna, since they had lived for several weeks now so closely alongside the Indians. But to Penny, it was all eye-poppingly exotic.

After everyone had gorged on the *birria* and could eat no more, and after the saguaro wine was exhausted, the sun set behind Black Mountain in a red and orange and yellow luster along the horizon. As darkness came, several of the men built a fire. It was much too hot to gather closely to it, but it attracted everyone in a wide circle around it. Magdalena sat with Joshua and Penny and Hanna.

Macario stood up, a little shaky from the celebratory wine, and spoke for a moment in Papago. Ignacio's face became sober, and then he too stood up after a moment and solemnly mumbled a few words. He sat down again. Magdalena leaned toward Joshua and whispered an explanation, that Macario wanted Ignacio to come back to the reservation to live, that the men would help him build his own adobe house, and that Macario was presenting to him a gift of his pickup truck. Ignacio looked around sheepishly, a small embarrassed smile playing on his lips and cheeks.

Again Macario started speaking in Papago, his face luminous in the darting flames of the campfire. And again Magdalena leaned over and translated in a whisper. Her grandfather was engaged in traditional *ha'ichu'aga*, telling stories, a custom for the elders of the tribe at any celebration. Now he was reciting the legend of *I'itoi*, one of the heroes of the Papagos. Magdalena translated slowly.

Then Macario changed to English. His voice became grave, and the twittering and laughter subsided around the campfire. "Joshua Rabb has been sent to us by God," he said.

Joshua looked up at the old man and felt extremely self-conscious.

"We put into his hands a most terrible choice: to act with mercy and compassion for an innocent man and be scorned by many of his own kind, or to take the safe way and ignore our need." Macario paused. "Joshua Rabb chose the only course that he knows, the path of honor and justice." He bowed to Joshua and continued speaking slowly.

"Many years ago when I was a boy, the wisest man in the whole tribe lived up here on Black Mountain. He had an *olas kih* right there." He pointed to a slight knoll on the hill. "And he used to sit up there against the rock all day and meditate. And one day, one of my friends decided that he could outsmart the wise man and make a big name for himself in the tribe. So he captured a small bird and fetched me and we went up the hill, right there to where the wise man was sitting and meditating.

"And my friend put the bird behind his back and said, 'Old man, what do I have in my hands?'

"And the old man said, 'It is a bird, my son.'

"My friend was very surprised, but he knew he'd still get him. So he said, 'Old man, in which hand do I hold the bird?'

"And the old man said, 'It is in your right hand, my son.'

"Well, now my friend was really surprised, but he knew that he could outsmart him with just one last question: he'd ask him if the bird was alive or dead, and if the sage said it was alive, he'd crush it. 'Old man, is the bird dead or alive?'

"The sage looked gently at my friend and said, 'It is in your hands, my son.' "

Macario looked at Joshua. "Joshua Rabb is precisely such a man of wisdom. He knows only how to act wisely and with goodness. We are honored to have him among us."

Joshua was loosened enough by all the wine that his already florid face showed no signs of blushing. He stood up and bowed to Macario and to several others around the fire and then sat down again. He was embarrassed by the intensity of Macario's tribute. Macario came around and shook Joshua's hand. He then handed the keys to his pickup to Ignacio. Ignacio took them, stood up and embraced his grandfather, shook hands with Joshua, and walked a little unsteadily to his grandparents' house, where the truck was parked. The others slowly drifted away from the fire. Magdalena remained in her *olas kih* for the night. She needed to be alone.

Joshua and Penny and Hanna drove back to the house. It

was almost eleven o'clock, and Hanna was very tired. She had drunk two cups of the saguaro wine. She went inside yawning. Joshua and Penny stood by her roadster, Penny leaning back against it, and kissed and touched for ten minutes in the darkness.

"I'm sorry to send you back into the house with this thing," she whispered, rubbing him through his pants.

"Want to take it with you?" he breathed.

"I want to take all of you with me."

"I'll save it for you till tomorrow night."

They kissed deeply. She got into the roadster and drove away.

~~~~~~~~~

Joshua slid slowly into consciousness. It was pitch-black in his bedroom, and a kettle drum was beating in his hung-over brain. No, no, it was not inside his head. He sat up abruptly. Someone was pounding on the front door. He looked at his watch. It was almost three o'clock. What the hell?

He got out of bed, pulled on his pants, and took the .45 revolver out of the nightstand drawer. He went to the window beside the front door and peeked out the edge of the curtain. It was Edgar Hendly. Joshua turned on the living room light and opened the door.

"Edgar, what in the—"

"There's trouble downtown," Edgar cut Joshua off. "I just got a call from Sheriff Dunphy. There's somethin goin on down at the shacks where Ignacio lives."

"Is Ignacio hurt?"

"I dunno. We'd better get out there," Edgar said.

Hanna came out of the bedroom rubbing her eyes. "What's going on?" she yawned.

Joshua came up to her and put his hand on her shoulder. "There's something happening downtown with Ignacio. I'm going down there. You have to stay here and keep the doors and windows locked. Okay?" He handed her the revolver.

She nodded solemnly and gulped.

Joshua went into the bedroom and dressed. He got into Edgar's Ford sedan. Edgar drove quickly to downtown Tucson.

They came down South Sixth Avenue toward the railroad switching yard and could see a tall fire as they neared the shacks by the yard.

At the east side of the yard was the city impoundment lot where the hulks of abandoned and wrecked vehicles were stored. It was unfenced and bounded on the east by about a dozen cardboard and tarpaper shacks which huddled around a central pit, forty or fifty yards around, where old tires were dumped. A mound of them rose like a small hill, and they were burning with a dancing blue flame, black smoke billowing off the top of the heap. Several people were standing around watching.

Edgar pulled up beside a sheriff's car. Marty Hankins got out and walked around to the driver's window.

"Sheriff Dunphy called me, said there was some trouble with Ignacio," Edgar said.

"Seems some of the boys got tanked up tonight over at the Esquire bar and decided to have a little fun with him," Marty said. "They came on down here and set fire to the tires, but the sheriff got a call from the bartender and he came down here and broke it up."

"Is Ignacio okay?"

"Well, a few of them hothead bastards took him off somewhere. We don't know where. The sheriff's out looking for them. Three other deputies, too."

"You have any idea where they went?"

"Nope." He shook his head and frowned.

"My God," Joshua gasped. "What will they do to him?"

Neither Edgar nor the deputy answered. Edgar struck the steering wheel with his palm in frustration. "Damn!"

"We've got to look for him," Joshua said.

Edgar shook his head. "Ain't got no idea where." He shrugged his shoulders. "Listen, Marty, we're heading back over to my house. Will you call me as soon as you know anything?"

"Yes, sir, I sure will, Mr. Hendly."

Edgar backed up slowly, and they drove silently toward the reservation. As they neared Valencia Road, they could see what looked like a bonfire on Martinez Hill, just east of the reservation and the Santa Cruz River bed. Instead of turning west on Valencia Road to go to Indian Agency Road, Edgar turned east to Nogales Highway and then onto a dirt road which wound up Martinez Hill.

A pickup truck sped down the hill and almost careened into the car. Edgar swerved and the car skidded off the road into a shallow ravine. He tried to start it, but it just whined and whined.

"Come on, we'll worry about it later," Joshua said.

They left the car in the ravine and ran up toward the summit of the hill. A Chevrolet sedan gunned down the dirt road toward them. They jumped to the side and the car sped away down the hill.

They reached the top a minute later, and the sight froze Joshua. Edgar turned around gasping and took a few steps down the road. He stumbled and fell to his knees.

Joshua shielded his eyes with his forearm from the intense heat and stepped toward the burning tree to see if there was any way to help Ignacio. It was an old dead mesquite tree, thick-trunked and full of spindly branches which were now burning with a whooshing sound interspersed with small explosions like firecrackers as pockets of desiccated sap burst into sparks. Two five-gallon gasoline cans were strewn empty on the ground. They must have poured gas over Ignacio and soaked the tree with it to get them to burn that intensely, thought Joshua. There was almost nothing left of Ignacio's outer flesh. As the ropes that had lashed him to the tree burned away, the charred black stiff corpse fell straight forward to the ground with a whomp. Joshua jumped away from it as sparks flew up. It was burning, smoldering. When it hit the muddy earth, it began crackling and sizzling and a stinking cloud of smoke swelled up around it.

There was no newspaper story about it the next morning. Nor could Joshua find a radio report. No one reported how he and Edgar had finally gotten Edgar's car started and put the charred corpse in the trunk and drove over to Macario Antone's house and roused him from sleep and then drove over to the cemetery and left the body there, just as it was, on the ground between the mounds of two graves. No deputy sheriff came to report to Joshua or Edgar that there was a search on for the lynch mob. No one came to offer the condolences of a shamed town. No one. Because this was only Ignacio Antone, a Papago Indian, a drunken *maricón*. This was not a person whom anyone wrote about or cared about or missed or sorrowed over. Morality, mercy, appeared to be the province of white people only in their dealings with other whites. And then only sometimes.

Joshua picked up Adam at the hospital at nine o'clock in the morning and brought him home. Adam wept as he listened to his father tell what had happened to Ignacio. Joshua made him take one of the tranquilizers that the doctor had prescribed for him, and he fell slowly into fitful sleep. At about two in the afternoon, he got out of bed, and he and Hanna walked slowly beside the ditch toward the reservoir.

Joshua spent the day in a kind of fog, a haze over everything that he did, so that it all seemed ephemeral, unreal. He hadn't felt as detached from life as this in over a year, not since he had lain for days on end with the throbbing pain in his foot and arm that he thought would kill him, or since he had been told of Rachel's death.

He sat down leadenly on the couch in the living room, and his depression was palpable, suffocating, and he felt himself breathing shallowly and his pulse squishing in his temples. For some reason, the scar over his rib cage where he had been shot and where part of his lung had been removed suddenly started hurting, and he thought that he was going to have a heart attack.

The last few days had been the nadir of his life, and it had not yet begun to rise. He had thought that nothing would ever affect him so penetratingly as seeing the dying inmates of that camp in Czechoslovakia, the little girl with the dead boys at her feet, Yossie Finkel, and all the many others. But he had been wrong. Seeing Ignacio's charred skull where his delicately handsome face had been just moments before was just as horrendous. Joshua had succored his pain, defended him, protected him, and freed him. Only so that bad people could reduce it all to nothing and set him afire. Pour gas on him and light him like a pile of rags. Poof. Gone in a scream. He gritted his teeth and blinked his eyes, but he couldn't hold back the flood of memories rushing before his mind's eye.

The road to Medzibiez and the town itself are under full American control now. Captain Goldberg comes into my office one evening and suggests that we go into town and look it over. Hanging around the concentration camp for the last week has been harrowing. We need to get away from it, if only for a few hours.

We drive into town in my jeep and stop beside what looks like a Gaststube. *In this part of Czechoslovakia, Sudetenland, everything looks like Germany, and many of the signs on the shops are in German. The sign on this place reads* ZUM BRAUHAUS GEIST. *We go into a dimly lit beer house with a few long tables at which several people are sitting drinking beer and eating sausages. The customers stare grimly at us, and turn back to their beer steins. We sit at a small table in the corner. A waitress in a white peasant dirndl with red lacy trim on the top where it encircles her huge breasts comes to the table and asks in German for our orders. We order bratwurst and beer, and the waitress giggles a little at the look Joe Goldberg gives her. She is tall and stocky with coarse hands like a farm girl, in her early twenties, and has curly blond hair and cupid's bow lips and hazel eyes.*

She brings the beer and sausages, and Joe says something to her in Yiddish, the closest he can come to German. The girl laughs lustily, and several of the other patrons stare resentfully at us. Joe asks her in Yiddish if there is a movie house in town, and the girl says there used to be, but it's just a pile of rubble from the recent artillery shelling by the American troops. Two men stare at Joe, listening to him chat in Yiddish with the German-speaking barmaid.

Joe and I drink several beers and talk about New York and our families and getting back, and Joe gathers energy the more he drinks. After an hour, I go into the pissoir at the back of the room. I come back a couple of minutes later and Joe is gone. I go up to the bartender and ask in German where my friend went, and the bartender points to the stairwell at the other side of the bar and the closed door on the landing. "Sie machen a bissele spass—*they're having a little fun," he says to me. I go back and sit down at the little table. I watch two men get up from the long table and go up the stairs, go into the room, and close the door. I get a little worried, and then I hear yelling.*

I jump out of my chair, pull my .45 automatic out of my holster, and run toward the stairway. I feel a powerful blow on the back of my head and sprawl facedown on the floor, unconscious. I wake up in the alley sometime later. My face is bloody from a deep gash on the back of my head, but otherwise I'm uninjured. I begin to stand up and suddenly see a body beside me. There is enough moon to see clearly. I roll the body over. It's Joe Goldberg. His own bayonet is buried to the hilt in his chest.

Joshua shook himself out of his tormenting reverie and got up from the couch to leave. Where? It didn't matter. Just anywhere. Just keep moving so he wouldn't have to think. But then the front door opened, and Hanna and Adam came in. And now he could not leave. Despite everything he felt, despite his need to weep and rend his garments and try to fathom the evil that had descended over them all, he gulped down his own anguish and smiled bravely at Hanna and mussed Adam's hair and sat back down on the couch to hold his children and comfort them.

～～～～

Macario Antone came to the door of the Rabb house at about four o'clock that afternoon. Magdalena opened the door. As old as he was, he looked somehow even older. His eyes were deeply recessed and red-rimmed, and he looked weak.

"Grandpa, I want you to go to a doctor over at the health services," Magdalena said.

"I'm okay. I'm okay. Can you come with me to see Father Hausner? We have to talk to him about a mass for Ignacio."

"Of course. But Mr. Rabb isn't here. He went to his office a few minutes ago. I can't leave Hanna and Adam alone."

"Then we'll take them. They can ride in the bed of the pickup. We have to see Father Hausner at four-thirty. He was very insistent. He doesn't have much time free today."

Adam and Hanna were on the floor listening to the radio.

"I get to ride in the back of the truck?" Adam asked.

"Sure do," Macario said.

"Wow! Thanks!"

They drove to the rectory next to the mission, and Macario knocked on the front door. A nun in a black dress and white head scarf opened the door. She wiped her hands on a dish towel. She still had a large purple welt on her cheek where Magdalena had slapped her. She cast Magdalena a vicious glance and silently led them into the living room. It was spacious and had a huge ornately hand-carved wooden dining table surrounded by Mexican-style wooden chairs with single thickness leather squares for seats and backs. There was a stone fireplace in the side wall. On the other side of the room, there was a long sofa and two matching upholstered chairs in a brocaded damask of rust and beige and gold. Indian rugs covered the terra-cotta-tiled floor. The high ceiling was saguaro ribs held up by rough-hewn timber beams.

They stood awkwardly, waiting for the priest. Out of politeness, Macario didn't remove his hat.

"Ah, Chief Antone," Father Hausner said, sweeping into the room. He held out his hand, palm downward, and Macario bent and kissed it. "It's been much too long since we've gotten together," the priest said. "Sit, sit. We'll all have some lemonade."

The priest sat in one of the upholstered chairs, and Macario sat in the other. Magdalena, Hanna, and Adam sat down on the couch.

"What brings you to me, Chief?"

"It is my grandson."

"Ah yes, indeed, I had almost forgotten. Ignacio was your grandson. How terrible a thing has been done."

Brother Boniface came in silently and stood behind Hausner's chair. Sister Mary Rose brought in a tray of glasses of lemonade and laid it on the coffee table. She left the room. Adam reached for a glass, saw that no one else was taking one, and sat back embarrassed. He peeked at Hanna and quickly averted his eyes from her scowl.

"We wish to have his funeral mass tomorrow morning," Macario said.

The priest raised his eyebrows and pursed his lips. "I am shocked that you would come to me with such a request, Chief Antone. Certainly you are a good enough Catholic to know that I cannot give a mass for a murderer, the murderer of one of our nuns, no less."

Macario's eyes narrowed. "He is no murderer. The judge let him free."

"I'm afraid it's simply out of the question, Chief. There is no doubt here that your grandson murdered Sister Martha."

"You mean that *you* have no doubt, Father Hausner," Macario said angrily.

"Have it your own way, Chief. I won't quibble over words. I have spoken about it with Steve Lukis and Buford Richards and Tom Delahanty. They all believe the same thing. They think your lawyer friend phonied up the evidence."

Macario's voice lowered, cracked. "If he does not have last rites, he cannot be buried in our cemetery. And we have no money for Forest Lawn in Tucson. He will have to be buried in an unmarked pauper's grave by 'A' Mountain."

The priest was silent.

"I beg you to reconsider this," Macario pleaded.

Hausner stirred uneasily in the large chair. "Father Boniface is a canon lawyer," he said slowly. "He has chosen not to be a pastor, but to be a monk. And he has chosen silence as a way to serve God. But perhaps in this matter he may be called upon to consider your request."

Boniface walked slowly from behind the chair. He put the cowl of his cassock down. He looked with soft, limpid blue eyes at Macario. "I well understand the turmoil of your soul," he said. His voice was incongruously soft, coming from this big man with the meaty, unpretty face. His blue eyes were gentling. "Did you speak to your grandson about this? Do you believe with perfect faith on peril of your immortal soul that he was innocent?"

"I spoke to him. He was not so overwhelmed with fear that

he would lie to me, or even could lie to me and make me believe it. He did not kill anyone or even know anything about it." Macario spoke pleadingly, his voice hoarse and cracking. He wrung his hands in frustration.

"But he was not innocent," broke in Father Hausner.

Macario's eyes kindled and he looked angrily at Hausner. "Mr. Rabb proved it. No Indian killed Sister Martha." Macario's eyes filled with tears of anger and frustration.

"Was Ignacio a good Catholic?" Boniface asked.

Macario breathed deeply to calm himself. "He was always a good boy, until he got turned down by the army. Then he changed, he started to drink. It was my fault. I was not a good father to him. I did not understand what had happened." Macario gritted his teeth and his cheeks twitched.

Boniface smiled benevolently. "Let Father and me speak of this for a moment. Would you wait outside?"

Macario stood up. Magdalena and Hanna and Adam followed him out the door. They stood silently, uncomfortable in the broiling late afternoon sun. Ten minutes. Fifteen minutes.

The door opened a foot. Sister Mary Rose peeked out. She smiled at Magdalena. "There will be no mass for him." She closed the door.

Macario was stunned. He teetered and almost fell. Magdalena and Hanna took him by the arms and walked him slowly back to the truck.

CHAPTER SEVENTEEN

Tom Delahanty came to the Rabb house at five o'clock that afternoon. Joshua answered the knock on the door.

"You don't look too hot today, Yehoshua. No sir, I guess all the excitement round here done got to you."

"What do you want?" Joshua's voice was gruff. His face was drawn and craggy.

"Well now, you ain't as all fired pleased to see me as you was the first time, huh, Yehoshua?"

Joshua stepped onto the porch and closed the front door. "Don't disturb my kids, they had some rough days."

"Well, I reckon they done at that, yes sir, no doubt about it. I was out at the hospital yesterday to see your pal Samuel. He wasn't doin so hot."

"Yes, I know."

"I talked to your acculturation girl out there too. She was sittin with him. She says that her and Sammy was *reclinin* over on Black Mountain. Sammy took out after somebody in a priest's cloak, and that's the last thing she knows."

Joshua nodded. "I know, I talked to her also."

"Mighty pretty girl, that one. Got a little education on her too, pretty damn high-toned for a Indian cunt."

"Watch your mouth!" Joshua's face was grim.

Delahanty smiled slowly. "Yeah, I done thought so. You got a powerful big attachment built up with that girl." He nodded his head and looked at Joshua intently. "Reckon you didn't like that Indian boy Sammy sniffin your private pussy, porkin your squeeze, huh, Yehoshua?"

Joshua gritted his teeth and said nothing. He clenched his fist.

"I didn't know you had such a hankerin like that about that Indian cunt."

"Get the fuck out of here."

Delahanty stopped smiling. He stopped hemming and hawing like a country bumpkin. "Well, I ain't got enough to charge you with bein the weird fuck that tried to snuff poor Sammy, but I'm workin on it. You pluggin your acculturation girl while Sammy was beatin your time. Plenty a motive there, huh, big shot? And you got quite a temper, don't ya? I done a little checkin up on you, called the FBI office in Brooklyn. They tell me you was arrested for bustin some guy's jaw in a bar fight over a whore. Damn near killed him. Yessir, there's more to you than meets the eye, ain't there, Yehoshua?"

He walked back to his car and drove off. Joshua stared after him.

〰〰〰

Penny sat in the lobby of the Cattleman's Hotel waiting for Joshua. It was much cooler down here, where there was air-conditioning, than in her room, where a small water cooler on the window whirred angrily and blew warm moist air. It had rained for an hour early that afternoon, and the heat and humidity were debilitating. She thumbed through a *Saturday Evening Post* and absently read a couple of the articles.

Two men came into the hotel, and Penny recognized the bigger one immediately. It was that FBI man, Delahanty, who had bothered her at her cabin. With him was someone she had never seen. She was sitting in the rear of the large lobby, and there were probably another ten people scattered around on the fat furniture. She slid a little deeper in her chair and held the *Post* up higher to shield her face from view.

They talked quietly with the desk clerk. The clerk turned the guest registry book around so that they could study it. They left after a few minutes.

Joshua came in five minutes later and limped toward the stairway to the rooms. Penny got up and went to intercept him. They greeted each other formally. There were too many people around for a show of affection.

They went outside into the growing darkness of approaching sunset. "Why are you using the cane again?"

He shrugged. "I've felt so bad lately, all I do is sit around and think. No exercise. My hip got kind of sore."

"I'll massage it for you later," she said.

He turned to her and smiled. "Best damn proposal I've had all day."

She took his arm and pressed close to him.

"You want to skip the movie and do the massaging right now?" he said.

"I wish we could. But we can't go upstairs in front of all those people in the lobby."

He frowned and nodded. They crossed Stone Avenue at Congress and went into the Fox Theater. *To Have and Have Not* was playing. It had made quite a splash, not because it was from a Hemingway story but because Humphrey Bogart had met his true love Lauren Bacall while they were filming it. Everybody was now using the line, "You know how to whistle, don't you? Just put your lips together and blow."

At least the theater was air-conditioned. They sat in the back row and held hands. There were only six or eight people in the theater. A couple sitting way over in the corner were engaged in feverish activity accompanied by heavy groans and a good deal of movement. Their show was better than the movie, at least far more graphic, and Penny and Joshua watched in fascination until it ended with the woman's head in his lap and him wheezing loudly.

"How about me?" Joshua whispered.

"Later," she whispered. "I'm a little more inhibited than they are."

He laughed. "Who isn't!"

Humphrey and Lauren left the bar hand in hand, and Penny and Joshua left the theater. It was nine-thirty and the vicious heat of the day had subsided.

"What do you want to do?" she said.

"I don't know. I don't feel much like going to a bar and listening to music. It's been too rough this week. I just feel like lying back and staring at the ceiling."

"Sounds good to me," she said.

They walked slowly to the Cattleman's Hotel. "You want something to drink?" he asked.

"No, not booze anyway. It's too hot. Maybe a beer."

They walked into the Owl Drug across from the hotel. He got four bottles of Lucky Lager out of the refrigerator. The cashier rang them up.

"You got a bottle opener?" Joshua asked.

The cashier opened a drawer and rummaged around inside. He pulled out a rusty metal can opener and bottle opener combination. "I got this old church key."

"How much?"

"Nickel."

Joshua handed him the money and he and Penny walked to the hotel. The lobby was almost empty now, and the desk clerk was sitting at the cash register with his back to them. They walked quickly and quietly up the stairs.

Her room was much more comfortable now that the swamp cooler had had a couple of hours of darkness to do its work. Joshua sat down on the edge of the bed and put the bag on the floor at his feet. He pulled out two bottles and the church key, popped the caps, and put the can opener on the bedstand. He handed one of the beers to Penny. She took a long swallow.

"I never liked this stuff until I got to Tucson," she said. "It's so hot here in the summer that a cold beer really tastes good. Cools you off." She sat down on the other side of the bed.

He lay back on the bed and rolled toward her and wrapped his arm around her waist. "I don't want to cool off."

She looked deeply into his eyes and unbuttoned her blouse. He reached behind her back and unhooked her bra. They undressed each other slowly and made love.

Joshua awoke at two-thirty. The light on the bedstand was still on. He dressed quietly, switched off the light, and left the hotel room, making sure that the door was locked. The lobby was deserted and dark except for a couple of lamps on tables. No desk clerk was behind the counter. He went out to the De Soto and drove home.

Penny heard a door click. She felt next to her for Joshua, but he was gone. She hated his having to leave like this in the middle of the night. She rolled over and nestled into the sheets. Suddenly she heard soft rapid footsteps on the carpet. She looked up, but her vision was blurry from sleep. Someone ripped the sheet off of her and a rough hand covered her mouth. She tried to scream, but the hand was smothering her.

She pushed at his face with both hands, and he punched her in the cheek. The pain spiraled through her jaw. She almost lost consciousness. She was too breathless and disoriented to scream. All she could think of was to get him off of her. She suddenly remembered the rusty church key. On the bedstand? She groped for it and found it. She stabbed at the man. She hit his shoulder, and he howled in pain. He swore "fucking bitch" in a guttural growl and sat up rubbing his shoulder. She stabbed him as hard as she could, several times. She caught him once on the side of the face. Both of his hands jerked up to cover his face, and he snapped his head back to get away from her. Her next blow hit his neck. She ripped down viciously. He fell off the bed and writhed on the floor, gurgling and gasping for breath. She grabbed the sheet and wrapped it around herself and ran out of the room screaming frantically. The man crawled after her, stood up, and lunged for her.

She ran down the stairs and into the lobby. The man had stopped following her. She ran toward the desk. A clerk was rising from a chair behind the huge counter with his mouth wide open in surprise.

"Help me, help me!" she screamed at him. "Help me! Someone's trying to kill me!"

The clerk ran around the counter to her. He was an old man, frail and small, and he looked at her in fright.

"Call the police," she sobbed.

"You stay here now, lady," the clerk said. "You sit down." He led her to a sofa and she sat down, sobbing hysterically.

"What room you in?" he asked, staring fearfully into her eyes.

"Three fourteen," she choked out.

He went behind the counter and picked up a baseball bat that was on the floor. He crept toward the stairs, bat up over his head in both hands, and crept slowly up the stairway out of sight.

Penny looked around cautiously as she regained her composure. She hugged the sheet close around her, feeling very cold, but she couldn't stop trembling. A few minutes later the clerk came running down the stairs. He stopped at the bottom and bent over and vomited explosively. He wiped his mouth roughly on his sleeve and coughed. He spat on the floor and ran behind the counter and dialed the telephone.

"Get someone here right away, Cattleman's Hotel. There's been a murder." He hung up and straightened up and stared at Penny in fear.

A short time later, a sheriff's deputy came into the lobby. The clerk went up to him and spoke in a low voice. He glanced at Penny and pointed toward the stairs. The deputy went up the stairs and returned in a few minutes. He walked behind the desk and telephoned. Penny was no longer paying any attention. She just sat staring into space, trying to stop trembling.

"You know who that is up there?" said the deputy, walking up to her.

She shook her head.

"Why'd you kill him?"

Her eyes opened wide. She looked up at him for a moment and then looked away and began weeping quietly.

"What happened? You get into a hassle over money?"

She couldn't speak.

The lobby began filling up with sheriff's deputies. First one, then two more, then two more carrying a canvas stretcher. They carried the body downstairs, and Penny looked over at the blood-drenched corpse. She had stopped crying and felt dazed. She could hardly remember what had happened. A deputy was talking quietly to the clerk, writing things down in a little notebook.

An elderly man with a big paunch and thinning gray hair sat down next to her on the sofa. His stomach bulged the buttons on his tan uniform shirt. "I'm Sheriff Dunphy. The registry says you're Penny Chesser. Can you talk?"

She turned toward him and sniffed and nodded shortly.

"You a hooker?" he asked matter-of-factly. "You get in a fight with him over payment?"

She shook her head vigorously. "He broke in and attacked me," she choked out.

His voice became harsher. "Come on now, Penny. Let's hear it. The doorjamb wasn't broke, the lock wasn't broke."

"Then he got a key from somewhere."

"All right, Penny, whattaya got on under that sheet?"

She looked at him fearfully and hugged the sheet tighter around her.

"Let's go upstairs, get some clothes on you. We gotta go down to the station." He stood up but she didn't move. He grabbed a handful of her hair and pulled her head up straight. "You'd better start listening to me, Penny, or you're gonna get yourself hurt."

She stood up stiffly, and he let go of her hair. They walked up the stairs to her room on the third floor. There was a great stain of blood in the middle of the carpeted hallway, followed by splatters of blood trailing into the room and on the white bed sheet. She walked to the closet and turned to the sheriff.

"Please turn around," she said in a thin whisper.

"Now's no time for bein dainty, Penny. I don't wanna get my throat tore out like your john. Just go right ahead there. I won't be shocked. But first drop that sheet. I gotta check you over."

She looked at him in terror. "Don't touch me," she whimpered.

He slapped her hard across the face. "Knock off that bullshit, Penny. Drop the sheet."

She clutched it around her. Dunphy grabbed it with both

hands and pulled it off. He held up one of her arms and studied it, then the other. She shuddered and crossed her arms over her breasts and sobbed uncontrollably.

"Let's see them feet."

She lifted her left foot toward him. He bent over and peered at it closely. Then he examined the other one.

"All right, turn around. Let me see the backs of your knees."

She turned around and faced the closet.

"Okay, you ain't on junk, that's for sure." He reached roughly between her legs and rubbed his finger in her vulva. He sniffed it. "But you been laid tonight, no doubt about that. What happened, he wouldn't pay you?"

She was still weeping and trembling. She reached out and took a pair of Levi's off the hook inside the door. She pulled them on. She took a simple white button-front blouse off a hanger and put it on. "Call Joshua Rabb," she gasped. "He's a lawyer with the Indian bureau. He'll explain this." She turned around and faced him belligerently.

He looked at her oddly. "How do you come to know him?"

"He was here tonight with me, before that animal came. I've been in Tucson all week visiting him and his family."

"All right," he said. "Get them sandals on and let's go back to my office."

Joshua hadn't even gone to sleep when he got home. The few hours of sleep with Penny made him feel rested, relaxed for the first time in many days. He heard the car drive up in the front yard. He had been reading in the living room. It was a little after five. What could it be this time? he thought. I can't take any more of this. He looked out the window beside the door. It was a sheriff's car. There was a loud knock, and he opened the door. It was a deputy he hadn't seen before.

"You Mr. Rabb?"

"Yes."

"A lady named Penny Chesser is down at the main station. Says you're her friend."

"Yes. What's happened?"

"Well, she killed a guy in her hotel room."

"What?" gasped Joshua.

"Yup. Chopped him pretty good. Cut a hole in his windpipe with a can opener. Bled to death."

Joshua was horrified. "Who was it?" he stammered.

"Well now, that's the interesting part, Mr. Rabb. It was Tom Delahanty, the FBI agent."

Joshua stared at the deputy in shock. "Where is she?"

"Down at the station by the courthouse. Sheriff Dunphy's with her."

"Is she okay?"

"She's a hell of a lot better than the FBI man." He shrugged.

"I'll take my own car," Joshua said.

"Okay, Mr. Rabb. Sheriff Dunphy just wanted me to let you know."

By the time Joshua got downtown, it was full sunrise. He parked across from the courthouse and limped to the sheriff's office at the rear. The desk deputy told him to go down the hallway to the room with the engraved wooden plaque on it that said SHERIFF. He knocked loudly and walked in. Pat Dunphy was sitting behind a metal desk, his hands folded on the blotter. He looked very tired. Penny sat in front of the desk. Her hair was down and uncombed. She still had the makeup on from last evening. The mascara and eye shadow were smudged from tears. Black streaks ran down her cheeks. She jumped up and hugged Joshua and started crying. He held her and let her cry herself out. Dunphy stared at them placidly. When she stopped weeping and trembling, Joshua walked her back to the chair and she sat down.

"I reckon this town didn't have much excitement 'fore you got here, Mr. Rabb," he drawled.

"Listen, Sheriff. Delahanty was crazy. He must have followed us to the hotel and waited for me to leave."

Dunphy gave him a sour look. "I know all about Delahanty. The girls down at the Catalina tell some terrible stories about him. I always figured it was just whore talk. But I reckon not."

He paused and held up a key. "My boys found this Cattleman's Hotel passkey in his pocket. Wonder how he got it?"

Joshua stared at it and then at the sheriff. "Who owns the hotel?"

"Evelyn Enterprises," the sheriff said. "Interesting, huh?"

Joshua nodded. "Interesting. You going to check into this?"

"Well now, Mr. Rabb," the sheriff drawled, "there's some kinds of things I do and some things I just *don't* do. Fuckin around with the senator's business is one of the second kind."

"Prevalent attitude around these parts."

The sheriff shrugged. "Well anyway, it's too bad it had to be the FBI man. Tough one to explain, 'specially to the bureau." He shook his head gravely.

"Can we go?" Joshua asked.

He nodded. "Yeah, you can go. Try to make this the last time I see you." There was no humor in his voice.

They got in the car. Penny slumped in the seat and wept. He held her.

"I can't go back to that hotel," she said, her voice quivering.

"Of course not, you're coming home with me."

"But people will talk."

"You'll sleep in Adam's room. Adam can sleep on the couch."

"They'll still talk."

"Fuck em," he said, his face grim.

He drove to the hotel, and while Penny waited in the car, he packed her clothes and brought the valise down. Everything was peaceful as they drove to Indian Agency Road and parked in front of the irrigation ditch. It was Saturday morning, and nobody was up and about this early. The drapes were still drawn on the front window of the house, so even Magdalena wasn't up yet.

"I don't want to go in right now," Penny said, her voice hoarse and low. "I just want to go for a walk."

They got out of the car and walked down into the irrigation ditch and up the other side onto the reservation. They ambled slowly through the field toward the mission. The monsoon rains had brought out a cacophony of wildflowers. Purple lupine and magenta locoweed, blue and white eryngo and crimson sky-rockets, coral bells and hummingbird trumpets peeking out from under rocks, and bright yellow snakeweed and rabbitbrush and goldenrod. The insouciant display of bold-colored little flowers in the midst of the otherwise relentlessly brown crusty desert vastness was startling.

Penny knelt down next to a small boulder and picked a handful of hummingbird trumpets. She sniffed them and held them up for Joshua to smell the sweetness.

"Now I know what Thomas Gray meant," she said, her voice low and sad.

Joshua said nothing, waiting patiently.

" 'Full many a flower is born to blush unseen,' " Penny recited, " 'and waste its sweetness on the desert air.' "

Joshua sat down on the boulder. "But is it really wasted?" he asked softly. "Only if you think that man is the center of everything, and that if the flower doesn't grow in Prospect Park for man's pleasure, then it's wasted. But out here, the hummingbirds and the gophers and the bumblebees and the diamondbacks are the center of everything, and for them none of it is wasted."

His face was soft, compassionate. She sat down on the boulder next to him. Slowly, interspersed with tears, she told him what had happened.

When she talked about Sheriff Dunphy ripping the sheet off of her and touching her, he had to grit his teeth tightly and swallow several times to suppress his anger, his desire to kill the fat bastard. He put his arm around her and held her tightly for an hour.

Then they walked slowly back to the house. Hanna was throwing corn at the chickens. She looked up and her mouth opened a little in surprise. She watched her father take something out of the De Soto and walk into the house. He was carrying a valise, *her* valise. Magdalena was in the kitchen making breakfast. Adam was on the floor in front of the radio playing with little toy cars. He looked up, and his eyes became big.

"Adam," Joshua said, "we're going to have a house guest.

She'll be staying in your room." Without waiting for a reply, Joshua went into Adam's room and set down the valise. Penny went into the bathroom.

"Is she moving in with us?" Adam asked, his face very serious.

"No, but she doesn't want to stay at the hotel anymore, and it's okay for us to have her as our guest."

Hanna came in and slammed the door. She traipsed into her bedroom noisily and slammed the door. Adam looked away quickly and began playing intently with his little cars.

Hanna came out of her bedroom in a pair of ragged-bottom Levi's shorts and a halter top. "I think I'll go down to the reservoir with Adam and Jimmy. Maybe I'll go swimming. Be back later."

She didn't even look at her father. She took Adam's hand, he stood up and got his BB gun, which was leaning against the living room wall, and they both left the house. Joshua looked after them with a frown on his face, but there was simply nothing he could do about it right now.

Magdalena came out of the kitchen. "There's hash browns and scrambled eggs all ready, Mr. Rabb. I'm going to spend the day at the hospital with Samuel."

Joshua shrugged apologetically. "I didn't mean to chase everybody off."

"Don't worry, Mr. Rabb. Hanna and Adam will get over it. Penny Chesser seems like a very nice lady." She smiled ingenuously and left the house.

Joshua turned on the radio and sat down on the couch. The shower went off in the bathroom. The door opened a crack, and Penny called out, "Could somebody bring me my suitcase? I need my bathroom stuff."

Joshua went into Adam's room and brought the valise into the bathroom. Penny was standing naked before the medicine chest mirror. She looked at him surprised. "The children—"

"Nobody's here but us."

"Oh," she said and smiled. "Maybe you'd like to take a shower, then. I'll scrub your back."

He locked the door and undressed. They got into the shower and she soaped him, all of him, and then he rinsed off under the faucet and turned the water off. He sat down on the edge of the tub and she sat on him and hugged him close. They made love, and then they just continued to sit there, looking at each other, smiling at each other, touching and kissing and loving.

"I almost forgot," she said as they combed their hair at the mirror. "What time is it?"

"A little after nine, I guess, maybe nine-thirty."

"We're supposed to be at the VA at ten-thirty to get your new arm."

"On Saturday?"

"Sure. Don't you remember? The prosthetician does a lot of his fittings on Saturdays so his patients don't have to miss work."

"Oh yeah, I forgot," he said, not very enthusiastically. "Are you really up to it?"

She shrugged. "I'd rather keep busy today, so I don't have to sit around and think about what happened last night." She looked at him quizzically. "What's wrong?"

"I'm going to feel kind of funny with that wooden arm. People will call me 'Captain Hook.' "

She turned and kissed his cheek. "Now, honey," she soothed, "nobody's that mean. You have nothing to feel funny about." She smiled warmly at him and kissed his cheek again. "You ready, Captain Hook?"

Both of them laughed.

They drove to the veterans hospital. The prosthetician and the physical therapist looked proudly at the contraption that they unveiled to Joshua and Penny. It was flesh-tone painted wood which looked something like a pickaxe handle bent forty-five degrees at the "elbow." On the top end it had a molded leather harness which covered his entire shoulder and stump. A three-inch-wide leather strap attached to the back of the harness and went around Joshua's back, under his armpit, and across his chest, where it buckled to the front of the harness. The wooden arm was attached to the flange of the harness just below the stump. There were two stainless-steel pincers attached to the "hand" end of the arm. The pincers were operated by two thin steel cables which Joshua would have to learn to manipulate.

Apart from the unaccustomed weight of seventeen pounds hanging off the end of his shoulder, the harness put painful pressure on the stump of his arm. He winced with the pain as the prosthetician took his hands away and stood back to watch Joshua try to adapt to his new appendage. The arm settled against Joshua's stomach, and he grimaced as he tried to lift it. He could only get it up about six inches.

"What's left of your biceps and triceps isn't enough to operate the arm, and your deltoid muscle has atrophied from lack of use," the physical therapist said. "You're going to have to build it up again. It'll take a few months. If you wear the arm for an hour a day at first, and every five days increase a half hour, you'll soon build up your strength. Now let me show you how to manipulate the hand."

He pulled on one of the cables, which was threaded through grommets imbedded in the wooden arm all the way up to the harness. "See, if you hold out the arm about a foot from your stomach and then rotate your shoulder backward, it immediately engages the cable assembly and both prongs open." The therapist held the arm away from Joshua's body while Joshua painfully rotated his shoulder. The shiny steel prongs opened an inch.

"Now if you want them opened fully to four inches, you bring your shoulder down like this." He pushed down on Joshua's shoulder. "Right, right, that's good. And you do the opposite to close the prongs, just push your shoulder up. The more intensely you push up, the more pressure is applied to the closure of the prongs. It'll squeeze up to four hundred pounds per square inch, plenty enough to rip someone's fingers off. So you've got to practice, practice, practice before you get into the receiving line at a wedding."

The therapist laughed a stale little laugh, enjoying the same joke that he had used on dozens of men in the same situation. Joshua wrinkled his cheeks, trying to smile approvingly, but the pain in his shoulder was too great. Beads of sweat burst out on his forehead and trickled down his face. The therapist brought the arm down and rested it against Joshua's stomach. Joshua let out a gasp of relief and breathed deeply as though he'd just been lifting weights.

"I can see that you're not particularly happy about it, Major," said the prosthetician, "but it'll get easier and easier until you don't even notice it anymore for a whole eighteen hours at a time." He smiled reassuringly. "That's enough of a workout for today." He unstrapped the arm and took it off.

Penny helped Joshua on with his shirt. They went back to the car.

"You drive," he said and tossed her the keys. "I feel like I just went ten rounds with Joe Louis."

"Want to go somewhere and eat lunch?"

"Sure," he said.

"There's a great little Mexican place downtown, El Charro."

"Sounds fine."

They rode in silence, and Joshua recuperated. Penny parked in an empty lot across from the restaurant, which was in an old converted stucco house. The name on the neon sign glowed garishly green on top, yellow in the middle, and crimson on the bottom.

"Think we ought to lock the car?" Penny asked.

"What for?"

"Somebody might fall in love with your arm and steal it."

"Let them have it," Joshua said.

Penny locked the driver's door and then walked around and locked the other. "Now, now, Captain Hook, let's not get pissy."

"You're a mean old broad," he said with a wry smile.

"I'm a nurse, tough as nails." She smiled.

They ordered *carne seca* burros enchilada style and beer.

"Well, I think last night solved the problem we've been having with bodies turning up in the irrigation ditch every few days." Joshua looked earnestly at Penny. "It was awful what you went through, and you ought to get the Nobel Peace Prize for it."

She grimaced. "Thank God you bought that five-cent can opener."

Joshua thought about the coincidence of it, the sheer luck of it. The vagaries of life, he thought, that life or death should turn on whether you just happened to stop for a beer and buy a nickel can opener.

"Now that the troubles are resolved, why don't you think about moving down the mountain?"

Penny took a swallow of beer and studied him. "I'm not sure I'm much of a fan of Tucson anymore."

He nodded his head and looked at her sadly.

"That's a pretty gooey look you're giving me, Captain Hook. Like you'd like to have me for lunch."

"Can't think of anything better to eat than you," he said.

She blushed a little and laughed. They ate the *carne seca* burros and glanced at each other from time to time and grinned.

"I've got to go back up Monday, you know," she said softly.

He nodded, unsmiling. "I know."

They finished lunch and drove to Joshua's house. As they parked, they saw Hanna and Adam walking toward the house from the reservoir. Jimmy was riding Charger. Joshua lifted his new arm off the backseat, and he and Penny went into the house. It was almost five o'clock. Magdalena came out of the kitchen holding a plucked chicken.

"Hi, Mr. Rabb, Miss Chesser. I thought it was Hanna and Adam. Do you know where they went?"

"They're down the ditch a little way, be here in a minute," Joshua said.

"I'll get the chickens in the oven. Dinner will be ready about six-thirty." She went back into the kitchen.

Joshua rested his arm against the living room wall. He turned on the radio, and he and Penny sat down on the couch.

Adam walked in followed by Jimmy. "Can we eat supper at Jimmy's?" he asked his father, not even looking at Penny.

"How come?"

"Well, they're having fried chicken."

"What do you do, check everybody's menu and then decide where you'll eat dinner?"

"Well, it's okay with Jimmy's mom. We asked."

Joshua was beginning to feel just a little annoyed by the way his children were treating Penny. "I think that you and your sister can eat dinner here tonight. We're having chicken too, and we have a guest." He glanced toward Penny and then looked at Jimmy. "We'd love to have you for dinner with us, Jimmy."

"Sure, Mr. Rabb, I'd sure like to."

Adam shrugged and walked to the door. "We're going to eat here and Jimmy's staying," he called out to his sister.

A moment later Hanna stomped up the porch steps and walked into the living room. "Hello, Miss Chester," she said.

Joshua heard the misplaced "t" and immediately remembered the anonymous note he had received. It gave him an instantaneous twinge of guilt.

"Hello, honey," Penny said with a smile. "Nice to see you again."

"What's that?" Adam pointed at the arm lying against the wall.

"That's my new arm," Joshua said.

"Yuk!" Hanna said.

"Gee whiz!" Adam blurted out. "Just like Captain Hook!" Jimmy giggled.

Joshua looked at Penny, and she burst out laughing. He chuckled.

"Can we look, Dad?" Adam asked eagerly.

"Sure, just don't drop it."

Adam picked it up tentatively, and he and Jimmy examined it. "Wow, this is really weird," Adam said.

"Yeah, look at them metal fingers," Jimmy said. "They're attached to them wires."

Both boys examined the arm in fascination. Then Adam laid it gingerly against the wall.

"I gotta take Charger back to his shed," Jimmy said.

"Yeah, I'll come with you," Adam said. "Be back in a minute, Dad."

The boys left. Hanna sat down on the upholstered chair and looked uncomfortable. "Can you really make that thing work?"

"After some practice, I think I'll be able to," Joshua answered.

She rolled her eyes. "Well, I have to wash horse sweat off my hands." She curled up her nose. "Horses are so *dirty*." She went into the bathroom.

"Well, at least she said hello," Joshua whispered.

Penny nodded and smiled.

Magdalena came out of the kitchen a few minutes later, wiping her hands on a dish towel. She sat down on the upholstered chair.

"How's Samuel?" Penny asked.

"He'll be all right," she said. She crossed herself. "The doctor said he'll have nothing worse than some scars on his scalp. Thank God."

Adam and Jimmy came back into the house. They sat down in front of the radio, and Adam took some toy cars out of his pocket. Jimmy had some too, and they lined up against each other for a battle. Magdalena went back into the kitchen to finish dinner. Hanna spent a long time in the bathroom and then went into her bedroom and closed the door.

Joshua and Penny sat lazily on the couch, listening to the radio, listening to the boys fight their battle. And then they all ate dinner, quietly, except for the occasional banter of the boys and a few murmurs from Hanna.

Penny was exhausted. She had hardly slept all night, so she went to bed a little after eight. Sometime during the early morning, she tiptoed into Joshua's room and turned the key in the lock.

She lay down next to him. "Hey, Hook," she whispered, "you alive?"

"I'm not sure," he said drowsily. "Touch me and see."

She rolled on her side and touched him. "Yes," she whispered, "you're definitely alive."

～～～～

Early Monday morning, Penny drove back up to her cabin on Mount Lemmon. Her vacation was over. And quite a vacation it had been. Joshua was depressed after she left, and Hanna and Adam left him alone. He stayed home from work all day and stalked around the house, brooding and sour.

The next morning, he pulled on his cream linen suit jacket a little before nine. As he got near the front door, he could hear his children's dolorous voices. They were sitting on the porch steps. He left the house and said good-bye to them, and they murmured good-bye. They silently watched him disappear down Indian Agency Road.

"He's in love," Hanna said to Adam.

Adam tilted his face toward his sister. "You mean like with Mommy?"

She nodded.

"Yeah, I thought so," Adam said miserably.

"I think we better find out all about her," Hanna said, her voice full of sorrow. "It looks like she's going to be around a whole lot."

"How do we do that?"

"Let's read what he's been writing in that big book."

Adam looked a little frightened. "What if Daddy finds out?"

"He won't. He'll be at work for a few hours at least. And Magdalena won't be back from the hospital till late."

"Well, if you really think it's okay."

"I do," Hanna said. "We have to find out what's going on with that Penny."

They walked into the house quietly, as though there were someone there whom they didn't want to disturb, and they went stealthily into their father's bedroom. They sat down on the side of the bed, and Hanna opened the bedstand drawer and took out the book with a plain black cloth cover that said JOURNAL. She opened it carefully. It had probably four hundred lined pages, three-quarters of which were closely filled with her father's quick, jerky handwriting. She turned to the last written page and paged backward to the beginning of the last entry, "July 22, 1946," which was the one he must have done yesterday when he sat on his bed writing feverishly for two hours after Penny left. Adam looked on, and Hanna began to read:

My company remained at the concentration camp outside Medzibiez for several days waiting for orders to continue our push to Vienna. Of the 511 inmates still alive when we liberated the camp, 174 died despite all medical efforts to save them. The survivors had nowhere to go. They came mostly from the Ukraine, and if they tried to go back there they would be hunted down and murdered by German soldiers or Polish and Russian partisan bands roaming the forests. So they had to continue to live in the same vermin-infested barracks in which the Nazis had imprisoned them.

Four of the survivors couldn't stand it any longer. Yossie Finkel, a yeshiva teacher from Lvov, and three of the boys who had once been his students, came to my office one morning. Finkel was only twenty-six years old, but like the others he had a shaved head and gray skin and haunted eyes which made him look sixty. They were all dressed in old U.S. Army fatigues and combat boots supplied by my men, but even the uniforms didn't make them look like soldiers.

"Mir kennen nit bleiben do," *Finkel said to me in Yiddish.* "Mir mussen nach heim gehn."

"Vus fir mishigass iz doss," *I answered him.* "*You have no homes left. And if you go off into that forest, you'll be dead in a matter of days, hours.*"

"*It doesn't matter to us anymore. Don't you understand? We cannot stay another minute in this place where our families and friends were exterminated like cockroaches.*"

"*But I can't protect you outside these gates,*" *I told them.* "*There are reports of bands of SS troops from this camp in the forest between here and Medzibiez. Believe me, you're better off waiting here until the war is over. It won't be long now.*"

Finkel and his friends had stood there stolidly, their jaws clenched resolutely shut. And I could not and would not hold them against their will. So I went with them to the mess sergeant and drew them each a week's provisions, and then I took them to the armory and gave them each a Luger, which had been left behind by the fleeing SS detachment. And then I stood dejectedly at the gate and watched them disappear into the forest, truly believing that they would be murdered within a few hours or days.

Three hours later, a scouting patrol from the camp reported finding four bodies of head-shaved men dressed in U.S. Army fatigues. They were on the north bank of the Kura River, about six miles from the camp.

I took a platoon of my men into the forest to flush out the killer or killers. We found the bodies by the river. They had all been shot in the back, and their faces had been stabbed so many times that all that was left were small puddles of bloody oozing mush. My men spread into the forest to round up the subhuman animals who had done this. I was alone, walking slowly eastward. I saw movement in the trees ahead of me, leaves rustling, a small sapling swaying, and I sprayed it with my Thompson submachine gun. There was a scream, and a voice hollered out something I couldn't understand in garbled German. A tall thin soldier in an SS uniform, supporting another wounded soldier, came out from behind a tree thirty feet in front of me. The wounded man's feet were dragging and his head lolled on his chest. The tall thin one called out in heavily accented English, "Enough, surrender, surrender, no shoot." And I leveled my submachine gun at them and fired a long burst, from right to left and back, and the Germans slumped to the ground. I did not even flinch, I did not even blink, as I stood over the bodies. I actually felt better than I had in many days. I pulled my bayonet out of its scabbard and bent over and stabbed the dead Germans in the face, first one and then the other, again and again until their faces were bloody pulp. I was gelid, emotionless.

"What does *gelid* mean?" Adam asked. His eyes were wide, shocked.

Hanna sniffed back her tears. "I don't know. I never heard it before." She continued reading.

Suddenly shots rang out. I felt the bullets rip into my chest and left arm. I didn't know who had shot me or from where. All I could focus on was the ugly stain of blood spreading over the front of my field jacket. It was April, and an early spring thaw had melted the snow and ice in the forest, and it was too warm for the wound to be anesthetized by the weather alone, as my leg wound had been last December at the Battle of the Bulge. The pain was excruciating. Medics deadened it as much as possible with morphine ampules in my thigh, but I remained semiconscious and felt cold and clammy. I was flown somewhere on a medical evacuation airplane.

I lay on the bed and tried to mesmerize myself by concentrating on the incessant whirring of the propellers.

Some of the words were very big and unfamiliar to Hanna. She stumbled over them as she read. There were tears in her eyes.

The propellers sounded to me like a long-drawn-out melancholy low string on a cello. A little grating, very mournful and distant, like a doleful dirge being played under my head for days on end, for nights without end.

When you are really hurt like this, your consciousness recedes behind your eyes into the murky, turgid center of your life until little by little you stop being aware of anything happening outside of you. The only thing you think about is the relentless pain, until the throb of it and the unceasing presence of it merge with the groaning of the propellers, and you know when one of them ends so will the other. Along with your life.

But it doesn't work that way when you finally open your eyes, when you reluctantly admit reality in again, when the airplane lands. They wheel you off and into an ambulance, and the cello dirge stops but the pain is still there. And they unload you like a side of beef onto yet another bed, this time in a hospital, and still the pain does not relinquish its penetrating vibrato, but now it is a guttural oboe playing a whispery sound like the hot wind rustling the drapes on the window. They shoot your shoulder full of something and your hip full of something else, and then you drift on that reedy whisper and float away from your pain, looking back at yourself like someone you had just visited in the hospital and were damn glad to be away from at last.

You awake slowly in the deep stillness and pale light of early morning, the next morning, two mornings later, ten. You do not know. You do not care. All you know is that the pain has finally stopped. You grope for the wound in your chest and your arm, and all you can feel is a huge bandage and little rubber hoses.

Somehow the days and weeks move steadily by, and first one tube comes out and then another, and then the bandages come off and the stitches are removed and healing happens. You are awake much of the time now, and they only give you the juice in the hip when you holler for it or when you cannot sleep at night. And now you look out the window and actually see that there are things out there, a tree with green leaves, a lawn of thick grass, a sky and clouds and rain.

Then you begin to remember, you see vividly the lugubrious faces of the inmates of that concentration camp, and they open their eyes wide to you in speechless pleas for mercy and help, but you are helpless. You must just watch them die, the gleam disappear from their eyes, their mouths fall open like the rictus of sparrows begging for food from their mothers. They were just like you, these once-persons, they committed no greater crime than you. And you feel guilty for being alive, for having the gall to begin to feel better. So they send a doctor to see you, a specialist in making you want to leave this place and go on living, and he comes again and again, and he tells you that an important part of the healing process is for you to keep a diary, write it all down, get it outside of yourself where you can objectify it and gain distance from it. So you do, almost every day. And then one day you wake up and the faces are gone, the visions are blurred, and you look at the tree outside the window and see that a bluebird is perched on a branch, and you hear it sing.

But I will never forget the camp.

And I will never forget the pain. Not just the physical pain, my arm, my chest. Morphine took care of that. But the searing pain of not ever seeing Rachel again.

I loved her. I love her. I remember our last night together as though it were last night. We made love, and she cried. And I lay there with the scent of her on my lips, and I cried too. Though I didn't let her see or hear me, because I didn't want to frighten her, for her to know that I was a coward, that I didn't want to go to war, I just wanted to stay with her and Hanna and Adam. Rachel was just a girl, and she died. And I couldn't even be with her in her last moments, I didn't even know about it. And then the agony of not being able to take Hanna and Adam into my arms and cry with them. That is the worst thing that has ever happened to me, to know that my children were grieving and in terrible pain, but not to be able to touch them and hold them and kiss away their tears. I know that they do not forgive me for this. I do not forgive myself. How can such things, which are so central to a man's life and the lives of his wife and children, be taken from him just like that, bang! gone. And then a general says that he's sorry, but that's the way it is. Your wife is dead but you can't go home, and here's a Silver Star and a promotion to deaden your pain. And you pray and cry out to God to help you in your desolation. But God does not answer. God does not help. God never helps.

Where are you, God? What the fuck are you doing up there?

There was more to read that Daddy had written, but Hanna could not see through her tears. She closed the book and her throat was choked with sobs. Adam stood up slowly and walked into his room and shut the door.

CHAPTER EIGHTEEN

Peace had finally settled over Tucson. A small story was in the newspaper on Monday about FBI Special Agent Thomas Delahanty being transferred to the Kansas City office.

No noteworthy incident of any kind marred the placid summer days and nights of late July and early August, and the only explosions were the daily afternoon thunderclaps and almost daily rains of the monsoon season. Edgar had taken his family on a vacation to the Grand Canyon "and any other damn place it ain't a hunnerd degrees!" Samuel was still in the hospital, but the doctor said that he was recovering well.

Hanna had been "bumping into" Mike Bowers at the Mexican market fairly often lately. It seemed that both of them went over there for an ice cream and a Coke at about three every weekday afternoon. Mike's parents owned a couple of hundred acres on Valencia Road, about a mile down, where they farmed carrots and onions and kept about two thousand Rhode Island Reds in long, stinking corrugated tin coops.

Hanna didn't care what Dad said, Mike wasn't a bad

boy. Maybe his father was a little crusty, at least when he had too much to drink, but otherwise he was just a plain and simple farmer, laconic, hardworking, and very polite to her. The two times she had gone over to the Bowers's farm to see Mike, his father had been very nice, apologized again and again for what had happened, assured her that they were decent God-fearing Catholic folks, and they sure didn't approve of any of the kind of things going on around here lately. Which didn't make much difference to Hanna, because the only thing that she was interested in was Mike Bowers.

Sometimes Magdalena would walk to the market with Hanna, and sometimes not. On Thursday afternoon in the second week of August, when the need for an ice cream and a Coke overwhelmed Hanna, Magdalena was over on the reservation doing something or other and Adam was down at the reservoir with Charger. The Hendlys had asked him to take care of the horse while they were on vacation.

At two-forty-five, Hanna walked down Indian Agency Road to the mesquite thicket and through the field to Valencia Road. A hundred yards farther west was the market. She walked to it and pulled a Coke out of the big ice chest outside. No one was inside except the old Mexican lady who ran the place and seemed to know only ten or fifteen words of English. Hanna gave her a nickel for the Coke and another nickel for the ice cream bar. The old woman went to the freezer and took out a Polar Bar and handed it to Hanna.

She ambled idly around the shelves of the little market—at least it was reasonably comfortable in there with the swamp cooler going—and ended up at the magazine rack looking at the covers. She stood there for ten minutes. The front door creaked open and she looked around. It was kind of a big guy, a little bit porky. Not Mike.

The wall clock said three-forty. Well, doggone it, Mike couldn't come today, Hanna thought. She suddenly had an odd sensation and looked up. The man who had come in was drinking a Coke, standing fifteen feet from her, partially hidden behind the end of a row of shelves, staring at her. He had a chubby face, was old, probably as old as her father, and he kept staring at her.

She walked outside and put the empty bottle in the wooden crate and threw the ice cream stick into the empty oil drum. The man came out behind her and just stared, his mouth open a little.

Hanna ran across the road and into the mesquite thicket. She turned around, and he was still standing in front of the market staring after her. She ran a little farther and looked back again. He was gone. She slowed down and walked home.

Joshua had just come home, and he came out of the bedroom buttoning up his shirt. He had changed out of his suit into the Levi's and work shirt he always wore around the house now.

"What's wrong with you?" he said, looking at her perspiry, red face.

"Some weird old man was up at the market staring at me."

"Well, if you keep wearing those tight shorts and that tube top, a lot of men are going to stare at you." He gave her a frown of disapproval.

"All the girls are wearing the same thing," she protested.

"All the girls don't look like you."

"Well, what am I supposed to do, sit around the house all day playing with dolls? I can't do that, I'm fifteen."

"Fourteen. Wear Levi's and a loose shirt and you won't get leered at."

"Daa-aad." She giggled, very pleased.

"Where's Adam?"

"Probably torturing frogs like usual."

"Is Magdalena going to be home for dinner?"

"Yeah, she said by five."

"Well, why don't you go on over to the reservoir and get your brother? Otherwise he'll never find his way home before dark."

"Can I go like this, or do I have to change into overalls?" She gave him a pouty look.

"Git!"

〰〰〰

The next evening, Buford Richards drove up to the Rabb house in his Security Police car and parked by the irrigation ditch.

Steve Lukis was in the front seat with him. Buford got out of the car and stood by the driver's door, looked over the hood, and called out to Adam, who was feeding the chickens, "Hey, boy, get along inside there and get the man out here."

It was almost seven o'clock, and the late sun cast weakening shafts of light over Black Mountain. Adam threw the rest of the corn on the ground among the pecking chickens and ran into the house.

Joshua came out and walked up to the passenger side of the car. "What do you want?"

"Take it easy now, son," drawled Buford in his best good old boy twang and grin. "I come to tell you that the senator's gone back to Washington. Some emergency."

Joshua nodded. "So?"

"Well, so's I'm here to tell you that old Jacob wants this shit to cease. He told me to tell you the war's over. There are bigger more important wars to fight. Them godless Russians [*ROOSH-ins*] are startin to act up just like old George Patton said they would."

The general had a quote for all occasions, thought Joshua inanely.

"Ain't that the damn way a the world, though," Buford said. "First we shoot Nazis and kiss commies. And now we gotta kiss Nazis and shoot commies." He shook his head sadly. "Damned if a old codger like me can keep up with this bullshit."

Joshua said nothing.

"Anyways, I'm here to tell you that the senator done put an end to this little war we been havin'. He even told me to tell you that you're a courageous man, and he respects you for it." Buford nodded. "And so do I. I'm tellin you true, I think you done a good thing there with Ignacio. Maybe you even taught us all a lesson we shoulda already knowed."

"Right. Now that he's been murdered, everybody loved him, just can't understand how it could have happened."

Buford shrugged. "Way a the world, boy. Just the damn way a the world."

"I don't get it, Buford. I'm just not following this real well.

All of a sudden I'm not an eastern shyster, I'm a 'courageous man.' And the senator gets the shit kicked out of him over his gold mine, but he doesn't mind that the *Indians* win this one? I don't buy it."

Buford's voice was flat. "Now we don't like to think of it as the senator bein whupped, Mr. Rabb. Let's just say that once the judge screwed us and the gold mine turned into a dust cloud, there ain't a whole lotta reason to keep fightin'. Like the man says, 'It ain't over till the fat lady sings,' and we reckon it's about time for the old broad to start singin'."

Joshua was still having trouble believing any of this. He watched Buford's right hand closely, waiting for him to pull his revolver out of the holster and shoot him in the teeth.

"Well," said Joshua slowly, "then I suppose that you'll want to pay some damages to the tribe because of that mine explosion. The senator will just be eager as hell to review the matter and see if we can negotiate a settlement."

Buford blanched slightly. His eyes narrowed. Then he caught himself and eased his expression. "Well now, son," he drawled, "I didn't say that we was ready to hitch up the buggy and go ridin off into the sunset. We didn't come here to talk bullshit, just to declare an armistice."

"The terms of the armistice for the Papago tribe will include the payment of damages."

Until now, Steve Lukis had been staring straight ahead. Now he turned his head slowly toward Joshua. "Listen to me, you low-life Indian fucker," he said in a quiet voice. "We have had just about all we can take of you. My father has asked me to resolve this thing by the time he gets back, and I'm trying to do like he wants. I'm sorry about the mine. Buford and me figured it was the right thing to do at the time, figured my dad wanted it that way. Well, we were wrong. He got pretty damn pissed off at us." He frowned and Buford nodded and shrugged.

"How about Delahanty?" Joshua said. "Was he just trying to make the senator happy?"

"Shit," Lukis muttered. "He didn't have jackshit to do with us. What he did was pure crazy, all on his own. Anyway, all we want now is our contract renewed with the tribe. Then you and your greaser pals can all jump into a tub a ratshit together and fuck each other in the ass."

"You are one hell of a negotiator," Joshua said, his face taut.

"Listen, you bastard, I'm gonna have a howitzer dragged up to your front yard one a these nights and negotiate this thing once and for all."

Joshua stared at him. "You have a real bad mouth there, Steve, a real bad mouth." He swallowed deeply to quell his anger and kept his voice calm. "Tell you what I'm going to do for you. I'll call a meeting of the tribal council over in Sells, any day you choose, and you can present your views to them, and maybe Chief Romero will be just happy as a bug in a rug to give you any terms you and your daddy want."

Steve's voice was a hiss. "Listen good to me, you fuckin low-life. I've got to leave for Washington, D.C., early tomorrow. But I'll be back in ten days, and you better damn sure have our contract signed and sealed or I'll smear you on the ground like birdshit."

Joshua turned and walked back into the house. He waited to get shot in the back by Buford Richards, but nothing happened. The car door slammed and the car pulled away.

Joshua closed the door behind him and stood braced against it. He breathed deeply. Hanna, Adam, and Magdalena had been peeking through the window.

"I think that's the guy who was staring at me at the market yesterday," Hanna said.

Joshua looked peculiarly at her, trying to focus on what she had told him yesterday, which he had dismissed offhandedly. "Are you sure?" he asked.

"I think so. But it was so dark out there right now I couldn't tell for sure."

"Well, you just stay away from the damn market for a while," Joshua said angrily. "Those people out there are crazy."

Hanna frowned but said nothing. Now wasn't the time. Her father looked scared.

CHAPTER NINETEEN

On Saturday morning there was a torrential downpour that became a drizzle at noon and didn't subside until almost four o'clock. Joshua waited restlessly for the rain to stop and finally left at five o'clock to visit Penny on Mount Lemmon. He would be back by midnight, he said.

Magdalena, Adam, and Hanna sat and listened to the radio.

"I think she's very nice," Magdalena said, "but you two sure haven't been very nice to her."

"I know," Hanna said, looking very apologetic. "I think she's nice too."

Adam looked troubled. "Daddy won't stop loving us if he loves her, will he?"

Hanna shook her head slowly and smiled at him reassuringly. "No, I don't think so. I think he'll just love us all."

At nine o'clock Hanna told Adam that it was time for him to go to bed. He was very annoyed. He wanted to stay up till ten. It was Saturday night, after all, and Daddy sometimes let him stay up late. But Hanna was insistent.

Daddy said nine o'clock. He sulked into his bedroom and slammed the door. Why should he have to be in bed when his sister got to stay up? She wasn't *that* much older.

Magdalena went to bed a few minutes later. She often stayed with Samuel in the hospital all day, and she got very tired and would go to sleep early when she got home.

Hanna sat on the couch with a little smile playing over her lips. So far so good. She had planned this for two days, since Daddy had told her that he would be going up to Mount Lemmon to visit Penny on Saturday afternoon and wouldn't be home until late. Hanna figured that she could handle Magdalena because she understood things. And Magdalena going to sleep early was even better. Now Hanna didn't even have to tell her. Everything was perfect, just like she'd planned it.

At nine-thirty she went to the bathroom and brushed her teeth. She had the lipstick that she'd bought just yesterday for thirty cents, and she put a little on and admired how it made her lips real red and stand out. She left the house and closed the front door very slowly so it wouldn't creak or bang and wake up Adam and Magdalena.

But Adam wasn't asleep. He was lying on his bed with four of his trucks, playing with them by the light of the almost full moon. The curtains were open wide on his window. He heard footsteps on the rocky dirt outside and saw his sister walking quickly down Indian Agency Road.

Hey, what's she doing? he thought. She's not supposed to be out there. He was still fully dressed and picked up his BB gun, ran to the door, closed it quietly behind him, and quick-walked as quietly as he could, following behind her about 150 feet. It was a tranquil bright night, and the stars looked like fluorescent snowflakes. This is neat, he thought. He felt like Cochise or Geronimo. He had tailed her just like an Indian warrior without being discovered, without making any noise, without being scared of the darkness.

Behind him a car engine turned over with a whine. The sound shattered the stillness. Adam turned sharply and looked toward the sound. He saw a big black car creeping up Indian Agency

Road toward him, going only a few miles an hour. Adam turned and looked for Hanna, but she had disappeared into the thicket of mesquite past the BIA. Suddenly he was terrified. The car was steadily gaining on him as though it were stalking him. He ran across the road into the empty lot where he and Jimmy had built their fort. From behind the west wall of the fort, he could see the car drive slowly past, stop, back up a little, then start again and drive quickly toward Valencia Road.

Adam walked carefully out to Indian Agency Road and couldn't see the car any longer. He ran to the mesquite thicket and cut diagonally through it. When he emerged from the thicket on the shoulder of Valencia Road, he could see two people framed in the dim lights in front of the Mexican market about a hundred yards down the road across the street. It was a short person and a tall one. They crossed the road and went into the thicket. Adam couldn't see any cars except one parked on the other side of the market. He began to calm down.

Quit being such a scaredy cat, he chided himself. I bet that's the boy Daddy told her she couldn't go on a date with and she got so mad and grouchy. He walked down Valencia Road until he could hear the sound of their voices and hid behind a broad mesquite trunk close enough that he could see their forms. He crouched and watched intently, trying to get his eyes to see into the night. He didn't want to go any closer. They might hear him and then Hanna would be mad and make him go home. But he wouldn't, because she couldn't tell on him without telling on herself. Ha! He smiled smugly, enjoying the adventure and the advantage he had over his sister.

Suddenly he heard a rustling to his left. He jumped, and his heart started beating like crazy. A coyote? A dog? He squinted and saw a form, a big man it looked like, except he was wearing something like a long dress or a robe with a big collarlike thing over his head. Oh God! Not again. He pressed close to the trunk of the mesquite tree and watched in terror as the form walked slowly, carefully toward the sounds of his sister's and the boy's voices. There was silence for a moment, and Adam couldn't see or hear anything. He held his breath. Then there was a whomp, like someone hitting someone or something. And then he heard his sister scream, a thin little scream, and then cry out, "No, no," and then start sobbing.

He was petrified for a moment, he couldn't move or even think what to do. But he had to do something. He crept toward the sound his sister was making, and a few feet away he could see them. The boy was lying flat on his back by the tree. The big man in the dress slapped Hanna and punched her and growled, "Shut up, bitch," and then threw her down on her stomach on the ground. Adam was ten feet away. He cocked his BB gun with the lever.

The man must have heard the click. He stopped and straightened and then wheeled around. Adam couldn't see his face but could see his form clearly in the moonlight filtering through the straggly mesquite branches. He shot toward the man's face. Nothing happened. The man lunged toward him. Adam quickly loaded again and shot, and this time the man let out a howl just like the dog that Jimmy had shot in the rump. The howl ended in a gurgled scream, and the man stopped and swayed and then started running, crashing through the thicket toward Valencia Road, groaning horribly.

Adam ran to Hanna. He put his hands on her shoulder and rolled her over. She shook her head and looked at him and then saw the boy lying near her, and she let out a strangled sob.

"Come on, let's get out of here," Adam said in a terrified, panicked voice. "He may come back."

She stood up. "Can't leave him," she sobbed.

"We gotta go to the market and tell," Adam said, getting a hold of himself. He took his sister's hand and tugged her away from the tree, and they both started running out of the thicket. They ran across the road and saw a car start up in the lot next to the market. It drove away with a squeal of tires.

———

Joshua drove down the mountain, sorry that he had had to leave. He had spent all evening in bed with Penny, but it was not long enough. He wanted to hold her, to fall asleep with her in his arms, to wake up next to her.

As he drove absently down Indian Agency Road, he suddenly became aware that there were lights on at his house. He glanced at his watch, one-twenty, what the hell is anyone doing up over there? Oh God, no! The house was lit up like an electrical storm. He sped up and turned in front of the irrigation ditch. A sheriff's car was in the front yard. Joshua's heart pounded wildly and his breath was short. He turned the key off and took his foot off the brake, and the De Soto jerked to a stop with a grinding of gears.

He jumped out of the car and ran through the open front door. Hanna was sitting on the sofa holding a washcloth to her face. She had a scrape on her forehead. Magdalena had her arm around Hanna's shoulders. Adam was sitting on the floor at their feet. The sheriff's deputy everybody called Marty was sitting on the couch next to her writing in a small spiral notebook. He put it down beside him and got up quickly and held up his hands.

"She's okay, Mr. Rabb. Much more scared than hurt."

Joshua rushed to her and she jumped up into his arms.

"Oh, Daddy, it was horrible," she gasped, sobbing convulsively.

"What happened?" Joshua asked in a frightened voice.

Hanna was panting and weeping too hard to speak.

"What happened?" Joshua asked, looking at Adam's drawn face.

"A man in one of those robes attacked her, Dad," Adam said hoarsely.

"A priest's robe?"

"Yeah, it had a big hood, just like the man who hurt me."

"Where? Here?" Joshua asked.

"No. In the field over across from the market."

Joshua's mouth dropped open. "In the field? What the hell were you doing in the field?" His voice was harsh, his eyes fierce.

Hanna stared at him round-eyed and kept on sobbing.

"Now take it easy, Mr. Rabb," Marty said in a soothing voice. "It seems your daughter met Mike Bowers over at the market at about ten o'clock, and your boy here had followed her up there and then followed them into the mesquite thicket across the way. And somebody clubbed Mike Bowers with a rock and tried to hurt your girl, but she's okay. Just some scratches and bruises."

Hanna's weeping began to subside, and she sat back down on the couch.

"Mike Bowers?"

"Yes, Mr. Rabb. A tall blond kid, plays—played pitcher for Tucson High. Good one, too." He hesitated. "He's dead."

Joshua flinched and stared at Hanna. She turned her face away. "Why were you with that boy?" Joshua yelled, still not fully understanding.

"Well now, Mr. Rabb, kids'll be kids. And I reckon Mike's about as nice a boy as you'd find around here. Anyway, Adam here saved your daughter's life."

Joshua stared at his son and then at the deputy.

"Yes, sir. Adam said he shot the guy with his BB gun. Must have got him in the eye or close to it by the way he took off running and howling."

Adam was on the floor in front of him, and Joshua tousled his hair. Joshua breathed deeply. "I was so sure it was Delahanty," he mumbled.

"So were we."

"It must be Father Hausner, that fucking pervert," Joshua said to Marty.

"Well now, Mr. Rabb, I wouldn't be jumping so fast to any conclusions. We got no proof."

"A big man in a cassock. Who else?"

"Could be that Brother Boniface. He's kind of a real weird duck."

"Well, one of them did it. I was over there at the mission six or seven weeks ago, just happened to be taking a walk at about midnight. I've got to do that sometimes, my leg gets to hurting. And I went into the church and one of those guys was buggering a boy, right in the church. I'm sure now the kid was Vittorio."

"Why didn't you report it?"

"Are you kidding! At the time who would've believed me? And who would've cared?"

Marty shook his head somberly. "Don't shortchange us. Most of us around here are decent folks, despite what's happened lately. I got no excuses. But this is the first damn thing like this that's happened here in my whole life."

Joshua breathed deeply. "Let's go over and see which one of those priests has a patch over his eye."

"Well now, we just can't be doing a thing like that. I got no jurisdiction to be going over on the res and investigating a crime. And you got no right at all. They'd be doing perfectly legal if they shot you for a prowler. Billy Fraker's been investigating it for the sheriff's department. He'll get my report first thing in the morning."

"Then what do we do, nothing?" Joshua looked angrily at the deputy.

"Nothing right now, Mr. Rabb. I'll talk to Sheriff Dunphy tomorrow morning. He'll get Billy moving on this thing. Then we gotta call the FBI in Phoenix. Till then, just take it easy. There's nothing you can do except calm your kids down and put them to bed."

Joshua choked back his fear and anger and breathed deeply several times. "Okay, let's get to bed. We'll talk about this in the morning."

Hanna and Adam went into their rooms.

"Thanks, Marty," Joshua said, holding out his hand.

"It's okay, Mr. Rabb. Your Adam really did a brave thing. A lot of kids would have just froze. Now you leave this to us, Mr. Rabb. We'll get him."

Joshua nodded. "But I was so damn sure that it was Delahanty, especially since everything has been so quiet around here since he died."

Marty nodded, shrugged, and left. Joshua sat on the couch staring ahead, seeing nothing but Hausner's face. Magdalena sat with him, silently. Then she laid her head in his lap and wept softly.

"*Madre de Dios, madre de Dios,*" she breathed over and over again and made the sign of the cross.

"Don't let either of them out of your sight tomorrow," Joshua said, "and stay here on the property. I'm going over to the mission. I think it's Hausner."

She sat up and gave him a shocked look. "Oh no, it couldn't be a priest. As mean as Hausner is, he still wouldn't *kill* anybody."

"I think he did," Joshua said. "And not only Mike Bowers. Vittorio and the nun and the other girl. A very bad man."

She looked at him dejectedly. "I thought it was Delahanty, too."

"We were all wrong," he mumbled.

"But Hausner isn't even there anymore," she said.

He looked at her askance. "What?"

"He's been removed as pastor. The rumors are that he and that Sister Mary Rose broke their vows. Father Boniface was sent to investigate, and he removed Hausner a few days ago. Sister Mary Rose was sent back to Minnesota last Monday. I don't know if Hausner's gone yet, but he's been recalled to the headquarters in Santa Barbara. Everybody on the reservation knows about it."

Hanna opened her bedroom door. "Daddy," she said, her voice weak, "I'm afraid to be alone."

Joshua jumped off the couch and ran to her. He hugged her, and she wept.

"It's okay, honey, you're safe," he whispered. She slowly stopped weeping and shaking. "Lie down again, and I'll sit with you."

Hanna climbed back into bed. Joshua got a chair out of the kitchen and put it at the foot of Hanna's bed. Magdalena slept on the couch in the living room.

Sometime during the night Joshua fell asleep, maybe for an hour or two. He awoke a little after seven and had a pounding headache. He went into the bathroom and took two aspirins and showered and shaved and put on his wooden arm. He knew how mean it looked, how intimidating the two shiny steel prongs were, sticking unnaturally out of a bent tree stump that substituted for his arm. He had been practicing wearing it and manipulating it for a couple of weeks now, just as he had been instructed by the therapist and the prosthetician. And today, it might just come in handy. He dressed in Levi's and a blue chambray work shirt and took the .45 revolver out of the night-stand drawer and put it in his back pocket. He peeked in on Adam, and he was sleeping soundly. He opened Hanna's door a crack and she was asleep. Magdalena was sleeping deeply on the couch.

He drove to the rectory at the mission and knocked on the door. It was seven-forty-five, and the bells in the towers were ringing, marking the beginning of mass in fifteen minutes. Indians were walking to the church.

Brother Boniface opened the rectory door. He smiled benignly. "Yes, Mr. Rabb. What can I do for you?" He stared at the hook on the end of Joshua's wooden arm.

Now Joshua was certain it was Hausner. Boniface had no patch over his eye, no marks on his face. "I thought you took a vow of silence?" Joshua said, hostile and accusatory.

Boniface nodded. "As a monk I was silent. Now I've been asked to become the pastor here, and silence would be quite inappropriate."

"I want to see Hausner."

"I'm afraid that's impossible, Mr. Rabb. Father Hausner did not come in last night."

"Bullshit!" Joshua hissed. He pushed open the door and Boniface stepped back, offering no resistance. Joshua looked through all of the rooms of the rectory. It was empty.

"What the hell's going on?" He stood menacingly in front of Boniface.

"What the hell's going on with you?" asked the priest, his eyes narrowed.

"My daughter was attacked last night by that pervert," Joshua said. "I want him. You can't hide him forever. The FBI will be out here."

"You're mistaken, Mr. Rabb." His voice had taken on a pastoral, soothing tone. "Father Hausner would not hurt your daughter."

Joshua left the rectory. He went into the church, into the sacristy. No Father Hausner. Two nuns came into the church and scowled at Joshua when he came out of the sacristy.

He left the church and went to the convent. The front door was unlocked, and the four small cell-like bedrooms were empty.

He was almost crazy with hatred and frustration. He could not stop what he was doing. He was incapable of slowing down, thinking about all of this. He had to find Hausner. He walked back to the rectory and knocked.

"Yes, Mr. Rabb," Father Boniface said, opening the door. "Has your quest been fruitless?" His voice was sardonic.

"I'd like to come in and talk to you."

Boniface stepped back and opened the door wide. Joshua went in and sat down on the edge of the brocaded couch in the living room. The priest sat on the chair and studied him.

"I hope that your daughter was not badly hurt."

"No, just terrified. But the boy she was with was murdered."

The priest made the sign of the cross. "Why do you think it was Gerhard?"

"The assailant was wearing a robe, most likely a cassock like you Franciscans wear. The same man attacked my son and Magdalena Antone and Samuel Santos. I'm absolutely sure of it."

Boniface frowned and shook his head. "Anybody could steal a cassock from the sacristy or even from here, Mr. Rabb, even you. We don't lock the doors. And I just can't believe it's Gerhard. He was not a good pastor to these people: he didn't love them as he should have, and his vow of chastity seems to have gone the way of all flesh since Mary Rose came here two years ago. But that happens. We are all mortal men." He looked openly at Joshua. "But not murder, Mr. Rabb. I've known Gerhard for thirty years. He's never hurt anything but his own immortal soul."

Joshua shook his head and chewed his lower lip. "Where is he?"

"I'm not certain. He was recalled by our superior in Santa Barbara, and he was supposed to leave last Thursday, but he refused to go. Then last night after supper, it must have been around nine, he told me he was going for a walk, and he simply hasn't returned." Boniface shrugged. "He had no money, at least not very much. I just don't know where he went. Perhaps to a hotel, just to sit and meditate."

Joshua breathed deeply but couldn't lessen the lancing pain of frustration that was filling his throat and mouth and eyes and smashing against the top of his skull. He shook his head and tried to think but couldn't focus. Where could the bastard have gone? He left here around nine, attacked Hanna at nine-forty-five or ten, then probably drove to downtown Tucson. It was about six or seven miles, and there were a couple of cheap hotels, the Presidio, the Coronado, even the Catalina.

"Okay, Father, I'm sorry for acting like a rodeo bull. I'm very upset." He stood up and walked toward the door.

Boniface followed. "I fully understand that, my son," he said quietly.

Joshua got into his car and sat pondering what to do. He gripped the steering wheel so hard his hand began to ache. He started the engine and drove slowly down Mission Road, just for something to do, hoping that movement would clear his head and give him an idea about what to do next. He found himself on the Nogales Highway and drove with increasing conviction into downtown Tucson.

His first stop was the Coronado Hotel. The deskman said that only four of the twelve rooms were occupied, and no one had checked in since Saturday. Joshua drove to the Presidio. He asked the desk clerk if anyone had checked in last night.

"You a cop?" the clerk asked, a man of about sixty with a grizzled three-day beard and a bulldog face and brown rotted teeth. He was about a foot shorter than Joshua. He eyed the wooden arm and the steel hooks emerging from the shirt cuff.

Joshua grabbed his shirt collar with the steel prongs and stared malevolently at him. "When I rip your fucking throat out it won't matter if I'm a cop."

The clerk's eyes bulged and he gasped for breath and turned around the guest register. Joshua held on to him and scanned the names. One man had checked in at midnight: "Fred Smith." Room 203. Joshua pushed the clerk away and the old man backed up and stood stiffly against the wall, eyeing Joshua cautiously.

He climbed the stairs—203 was the second door. He knocked and waited. He knocked again and waited. He pounded, and the door opened. Gerhard Hausner was reeling drunk. He was dressed in Levi's and a T-shirt and sandals. His cassock was on the floor by the tousled bed. There were no marks around his eyes except the broken blood vessels of an alcoholic on the tops of his cheeks. They were livid now, but Joshua had never noticed them before. Hausner squinted at him drunkenly.

Joshua walked slowly down the hallway and the stairs and he heard the door slam shut. He felt totally defeated and deeply depressed. His shoulder hurt like hell from grabbing the clerk by the collar. He drove home. Hanna and Adam were both very subdued, still frightened by what had happened. And so was Joshua. They listened glumly to the radio all morning and afternoon and evening, ate rabbit stew prepared by Magdalena, and went to bed early.

~~~~~~~

Joshua sat in his office the next morning, and he drummed his fingers on the desk blotter. He had left his arm home, because the effort of restraining the desk clerk with it yesterday had made his shoulder very sore. In fact, every part of his body seemed to hurt, probably from frustration, and he had taken his cane with him this morning.

Could it be? he pondered. He had thought about it all night, weighing the facts, mulling over the possibilities. He had been sure it was Buford Richards the night that Vittorio was murdered. He had simply been certain. But then he had lost sight of Richards in the confusion of other possibilities. Now he brushed aside the distractions and saw the situation with crystal clarity for the first time in weeks. He looked for a number in the telephone book and dialed.

"Hello, Dr. Wolfe? This is Joshua Rabb, remember me?"

"Yes, of course."

"I need to ask a medical question."

"Sure."

"How would I go about finding the blood type of a particular individual?"

"Well, I only deal with the dead ones. You talking about someone alive?"

"Yes."

"Male or female?"

"Male."

The doctor pondered a moment. "I guess there are a few places. If he's been in the service, it'll be in his service records. Otherwise, if he's had an operation that required a transfusion, he'd have to be typed by the hospital." He paused. "I can't think of any others."

"Do you have access to hospital files?"

"Yes, sure. I'm the pathologist at Tucson Medical Center and I have staff privileges at Saint Mary's."

"Can you check for me?"

There was a pause. "Let me ask you this, Mr. Rabb, just what the hell are you after?"

"I'm after Sister Martha Robinette's murderer, and Mike Bowers's, and probably Vittorio's and the other Papago girl's."

"You think one man killed all four people?" The doctor did not sound incredulous.

"I think one very sick animal may well have killed them all."

The doctor breathed audibly. "Who do you want me to check?"

"Is this confidential?"

"Yes."

"Buford Richards."

There was a long silence on the line. "You don't mean the guy who's the chief of security for Senator Jacob Lukis?"

"Yes, I do."

More silence. A deep sigh. "I don't know about this. Checking on the average nigger is one thing. Pulling records on Buford Richards is a whole other matter."

"I think he attacked my daughter two nights ago. I don't jump to these conclusions just on a whim."

"I know," the doctor said soberly. "I know. And I just read the police report on poor Mike Bowers."

"It's absolutely vital that we find out if it was Richards," Joshua said.

"Where can I reach you?"

"I'll give you the number here at the BIA. I'll be here until about four, four-thirty. Three-two-seven-four-one."

"Okay, I'll see what I can do."

It was three o'clock in the afternoon when the doctor called back.

"Mr. Rabb?"

"Yes, Dr. Wolfe."

"On August 5, 1944, Buford Richards was admitted to Tucson Medical Center with a burst appendix. He had peritonitis. He underwent emergency surgery and received two units of AB blood."

Joshua breathed deeply. "Thank you, Doctor."

"You didn't get it from me," he said.

"I didn't get it from you," Joshua said.

～～～

Joshua swiveled in his chair and gazed out the window. Now what do I do? he thought. He sat fidgeting, adrenaline making him twitch and breathe quickly. He heard running footsteps in the hallway, and Magdalena ran into his office.

"I'm sorry, I'm so sorry, Hanna ran off. She was in her bedroom, I didn't know she was going anywhere. I went in there and the window was wide open and she left this note." Magdalena handed it to Joshua. He jumped up and came around the desk.

Daddy, there is a rosary service for Mike Bowers at St. Augustine's Cathedral. I just have to go. I feel so bad. But I know you would be afraid to let me. I'll be okay, and I'll come right home. Don't worry. Love, Hanna.

Joshua rubbed his face hard. Take it easy, he chided himself, nothing terrible is happening. She's just going to a church and she'll be okay. It's broad daylight outside. I'll go down there and pick her up. She'll probably want to go to the funeral tomorrow. Well, she should. I'll go with her.

"How would she get there?"

Magdalena shrugged. "Bus, I guess. One picks up at the market. She could transfer at Nogales Highway and go straight downtown."

"Okay, it's all right, Magdalena. It's not your fault, it's mine. I should have realized she'd want to go to the service." He put his hand on her shoulder and kissed her teary cheek to calm her. "Where's Saint Augustine's?"

"I'll go with you."

"No, it's all right. You go back and stay with Adam. Don't leave him. Just tell me where the church is."

"It's a few blocks this side of the federal building in the Mexican section, a real tall cathedral, you can't miss it."

"Okay, I'll bring her home." He took his cane and limped quickly down the hallway out of the BIA and drove to downtown Tucson. The church was an imposing Spanish Colonial cathedral rising majestically above a sparse neighborhood of stucco and corrugated tin-roofed shacks. He parked in the large dirt lot beside it and walked around to the two huge wooden doors in front. There was no one outside. He walked into the semidarkness and let his eyes adjust. There were some twenty people sitting in pews, a few praying, others just sitting. Hanna was not among them. A casket lay on a table in front of the altar rail. It was covered with flowers, except for the one-third section of the top which was open. Beside the casket sat an elderly woman in a black dress that came all the way to the floor. Next to her stood the man who had brandished a torch at Joshua a few weeks ago. Joshua walked up to him.

"Mr. Bowers, I wish to offer my condolences for what happened. It's a terrible tragedy."

The man was dressed in a shabby dark gray suit that was threadbare and ill-fitting. His white shirt had an oft-washed frayed collar. He gave Joshua a look of ineffable sadness and shook his hand limply.

"Thank you for comin', Mr. Rabb. Your daughter was just

up here." He cleared his throat and sniffed. "They was a nice pair a kids together." He nodded slowly and sniffed again.

"Yes, they certainly were, Mr. Bowers."

"And I want ya to know I din't have nothin to do with Ignacio Antone. They wanted me to come, but I told em not this time, I ain't taking no part in such a thing. I knowed it was dead wrong, Mr. Rabb, but I couldn't stop em, they done it anyway." He shook his head sorrowfully.

"Thank you, Mr. Bowers. Did you see Hanna leave?"

"Yes, sir, not ten or fifteen minutes ago."

"Did she say where she was going?"

"Well, I reckon she was headed back home. There was one a them priests here from the mission, and I think they left right about the same time. I reckon he prob'ly gave her a lift."

Joshua was instantly chilled. He gasped, and Bowers looked at him oddly.

"Did you recognize him?" Joshua asked.

Bowers shrugged. "Well, now as you say it, I don't rightly know. He was standin in the back over there with his hood up over his head, you know, just prayin'."

Joshua limped quickly down the aisle and out of the church. He was almost paralyzed with fear. He knew that it was Buford Richards, but he had no idea where to look. It was only four o'clock, the sun was shining brightly high in the western sky, and Richards couldn't take her where someone might drive by and see them. Where then? To his home? Where the hell did he live? Joshua had only seen him at the Lukis house, way out in the remote desert. Steve Lukis was in Washington with his father, and the senator's wife and household staff were undoubtedly there too. A man like Senator Lukis traveled with his whole entourage. Buford would be left to guard the house. That had to be it. At least it was all that Joshua could think of. He had to do something.

Panic made him gasp for each breath. He got into the DeSoto and sped as quickly as he could to Oracle Highway, north to Orange Grove Road, and then west to the dirt road into the Lukis property. The Security Police car was in front of the house. There was also that fancy red sports car out front. One car was missing from the garage, the Cadillac convertible that Joshua had seen there. It was parked with the top up in front of the guesthouse, sixty yards to the left. Joshua leapt out of his car and limped to the front door. He pounded on the door, waited an interminable terror-filled minute, and pounded again and again. Nothing happened. He ran limping to the guesthouse and beat on the door with his cane. He was so panicked that it didn't occur to him that he was unarmed.

Buford Richards opened the door. He was wearing his uniform and his holstered revolver. His shirt was sweat-stained and disheveled, halfway out of his pants. The knuckles of his right hand were raw and bleeding. His right eye was severely bloodshot and almost swollen shut.

"What the fuck d'*you* want?" he muttered.

"I want my daughter."

"She ain't here."

"I want to see."

"Whattaya, nuts? This is the senator's house!"

"Then why are you here?"

"Because I live here, shithead!" Richards rested his hand on the butt of his gun. "Get your ass outta here, boy. This ain't a good time to come callin'."

Joshua swept his cane up viciously between Richards's legs. Richards let out a yelp and doubled over, groaning. Joshua pushed the door open, dropped the cane, and quickly took the revolver out of Buford's holster. "Where is Hanna?" he said.

"You crazy bastard!" Richards gasped, straightening up slowly. "You outta your mind? This is the senator's house."

Joshua heard music playing. He limped into the bedroom. The door was open, and the jamb was splintered. A Victrola was playing a Gene Krupa album. A dim lamp was on, and it cast shadows over Hanna, lying in a heap on the floor beside the bed.

Joshua cried out and ran to her, tucking Richards's revolver into his belt. He fell to his knees and lifted her head and shoulders. Suddenly he was struck on the back of his head and a shattering pain shot through his scalp. He pitched forward on his daughter. Another blow hit him between the shoulder blades.

He shook off the painful haziness and rolled off of Hanna and looked up, dazed.

Buford Richards leapt at another man and smashed his fist into the man's side. The cowl flew back from Steve Lukis's head and he slumped to the floor on his knees beside Hanna. Lukis was wearing a brown cassock, splattered with blood. His face was bloody, his lips and nose smashed, and he had a small gauze patch over his right eye. Richards hit him again on the back of the neck, this time with both fists locked, and Lukis keeled over on his side.

Hanna had a livid bruise on her cheek, and her lips were swollen and bleeding. She opened her eyes slowly, dizzily, and began to whimper. Joshua lifted her gently and carried her out of the guest house. He put her in the passenger seat of the De Soto.

"You're all right now," he said. "Nothing is going to happen."

She nodded and wept gaspingly and wiped blood off the side of her mouth.

"I'll be back in a minute," he said softly. "Are you okay?"

She nodded again.

Joshua walked back into the guesthouse and into the bedroom. Lukis was sitting motionlessly on the edge of the bed, his face dripping blood onto the front of the already-saturated cassock.

"I'm taking him to the sheriff's department," Joshua said, pointing the revolver at Lukis.

Buford shook his head. "I can't let you do that, Mr. Rabb. The Lukis family has a hundred years of honor surrounding it. It can't all be destroyed by this."

"Then why didn't you stop him?"

Buford gritted his teeth and sighed deeply. "I didn't know it was him, Mr. Rabb. Nobody knew. I first figured it was Delahanty. I reckon all of us did. But then I guess I suspicioned that somethin was crazy with Steve the night that Sister Martha got killed. Steve had been riled up somethin fierce about her since the July Fourth picnic earlier that day. She'd cornered him and old Jacob and called em ever'thing but niggers for mistreatin *her people*. Man, she plum drove Steve outta his mind with hate when she talked that way to his father. Steve thinks the senator's the next thing to God. But when I found Ignacio, well hell, I didn't think nothin more about Steve. I figured Ignacio had done it for sure." He shrugged his shoulders and stared miserably at Steven Lukis. "I sure never thought Steve would do such terrible things, thinkin he was helpin his father out. Blowin up a mine tunnel is one thing. But this other stuff, hell, that's another thing altogether. I knowed Steve since he was a baby. I just couldn't believe it." He shook his head. His voice was mordant. "Then I heard Steve screechin up in that Caddy ten minutes ago and go slammin into the guesthouse—he don't live here, he lives downtown—and he wouldn't open the bedroom door when I knocked. I hadda break it in. And when I saw the priest's outfit and your girl, I knew."

He gulped and looked grimly at Joshua and shook his head sadly.

"What are you going to do?" Joshua asked.

Buford shrugged and sucked in his breath. "Well, I already pret' near beat him to death."

"That's not enough," Joshua said.

"What the hell you want?"

Joshua pointed the revolver at Richards. "Stand away. I'm taking him to the sheriff's department."

Buford rubbed his chin and shook his head. He took two steps away from Joshua. Joshua tightened his finger on the trigger of the revolver and pointed it at Steve's face.

Suddenly Joshua's arm was twisted painfully around his back and the gun fell to the floor. A hand pressed his head forward, and he thought his neck was going to break.

"Don't struggle, Mr. Rabb," came the deep gravelly voice of Senator Lukis. "Manuel will snap your head off your shoulders like a fig off a tree."

Joshua stood very still. The man holding him was as strong as a gorilla.

"I'm very sorry about what Steven has done, Mr. Rabb." The senator's voice was funereal. "He thought he was helping me, but he has brought great shame upon us. But I'm sure you'll understand that it would hardly be fitting to have him brought like a common criminal to the sheriff. All that publicity, a shocking trial. It would destroy everything my family has worked for."

Joshua grunted.

"All right, Mr. Rabb. Manuel is going to release you now. Please don't do anything stupid."

Joshua rubbed the back of his neck and rotated his head painfully. Manuel was shorter than Joshua but at least fifty pounds heavier. He was dressed in Mexican duck cloth pants and a long-sleeved coarse cotton shirt. His straight black hair was tied in a braid.

"I thought you and your son were in Washington," Joshua said hoarsely, rubbing his throat.

"I had to come back on Saturday, so Steven never even left for Washington." He paused. "My wife had a stroke late Friday night. She is very ill." He scowled and shook his head. His voice quavered. "And now this. The publicity, the trial. It would kill Alice."

The senator stepped toward his son and his chin and cheeks trembled. Then he began to cry, noiselessly, and tears rolled down his cheeks.

"I guess this is something I must do myself," he murmured, wiping away his tears brusquely with the back of his hand. He walked over to Joshua and picked up the gun which Joshua had dropped on the floor. He raised it toward Joshua's face and pointed it between his eyes, six inches away. Then he turned slowly and stepped directly in front of Steve, pressed the revolver to the middle of his forehead, and pulled the trigger. The bullet embedded in the far wall. A mist of blood and brains and bone fragments exploded from the back of his head. Jacob Lukis threw the revolver across the room.

Joshua walked to the doorway. "You hear that?" he said quietly.

Buford turned toward him, his eyes morbid and distant. "Huh?"

"That's the fat lady singing," Joshua said.

Buford gritted his teeth. The senator turned his tortured face toward Joshua, then looked away slowly.

Joshua walked out to the car and drove home.

≈≈≈≈

The next day at noon, Joshua walked briskly to the Mexican market on Valencia Road. He needed the exercise. He bought a copy of the *Arizona Daily Star* and stood under the cooler vent reading it. The headline read, SENATOR'S SON DIES IN FIERY CRASH.

by J. T. Sellner

The charred remains of Steven Lukis, the thirty-nine-year-old son of Senator Jacob Lukis, were found late last night in the custom Bugatti that he always drove. Lukis was apparently the victim of a one-car accident when he failed to negotiate the sharp hairpin curve on the Oracle Highway 17 miles north of Tucson, and his car rolled and burst into flames. His remains were positively identified by the Pima County coroner through dental charts and X rays.

Steven Lukis was never married. "He was married to his work," said his sister, Jennifer, the only other child of the senator and Alice, his wife of 54 years, the former Alice Hanner of the pioneering Hanner family of Phoenix.

The family is in seclusion today. The senator has asked that in lieu of flowers, remembrances be made in his son's name to Casita de los Niños, Tucson's orphanage, which has always been a primary charity of the Lukis family and particularly of Steven.

Buford Richards, a family spokesman, told this reporter that the senator had often warned his son about excessive speed, especially at night, "but Steve was a man who loved life and wanted to live every day to the fullest. His warmth and good humor will be sorely missed. May God grant his soul eternal peace and comfort."

"May God not," Joshua mumbled.

≈≈≈≈

It was seven-thirty Thursday morning. Magdalena served Joshua and Hanna and Adam some scrambled eggs. She sat down at the table with them and ate quickly. They heard the mournful bell ring at the mission, every ten minutes since seven o'clock.

Magdalena glanced at the rooster clock. "I better go. The mass will be starting."

"You sure you don't want us to come?"

"Yes," she said, her eyes teary. "It will be too sad. I don't want Hanna and Adam to see."

She left the house. Joshua toyed with his food, Hanna was glum and silent. Tears fell down Adam's cheeks.

Yesterday Father Boniface had told Macario Antone that Father Hausner's decision had been wrong, and that Ignacio would be given a funeral mass and burial in the Indian cemetery. The old man had wept openly and then driven over to tell Magdalena. They picked up four friends and drove to the paupers' graves at "A" Mountain and dug up Ignacio's shallowly interred plain pine coffin. They brought it to the cemetery and dug a grave and left it beside the grave.

Joshua sat on the couch in the living room and stared vacantly at the wall. So much had happened. Too much. He was exhausted and depressed. Hanna and Adam saw the look on his face and knew better than to bother him. They went quietly into their own rooms and left the doors open.

A half hour later, maybe an hour, Hanna and Adam both walked out of their rooms and looked inquiringly at each other. Their father was slouched on the sofa, staring somberly at the wall.

"What's that?" Hanna asked. Adam opened his eyes wide and shrugged.

"What's that, Daddy?" Hanna asked again, walking into the living room.

Joshua sat up stiffly. "What?" He listened. It sounded like a lot of people singing, getting closer. "I didn't even hear it."

He went to the door and opened it and walked out into the yard. The others followed him.

It was Ignacio Antone's funeral processional from the mission. They had taken a very wide detour to the irrigation canal. At least five hundred Indians stood just across the ditch from the Rabb house singing a song in Spanish. In the middle, in front, was Macario Antone holding a whitewashed rough-hewn wooden cross that would be Ignacio's grave marker. Next to him was Magdalena. Beside her stood Father Boniface in his brown cassock with a simple white satin stole around his shoulders, also holding a whitewashed wooden cross. He smiled and nodded and bowed low toward Joshua.

Hanna took her father's hand. Adam walked up beside them. And Joshua could not hold back his tears.